Late Bird

Jason Kraus

TO HEATHER:

FREEDOM FIRST!
FREEDOM ONLY!

*"**Late Bird** tells a captivating story, with touches of humor, sensitivity, and slices of small town America; then in a flash, catapults the characters into the workings of politics, accompanied with insightful, thought-provoking common-sense solutions to solve the problems of our country ... thrilling and amazing!"*

"The line, America needed a leader, not another president, exploded with truth, and my imagination ran red, white, and blue. The innocent face of a child on the cover, painted to resemble the American flag, set the tone of this exquisitely told novel, and I was not disappointed as to what lay amongst its pages. The characters were unique; emoting memorable voices distinctly their own, while the prose and descriptions brought the story to life. The pace was riveting, the tales were filled with pathos and elation, and the promise of an answer to our countries woes was plausible. I laughed, cried, and cheered as our hero Falcon faced each obstacle. But as the book came to a close, I hated to say goodbye to the characters, and mourned the hope momentarily instilled for the future of our country. What a grand world this could be if we had more Falcon Sanes. God bless Mr. Kraus for such an inspiring message."

*"Have you ever sat in front of your television set after a hard day's work and watched our politicians, whether local or national, and thought, "Where have all of this country's morals and values gone?" You think to yourself, "Why can't we have politicians who actually work for the citizens, don't take contributions for their campaigns and actually do the right thing?" Well, finally, there is a person, Falcon Sane, the **Late Bird**. Follow Falcon from*

boyhood to adulthood and you will soon realize it is all about family and friends who influenced his life. I thoroughly enjoyed this book and found myself rooting for Falcon to achieve his ultimate goal, to become the leader of our country."

LENNY PATANE, FIREFIGHTER/PARAMEDIC

*"The book cover grabbed my attention. I found myself wondering what importance lay behind a portrait of a child with the American flag on his face. I read the jacket. Politics and reality are not my preferred genre. I escape into romance and sci-fi. But the line, "United we can make a difference," sparked something inside me. I was immediately swept up as the story line unfolded; the progression of events were engaging, and the characters sprang off the page. Remaining intrigued as Falcon Sane matured was not a chore, as **Late Bird** put into print what every true American should be, dedicated and loyal. The story became personal as the hero inspired me to hope for the future of our great country, America. A hope that was believable, when seen through the heart of one child. Bravo!"*

KATY LEE, EVENTS COORDINATOR, AND ARTIST

*"I applaud this first novel by Jason Kraus. **Late Bird** was engrossing and a smooth read. I could relate to the struggles of the young boy as he forged his way through life; stood up for those who were weaker, and grasped the value in remaining true to him-self. Despite difficult challenges, Falcon's honor and character never waver, which helps to develop him for positions of leadership. With that insight, came wisdom and a visionary plan; to solve a complex tax problem by creating equality for all, to call failed politicians to task, and to reunite America. A must read."*

PAUL DOUGLAS, BUSINESS OWNER, UNITED STATES ARMY, VETERAN

Library of Congress Control Number: 2014948636
ISBN: 978-0-9905746-2-0
Late Bird Softcover Edition 2014
Printed in the United States of America

For more information about special discounts for bulk purchases, please contact 3L Publishing at 916.300.8012 or log onto our website at www.3LPublishing.com.

Book design by Erin Pace-Molina

The greatness of America isn't found in our differences. It lives—within our truths. In our agreement with one another to pursue happiness: to engage life in its fullest capacity.

America isn't easy. She isn't supposed to be. Easy belies weakness. America is hard, like the hands of a farmer or the backbone of a soldier. She gives unconditionally, allowing for the growth of her people. Despite our struggle with right and wrong, she is the beacon guiding us through the night, into safe harbor, providing the most important lesson the world has ever known: The lesson of freedom.

It hasn't been said lately and never enough.

We thank you America.

We won't let you down.

Acknowledgement

*T*hrough this journey I have garnered knowledge, experience, and help along the way. I would like to thank my beautiful mother. Mom, even though this book is over 500-pages long, I simply don't have the words needed in order to thank you. So instead I will use yours. Words you have given to me my entire life. I love you. It's all done Duffy Moon. :)

To my wonderful father: Dad, I've spent my time on Earth trying to be half the man you are. This will be the one goal I've set in my life I already know I will never obtain. You are the backbone of America. You are my hero. I love you.

To my amazing wife: Through you sweetheart I finally know joy. Your support, love and strength know no bounds. The best part of my life is when you are near. You are my favorite everything. I love you Dawnie.

To my editor(s) and publisher: Michelle, Erin, and Britney. Great job ladies. Wasn't that fun? :)

To the greatest country in the history of man: God bless you, my sweet America. Thank you for my life. Thank you for my freedom. I'm coming as fast as I can.

Finally, to the Big Fella: Thank you for my free will. I pray I am using it properly.

Jason Kraus

1

*N*ovember 4, 2016. The Democratic presidential candidate paced in her rented hotel suite above the fray. Downstairs, multiple TVs blared in unison with the musical loop of Springsteen while Jay Z reverberated through the rented ballroom at the Democratic Headquarters in Chicago, Illinois. Balloons and streamers frozen in place appeared to defy gravity. Cristal, Heineken, and a rowdy crowd waited for the signal to cut loose. Hushed groups of exhausted year-long campaign volunteers huddled to watch a collection of news networks break down every possible voter scenario. A drunken sex-fest was going to happen, one way or the other.

In Tallahassee, Florida, the Republican presidential candidate stared out the window from the sixth floor in his rented hotel suite above the fray. The Republican headquarters multiple TVs blared in competition with a mariachi band. Based on amnesty, the party had stretched their plan to court new voters as far as they could. Balloons and streamers suspended in place appeared to defy gravity. Margaritas, Coronas, and a riotous crowd waited for the signal to cut loose. Hushed groups of exhausted yearlong campaign volunteers gathered and watched a collection of news networks break down every possible voter scenario. A drunken sex-fest was going to happen, one way or the other.

The Independent candidate Falcon Sane stood on his deck

in Liberty, California admiring the mountains surrounding his home. He squeezed the hand of the woman beside him. After 15 years together he still thought of her as his beautiful bride.

A sprinkling of close friends gathered with anticipation in the couple's understated 1,800-square-foot house nestled at the top of the valley. Over the years as Falcon's disillusionment with manipulative politicians grew, he hoped a real leader would emerge. None did. Trusted colleagues and family suggested Falcon toss his hat into the literary ring, and a new voice was born. A positive message chronicled through his life's challenges, triumphs, and loves. A song of freedom, with devotion to country Americans could relate to. It became his platform, and the very spark the nation desperately needed. The outcome of this election would determine if his message reached their hearts.

America needed a leader, not another president.

The people hadn't elected one in decades ... would they do so tonight?

2

*F*alcon Sane entered public school as a Late Bird.

Late Birds were quick, exceptional learners and required less attention than their subordinates, the Early Birds, who like the proverbial worm flocked to school first in hopes of catching reading and math skills. Late Bird felt sorry for Early Birds. Forced to the bottom of the pecking order, they were picked on, labeled retarded, and missed morning recess, which to a six-year-old was worse than death. Little kids barely out of the shoot and already branded with a scarlet "E".

Falcon was branded too, long before he started school. Not because of his good looks, although he could've posed for a Gerber Baby ad sporting strawberry blonde hair, creamy skin and blue eyes. Nor was it because of his amazing athletic skill that sprung to life as a toddler. No, the brand placed on Falcon was God-given. He had a spirit full of love and compassion, and a heart magically touched by the maker. It was the best part of Falcon, and too often his undoing.

He was unaware of Watergate as it devoured a president, the Cold War between the United States and the Soviet Union, or the reason behind the enforcement of the 55-miles-per-hour speed limit. Gas rationing and politics, which would serve as an omen of poor leadership destined to come, were not on the mind of a six-year-old. As Woodstock and Vietnam faded into the backdrop, the last remnants of the previous generation were barely bookmarked by monuments of a soon-to-be-forgotten society. But solidly holding its place in history was one small dedication. Douglas MacArthur Elementary located in Lakewood, California, directly across from Falcon's house. It was the boy's second home, where in first grade he had begun to taste the world around him, acquire new friends, and master the art of kickball.

Falcon's mother Rachel stood in the doorway of her son's room and sang, "Good morning to you, good morning to you, we're here in our places with sun shiny faces and this is the way to start a new day. Are you ready for your first day in second grade honey?"

Falcon tossed back the covers and his bare feet hit the floor. Lunging into Rachel's body he wrapped his arms around his mother.

Rachel felt the same about Falcon and kissed the top of his head. "Well?"

"I wish you could come too."

"I know baby." She smoothed his hair. "You can tell me all about it at lunch time."

"Okay Mommy."

After bouncing several times on his bed, Falcon's five-year-old brother leaped fearlessly into the air. "Catch me Mommy!"

"Deeter!" Rachel jumped to his command. "One of these days you little spider monkey, I'm going to miss."

"No you won't, you love me too much," he beamed.

He kissed her quick and shimmied down Rachel's body like it was a tree. Falcon and Deeter dressed and trailed the enticing aroma of fresh-baked banana bread coming from the kitchen.

Rachel admired her two sweethearts as they devoured eggs, apple slices, and the warm bread smothered with melting butter. "Daddy said he'd be home early today so you three could play football."

"Woo-hoo!" The boys rounded their arms and squeezed their tiny hands into fists. "Football, football, football!"

Deeter made grunting noises and scrunched his shoulders to his ears. "Look Mommy, I'm a no neck."

She laughed at her toe-headed monkey who mimicked her name for football players. "Eat up my little linebacker. School is waiting."

Once the boys finished, Rachel said, "Please clear your dishes and go brush your teeth."

"Aw," said Falcon. "Do I have to? My teeth are white, see." He grinned like the Cheshire Cat.

"Yes they are." She patted his head. "And I want them to stay that way."

His bottom lip slipped into a pout. "Rats!"

Deeter said, "Come on Falcon it'll be fun. We can have a spitting contest."

"No spitting, just brushing," said Rachel.

The two boys shrugged and raced down the hall.

Combed and kissed Falcon asked, "Can I cross the street by myself today?"

Letting go of her baby was hard, but ..."What's the rule?"

"Go all the way to the crosswalk, look both ways, and walk, don't run."

They have to fly sometime. Rachel nodded.

The little rule-follower sprinted to the corner, crossed safely, and blew kisses to Rachel who stood on the porch watching, unaware that in the time it takes a second hand to circle a clock, Falcon's precious innocence would be tainted forever.

Excited and revved up for kickball, Falcon ran toward the playground. Rounding the building he noticed a half-dozen larger boys encompassing a kid crouched on the ground. Falcon had witnessed this scene once in first grade, and along with the other children hustled by like a herd of animals leaving the weak behind. He never forgot it as it filled his mind that night with disturbing dreams that disrupted his sleep. From then on he realized he could never again pass someone in trouble. If Falcon didn't stand up, he wouldn't be able to lie down at night and for that reason he inherently understood he was different from his peers. Had Falcon been bigger, tough, and more mature, he might've joked or talked the problem away. But at the moment, he was a Late Bird and only six.

Taking a deep breath, he approached the gang and muttered, "Leave him alone."

The half-dozen boys spun around as if controlled by a puppeteer.

One kid snarled, "What'd you say you red-haired little fucker?"

The Late Bird blinked and swallowed hard. His courage intact, he lacked the skill and experience to handle such a situation. Out of the corner of his eye he saw the little kid on the ground scramble to his feet and run away.

"I meant, why don't you leave him alone? What'd he do to you?"

The third-grade mob surrounded Falcon and spewed a flurry of obscenities.

Their threatening voices created a crescendo in his head, his body trembled, and he could barely breathe. Realizing there was no way out desperation took hold. *Wait!* He spotted a teacher several yards away. *No not a teacher... a recess monitor.* It was her *job* to keep this very thing from happening. Falcon lost vision of the monitor as the biggest third grader he'd ever seen stepped forward, towered over him, and blocked out the sun.

"Tell you what, freckle face." He flicked Falcon's forehead hard.

Falcon flinched.

"Let my kid brother beat you up and we won't touch you. But if you fight back we're all gonna kick your ass!"

Late Bird looked at the little brother. They were in the same class. He was an Early Bird.

"Go on." The huge third grader shoved his brother. "Jump him!"

The two victims stared at each other, neither one knowing what to do.

The little brother slid his hands into his front pockets, and then looked up at Late Bird who was taller.

"Lay down," screamed the big bully. "Let him jump you!"

A mass of kids gathered and started chanting "Fight, fight, fight!" while the bully and his buddies closed ranks.

"Get on the fucking ground!" Two of the bullies grabbed Falcon and slammed him into the dirt.

Late Bird remembered the playground monitor. *Where is she*? He lifted his head and scanned the blacktop.

She stared straight at him, their eyes locked as she pressed the whistle to her lips.

Fists began to pummel his head and back. The words *please help me* stuck in his throat. To this day Falcon can't explain what happened next. It's a puzzle he'll never have an answer to because there was no excuse. The recess monitor let her whistle fall, turned, and walked away.

Defeated the six-year-old child had no choice.

Late Bird lay down.

Like his father, Falcon was proud. He didn't want to admit he'd taken a beating that morning, even though he'd been outnumbered. Ashamed and embarrassed, Falcon was incognizant of his heroic behavior. It was the right thing to do, what choice did he have? Deciding to keep the incident a secret from his parents, he brushed himself off, stuffed the memory into the deepest recesses of his brain, and tried to ignore the damage to his heart.

It was clear early on, second grade did not challenge Falcon. His teacher recommended he be advanced to third, but already much younger than his peers, his parents declined. Instead Rachel fortified his education with math flashcards and Scrabble and introduced sign language. She provided art supplies, encouraged Falcon and Deeter to follow recipes, taught her boys how to dance, and instructed them on the proper usage of utensils. The boys' father, Mitch, shared political insights and opinions with his young son about Governor Ronald Reagan and President Jimmy Carter. While father and son sat in gas lines, they discussed stats on the back of baseball cards, which Falcon had memorized, and the questions of a curious little boy.

"Hey Dad ... what is Iran?" Falcon asked one day while sitting in the car, waiting to gas up, and listening to talk radio.

Mitch wiped sweat from his brow, edging the car inches ahead in line. "It's the exact opposite of America. It's a place where people aren't free."

Falcon thought about that for a second. "What do you mean free?"

"You know how you don't like it when I tell you to do your chores?"

Falcon nodded. *I hate anyone telling me what to do.*

Mitch rolled his words over in his head. He didn't want to scare his son. "Over there if you don't do your chores you don't get to eat," Mitch said, turning the dial to a Rock'n'Roll station.

Mitch worked two jobs to provide for his family, heading

out the door before the sun rose and too often arriving home after it set. As an honorably discharged Army medic he continued in the field as a hospital orderly. But quickly having two children, he switched professions to follow the money, first employed as a checker for a big grocery chain, and then driving semi tractor-trailers. After hours he swamped produce at a potato house and unloaded huge metal crates until every trailer on the dock was emptied. Along with his paycheck the potato house threw in a 10-pound bag of spuds each week. Rachel, an excellent cook, became a potato savant and built her menus around the root vegetable as it was the one thing guaranteed in the refrigerator every day.

Falcon's life was a blur of school, getting dirty tearing up the neighborhood with friends, and eating lots of nutritious homemade food, until Mitch's accident. Falcon and Deeter had flipped a coin to see who would ride with Mitch to the store that fateful day. Deeter won the toss with a call of "heads". Then strapped into his booster in the back seat of the car, he waved to his big brother as he and Mitch drove away. Ten minutes later a driver in Mitch's lane came head-on, which gave him two choices. Crash into the steel maniac hurtling toward him or veer into the wall of vehicles parked along the curb. Mitch chose the wall of cars and probably saved both of their lives. His decision wasn't without consequence though.

Mitch inhaled and gritted his teeth. "Are you okay, Deeter?"

"My head hurts Daddy," Deeter began to cry.

"Does anything else hurt?"

"I bit my tongue and it's bleeding a little."

"Okay buddy, sit tight." Mitch tried to move his right leg and sweat exploded all over his body.

Mitch looked down quickly. Having been an Army medic he knew instantly his leg was broken. His breath became shallow, his skin turned clammy and he felt faint. He stretched his right arm over the back seat. "Take my hand Deeter." He didn't know how long he could hold out before his body went into shock. The last thing he remembered was the wail of a siren coming closer, and his words, "Hold on son. Help will be here soon."

The reckless driver was not insured. The Sane's own insurance company only replaced their car. With the breadwinner laid up for months with a broken femur, time became the Sane family's enemy. Rachel dug in immediately when Mitch was first hospitalized. All her volunteer time at MacArthur Elementary paid off when an opening for a teacher's aide presented itself. She then found five school-aged children who needed morning- and after-school care. Mitch's paychecks stopped as did the 10-pound bag of spuds, but they were still inexpensive and nutritious so they ate potato soup, cottage potatoes and potato pancakes. Clothes and shoes came from the thrift store, and the local swimming pool and the library became their sources of entertainment. After months in traction, Mitch at last came home. His entire leg confined in a cast, the good man's spirit trapped in a bad dream. With disability running out, and most of their savings gone, Mitch's worst nightmare was coming true. They were broke. Being a cash-and-carry couple, their only debt was the small house they'd purchased using Mitch's GI benefits. Rachel's income covered the payment, but the little left over wasn't enough.

One morning Mitch hobbled into the kitchen on crutches and approached Rachel.

"I saw an ad in the paper about house advertisement delivery," he said. "I just called for more information."

Rachel dried her hands and turned to face her husband.

"It'll be a lot of work," Mitch told her, "but if you set me up in a chair out back with the newspapers stacked around me, I could layer, roll and stuff them into the plastic bags. We'd pack the Datsun and once your after-school kids are picked up, you, me and the boys could deliver them."

"How would we deliver them?"

"Each bag has to be hung on the doorknob. I can rest my cast on the passenger seat and drive with my good leg. You'd carry papers for one side of the street and the boys would cover the other side."

"I don't know. They're only little boys."

Mitch stood silent for a second. "We can do this Rachel. We have to, we need it."

Rachel sighed. When her husband was healthy he almost brushed six feet and had the strength of a bear, while she stood five six and slender with the frame of a dancer. Looking at her sons, she still saw babies.

"You know I don't want to, but maybe we should apply for welfare until you're back on your feet."

Mitch closed his eyes and shook his head once.

"No Rachel." He stared at her, his face grim. "No way am I doing that, understand?"

She understood pride and self-sufficiency, she had her share, but several weeks later out of desperation Rachel prepared to take Falcon and Deeter to the Public Assistance Office. She hated exposing her children to what she imagined would be awaiting them, but was told over the phone a social worker would have to actually see the boys.

"Where are you going?" Mitch asked, propped up in the garage as he rolled and stuffed newspaper advertisements for later delivery.

"To the library and then the park," Rachel lied.

Mitch nodded and continued the only work he could find that might help him keep his family secure.

Falcon was unaccustomed to the mixture of people filling

the welfare office. Cigarettes hung from turned-down mouths, missing teeth seemed a common denominator, horrible body odor hung heavy in the air, and one man had scary-looking tattoos that covered his arms. A screaming woman stood at the counter while another wailed she had nowhere to go. A crying baby was ignored, and a little kid with snot caked on his face kept whining he was hungry.

"Mom," said Falcon. "I don't like it here, let's go."

Deeter squeezed against his mother's body trying to disappear.

"I know honey, neither do I. Stay close and we'll be out of here soon."

Rachel's eyes stung. Horribly uncomfortable and trying to put her children at ease, she guided her startled chicks toward an empty corner, lay tissues on the disgustingly stained chairs, and pulled them together like a nest. The boys kept busy with books and coloring as the young mother focused on the procedures, paperwork and appeasement of Falcon and Deeter during the three-hour wait. She could not help but overhear conversations around them about how another baby got more money, how to falsify documents, and flat-out lies to manipulate the system. She prayed her children were not listening. Finally their number came up.

The social worker, a rigid, prim, young woman with a heavy accent glanced over the forms Rachel had meticulously filled out. Narrowing her eyes at Rachel she said in a high-pitched, halting tone, "You look perfectly healthy to me."

"I am, but—"

"Then why are you coming to me for a handout? Why don't you get a job and take care of your family?"

Rachel's neck and face grew crimson.

"Well?" the woman snapped.

Falcon stood up. "Let's go Mom."

"Me too, Mommy," said Deeter. "I wanna go."

After quieting the boys Rachel replied, "You can see I have two children, and as I said on my paperwork my husband can't work."

"That's no excuse for not finding a job. Plenty of women do it."

Rachel wanted to verbally slap the woman. Her lack of compassion made her a poor candidate for such a position, but for the sake of her family Rachel swallowed her pride.

"I have a job but it isn't enough. My husband is stuck in bed or a wheelchair, using crutches just long enough so I can change the sheets. He can't even hold himself on the toilet. I married at 17 and don't have a high school diploma. What kind of job do you think I could find that would make enough money to pay someone else to take care of my husband and children while I'm at work?"

"That's not my department or concern. I am here to determine whether you qualify for financial aid."

She initialed the forms, inked, and ferociously stamped the top in bold red letters: DENIED.

"But—"

"Since there is a man in the house and you are able to work the two of you do not qualify for assistance. Look into the public school lunch program and get another job. I do not promote welfare queens."

She stood up, looked straight through Rachel, and called the next number.

Fighting tears, Rachel escorted her children away from the horrific place as quickly as possible. She hoped her boys didn't understand the outcome, and Rachel had no intention of telling Mitch.

"That wasn't fun, was it?" Rachel fastened Deeter's seatbelt.

"No Mommy," Deeter said, "let's not do that again ever. That lady was mean."

She kissed his head and slipped in behind the wheel. "You boys were angels. I'm very proud of you."

Falcon sat in the backseat and stared out the window.

Rachel glanced at her oldest son in the rearview mirror. "Falcon, please don't say anything about this to your dad, okay?"

Falcon continued to stare. "I won't Mom."

She forced a smile. "You're my hero sweetheart."

"Me too Mommy," said Deeter. "I'm your hero too."

Rachel's heart lightened. "Yes baby. I'm the luckiest mommy in the world to have two such handsome heroes'."

Falcon said, "You know what Mom? When I grow up, I'm going to be President of the United States."

Deeter said, "I thought you were going to be a baseball player?"

"I am. I'll be the President after that."

"Why do you want to be the President?" Rachel asked.

Falcon was silent for a moment, thinking about what he'd just witnessed. "Because I want to help people."

She wasn't surprised at his response. "You would make a wonderful President honey. America would be very lucky to have you as Commander in Chief."

Rachel held Falcon's gaze in the rearview mirror.

"Commander in Chief," Falcon rolled the title around in his mouth. "I like that."

"So Mr. President, what would be your first ruling?"

"I'd make sure everyone had enough to eat."

Rachel put on a brave face and smiled at her loving son. "I believe you would." Trying to change the subject she asked, "What would be next?"

"That's easy." He grinned. "I'd make ice cream free every day."

"Yeah, that's a great rule!" said Deeter, the sugar hound of the family.

"Then why don't we drive to Thrifty and get you started," said Rachel.

Falcon thought about that for a second. "Can we afford it, Mom?"

"I thought it was free?" Deeter chimed in.

"No, nothing's for free Deeter," said Falcon in a voice too serious for a six-year-old.

Rachel sighed. No, they couldn't afford it. Two cones cost the same as a gallon of gas or a dozen eggs, but sometimes in life you can't afford not to do certain things. She said a silent prayer and checked the ashtray where Mitch occasionally tossed loose change. Twenty five, .35 ... .70 cents. She rattled the unexpected fortune in her hand like dice. "Can we afford it? You betcha baby!"

While the Thrifty's cone erased the welfare office for Deeter, there wasn't enough ice cream in the world able to remove the memory for Falcon.

The advertisement delivery job was a challenge. Mitch and Rachel spent hours enduring paper cuts, ink-stained bodies and clothes while coaxing hundreds of sale ads into plastic sleeves. With the Datsun loaded, the family of four headed out in the evenings. After situating Mitch behind the wheel of the car, Rachel loaded her canvas newspaper bag front and back until she could barely stand.

"Ouch, Mitch my hair's caught." She leaned her back against the car door.

He gently freed his wife's waist-long blonde hair and then pinched her fanny.

"Mitchell, stop that!" She tried to pull away but loaded like a pack mule she wasn't going anywhere.

"Oh you know you love it," he teased.

Deeter slipped in beside her and gave her behind a pinch too.

"Stop it you guys," said Rachel as she leaned forward and tried to stand. "Mitch I'm falling."

He reached his massive arm out the window and around her and pulled her to her feet by the front bag.

"Don't worry Rach I've got your back."

He did too. Rachel married Mitch when she was 17. Running away from a tortured past, one that sometimes haunted her still, he offered her a home, family and security. Mitch grew up poor and in a rough neighborhood, and the challenges they faced in their youth established a common bond.

As Rachel made her way across the street her husband let out a wolf whistle.

"Hey babe, how about a ride?" he hollered.

Rachel turned. "Don't start something you can't finish mister."

He winked. "Come on back here and I'll finish it."

She flipped her hair and sashayed away with her pouches to deliver her side of the street.

Mitch made a game out of it with Falcon and Deeter. He threw the bags over the roof of the car like footballs and each time the boys raced to hang them on the front door of a house they yelled, "Touchdown!" It was exhausting, and a car nearly hit Falcon once when a huge dog jumped the fence and chased him as he screamed into the street. But the kids were good sports, and the little family struggled on.

Rachel stretched their grocery budget and (as suggested) looked into the school lunch program.

"You can eat at the cafeteria whenever you want to now," she announced at breakfast one morning.

Falcon was overjoyed as he often begged for that indulgence.

He dreamed of French fries, pizza and cookies made with white sugar. His mom was a great cook, but *healthy* and *balanced* were words always connected to her meals. At 11:30 a.m., Falcon's teacher instructed the children to sit in a circle and prepared to pass out lunch tickets. Lost in thoughts over his first chance to eat "cafeteria food," he wiggled in his spot on the floor. Then he remembered his mom had not given him any money. He hurried to tell his teacher.

"Don't worry Falcon," she said, "it's been taken care of. Please sit down."

Mom must've paid. He danced back to his seat humming, already tasting the French fries.

His teacher motioned for silence and began calling names. She tore the blue tickets from the roll as she handed one after another to the children marching up front to retrieve their prizes.

When the blue tickets ran out Falcon began to feel anxious. *Maybe she forgot to write my name down.*

The teacher then produced a roll of yellow tickets that had disappeared into her lap.

Although Falcon had never received a lunch ticket before, every child in the room knew the difference between the different-colored tickets, blue for students whose parents paid, yellow for families on welfare. Every day he'd watched the second group slump to the teacher to receive their yellow tickets. His heart began to race as she continued through the alphabet. Closer and closer she came to his name. He wanted to scream. *Stop, don't call my name! I don't want that ticket!*

"Falcon Sane," she said.

His eyes began to sting. He lowered his head and felt the floor drop beneath his feet.

A flurry of noises erupted from the surprised children as they'd never seen him get a lunch ticket before. Especially a yellow one.

Defeated, the Late Bird walked toward the teacher.

He stared in disbelief as she extended the putrid yellow piece of paper. He didn't want to, but the rule-follower in him took control. Grabbing it like a piece of flaming trash, Falcon went hurrying back to his place in the circle. Instructed to line up at the door, everyone did, including Falcon. But as the children exited the room he stepped away from the group, marched to his teacher's desk, and said, "I'm going home for lunch today." He held the ticket out to his teacher. "I'll be going home for lunch the rest of year, so you don't ever need to call my name again."

The teacher took the ticket from her star pupil. "Are you sure? Is this okay with your mom?"

"Oh sure, I already talked to her," he lied. "So never call my name again, *ever*."

"All right."

The Late Bird rushed from the room and headed home. He knew his mom would understand. But whether she did or not there was no way he was taking that yellow ticket. *I'll starve first.*

Barely hanging by a thread the Sane family financially limped on. The YMCA offered free baseball during the summer break at the local park and seven-year-old Falcon begged to play.

"Please Mommy please! I promise I'll never ask for anything else, ever!"

His parents laughed, appreciative of their boy's passion, and signed him up. The neighborhood coaches, parents and peers immediately recognized Falcon's athletic ability. He ate up the encouragement and coaching over the summer, and throughout the next year participated in different sports. It was understandable then that it felt like his young world was coming to an end when in November he and Deeter got the news. They would be moving over Christmas break. The pain in Mitch's leg had never gone away. Now back to work with a limp and the pain increasing every day, Rachel finally talked him into seeing another doctor.

"I can't believe what I'm seeing in these X-rays," announced Dr. David Drucker the talented surgeon the Sanes found after a year of searching. "Your leg is still broken. You're facing a long recovery period — that is, if I'm able to save your leg at all."

Mitch and Rachel stared at the physician stunned. *Did he just say another surgery with a long recovery period, if he's able to save the leg at all?* There seemed to be no light or end to this tunnel, just the tunnel. Running out of options the decision was made to sell their home. Mitch's sister Karen and brother-in-law Jack had a desire to quit city life and move to the mountains. A small RV park and store for sale in Northern California might be the answer for them all, if they pooled their resources. Then if Mitch never got back on his feet following surgery, his knowledge of the retail business would be invaluable. Fortunately the housing market was in an upswing and the sale of their last resource brought a good return. With some trepidation, the two families headed to Northern California dreaming of a new start. Mitch had plenty of experience in the grocery business and liked the idea of owning their own business. Rachel on the other hand had some concerns. The location was remote and sandwiched between a treacherous two-lane-winding highway and a dangerous river. She worried her boys might drown or fall prey to a landslide or careening car. But she wanted her children to be away from the crime and drug scene silently creeping into Southern California, and whether she liked it or not they had to move.

The day after Christmas, resembling early settlers the two families packed up and caravaned in three separate vehicles. They traveled 650-miles north past Bakersfield, Sacramento and Redding. By the time they made it to Highway 299, it was dark, and the winding road went on relentlessly. It was a grueling 13-hour drive for Mitch who was encased in a body cast from his second surgery. But staunch as early settlers, other than an occasional, "Are we almost there?" from the children, no one complained.

Because Mitch needed to lie down in his sister's van, Falcon and Deeter rode alone with Rachel. She'd never felt so tired and prayed they would come to their destination before the darkness lulled her to sleep.

"Mom?" asked Falcon, "did you see that sign? It said Del Loma and the number 30 next to a long P word. What's that mean?"

"Population," said Rachel. "It means how many people live in the town."

Falcon unclipped his seatbelt and leaned over his mother's shoulder. "Only 30 people live in this town? Are you sure, maybe some of the numbers fell off?"

Rachel forced a laugh and focused back on the road.

"No sweetie it's correct." She hoped the boys would see how beautiful it was here before the isolation took hold; but even in the vast darkness, Falcon didn't miss much.

Deeter asked, "Are there any kids here?"

"I'm sure there are honey. You'll see them at school."

"But I mean to play with after school?"

"I don't know," said Rachel.

Falcon plopped back into his seat and whispered, "I sure hope so."

It was late when they pulled into the RV Park. One four bedroom double-wide mobile home was included in the deal, and the two families planned to share it for now. The weather had turned cold, and there were patches of snow on the ground. As they made their way up the front stairs Deeter found a note taped on the door and handed it to Rachel.

"What does it say, Mom?"

"I don't know. I can't see it by the headlights. Wait until we get inside."

But inside wasn't better. The light switch clicked on and off without a result. Rachel returned to the car and dug out a flashlight from the glove box.

"Hey flatlanders," she read, "powers out, septic tank is full, water line is broken. Fix them." She laid her aching head against the seat blinking back tears.

Deeter ran in place stomping his feet on the ground. "I'm cooold Mommy! Can we go inside?"

"Get back in the car," she said.

Jack, Mitch's brother-in-law sidled up to the open car door. "What's up?"

Rachel handed him the flashlight and held the note up for him to read.

Mindlessly Jack twirled a corner of his mustache as he perused the friendly welcome. "Looks like we have a full schedule tomorrow. I'll dig the lantern out of the camper. You and the kids stay in the car until I get the woodstove going inside. I'll tell Mitch and Karen to do the same."

Rachel closed her eyes and rubbed her temples.

"Mom?" asked Falcon, "what's a flatlander?"

"People who live on flat land, I think."

"Are we flat people?" asked Deeter.

She managed a weary smile. "No baby, not anymore."

"What kind of people are we then?" he asked.

The worried kind, thought Rachel as Falcon stared into the night.

Morning came too soon, and the sun streamed through every window while Karen rustled up some food from their camper. Sleeping bags on the floor worked for everyone but poor Mitch, who'd spent the night in his reclining wheelchair he jokingly called the Cadillac. The boys and Jack and Karen's five-year-old daughter Maggie scarfed down donuts and dry Lucky Charms. Falcon and Deeter were in heaven and in no hurry to finish such a decadent breakfast.

"Guess what Deeter?" Falcon grinned at his little brother. "We don't have to change our clothes or brush our teeth or anything."

Rachel said, "Clothes no, but teeth and hair, yes."

"Do we ever have to change our clothes again, Mommy?" asked Deeter.

"You're home free today, but if we get some water, baths and clean clothes are tomorrow."

The boys were anxious to get outside. Surrounded by dense forestry and massive mountains was a new experience for them. Oak, Pine, Madrone and Redwoods covered the valley washing the land with an ocean of green. Islands of old snow lay melting on the ground while high up, the mountaintops appeared to be floating in clouds. Wild blackberry bushes and long-forgotten apple orchards produced treats in the summer for wildlife and the occasional resident daring enough to suffer thorns and bees. But considering the immense mountain range surrounding the town, the size of Del Loma was amazing. Locals stated if you blinked while driving on the highway, you'd miss it completely. As funny as that sounded it wasn't a joke. Still the old mill town located on Highway 299 was something to see. Tiny log cabins sufficed as a motel. A rambling building, which was sometimes used as a restaurant, was attached to the country store that now belonged to the new flatlander families. The paved streets and cookie-cutter homes of Southern California were long gone replaced by gravel, dust, single- and double-wide trailers. There were more dogs than people and more snakes than dogs. Fortunately the canines helped keep the slithering population low, at least around the campground.

Falcon hunted Rachel down as she unpacked their belongings.

"Mom, Mom! Uncle Jack found some people this morning, and they're going to show him where the water line is broken. Can Deeter and I go along, please? He said it's okay with him."

"Please Mommy!" Deeter hugged Rachel's waist and poured on the charm. Even at seven, the light that shined from his perfect cherub face and deep blue eyes always worked magic on her heart.

"Yes, you can go. Stay out of the way, but not out of Uncle Jack's sight. I don't want you getting lost or eaten by a bear." Rachel chuckled to herself knowing that bear part would keep the boys in-check.

"Are there bears out there?" asked Falcon, scrutinizing his mother.

"Yes honey, bears and lots of wildlife live here. So you must always be careful."

Deeter bragged, "I don't care. I'm not afraid of no bear. I'll just run, climb up a tree, or hit him in the nose with a stick."

"Brave words my little man." She patted his head. "Until one chases after you."

With wide eyes both boys scurried out the door.

Mitch, eager to get to work, hobbled on his crutches around the store, worked the top shelves, and directed Karen to anything that required bending over. Jack made calls early that morning. The power was promised to be on before the sun went down, a honey wagon was en route to empty the septic tank, the propane and gasoline drivers already left a dump, and a few locals dropped by to introduce themselves and check out the rookies. Rachel found enough seasoned wood stacked beside the trailer to promise weeks of warmth, hot water and cooking in an emergency. Beds would be up by nightfall, a warm meal scavenged from the inventory in the store, and after their first full day in Del Loma, everyone rested up for the marathon of work that lay ahead.

The three little flatlanders, as locals insisted upon calling them, Falcon, 9, Deeter, 7, and newly turned six-year-old Maggie, discovered a handful of kids in Del Loma. The half-dozen kids were much older, but by Falcon's excitement, you'd have thought he'd discovered gold, which was quite plentiful in the Trinity River that roared at the back of the campground.

Christmas vacation passed, and Karen and Mitch headed back to Southern California. Mitch was still under his doctor's care, and the sale of Jack and Karen's house fell apart shortly before they'd headed north. She'd have to keep working in Southern California to make the payments, as the purchase of Del Loma and getting it afloat rapidly ate the two family's resources.

The school bus stopped at the store twice each day, picked up and dropped off. But their first day, Rachel drove the children upriver to Cox Bar, the two-room schoolhouse.

Mrs. Wallace was the elementary teacher and a genuinely dedicated spirit. Accustomed to teaching multiple age groups, she was perfect for the three new comers.

Fascinated with learning again, Falcon couldn't stop talking about his teacher. "Mrs. Wallace is so smart Mom. She asked today if anyone knew what the letters E.R.A. stood for. I raised my hand so fast she looked surprised. She said, 'Go ahead Falcon, what do those letters stand for?' I sat up as straight as I could and told her E.R.A. stands for Earned Run Average!"

Rachel smiled and tried not to laugh.

"Her face looked just like yours Mom." Falcon paused. "Anyway, she said I was right, but they stand for something else too: the Equal Rights Amendment. We talked about the Constitution, when it was written, and how it protects all Americans because we're equal, no matter if we're boys or girls or what color we are. I never thought about that before."

Rachel admired Falcon's bright mind and placed a plate of sliced apples and peanut butter in front of him as she continued to listen.

"I told her the best people I know are my mom and dad, and they're equal. We talked about slavery, and I told her I'd seen the movie *Roots* and it made me sad. 'Why?' she asked. I told her because people hurt each other. She looked at me and told me I would do great things one day because I had such a good heart." He dipped apple in the peanut butter. "Isn't Mrs. Wallace smart?" Falcon took a bite and grinned.

Mrs. Wallace challenged Falcon far beyond his grade level and under her tutelage he flourished.

At seven, Deeter still could not read. Rachel sensed a problem early on when he had returned home from preschool and had complained of a hard day because he had to color and cut. Mrs. Wallace loved Deeter's joyful disposition, sharp wit and charm.

"He'll read one day," she assured Rachel. "Don't worry so much Mom."

As the children blossomed, so did nature. Although Rachel and Jack worked more hours than they could count, aside from introducing the children to the land of poison oak and ticks, it appeared the two families made the right decision.

Spring quickly turned to summer, and Falcon stirred like a racehorse waiting to break free of the gate. The sparkling Trinity River was a short walk from anywhere in town, and he longed to swim and try his skill at tubing the rapids. Steelhead and trout gave way to the awesome sight of thousands of salmon jumping and swimming upstream, returning to their birthplace to spawn. Soreheads led the way for the new trainees and then expired as the cycle of life repeated. Falcon wasn't a fan of bears waking from hibernation that ransacked the trashcans around the trailer park nor rattlesnakes and scorpions revived by the heat. But the purity in the air, the calming gurgle of the river, and strength in the trees convinced him living here was worthwhile. It had been difficult for the sensitive little boy to leave hard-earned friends, baseball, and school behind. Cox Bar was the third school he'd attended in five years. Each change brought a challenge more difficult than the last for a child who thrived on routine. At the time Falcon didn't know this would become a pattern, but attending three more schools before graduating high school would leave him with a constant desire to relocate every few years. So far, Cox Bar had been a smooth transition. Or so he thought.

3

*T*hankfully Mitch's surgery had been successful. He was almost like new and back in Del Loma with his family just in time for the busy summer season. Throwing up the latest stock delivery in the small store, he greeted his neighbor and fishing buddy.

"Hey Jerry, how's it hanging?"

The bell on the door jingled as he shut it.

"Not bad Mitch. Say, listen. I'll be out of town for a few days and need someone to feed my chickens. Do you think your boys are up to the job?"

"I heard feeding your chickens is like trying to bathe a cat."

Jerry laughed, "Nah, mostly it's the rooster. That's what I keep the rake beside the coop for."

"They'll be back in a minute with my lunch, you can ask them yourself," said Mitch.

Falcon and Deeter came running in the backdoor.

"Here Dad," Falcon laid a covered plate on the counter. "Mom said we could have a candy bar or an ice cream."

Deeter, who was already caressing a candy bar in each hand, switched back and forth inhaling deeply one after the other.

"Make a choice Deeter," Mitch said. "And put the other one back."

"I'm having an Eskimo Pie." Falcon slid the lid of the

refrigerated glass case open.

"Yeah!" said Deeter, "Me too." He plopped the two candy bars back into their boxes on the shelf and crowded behind his brother.

Jerry offered to pay the kids 50 cents each, and they could take the eggs home to their mother. They would have done it for free, but Falcon, the budding capitalist, eagerly agreed. Before their handshake sealed the transaction, Falcon was already calculating how to turn his 50 cents into a dollar.

The next morning the two working gents, Falcon and Deeter headed to Jerry's land. Tossing rocks at trees, snagging juicy wild blackberries, the brothers discussed plans to go tubing that afternoon and more importantly, who would hold the rooster at bay with the rake.

"Don't worry," said Falcon. "I'll do it."

"But what if the chickens peck me when I try to take their eggs?"

"Okay, then I'll get the eggs," said Falcon.

"But what if the rooster—"

"Listen Deeter, I can't do both. When you put the chicken feed in the trough, the hens will get off their nests."

Deeter's face lit up, looking even cuter than Mikey the little kid in the Life cereal commercial. "Hey, that's a great idea. You're sure smart."

Falcon beamed at his kid brother whom he had always adored.

Reaching the top of Jerry's driveway, the two boys froze. A man darted from behind some bushes, past their neighbor's mining dredge, peered over his shoulder at them, and disappeared into the woods. Living in the mountains one could quite easily stumble into the path of a bear, coyote or mountain lion.

Falcon signaled with his hand to stop and stepped in front

of Deeter. Narrowing his eyes, he slowly perused the area.

Deeter whispered, "Do you see anything, Fal?"

"No. But that guy acted scared." Falcon continued to scan. "Do you see anything?"

Deeter pressed against his big brother's back, "Un-uh."

Everything appeared calm, but last winter the boys had heard the throaty call of a mountain lion while walking in the woods, then a doe had bounded through the brush scared out of her wits. They had followed the doe's cue. It paid to be careful. Falcon looked once more. The only thing that seemed different was the blue tarp, which covered Jerry's dredge, had blown off to one side.

Falcon shrugged, "It's clear, come on Deed, help me cover the dredge back up."

They did and walked toward the hen house.

Deeter said, "I think that man was Butch. You know Mike and Billy's stepdad."

"Yep, it was." Falcon grabbed the rake, "Ready Freddy?"

"Wait!" Deeter stopped his brother from turning the latch on the coop. "I don't think 50 cents is enough to face the devil rooster."

"The devil rooster!" Falcon whooped, "Maybe not, but it's the deal we made. Come on."

The chickens were fed, the eggs were collected, and the two businessmen survived the ordeal. As they stepped back outside the coop Butch came tromping down Jerry's driveway.

He snarled, "What're you boys doing down here?"

"Taking care of Jerry's chickens," said Falcon.

"Are ya finished?"

The boys nodded in sync.

"Did ya see anybody down here before?"

Falcon didn't know the man firsthand, and he didn't want to. One day in front of Falcon's home, Mike, Billy, and he were tossing a football around when a swerving pick-up truck circled the boys encompassing them with a cloud of dust.

Butch had yelled out the cab window, "Get in the back!"

"We're not done," said Mike.

Butch had then jumped out of the cab, grabbed a hunk of wood, and chucked it at Mike's head.

"You're done when I say you're done now get in the fucking truck!"

Remembering the man's rage, Falcon couldn't help but be frightened as Butch stumbled closer to him and Deeter.

"Did you hear what I said? I asked ya if you'd seen anyone before I got here."

Falcon was raised not to lie. Work hard, tell the truth, and be respectful, but this man didn't want truth and didn't deserve respect.

He pulled his brother close beside him and whispered, "Start walking."

"Well?" asked Butch.

Falcon told the truth. "The only person we've seen is you."

Shoulder to shoulder the two young boys angled their way up the steep drive. Falcon kept his eyes riveted on Butch.

"Keep going." He nudged his little brother.

Butch glared at the boys and spoke in a low, threatening growl, "You mean right now, dontcha kid? You're seeing me now, right?"

Falcon could hear Deeter wheezing. Being scared sometimes brought on an asthma attack. He turned and slipped his baby brother behind him.

Barely an arm's length away from Butch, Falcon couldn't help but notice the holes in his filthy white wife-beater shirt and the stench of stale beer.

Sounding braver than he felt, Falcon answered, "Didn't see

anybody, just getting the eggs."

As they passed the man, Deeter started to pick up the pace. "Let's run for it Fal," his breath whistled.

"No." Falcon snuck a peek over his shoulder where Butch watched and smirked. "Never run. Things chase you when you run."

A few days after the Butch incident Falcon bounded into the family store and hoped to help his dad. Summer brought tourists, forest fighters who lined up for showers in the trailer-park bathrooms at a buck apiece, and enough gold dredges that floated on the Trinity one could almost walk to town on them. The family wasn't getting rich, but began to see a profit. The budding entrepreneur reveled in the business as he rang up orders on the antique cash register, smiling each time the bell rang and the drawer sprang open. Falcon counted back change, bagged groceries, mastered the credit-card procedure, pumped gas, and stocked shelves. But his favorite thing was counting the register at closing time. He loved to touch the money, especially the $20 bills. The only thing he wasn't allowed to do was sell cigarettes and alcohol, which was fine by him. Falcon slipped past his father, who was refilling the beer and soda coolers and headed toward his throne. Standing proudly behind the counter, he took a deep whiff of the coffee his Dad always kept brewed for the locals.

"Can I have some coffee?" he asked.

Mitch broke down the cardboard soda flats and tossed them in the backroom.

"You won't like it." He walked to the front of the store.

"It smells good Dad. I think I will, please?"

This conversation wasn't new. Mitch relented and filled a Styrofoam cup halfway. "Here you go."

Falcon reached for the sugar.

"Hold it. You didn't say anything about sugar. You said you wanted coffee." Mitch grinned mischievously. "Drink it black son, like a man."

"Okay, thanks Dad," Falcon said excitedly. He brought the cup to his lips and paused. Although his brain warned it was too hot, he'd been begging for months and wasn't waiting a second longer. He made a loud slurping noise.

"Blech!" He spit the nasty liquid back into the cup and sucked air to cool the raging fire in his mouth.

Mitch roared with laughter, poured himself a cup and then like a fire-eating dragon, gulped it down without a blink.

"That stuff's horrible!" Falcon shivered and tried to rub the taste off his swollen tongue with his fingers.

The front door opened and banged against the shelves as their neighbor Jerry hustled in. He pointed an accusing finger at Falcon. "You're just the person I want to talk to."

Falcon instantly forgot about his burning orifice.

Mitch said, "Why Jerry, what's going on?"

Jerry placed both hands on the counter and loomed over Falcon.

The boy stepped back. The attitude toward kids in Del Loma was not to spare the rod, and he'd seen Jerry tee off on his own son before.

"Did you or your brother touch anything at my house?"

Mitch studied his startled son. "Sure they did. You asked them to take care of your chickens."

"I know, I know." He waved Mitch's answer away. "But did they touch anything else?"

Mitch said, "Falcon, did you guys touch anything other than the eggs?"

"No sir we just grabbed the eggs. The rooster almost got out once, but we pushed him back with the rake. He's mean."

"You didn't touch anything else?" said Jerry.

"No sir."

"Are you sure?"

Mitch was an easygoing guy up to a point — and that point had arrived.

"He just told you 'no'. What's the matter with you?"

"Someone stole my dredge. Did you see anybody over at my place?"

Falcon flashed back to their encounter with Butch. He'd forgotten all about it. "Yes sir," he said and filled in all the details.

"That mother fuck—" Jerry stopped himself. "Sorry. I just talked to that A-hole—sorry. Anyway, he said he saw Falcon and Deeter, went over to check for me, and found them messing with my dredge. Now I think he stole it and blamed it on your kids!"

Mitch stood on his good leg and straightened to his full height. "Well it sure wasn't my kids."

As Falcon listened to the adults, he knew this wasn't going to end well. Suddenly he agreed with Deeter, 50 cents didn't seem like enough.

"I already called the sheriff, are you willing to tell him what you saw?"

Mitch nodded at Falcon.

"Yes sir."

Jerry said, "Good, he'll be here in … well, you know how long it takes the cops to get out here."

They knew. The only law enforcement was the Sheriff's Department located in Weaverville 40 miles away. Sometimes a CHP would drive by, but that was as rare as Haley's Comet. Once a dead man washed up on one of the swimming beaches along the Trinity. It took the Sheriff's Department a full day to get someone to haul him away. When a deputy finally arrived on scene, someone asked what took so long? He replied, "He wasn't goin' nowhere was he?"

The people of Del Loma and the other minuscule towns scattered along Highway 299 knew exactly who to count on if trouble arrived — themselves. Gun racks decorated rear windows in pickups, while men and women carried a variety of knives (pocket or otherwise). There weren't enough inhabitants for the town to be compared to the days of the Wild West but more than a sprinkling of pot farmers, ex-felons and miscreants up and down the river made life difficult for law-abiding citizens often enough.

It reminded Falcon of a line in a Louis L'amour western novel when it came to self-preservation. *Better to be judged by 12 than carried by six.*

Rachel took to small town life like a kid riding a bike uphill. It was hard work, but sure fulfilling on the way down; getting fire wood and keeping the wood stove full, washing the dogs in the river, picking wild blackberries, cutting her babies' hair, and keeping them tick free. Her latest project found her growing and canning food for her family. With books from the county library in Weaverville, she planned and put in a garden near the front of the store. When business got slow, she enjoyed the majestic forest and watched the boys play.

Falcon hated his mother's garden.

"It's the size of a baseball field," he complained, the evening Mitch sent him to help his mother with weeding.

"It only looks that way because it isn't fenced in yet," Rachel said.

"Why can't I just work in the store?"

"It's good for you to learn about nature." Rachel stretched her back and retied the red bandana wrapped around her blonde hair. Her bare toes squished into the soft dirt and she itched her nose with the back of her soil-caked hand. "Like changing the oil in the car or washing your clothes, one day when you're grown you'll be glad you know how."

"No I won't," grumbled Falcon. "When I'm grown up, I'll be rich and pay other people to do it for me!"

Rachel laughed, "You're probably right honey, but you're going to learn anyway."

"There's no probably about it," he muttered under his breath.

They worked side by side until the summer sun began to fade. Rachel coerced her Grumpy Spider into singing Kenny Roger's *The Gambler*, Falcon's favorite song, and they ate sweet strawberries from the garden bigger than unshelled hickory nuts, as they weeded.

Deeter shouted from their single-wide trailer, "Hey Falcon, *Little House on the Prairie* is on!"

Falcon mumbled, "I'm living *Little House on the Prairie*."

Rachel stifled a giggle, "Go ahead; you've done a great job honey. I'll take care of the rest."

"Really Mom? I mean I'm kind of getting the hang of it now."

Falcon prayed she wouldn't take him up on his offer.

"Really, and you two may have some canned peaches with ice cream if you like."

Falcon nearly knocked her over with a hug. "I love you Mom."

"I love you too baby."

She kissed the top of his head and watched her beloved child disappear into the trailer. Left alone to finish, Rachel knelt down to thin the newly sprouted carrots. She heard a crunching noise and raised her chin. Startled at first by the sight of a horse snout only inches above her head, when her eyes focused on the rider she suppressed a gasp: Rotten Robert.

When men were released from prison in California, they received a one-way bus ticket to wherever they wanted to go. Too many of them sought out places like Del Loma, where they hid from law enforcement and wreaked havoc with little interference from authorities. Robert was just such a man. Rumor was he stabbed a man in a knife fight while the man was walking away. About medium build and a raggedy demeanor, he looked more like a bum than an outlaw. Locals guessed he crowned himself "Rotten" to sound more dangerous, but since cowards can be unpredictable, he probably was.

Before Rachel could respond Robert spoke.

"Ya knooow ..." he dragged out the word "know" as though he'd said something really important. "I saw them dogs of yours chasing deer in the woods the other day. If a ranger got wind of that, they'd put your dogs down."

Robert hated the boys' Australian shepherds, Amber and Bootes, and the feeling was mutual. Protective, intelligent animals, they'd sized Robert up on their first meeting. Because the store had been broken into at night a few times Mitch and Rachel had decided to lock the dogs in there at night. This stopped the break-ins from happening again. Robert was the prime suspect since his brand of cigarettes and beer were always missing after each robbery. Although the dogs couldn't speak, their behavior said it all as they had to be restrained anytime he showed his face.

The young woman remained poised on her knees. "It's none of your business what my dogs do."

"Well, being a upstanding citizen, it just might be my duty to turn 'em in. Better yet, I'll save the law the trouble and maybe shoot 'em myself."

He showed his yellow, rotten teeth while caressing the Colt .45 riding on his thigh.

Rachel stared at him as he continued.

"Nope, don't care for them dogs at all. Or your snotty kids neither, especially that redheaded one always looking at me like he's better or somethin'.'"

Rachel could feel blood scorching her neck as her heart banged a cadence in her ears. Growing up in an abusive home, she feared and hated violence. She couldn't spank her kids and cried on the rare occasion Mitch gave them a swat or two. But something inside her snapped.

She rose without hurrying, closed the gap between them, and spoke in a low, steady voice, "You think you're a big man, don't you, Mr. ... Rotten ... Robert?" She scoffed at the coward who sat high in his saddle. "I'm not afraid of you. And if you ever come near my children, it'll be the worst day of your sorry life. You're not the only one who has a gun ... and I swear you'll beg me to use it on you before I'm through."

She stared him down without a blink and then broke into an eerie smile.

Visibly shaken, Robert flinched and pulled on the reigns and backed up his horse. *That bitch is crazy.*

Rachel clapped her hands at the horse.

"Now get out of my garden and stay off my land!"

The next day Rachel reported the episode to the sheriff's office.

"I'm coming your way," said the deputy. "I'll stop by and you can sign a complaint for the judge to file a restraining order to keep him off your property. But if Robert was found floating face down in the river, it would sure save us all a lot of trouble, so long as it's in Humboldt County."

Rachel couldn't believe what she'd just heard. Did the sheriff actually expect her to kill a man? Del Loma was looking less and less like an innocent small town.

A few days later Mitch was doing inventory when Jerry walked back into the store.

"The deputy called me an hour ago. He said he was on his way."

Jerry had regained his composure since his last visit to the store. Falcon and Deeter were good kids, and Mitch was his friend. Never mind the fact Mitch was a bear of a man. "Sorry about last time. I was a little heated."

Mitch waved him off and nodded his head, "If you'd gotten too far out of line I'd have let you know."

Jerry was sure of that. "Yeah I know ... sorry anyway."

"Forget about it."

"Thanks." Jerry paused for a second, "If you don't want your kids to say what they saw I'll understand."

Mitch shook his head. "That wouldn't be the right thing to do. They're strong kids. They'll be fine. "

Falcon bolted into the store as he hoped to work the register and screeched to a halt when he saw Jerry.

"Sheriff will be here soon to get your story," Mitch told his son. "Why don't you hang out with us for a little bit."

"Sure dad, can I work the register?"

Mitch smiled at his boy. He always wanted to be around the money. Deeter loved the candy bars. Falcon loved the cash.

"Sure, get behind the counter and count the till for me."

The young tycoon in training jumped behind the counter, cranked the register, lifted the tray, and began to fondle the twenties.

While waiting for the Deputy Sheriff the two men talked.

Jerry said, "I heard you had a little problem with Wild Bill?"

Mitch shook his head like a lion in the Serengeti that tried to shake off flies.

Falcon knew the whole story.

With the purchase of the campground came several small trailer houses they rented to locals. A young pregnant woman on welfare named Hazel, and her one-year-old son, lived in a singlewide. A man who claimed to be her husband showed up at the store one day. He called himself "Wild Bill" and appeared to be another society deadbeat — just what Del Loma needed. Mitch discovered Bill had been beating his wife, and since his name was not on the lease, he kicked him out. Unfortunately the woman snuck him in and out at night, and the beatings continued. After several weeks, Wild Bill grew bold and moved back into the trailer where a series of problems followed. The park's cable line was spliced in two and those citizens who paid for the service had only a snowy TV screen. A forest ranger discovered pot growing in their community garden, which the Sanes could be held liable and prosecuted for. The woman continued to carry bruises and facial wounds, blaming this on her own clumsiness. All these things pointed to Bill; but the day Mitch saw Bill's motorcycle parked and noticed smoke billowing through a jerry-rigged stovepipe cut into the roof of the rented trailer, he'd had enough.

Mitch banged on the door. "Bill I know you're in there, don't make me come in after you."

A male voice returned a warning with obscene words.

"You'd better open this door," Mitch replied.

"I said fuck you!"

Mitch was a good man and easygoing but once his temper took over, God help the fool who stirred him up. Prepared to rip the door off its hinges, he was surprised when it suddenly swung open. The seven-month pregnant woman stood there dazed. Blood dripped from her nose, top lip swollen, and her pupils were dilated. Reeking of pot, she staggered forward, waddled down the stairs, and sat on a tree stump.

Mitch shook his head as he struggled with a combination of pity and disgust.

Bill appeared in the doorway dressed only in cowboy boots and filthy jeans.

"Get the hell off my porch!" he bellowed and took a swing at Mitch.

Mitch ducked and threw a rib-cracking punch into Bill's pasty beer belly. Collapsing to his knees, his bravado gone, he gasped for air like a beached fish.

As Mitch backed down the stairs he felt a sharp blow between his shoulder blades. Hazel had clouted him with a fist-sized rock. Turning he stared at the woman he and Rachel gave free rent to the previous month, and the same woman they'd given food and diapers to. The same woman they'd driven to the hospital for pre-natal check-ups and stitches from the last beating.

Mitch grabbed the rock from her hand. "Sit down and don't move."

Mitch angled his body to watch the woman as Bill attempted to rise.

"I'm gonna kill you," said Bill.

Bill's voice was raspy as he struggled to stand, but he was no match for Mitch — and they both knew it. Mitch grabbed Bill by his dirty ponytail, yanked him off the porch and dragged him to his bike.

"I'm saying this once. You've got 60 seconds to mount up and get the hell out of here. If I see you again, I'll drag you into the woods. This is your last warning. Are we clear?"

Bill, who appeared not so wild, stumbled to his bike and shouted obscenities once he was out of Mitch's reach.

After collecting the woman, her son, and their few belongings, Mitch and Rachel drove them 40 miles to Weaverville and the only hospital in the county.

Hazel was crying.

Rachel struggled to not do the same. "I packed the gifts from the baby shower in a plastic bag so they'd stay clean." Rachel placed it at the foot of the hospital bed. "Your other things are over there in the corner. Someone from social services is here to take your son where he'll be safe." She opened her purse. "Mitch gave me a hundred dollars. I'll put it in your pants pocket. I'm sorry things haven't worked out better for you, but you can't come back to Del Loma anymore. Good luck honey." She gave her a hug.

Mitch stood talking to the doctor at the front desk. "She doesn't have anywhere to go. She's burned her bridges with us."

The doctor nodded. He'd seen it too many times before.

After Mitch finished his story, Jerry helped himself to the complimentary coffee permanently stationed on the counter. "The town is better off without that scumbag, Mitch. I'd have done the same thing."

Mitch wondered if that were true.

At last the sheriff's deputy arrived to take the report about the stolen dredge. "We don't usually become involved with this kind of situation," he stated sounding surprised. "Most times it's taken care of with a beating and the return of property. If someone got too messed up, then there might be an arrest."

Falcon grew motionless behind the counter as the three men discussed the details.

"So you think it was your neighbor?" asked the deputy.

"Yep. Mitch's kid," Jerry motioned toward Falcon, "saw him take it."

The three men focused on Falcon; his heart stopped and started again.

"Did you see him take it, son?"

"I saw him playing with it."

"Playing? What exactly was he doing?" asked the deputy.

"He was looking under the tarp, and when he saw us coming, he took off."

"Who's us?"

Mitch said, "Both of my sons were there. Falcon here is the oldest."

"I see, then what?"

Falcon said, "About 10 minutes later he came back and asked what we were doing."

"Okay. Anything else?"

"No sir."

He wrote something in his book. "Jerry, you stay here. I'll talk to the guy alone. Maybe he'll give it back, and we can chalk it up to a big misunderstanding."

The conversation between Butch and the deputy resolved nothing. The deputy drove the 40 miles back to town and filed his report. It was up to the district attorney now.

Falcon and Deeter were immersed in summer vacation — building a tree fort, swimming and tubing in the river, and trying hard to avoid poison oak while exploring the forest and canyon that encompassed them. Shortly after the sheriff's visit, they were running down a deer trail when Butch's step-kids appeared on the path to block their way.

Mike, practically a grown man with facial hair and biceps, and Billy not far behind, positioned themselves on either side of their 17-year-old sister.

Falcon eased his body in front of Deeter, tried to swallow the sick feeling in his stomach, and knew his action wouldn't help or matter.

Mike grabbed Falcon's neck and slammed him against a nearby tree.

Billy pushed Deeter to the ground and wrenched his skinny arm behind his back.

The sister pointed at Deeter.

"Don't let that white-haired chicken shit loose." Then she turned toward Falcon. "Listen up you red-headed little faggot. The cops arrested our stepdad because of you. He's home now, but has to go to court next month."

She slapped Falcon across the face — hard.

Deeter struggled to get loose.

Billy yanked his arm up.

Deeter let out a cry.

Then planting a knee in the little boy's back, Billy said, "Sit still or you're next."

Falcon's eyes began to water, and he tried in vain to escape.

The sister slapped him again and banged his head against the tree.

"You're the only one saying you saw Butch steal that dredge. If you say it in court, we're gonna track you down just like today and kill you!"

She smacked his face again as hard as she could.

Falcon's emotions betrayed him, his body slumped, and he started to cry.

Deeter flailed on the ground.

Billy pushed the boy's face into the dirt. "Knock it off!"

Deeter began to wheeze and started to cry.

The sister raised her hand to strike Falcon again.

Mike let go of the trapped boy's neck and blocked her arm. "That's enough."

Falcon crumpled to the ground and covered his face.

Mike muttered under his breath, "That damned Butch. This is all his fault." *If he hadn't stolen the dredge, got arrested, and let out on bail, Mom wouldn't have told me to, 'Shut those little liars up.'* At first Mike had refused. Then after she slapped him, apologized and cried, he had finally agreed to do her bidding. Doubting Mike's resolve, she had sent her daughter along to make sure the job was done right.

Falcon remained crunched into a ball in the dirt.

The sister cocked her leg and aimed a kick at Falcon's head.

Mike pushed her before it reached Falcon and growled, "I said that's enough!"

Billy let go of Deeter who scrambled to his brother.

The menacing trio began to walk away.

"Remember what I said you little snitches," the sister yelled over her shoulder, "And you better not run home and tell your daddy and mommy either."

Mike pushed her, "Shut up!"

Deeter helped Falcon to his feet.

Leaning on each other for more than physical support, they headed in the opposite direction of their tormentors.

"It's okay Fal." Deeter's breathing was thin as he tried to help his brother.

Falcon knew it wasn't. His dirty tear-stained faced burned, the back of his head hurt, and that wasn't even the worst part. Two weeks ago he told the story to the District Attorney. The DA asked if he was willing to testify in court and he'd said, "Yes." Now if he did or told his parents, he and his brother might be killed.

The boys limped home and found their parents in the kitchen.

Once Falcon looked at them, he started to cry again.

"Honey!" Rachel flew to his side. "What happened to you? What's wrong?"

Fear, humiliation and pain overwhelmed Falcon and his little heart shattered.

"Sweetheart," Rachel held him to her chest.

Mitch ordered, "Stop crying Falcon and tell us what's wrong."

Deeter who always let Falcon do the talking couldn't stand to watch his brother suffer; in staggered breathes, he blurted out the whole sordid tale. "And they're going to kill us now!" And having told all he began to cry.

Rachel included Deeter in her embrace to comfort her babies.

"Mitch, get Deeter's inhaler from the ..."

The screen door slammed shut.

She glanced around the kitchen. Her husband was gone.

The transmission in the little yellow pickup bore Mitch's anger as he ground the gears. A wake of dust and gravel filled the air as the truck peeled out of the drive and powered down the highway. Still rolling when he reached Butch's house, Mitch jerked the emergency brake and jumped out leaving the engine running. In three strides he stood staring through the screen door at the coward who'd just threatened his children. He yanked the door open.

Butch clamored to his feet and threw a chair at him.

Mitch, a bull of a man, brushed it away like a strand of loose hair. Two steps later he clutched Butch by the throat, lifted him off the ground, and pinned him against the kitchen wall.

Butch's wife hurried out of the storm, flattened herself against the refrigerator, and froze.

Mitch's grasp was so tight, his prey began to gasp and struggle for breath. Fury gave way to rage, rage calmed down to anger, and as Butch's face turned purple Mitch regained control. He loosened his grip a little.

"If you or your kids ever *threaten* or *touch* my children again you're done! I'll come back and beat the fucking life out of you, you piece of shit. You got me?"

Butch tried to nod but couldn't.

Mitch opened his hand and threw Butch to the ground. Standing over him he spoke deliberately, "Do ... you ... understand ... me? I'd hate to think you didn't."

Cowering on the floor, Butch nodded.

Three weeks later 10-year-old Falcon Sane stood in the witness box with one hand on the Bible. Because children were involved, the judge ordered a closed session.

Rachel sat beside the DA, across the aisle from Butch and the public defender. The animal that had caused her children to be hurt smirked at her when everyone stood during the judge's entrance. Every fiber in her body wanted to attack him and gouge his evil eyes out. She thought it best to keep Mitch clear of him, and they agreed he would wait outside in the foyer with Deeter in case his testimony was needed.

The judge turned to Falcon, "Do you know what you just swore to son?"

"Yes sir, to tell the truth."

"And what does telling the truth mean?"

Falcon said, "It means not to lie. My mom and dad say everyone makes mistakes, but we cannot lie because then no one can ever trust us, not even ourselves."

The judge nodded. "Good enough."

The DA approached the boy. "Falcon, do you know why you are here today?"

"Yes ma'am."

"If it pleases the court because of the age of the witness I would like to ask him to simply tell us what he saw."

"Granted."

"Thank you your honor."

Falcon recounted the scenario of that Saturday morning that unleashed a myriad of troubles upon him. "Then my brother and me came home and watched Super-Friends and a cartoon about how a bill becomes a law."

"Very impressive," she said. "Perhaps one day you will be in here helping us enforce the laws."

"I don't think so. I'm going to get a college scholarship for baseball, play in the pros, and then be the President."

Soft laughter followed his response.

"Those are some lofty goals," said the DA. "Maybe you will play for the Giants one day."

"Nah. When I make it to the majors I'll be with the LA Dodgers. I want to play with Steve Garvey, Ron Cey, Bill Russell and Davey Lopes."

"Don't you want to play with Steve Yeager?" asked the bemused DA and staunch Giants fan.

"Nope, my dad says Joe Ferguson is better. Besides once I waited for half an hour to get Yeager's autograph. I was next in line when this girl showed up and he told me to beat it. Then he gave her a real Major League ball."

The judge smiled at Falcon. "You'll have to remember that story when you're in the pros and make certain your young fans aren't disappointed."

"I will sir," Falcon said solemnly.

The DA continued with her questioning. "So Falcon, the man you saw that day, do you mean the defendant?"

"Defendant?" Falcon furrowed his brow and shrugged. "I only saw Mike's stepdad, Butch."

"I apologize Falcon, is that person in the room here today?"

"Yes ma'am," Falcon said braver than he felt.

"Could you point to him please?"

Falcon looked at the man sitting a few paces away.

Butch glared and sneered at the boy the same way he had intimidated the children before.

Falcon's heart jumped, and he scanned the room for his mother.

Rachel gave him a reassuring glance and a slight nod of her head.

The judge said, "It's all right son. Don't be afraid."

Falcon turned back to face Butch and that smirk on his face turned the child's fear into anger. He remembered being banged against a tree and slapped over and over. He'd felt helpless to free himself or Deeter, and he didn't like that feeling. He took a gulp of air.

"Right there!" he nearly shouted and pointed at Butch. "He's right there!"

"Thank you Falcon," said the DA. "Please let the record indicate that the witness identified the defendant, Butch Clinton, as being at the scene of the crime."

"Objection," said the defense attorney

"On what basis?" asked the judge.

"The age of the witness your honor."

The judge said, "You're objecting to the witness' age?"

"Due to his age his memory may not be as precise as an adult."

"This young man's testimony of the events he witnessed seem quite precise to me, overruled."

"Then I object" whined the defense attorney, "based on no other corroboration."

The DA said, "His younger brother is right outside waiting to corroborate his story if need be your honor."

The judge was not about to allow another innocent child to be frightened. He lifted his glasses and stared at the defense attorney.

"Overruled."

Falcon listened intently to the barrage of words. He wasn't sure what just happened, but the DA was smiling, the defense attorney sat down looking defeated, and Butch's smirk was fading.

The DA winked at Falcon, "The prosecution tenders the witness."

The boy sat up taller in his seat.

The young defense attorney tightened his tie, stood, and walked to the center of the room. His style was a bit bookish, but he had to play the game in hopes of carving out a career for himself. Like many of his cases, he felt he had zero chance of winning. He'd told Butch if he returned the dredge the matter might be dropped. Butch implied he couldn't which meant it had already been sold. Taking his time in approaching the boy, the defense attorney pondered as to what question he might ask that would help his client and not piss off the judge. Everyone in the room knew his client was guilty. Sadly the time, effort and money wasted on one scumbag was the American justice system at work. He looked at the cute, little Dodgers fan and knew he'd better tread lightly or the judge would hammer him, not to mention, he'd heard Falcon's father was a monster if anyone messed with his kids. His own client said the man grabbed him by the throat and threw him across a room. He smiled inwardly remembering that story. *I'd like to do that too.* The rumor going around about the mother was hard to believe, though. The petite, fetching, well-dressed woman who sat beside the DA did not seem the type to mix it up with the likes of Rotten Robert. But the sheriff said Robert sniveled like a baby at his last parole check-in about her. *The Sanes sound crazy.* A kind of crazy he admired but didn't want to be on the receiving end of.

The judge cleared his throat, "Do you have any questions for the witness or not?"

"Yes your honor. Thank you."

But his questions were useless. Not only were there two eye witnesses, frightened little kids at that, but his client's stupidity in confronting the boys had seared the information into their memories. He didn't dare bring in the younger brother in case he started to cry. *The judge would cream me for sure.* He folded his hand, resting his case knowing there weren't enough cards in the deck to win this round.

The witness was excused from the courtroom, and the bartering began. The judge let it be known that the river carried news faster than a raft on the rapids, and he'd heard about the skirmish and threats the two boys had suffered at the hands of the defendant's much older step-kids.

"If anything should happen to the Sane children," he warned Butch, "I guarantee you will be the one held responsible."

He hoped that would fend off any future danger and remove the possibility of Mr. or Mrs. Sane being brought into his courtroom one day because they'd been forced to do what any real parent would — defend their children.

Butch pled guilty and agreed to apologize on the record to Falcon Sane. Once the plea agreement was made Falcon's parents took their boys home.

Mitch said, "No need hanging around to hear an apology that isn't sincere or going to fix anything."

Scheduled to serve a three-month sentence in the county jail, Butch was let out after two months for "good behavior." He lay low in Del Loma the last part of the summer with his wife until her parents kicked them out of their house for good. They slithered back to Los Angeles where rumor had it he'd been beaten to death in a bar fight.

Rachel's garden had become a showpiece. Magazine-quality tomatoes, succulent cantaloupe, towering beanpoles, sweet peas, nasturtiums, daisies and more beckoned the eye and tempted the pallet. Mac, a retired fireman, and Ernie, the local storyteller shared strawberry cuttings with Rachel. After digging up more rocks than sat in a riverbed and tilling in chicken manure from Jerry, everything she planted burst into being. The strawberry patch was picked each morning, but the fruit growth surpassed her ability to use it up so she began selling baskets of the fragrant crimson berries in the store.

Falcon leapfrogged off his mother's idea and enlisted the aid of Deeter, their cousin, and Jerry's two kids. He called the workers together with the enthusiasm of a circus barker, convincing them of the riches awaiting them by picking wild blackberries.

"Fill these baskets my mom gave me," he said, "And I'll pay you 25 cents for each one."

They scattered like a circle of marbles on one solid hit and spent hours combing the brambles.

Falcon kicked back and played fetch with Amber and Bootes as he slurped juice pops from his parent's freezer. When the workforce returned he happily paid 25 cents for each full basket to the weary, scratched and hungry bunch and threw in a juice pop as a bonus. Then sorting the fruit, he meticulously filled baskets only half-full, taped paper on the side that read, "$1.00," placed them in beer flats, and headed to the store.

"Mom, can I put my berries on the counter too and sell them?"

"Wow, that's a lot of berries. You must've been picking all day. Sure honey."

By the time the store closed all the berries had sold, and the ingenious industrialist was counting out money like a banker $10 richer.

The summer finished for Falcon and Deeter without any big issues. Mild sunburns on their knees and shins from tubing the river too long occurred. Regular workdays in the forest with the men getting wood for the winter and several cases of poison oak in their privates made Rachel wonder what the heck they were doing out in the woods.

Mitch said, "They're probably too lazy to come into the house to pee and just petting the dogs could transfer poison oak."

They played baseball in the field until dark, watched the

miners clean their sluice boxes, and paid other kids to buy candy for them in the store as they tried to get around their mother's rules. Most importantly, they didn't see Mike, Billy, or their mean sister.

The new school year was upon them and brought excitement and trepidation for Falcon and Deeter. The school bus route for all of Highway 299 started in front of the store and collected every school-aged child along the river. Mike rode the bus too, and this year he and Falcon were assigned to the same class of the tiny two-room school house. One twist of luck for Falcon was the exit of Mike's mother, his brother Billy and his sister. Mike's grandparents were staunch citizens of Del Loma, and after the dredge incident they gave their daughter an ultimatum: Get rid of Butch or move out of their home. Mike had had enough of his flaky mother and cruel stepfather and refused to go.

Falcon had never prayed before, but he gave a mental tip of his Dodger cap to God and said thank you, "Two down Lord, one to go." A few months away from turning eleven, Falcon grew, but he could grow all day and night and never catch up to Mike.

Falcon and Deeter climbed into the bus and sat near the front.

Mike spread out in the middle while the high school group headed to the rear. The cooler you were the further back you sat. The bus ride took 20 minutes for the kindergarteners through eighth graders. Their school wasn't named after anyone famous like Mac Arthur, it was called Cox Bar Elementary.

Maybe Cox did something special here, Falcon wondered.

The bus stopped and Falcon and Deeter walked quickly toward their classrooms. Deeter was two grades behind Falcon and in third grade and luckily still had Mrs. Wallace. She was smart, sweet and playful with her students. Best of all she liked kids.

Deeter worried about his brother, but felt relieved Mike was not going his way. "Good luck Fal. See you later."

Falcon hoped so. Trying to sound casual he said, "Sure Deed." He took a deep breath and sensed the tension in his day had only just begun. Aside from Mike, Falcon had to face Mrs. Boochie. He'd told Rachel last spring that the upper-grade teacher reminded him of the Wicked Witch of the West.

"I swear Mom, she looks just like her, and she's mean too. She called a boy stupid for having trouble with math and yelled at a girl for sharpening her pencil. She said she doesn't know why she's a teacher because she hates kids."

Now he would be stuck with her for the next four years. Vacations couldn't come fast enough. Falcon removed his Dodger cap as he entered the room. The desks weren't clustered by grade or set apart like Deeter's. His brother got easily distracted, and Mrs. Wallace gave him a special cardboard cubicle he could take on and off his desk. In Mrs. Boochie's room each desk was lined up military style five across, four deep, and so straight he wondered if she used a yardstick to position them. The bell rang.

Mrs. Boochie said, "I've organized the seating alphabetically, it's easier for me to call roll. Locate your seat immediately by reading the place cards and sit quietly."

Falcon hung his hat on the coat rack and searched for his name. Three seconds later he realized his day just got worse. Like his own, Mike's last name started with an S. "Oh man," he spoke beneath his breath. Falcon never used profanity. First, it was against his parent's rules, and he was a rule follower. Second, he never thought about life in a profane way. He'd heard it plenty on the playground and saw kids flip each other off, but it just wasn't in his nature. That morning as the witch bellowed through role call and the reality of sitting next to a guy all year who'd threatened to kill him sunk in, the only word he could think of to truly describe his situation was ... *fucked.*

He silently slipped into the desk next to his giant tormentor.

The witch droned on about something Falcon didn't care enough about to even try and follow. He'd always loved school, but could see that until he graduated to high school, survival would be the only lesson he needed to learn. Finally the sweet release of morning recess arrived.

"Listen for the bell," barked Boochie. "Anyone not in their seats on time will be sitting in the corner with their nose to the wall."

Falcon mumbled, "I might be safer there." He stood and started for the door.

Wham! A shoulder rammed into his head knocking him into a desk.

Mike smirked and walked by as if nothing happened.

Falcon paused and looked toward the witch.

She stared at Falcon then turned away. *Not my problem.* She couldn't wait for Mike to graduate. He was bigger than her and often intimidating.

Falcon shook it off and thought about his options. He lived for recess, but it might be safer staying in the classroom. *Not even Mike would try and kill me in front of the witch. Would he?* In the end he had no other option. Deeter would be out there, and Mike knew Falcon wouldn't let anyone hurt his brother without a fight. Trudging toward the door he reached for his cherished Dodger's cap then thought otherwise. *Better leave it here. This isn't going to be pretty.* He approached the playground like a man headed for the electric chair. He didn't have to wait long.

On the basketball court eight kids stood shoulder-to-shoulder holding various balls. Mike towered behind them glaring at Falcon.

Falcon scanned for Deeter and realized his class wasn't out yet, and there wasn't an adult in sight. Although Falcon demonstrated natural athletic ability, fighting wasn't in him yet; but neither was running. Fleeing wasn't an option as self-respect won that battle. He sized up the battery in front of him. Aside from two of Mike's friends, the rest liked Falcon. *Mike probably threatened them too — his standard mode of operation.* Everyone held a ball but the giant. Falcon noted one of Mike's buddies clutching a baseball and made a mental note while preparing for the bombardment sure to ensue. This situation was going to change today one way or the other.

Mike spoke first, "Say you're sorry."

"Sorry for what?"

"You know."

Falcon struggled to find his voice. "I don't. Why don't you tell me?"

Mike stared at the little kid. *Scared shitless and the runt still won't back down.* He'd felt bad last summer as he had grabbed Falcon by the neck while his sister had slapped him. When he heard that Mitch threw his stepdad across the room he smiled inside wishing he'd seen it. He hated Butch. But in Mike's mind Falcon was winning the fight, and he couldn't let that happen. He didn't have a good family or a future like Falcon. The only thing he had of value was physical power, and they both knew it.

"Last chance."

Falcon defied him, "Or what?"

Any opportunity for emotional growth became nil as Mike's fragile ego could not sustain being challenged.

He screamed, "Fire!"

Falcon immediately focused on the baseball knowing it could do the most damage. The kid's aim was poor and it went high and to the right. Falcon jumped, snagged it, and threw it back as hard as he could. He had been making such plays since he was little, and the kid was caught off guard at the speed. Instinctively the kid ducked, the ball sailed over his head and hit

Mike square in the face.

The group gasped, the bombing stopped, and the kids slunk away from Mike.

Embarrassed and in pain, Mike stormed toward Falcon.

"Now you're gonna get it you little fucker!"

Falcon froze as Mike closed the gap between them. He knew he couldn't win, but it was time to make a stand. He raised his fists.

Mike threw a punch.

Falcon ducked and spun around.

Enraged and out of control, Mike swung wildly as Falcon ducked again.

The scattered children inhaled as Falcon threw a punch that landed on Mike's cheek. *Maybe he could win.* That victory was short-lived as the beast lifted him in the air and slammed him to the ground and crushed the boy with his full body weight.

Struggling to get free was impossible but Falcon tried gamely.

"Are ya done?" Mike asked Falcon

That stirred Falcon's outrage, and he tried to get loose again.

Like a boa constrictor Mike's grip tightened further on his body. "Are ya done now?" he asked.

Falcon thrashed his legs but the monster weighed too much.

"Just stop moving," Mike breathed in Falcon's ear. "And I'll let you go."

Helpless in the dirt, Falcon knew he couldn't budge him. Struggling to breathe and wanting to cry he clenched his jaw and bit the sides of his mouth. His crying days in front of others was over.

"Seriously," Mike almost pleaded, "if you stop moving I'll let you go."

Exhausted and subdued Falcon stopped. One second turned

to two, then three. "I stopped! Let me go!" he screamed.

"Calm down. I am."

Mike knew he could handle Falcon, but the kid's attitude changed drastically since summer. He just proved he'd fight, and Mike figured Falcon might kick him or at least try to when he let him go.

When Falcon felt the teenager shift his weight he coiled his leg into a position as he planned to kick him in the head.

Mike was ready and jumped back out of reach.

Falcon scrambled to his feet and glared at Mike for a few seconds, then turned and headed toward the bathroom. The words, "don't cry, don't cry" wove through his brain like a man-tra. Alone in the bathroom he stared at his ravaged reflection in the mirror and pain pierced his heart.

"You will not cry. You will not, never, ever again."

His eyes hardened and he felt the door slam on his childhood.

As Falcon stared into the mirror the bathroom door began to inch open. He kicked it shut.

"Hey, you okay?" asked Chuck, Mike's henchman, the one who ducked and missed the power of Falcon's right arm. "Mike wants to talk to you."

Falcon took stock of the situation. He'd had enough. He wasn't afraid anymore. "I'll pass."

"Whattaya mean?" Chuck asked incredulously.

Falcon ripped the door opened and Chuck jumped back.

"Are you deaf? I said ... 'I'll pass.'"

"But—"

Chuck was older but not much bigger. As Falcon stepped toward him he spoke in striking staccato syllables, "Get—away—from—me!"

Chuck backed up. *This kid is crazy, crazy enough to take on Mike. I didn't want to deliver the dumb message in the first place.*

"Take it easy Falcon."

He made a quick escape.

Mulling over all that transpired Falcon brushed off his pants and shirt. The bell rang, and he strode back to his classroom. Shoulders square, eyes forward, he sat down at his desk. Beaten, but unbroken, Falcon Sane was a brand new man.

His opinion of his teacher immediately turned from fear to disrespect. He didn't need her guidance, a kind word or approval anymore. Not that those things were happening anyway. She'd displayed her character by succumbing to her own fear of Mike and ignoring her most important duty, the safety of her children. Although his young mind couldn't explain his change toward her in that fashion it was really very simple. As an authority figure she'd let him down. Disrespect earned, disrespect given. His attention turned to his history book, devouring information about General George S. Patton's drive across Europe during World War II. Patton served to strengthen his resolve. *I might be only an army of one, but I too will push on.* After an hour and a half of history and English it was almost time for their next recess break. Falcon watched the clock and readied himself to plow through the door regardless of who stood in his path.

Mike's body shifted as he too prepared to overtake the door with the bell.

Falcon did the math as he counted out the steps to the door. *No way will I make it to the door first.* His heart raced and adrenaline burst through his veins as he prepared for another fight. Fifteen seconds left. *Just blow through the door and take him with you.* Then inexplicably a strange sense of peace washed over him and an alternative plan came to light. As his young mind put the plan into place he smiled secretly.

The second hand passed the 12 and the bell rang.

Mike bolted for the door.

Falcon remained still; he made no attempt to look around as the room emptied.

Boochie glanced at the boy, uncomfortable with his silence and then left as well.

After the classroom emptied he slowly walked outside, paused and scanned the playground. A game of dodge ball limped along. Like a soldier, Falcon marched to his destination, the only jungle gym on the playground. The bars were on a hill overlooking the other students. Patton would've been proud. Falcon had taken the high ground. His plan was simple. His physical strength was insufficient at present, but his leadership and athletic competitiveness were prized by the older kids, especially Mike. By removing himself from the equation and refusing to engage, the other kids would be hard-pressed to enjoy recess. By choosing his turf wisely, he was in a prime spot to defend should anyone decide to attack. Twenty minutes passed, as Falcon endeavored to entertain himself on the bars. It was grueling as his entire body ached for athletic competition, but he waited, watching with detached eyes as the pathetic dodge ball game whimpered out.

The bell clanged releasing the tension.

Falcon walked purposefully to class neither looking for a fight nor giving ground. He took his seat and began to work on his math never acknowledging his Soviet Union barely inches away.

Chuck turned to sneak a peek at Falcon.

Falcon felt eyes on him, raised his head, and shot Chuck down with a piercing glare.

Chuck looked to Mike.

Mike stared at the chalkboard in front of him lost in thought.

I'm not doing that again, thought Chuck.

Falcon's thought process was morphing. Though he preferred peace, a passage in a book he'd read recently started to make sense. It read, "Men are easy to understand if you know which kind they are. Do they aspire to be liked, respected or feared?" When asked why you couldn't be all three, the character replied, "You can be liked, but evil has no respect for that. You can be respected but evil has no self-respect, so respect for others is impossible. Or you can be feared, knowing full well people who fear you will never like you. The choice is yours. But don't try to be more than one. You'll only get yourself hurt or worse."

The expression on Chuck's face told Falcon all he needed to know about survival. Falcon was done caring about being liked. It was now down to respect or fear.

Mathematics gave way to Social Studies and Boochie railed on about the E.R.A.. Falcon listened to Boochie's thoughts for a while and then completely dismissed anything she had to say about women's rights. Mrs. Wallace had explained this issue to him last year and engaged him in dialogue about freedom and personal responsibility for all regardless of gender or race. These ideas resonated with him and matched the values and ethics he'd been taught by his parents and were completely opposite of the drivel coming from Boochie. Just as Boochie worked herself into a lather and denigrated males everywhere including her students, the lunch bell rang.

Falcon sat peacefully at his desk while the room emptied. Boochie gave him a rude look then left him sitting alone. He grabbed his lunch and headed to his new bunker to eat in self-appointed solitary, save one.

"Hi Fal," Deeter raised his lunchbox like a wave as he walked up the hill.

"Hey buddy."

No other words were spoken. The two brothers opened their lunches and ate silently. When they finished Falcon pointed, "Put your box over there behind the rock."

"Why?"

"They'll be out of the way in case we have trouble."

Deeter's eyes got big. "What kind of trouble?"

"Don't worry, let me handle it."

"What should I do?"

"Leave your box and go back to your class. I'll bring it later."

"Should I tell my teacher?"

"No. Just get away quick."

"Falcon if there's trouble I don't want to leave you all ..."

"Trust me Deed, I can take care of it easier if you're not here."

Deeter wondered if Mike had threatened his brother during recess. He might be just a skinny little kid, but he could smash Mike with a rock or something.

"I'll stay with you Fal, I'm not afraid," he lied.

Falcon knew Deeter was afraid, but he admired his loyalty.

The two boys sat watching. One by one the younger kids ventured off doing little more than separating themselves from Mike's gang who lounged around the picnic table. The bell rang and everyone returned to class.

Falcon continued his plan the following week, accompanied by his brother. It was now "Day Five on Bunker Hill," so aptly named by Falcon in reverence to Americans long ago who just like him had had enough.

Deeter stirred and finally asked a question he'd been sitting on for the last couple of days. "How long are we gonna sit here?"

It was a fair question, a question Falcon didn't have an answer to. "Until someone makes a move."

Deeter slumped at his big brother's answer.

"You don't have to stay."

"I know, but I'm not going back without you."

Falcon thought about it and nodded.

"I'll grab a football next time and we can throw it around up here."

That lifted Deeter's spirit.

"Good idea, Fal."

Two weeks into the stalemate the brothers marched to their hill and tossed a football around. The playground activity had halted since no one rallied the kids or organized teams. A few young stragglers asked permission to play with Falcon, and he made it look like they were having the time of their lives. It was just enough to weaken Mike's hold.

"This is boring Mike," said Burt, a kid in Mike's grade and near his size. "Recess is the only good thing about school." He pulled a buck knife from his boot and flipped it into the dirt.

"Yeah Mike," said Chuck. "When are we gonna do something?"

Mike glared at Chuck. "With who? There's no one to play with."

Burt thought about that and chimed in, "Let's make Falcon play with us or you can beat him up again."

The last two weeks had been eye-opening for Mike, although he didn't quite know what to make of Falcon. School was easy enough, and he played sports better than most, but he'd never been a bully. Having had three stepfathers, Butch being the worst, Mike had plenty of practice on the receiving end. He didn't like it. Butch was a drunken, skirt-chasing loser. The guy even flirted with Mike's sister. One night his grandfather had had enough and called Butch on it. He pushed the old man down hard and laughed. Mike jumped in to defend his grandfather and caught a fist on the jaw. Butch had been aching for an excuse to beat Mike's ass. The unmistakable sound of a shotgun being racked froze the drama's momentum.

"One more step Butch, and it'll be your last."

Mike's grandmother leveled the double barrel shotgun at the abuser.

"Ma!" screamed Mike's mother. "Put that down!"

Unshaken the grandmother stared down the sights and took up the slack in the trigger.

"Butch, get out! Get out before she shoots ya!" Mike's mother pushed the man out the front door. With her man now banished from the house permanently, she took Billy and her daughter, and left for good the next day.

"Make that lying little prick Falcon pay," she told Mike when he refused to leave with them.

Mike had felt bad when he hurt Falcon the first time and only harassed him because he'd promised his mother. When Falcon hit him in the face with the baseball, he had lost his temper. Now Burt wanted to force the kid to play with them or beat him up again. *This is just stupid ... and wrong.* He looked at Burt.

"You want to beat him up because he won't play with us?"

"Why not, he's a punk. Who does he think he is anyway playing up there with his little brother? If he doesn't do what we say let's just beat his ass, better yet ..." Burt lifted his jeans a few inches to show the buck knife sheaved in his boot.

Mike studied him carefully. "You can't beat someone up because they won't play with you asshole." *What a mess.* A mess caused by a prick who'd gone to jail and was now in Los Angeles out of Mike's life. Mike looked up the hill at Falcon — the kid hadn't done anything wrong. In fact, he'd actually done the right thing. *This has to stop, now.* "Chuck, go tell Falcon I want to talk to him."

Chuck whined, "But, that didn't work last time."

"You pussy, I'll do it; I'm not afraid to tell him." Burt turned toward the hill.

Mike shoved Burt back. "Shut the fuck up."

Falcon stood on Bunker Hill out of earshot and watched Mike and his gang argue and glare at each other, while Mike's face turned red as a hot thermometer. Falcon decided something was coming. *Maybe it'll be that crazy Burt, who always brags about what he could do with his buck knife.*

"Deeter, hand me that stick we hid by our lunchboxes the other day."

Deeter scurried to retrieve the weapon. "Whatcha gonna do with it?"

Falcon grasped the three-foot long, two-inch thick solid piece of oak as if it were a Louisville Slugger. He didn't answer his brother, just swung the stick nice and easy like a baseball bat although the message was anything but playful. Keeping his eye on the gang, he continued swinging the stick finding his rhythm.

"Remember what I said Deed. If they come up, you run back to class."

"But—"

Falcon glared drilling him with the same "I-mean-it" look that their mom used.

"O-kay."

Falcon watched Mike and his two henchmen as the conversation quieted. A decision had been made. He tightened his grip on the sturdy piece of wood.

Chuck peeled away from the group and headed up the hill.

Falcon focused and counted his steps. If all three of them came at the same time the halfway point on Bunker Hill was where Falcon would make his stand. Patience was his first line of defense. The words he'd read in his history book from a *Revolutionary American Colonel "to wait until you see the whites of their eyes"* before attacking reverberated through his head. With a little luck they'd all block each other while he attacked and escaped. Defending the hill was a lost cause, but as brave Americans centuries ago had realized, one lost battle didn't matter as long as you won the war.

Chuck's eyes stayed glued to the stick as he drew closer to

the swinging club reminding him of the baseball that flew over his head. *This kid's fucking crazy.* He shook his head, but continued to advance, too young to grasp at the moment, his entire life was being marked by the decisions he made. Chuck would undoubtedly be the deliverer of other people's words. He would forever wait to be told what to do, forever a follower. Chuck halted at the bottom of Falcon's hill.

As pleasant as he could he said, "Mike would like to talk to you."

Falcon waggled the stick in the air and listened.

"Mike says he wants you to come back. He wants this to be over."

Mike couldn't hear Chuck, but nodded when Falcon looked at him to signal that Chuck spoke for him.

"Is this a trick?" asked Falcon

"No! Not at all. He wants you to come back. We all do."

Chuck threw in a smile and tried to convince Falcon.

"What about Burt?"

Sensing a chance at a truce Chuck lied, "Burt too."

Falcon was pretty sure Chuck had just lied to him, although he couldn't pinpoint what part. "I'll think about it."

"Sure, sure, take your time." Chuck felt elated. "I'll tell Mike."

The messenger scurried back to the pack.

Falcon mulled his options through again. *I can fight. I can stay on the hill until Mike graduates to high school, or ...*

"Well?" asked Mike.

Chuck said, "He wants to think about it."

"What's to think about?" Burt sneered, "That little bitch!"

"I'm not telling you again Burt, shut up," ordered Mike.

Falcon turned to Deeter and smiled. If he was right, the group realized they needed the glue of a leader, and even Mike knew that glue was standing on the hill swinging a club.

"Are you going down there, Fal?" asked his brother worriedly.

Falcon nodded.

"Are you taking our stick?"

He wanted to, but intrinsically knew for this to be over he had to show good faith. Mike had reached out. It was time to do the same.

"Nope, the weapons for peace are strength and trust." He tossed the stick aside.

"Be careful Fal, I love you."

"Thanks buddy, I love you too."

As Falcon drew near the group he was surprised.

Mike smiled and extended a hand to shake.

Falcon did the same.

"Sorry about all this," Mike said.

Falcon took a deep breath, "Thanks. Sorry I hit you in the face with the ball."

Mike laughed, "No you're not."

"Yeah," Falcon grinned, "you're right."

Mike still held the young boy's hand.

"Really, Falcon, I am sorry ... about everything."

Falcon felt the sincerity in Mike's voice and could sense the war was over. It was time to sign the peace treaty.

"Let's forget it ever happened and play some dodge ball!"

The playground magically morphed back into its former creation, *ground on which to play* as the other children joined again from all over the schoolyard.

That night the two Sane brothers lay in their bunks talking into the darkness.

"That was a close call today," said Deeter. "If anyone tried to hurt you, I was ready to grab that stick and whomp 'em."

Falcon felt warm inside knowing his kid brother would've tried to watch his back. *Thank God I didn't need that.*

"You know I would!" Deeter added.

In a few years his little brother would be a fierce warrior when someone stirred him up but right now he was still a little dude.

"I know you would've you crazy Spider Monkey."

"Go to sleep boys," said Rachel from the other room.

The boys giggled and drifted peacefully into dreams, unaware that one more battle waited in the morning.

The world appeared to have changed overnight as Falcon and Deeter rode the school bus the next day. Falcon and Mike behaved like lottery winners, grinning and chatting with everyone. Even the crotchety bus driver noticed the change and cranked up his cassette tape of Creedence Clearwater. The bus was rocking, and the kids were having a blast as the big wheel kept on turning into the next stop where Burt and a few others got on.

Burt hesitated next to Falcon's seat and then moved toward the rear.

No one thought much of it except Mike.

Falcon felt like a new man. The collapse of his Soviet Union brought reborn excitement to his life. Once again he thought about books, baseball, school and girls! The bus driver apparently had a mixed tape as Lynyrd Skynyrd blasted *Free Bird* over the jovial kids and Falcon sang along. His world was back on track, and he was ready to run free.

Mike sat across from Falcon but watched Burt, who seemed fixated on the kid. Burt was always a little strange but he and Falcon had never had a problem before Mike stirred things up.

A couple seats back Burt reached down and checked his buck knife. Tracing a finger over the smooth deer antler handle, he knew the blade would be reliable after sharpening it all night. Staring at the red-haired kid in front of him he wished for the old days when you could scalp someone.

He muttered to himself, "You're lucky we aren't back there, Red."

Mike leaned toward Burt, "What'd you say?"

"Nothing."

"You sure?"

Burt shrugged.

Mike took a deep breath. He'd just fixed the mess he'd caused, he wasn't about to let this happen. Pretending to stretch his long legs he slipped into the seat, which separated Burt and Falcon.

"What's up?" Mike asked Burt.

Burt didn't answer him.

Mike looked at the menacing teenager. "Where's your knife?"

Burt bragged, "In my boot like always."

"Make sure it stays there."

"Says you."

Mike slammed a fist against the back of his seat that caused Burt to jump. "Yeah says me."

They locked eyes, but Burt looked away first. He was no match for Mike, and they both knew it.

The bus arrived at Cox Bar and laughing, enthusiastic children emptied out.

Falcon was still humming, and it was all he could do to refrain from running. He'd stayed up late finishing a 12-page report on Nathan Hale the American Revolutionary hero. Today he planned to start on Benjamin Franklin.

Burt slipped behind Falcon and knocked him to the ground.

His notebook, lunch and papers scattered, and all 12 pages of his report took flight. A breeze even blew some up to Bunker Hill. His joy evaporated as he stared at his hard work fluttering around him.

Burt laughed, "Looks like it's raining paper."

Falcon lay there stunned. He'd thought his troubles were over, now here he was in the middle of it again. But he'd had enough. He remembered the words, like, respect or fear. Like and respect didn't appear to be working. It was time to deliver some fear. He got up and squared off with Burt.

Burt's smirk disappeared as he reached into his boot.

Falcon didn't care. He was fed up and stepped forward when a strong hand grabbed him from behind, yanked him backward almost off his feet, and briskly pushed him aside — that hand belonged to Mike.

"Put that fucking knife away Burt!" Mike ordered stepping in front of Falcon.

The bus driver saw the situation, closed the doors, and drove off.

"He's just a punk, you said so yourself."

Mike said, "He's my friend now, and I'll beat your fucking ass right here and keep that knife forever."

Confused by this sudden turn of events, Burt put the weapon back in his boot. It wasn't worth taking a beating or losing his identity over. "Whatever."

"No ... not whatever," said Mike. "It's over, got it?"

"Yeah I got it."

Mike said, "Good! Now help me pick up Falcon's papers."

The three boys collected the cherished report.

Burt handed his pages to Falcon. "Here you go. Sorry."

Mike smoothed the pages and handed the rest to Falcon. "That's all of them."

"Thanks Mike."

"No thanks needed. This was my fault. I'm just glad he didn't stab anybody."

Falcon gulped, "Me too."

Mike laughed at Falcon, "He's almost as crazy as you!"

As the two friends walked to class together, respect and fear traveled through Falcon's mind. He wasn't so sure about respect or fear anymore. He was starting to like Mike.

The school day finished, and the bus dropped Falcon and Deeter off in front of the store.

"See you later Mike," Falcon said.

"See you later Falcon."

Life felt normal again.

The boys waved through the store window to Uncle Jack and walked home. They hugged and kissed Rachel who was cooking supper and then headed off to do their chores.

Thirty minutes later Mitch came home. He'd been in the trailer park where he fixed a fence. In his hand was a beautiful pie still warm. He set it down on the kitchen table.

Deeter slid by trying to get as close as he could to the delicious smell. Inhaling deeply he grinned at his parents.

"Can I have a piece?" he asked as sweetly as he could with his little eyelashes batting innocently.

Rachel started to say no, but Mitch winked at her and nodded to Deeter.

"Go get your brother. You can both have a piece, in fact you can have as much as you want."

Deeter's eyes expanded to the size of dinner plates. He raced down the hallway then yelled out the backdoor, "Falcon! Hurry up and get in here! It's an emergency!"

With his message delivered, he sprinted back to the table and angled for the best position.

Falcon crouched behind the house and dumped black sand into a mini-sluice box made by one of the gold miners who lived in the trailer park. The shiny black sand sucked up by a dredge from the Trinity River held flecks of gold. It was a tedious job, but with enough patience and water applied the sand washed away and left the gold behind. The miners didn't mind the young entrepreneur who dug through the black sand and looked for treasure. They appreciated his passion since they felt the same about the yellow metal. Falcon heard Deeter's call about an emergency and headed toward the house. He knew it wasn't an emergency by the tone of his little brother's voice. Deeter was hilariously dramatic when excited. *I'll bet it's something to eat.* He laughed to himself. Immediately the aroma caught his attention as he walked down the hallway and into the kitchen.

Deeter was almost beside himself as he chattered, "You promised Dad. You said we could have as much as we want! You heard him, Mom."

"That's what I said." Mitch winked at Rachel again.

Rachel studied her husband quizzically.

Falcon approached the kitchen table and Deeter cut in front of his brother.

"Falcon's here. Can I paleeassse have some now?" Deeter smacked his lips with sugary anticipation.

"Sure go ahead," said Mitch. "Have as much as you like." Falcon's head snapped around. He knew the rules. No sweets before dinner. "As much as we like Mom?"

"Aw Rach," Mitch said. "They're only kids once. Sometimes you have to bend the rules a little."

The boys looked to their mom.

She shrugged, "I guess it'll be okay."

Deeter lunged forward and completely ignored the idea of a fork or plate.

"Whoa, whoa, whoa!" exclaimed Falcon. "I thought I was going to get some!"

Mitch smiled. "Sure buddy you can have as much as you like too."

Rachel watched the scenario unfold knowing something

wasn't quite right. But all of her men seemed so happy she went along with the program while instilling some decorum.

Rachel said, "Let's cut one piece each for you two."

Deeter wasn't having it, "Dad said we could have as much as we like!"

"And there's more where this came from too," Mitch said.

Spider Monkey nearly fainted at the thought of endless sugar.

A tiny voice in Falcon's head told him something wasn't right, but he shut that noise down immediately when dollar signs flashed before his eyes. *Maybe when I'm full I can sell it to the other kids in town.*

Rachel laughed at all the excitement and energy.

Falcon announced, "If we can have all we want then I want the whole thing."

Deeter went ballistic. "I'm the one that told you it was an emergency Fal! I deserve the pie more than you do!"

Mitch offered a solution. "Why don't you split this one and if you want more we'll get some more."

"Woo-hoo!" hollered the boys. They raced to get plates.

Rachel shot Mitch a questioning glance, and then restored order before Deeter climbed over Falcon's back for first crack at the delicious dessert.

"Okay that's enough. Falcon you cut the pie in half, and Deeter can choose first which half he wants."

This was Rachel's standard technique utilized whenever they had to split things. It worked well except for soda pop. Deeter had a nasty habit of backwashing. The new rule worked out by the brothers on soda sharing was Falcon could take the first drink and then Deeter could have the rest. Deeter always ended up with more, but Falcon couldn't stomach floating food in the bottle.

Falcon's tongue sat on his top lip as he excruciatingly and

deliberately cut the pie in two equal portions.

Deeter bounced on the balls of his feet in sheer delight. "After this half, I'm getting a whole pie for myself. As much as I want, right dad?"

"Yes sir."

Falcon finished and turned the pie to his brother. "Which one do you want?"

Deeter leaned over, his mouth salivating, and licked his chops. "I'll take ... that one." He pointed with the certainty of a commanding general.

Falcon cut his own piece in two and lifted both to a plate. He then pushed the tin toward Deeter with his half of the pie.

Deeter didn't need any encouragement. He grabbed his fork like a starving man and dug in. Spearing a bite three times too big for his mouth, he started to shove the entire piece in.

Mitch stopped him. "Hold up a minute Deeter. Let Falcon get a bite too."

Deeter's fork stopped in midflight as his face contorted into a pain only known to sugar fiends. "Hurry up, Fal!"

The boys closed their eyes simultaneously and put the delicious pie into their mouths.

Instantly Deeter's taste buds screamed.

Falcon spit his bite back onto the plate. "Blech! This is horrible!"

Deeter was still trying to get the monstrous bite out of his mouth. He grabbed a napkin and began to ferociously wipe his tongue.

Mitch jiggled from silent laughter as tears streamed down his face.

"This pie is rotten Dad!" Falcon saw his pie profits disappearing. *Nobody will buy this!*

"Yeah Dad, this pie is rotten!" Deeter continued to evacuate the gargantuan piece that only seconds ago looked too small.

Revolted, Rachel accused, "You gave them rotten pie?"

"No ... no ... it's not rotten." Mitch stopped laughing long enough to say, "It's green tomato."

"Green tomatoes?" repeated Falcon. "I don't like red tomatoes. Who wants to eat green-tomato pie?"

"Apparently not too many people. Does this mean you guys don't want any more?"

"Yuck! No way," said Falcon.

It wasn't that cut and dry for Deeter. He took an unlimited sugar offer a bit more personally. He didn't want to believe his dream come true had a hitch. "So this isn't rotten ... they all taste this bad?"

Mitch began laughing again.

Rachel shook her head and started to clean up the pie debacle. "Falcon, please take the pie outside and see if the dogs will eat it, and Deeter I need you to set the table."

Deeter stared at the pie as his brother dumped his pieces back into the tin. *So close ...* and his heart sank when his sugar dream was dumped into the dogs' bowls.

Amber and Bootes sniffed it twice and walked away.

They wouldn't eat it either.

4

Mike outgrew Cox Bar and headed to high school, while Falcon just grew and grew to six feet and sixth grade. His regular chores of cutting and stacking wood and helping his parents maintain the store and trailer park were beneficial as his body became strong. The "townies," (people who lived in Weaverville upriver from Del Loma) called the kids living along Highway 299 "downriver". This was meant as a slight since Weaverville was supposed to be more upscale than the little mill towns heading west along the Trinity. Falcon ignored the labels. He was born in Southern California and raised in the mountains. He didn't consider himself a city or mountain kid; but the idea of labeling seeped into his consciousness, and it came full circle one day when Boochie started on another rant. She had a new favorite *ism* to play with. She traded in feminism for racism.

During social studies one day she said, "Falcon, can you give an example of something that describes you?"

He thought about it for a second. "I'm an American."

"Yes, but can you add to that?"

"My name is Falcon Sane, *and* I'm an American."

"Let's try it a different way. What color are you?"

Falcon examined his arm, "Kind of pink with tan freckles."

"That's not what I am talking about!"

Falcon had no idea what she was talking about.

"Your skin is white," she announced.

"Okay?"

"Do you believe you are special because you have white skin?"

"I don't know what you mean," he said.

"Being a white male doesn't make you better than a black man."

Falcon scanned the room to look for an answer. Everyone else appeared confused too.

"You downriver kids are so ignorant. You'll never amount to anything. It's a good thing there's welfare."

Falcon was bewildered about her skin color questions, but he didn't need an interpreter to know she'd called him stupid. At the dinner table that evening he posed the subject to his parents.

"My teacher said being white doesn't make you better than being black."

Rachel's eyes tightened as she listened to her son. She'd worn out her welcome at Cox Bar the past two years with scheduled and nonscheduled visits due to the teacher's abusive rhetoric, inconsistent teaching patterns, and wildly inappropriate choices of classroom topical discussions. She'd taken her concerns before the principal also to no avail, as he was Mr. Boochie. Falcon was bright and loved to learn. He politely and respectfully followed the rules authority figures set before him. His teachers in the past had praised him, even commenting that students like him made their jobs a joy. He loved school — that is, until her. Each day his grievances grew stronger, and his mood as he stepped off the bus became darker until at last he said nothing at all.

"The color of someone's skin doesn't make them better or worse," Rachel said.

"Then how can white men keep black men down?"

Falcon's parents shared a disgusted look.

"And she said," continued the boy, "downriver kids are ignorant and it's a good thing there's welfare."

Rachel drove her boys to school the following morning and walked into Mrs. Boochie's classroom.

The teacher turned. "What are you doing here?" she snapped. "We do not have an appointment."

Rachel's desire for civility vanished. "Did you tell the students yesterday being white does not make them better than being black?"

"It doesn't—"

"And did you call my son a downriver kid and say it's a good thing there's welfare?"

Mrs. Boochie glared. *How dare this downriver white woman question her teachings? Who does she think she is?*

"Your son's a liar, and he's manipulating you," she said.

Rachel stepped forward.

Boochie stepped back.

Quietly Rachel said, "The only liar in this room is you. I warned you I would take my children out of here if you didn't stop. You don't deserve to call yourself a teacher. The only subjects you're teaching are hate, guilt and distrust. Shame on you." She turned and left the room to seek out the principal.

"Beginning today, I am taking Falcon out of your wife's classroom. In the fall both of my sons will be enrolled at Junction City. I told you the next time would be the last time. You should be ashamed of yourself and your wife."

The principal sighed. He actually agreed. His wife was out of control, ranting about freedom for the black man, woman's liberation, and how the white man was holding both of them down. She was free to have her opinions, but the classroom needed to remain off bounds. Ironically, the fact that Mr. Boochie was a

Jason Kraus   77

white man seemed to be lost on his wife. "She'll be retiring in two years."

"That's two years too late."

"There's only a month left in school. What if I place Falcon next door with Mrs. Wallace? I'm sure she won't mind."

"What about the other children? This isn't only about my sons. She isn't fit."

He said, "I understand your concerns. Can we address one thing at a time? I'll sit in on her class the rest of the month. Can we please try and work this out?"

Rachel considered his offer. A transfer request required a hearing, which could take weeks. Falcon needed to be free of that woman now, and although the bus ran all the way to town, her sons would be exempt from riding it if she chose to move them. That meant driving a 60-mile round trip, twice every day. If she waited until fall, the sale of the campground and store would be complete and her schedule open. That settled it. Both boys were transferring in the fall. "That will work but believe me; if she so much as looks at my son I'll file a complaint with the board."

"I understand Mrs. Sane," said Mr. Boochie.

Rachel added, "I'll be checking back regularly. If you aren't in that classroom with the other children I will report the two of you to the superintendent."

The ending of the school year also brought the sale of the two families' business. The store and trailer park had served their purpose in finding a new start but neither of them was profitable enough for one family to survive on let alone two. The store and park sold and new businesses purchased. Uncle Jack and Aunt Karen moved to Weaverville and bought a store called Western Auto that sold auto parts and a myriad of house and garden supplies. The Sanes purchased a local dairy distributorship that delivered milk, cheese, ice cream and ice (among other things) up and down the river.

With the purchase of the distributorship Falcon, 11, and Deeter, 9, spent the summer working 12- to 14-hour days, three times a week. The bumper sticker on the ice trailer read, "I drive Highway 299 — pray for me." Mitch was an excellent driver but rockslides, deer and other drivers kept him wide awake as they traveled the treacherous highway that wound through Trinity and Humboldt County. The boys crashed in the sleeper in-between stops. Mitch did the small accounts, schools, country stores and the restaurants, but he would shake the boys out for the super markets, Indian Reservation, and the hospital. The front trailer carried cold items, except for the back portion which held ice cream.

Deeter always volunteered to work the freezer compartment.

"Hey Dad," he'd say, "This box of ice cream sandwiches came open, can I have one?"

"Why is it the ice cream sandwich boxes only break open when you're in there, Deeter?"

"I don't know," he grinned. "Just lucky I guess."

The second trailer carried nothing but ice, thousands of pounds of frozen water cubes, and 12-pound blocks. Loading ice into the machines hardened Falcon's body and taught him what work really felt like. This type of training set the stage for his life.

The transfer to Junction City and seventh grade for Falcon was as smooth as it could be. Rachel drove her sons to school every day, dropped them off, and returned home. In the afternoon she traipsed back to get them repeating the 60-mile-round-trip drive. Grudgingly the powers that be finally relented at the end of the year and allowed the boys to ride the bus home from school, which saved their mom one trip a day. But the message was clear. Leave the Sane kids' mother alone.

The business started to grow under Mitch's hard work and salesmanship and needed a dock to receive their merchandise being trucked in by tractor-trailer. Falcon and his family bought four acres and moved into town over the summer.

Weaverville was a historic mining town with a population of 2,500. It held a movie theater, bowling alley, supermarket and ice cream shop. To Falcon it was a whole new life and most of eighth grade passed quickly. A wonderful high school senior named Miranda coached the local 13 and under traveling boys' soccer team. Falcon joined and became an instant All Star. One day at the end of practice, Falcon was elated as he recognized an old friend from Del Loma coming toward them.

Mike extended his hand to Falcon. "Boy you sure got big."

"Maybe you just shrunk," Falcon teased.

Mike was now a junior in high school, a football star, and drove a car. "Miranda told me she had this red-headed, freckle-faced kid who could run like the wind on her team. I said if he has a smart mouth I know that kid."

"Just because I'm smarter than you doesn't make me a mouth." Falcon smiled. "By the way, it's strawberry blonde."

Mike laughed. *You had to love this kid.*

Both boys had grown. Mike was six feet and weighed 180. Although Falcon stood just as tall, he barely eked out 135 pounds.

Mike grinned and tried to grab him. "Come here you little fucker." Falcon spun away and jumped on Mike's back.

"Yaw! Yaw! Get along little doggie!" Falcon whooped as Mike tried to throw him off. After a few seconds Falcon fell, landing on the ground.

Mike reached down and pulled him up. "It's good to see you."

"You too, I read in the paper you had over 100 yards against Hayfork Friday night."

"Yeah, but we didn't win. Our quarterback got crushed on

the goal line. Some of those Patton kids hit hard."

"I think they're brothers or cousins or something," Falcon said.

"They're something all right. How you been?"

"Good. Playing baseball and soccer. School's almost out. I'll be seeing you next year in high school."

Mike smiled, "That's right. You'll be a little freshman. Maybe I'll trash can you."

"You can try," challenged Falcon.

"Nah, you know I wouldn't do that to you. As long as I'm around I'll always have your back."

"I know, I was just kidding."

"But I better not catch you checking out my woman," Mike pointed to Miranda.

Falcon said, "My coach?"

"Yep."

Falcon made little kissing noises with his mouth and they both laughed.

Miranda watched them from the middle of the field. Her heart ached whenever she saw Mike. He was the light in her world. They planned to get married after he graduated. She also loved coaching Falcon. The combination of talent and fire the young boy carried was a coach's dream. She had no idea they even knew each other until she mentioned him to Mike a few days ago. "I got this new kid. Unbelievable! He's faster than most adults right now, and he hates to lose more than I do!"

"Does he have red hair and freckles?" Mike had asked.

"How'd you know that?"

"Just a guess. Maybe I'll drop by practice and see for myself."

Miranda had sighed, "You know you can come by anytime."

She observed the two of them playing around and smiled at how comfortable they were with each other — like brothers. Mike gave Falcon a man hug and headed back to Miranda.

"I guess you know each other?" she asked.

Mike pulled her close. "Yeah we go back a ways ... great kid. You think he's good at soccer you should see him play baseball."

Miranda said, "That's funny. When I told him he could be good enough one day to get a college soccer scholarship he said he was going to get one in baseball."

"I'm sure he will. You'll probably see him on TV one day."

"Playing baseball?"

"Maybe, maybe not. He's just that kind of kid — you know ... special."

Miranda nodded at the love of her life. "You're pretty special too."

"I love you girl."

"I love you too."

Miranda gave Mike a kiss and a big howl went up from her team. "All right enough of that!" she said. "Falcon, take 'em around the field three times! You guys sound like you have too much energy!"

"It looks like the big man needs a nap," Falcon teased Mike.

Mike grinned. "That's called working the late shift at the pizza place."

"Better get some sleep then buddy!" Falcon winked and led the team around the field.

Mike nodded and the two friends waved as he walked back to his truck.

Eighth grade was almost a memory and while Falcon looked forward to high school, his favorite time of year was only a month away. Summer, three months packed with baseball, soccer and work, but today was about soccer. Noted for being early, Falcon arrived Saturday morning to an empty field. He bounced headers against the goal frame, ran sprints, dribbled, and kicked the ball from net to net. Twenty minutes into it his teammates began to show. By 8:00 a.m. everyone was present but Miranda, who was never late. Five more minutes passed, and Falcon took charge. He knew the routine and started the team running drills. Although he enjoyed the role of coach, he couldn't help but worry about Miranda. After an hour he wrapped up their impromptu practice.

"I'll give coach a call," Falcon told his teammates. "Maybe she was having a bad hair day. You know girls."

Everyone laughed and nodded in agreement.

"Okay, I'm going home." Falcon began the two-mile trek. Walking along the road was common in Weaverville. There were no sidewalks and everything was within a moderate radius. One of the perks of small-town living was everyone knew each other, and it wasn't unusual to be offered a lift. About halfway home Falcon was offered such a ride, and he climbed into the car of a neighbor.

"Where're you coming from?" the man asked.

"Soccer practice, only our coach Miranda never showed."

"Didn't you hear about her boyfriend?"

The hair on Falcon's arms stood up. "No, what's up?"

"Last night after work he drove off the big cliff outside of town."

Falcon's chest tightened. "Is he okay?"

"No," said the man, "he's dead."

"Dead," Falcon repeated. "Mike, you're talking about Mike Stockdale?"

"Yes," the man studied Falcon's face as it grew white. "Are you okay son?"

Falcon couldn't believe it was true. "You're sure?"

"Yes, I'm sorry to have sprung it on you that way. I didn't know you two were friends."

Falcon's pulse banged in his head like a bass drum, *dead,*

dead, dead. He couldn't breathe. He'd just seen Mike, how is this possible? He started to ask again, "Are you sure ..." But he couldn't bear to hear the answer once more. He felt sick. "Could you let me out here?"

"Are you sure? I'd be glad to take you home."

"No ... no thanks ... I'll walk." Falcon stumbled out of the car.

"You sure?"

"Yeah ... thanks anyway."

"I'm really sorry Falcon."

Falcon nodded and headed for home. As the car pulled away he started thinking. *Maybe he's wrong. Maybe it's a different Mike. Adults get teenagers mixed up all the time.* Then the reality of Miranda's absence that morning hit. His feet stopped while his brain connected the dots. What little breakfast was left in his stomach crept into his throat, and he swallowed the bitter substance. Somehow his legs propelled him home seconds before the tears pooled in his eyes and spilled over.

Rachel heard the backdoor slam and called from the kitchen, "Who goes there ..." she saw Falcon's pained face. "Honey what's wrong?"

"Mike's ..." He couldn't make his voice say the word because once he did it would be true.

"What about Mike?"

He spit the staggering news out as if the very phrase burned his mouth.

"He drove off the big cliff last night, Mom," he choked. "Mike's dead."

Rachel gasped, "Oh sweet Lord! I'm so sorry baby."

She tried to embrace her son, but he pulled away. Deeter had told her about the fight between Mike and Falcon once things were resolved. The uplifted attitude in her child had not gone unnoticed, and now the agony on his face told it all. The boys had become more than friends.

"Falcon?"

He shook his head and headed to his room to grieve alone.

Mike's funeral took place three days later.

Falcon planned to stay away. "Why do I have to go?" he asked his mom.

"To pay your respects honey ... and to say goodbye."

He'd been to a funeral before and felt helpless to soothe crying, hurting people. He sure didn't want to be one of them, but she was right. It would be wrong not to go to his friend's funeral. He dressed up, and Rachel drove him to the chapel. "Do you want me to sit with you?"

"No, that's okay Mom."

"All right, I'll sit near the back if you need anything."

"Thanks."

Outside the double doors, a huge picture of Mike in his football uniform was on display. Falcon placed his hand on the Trinity insignia on Mike's chest. It felt warm. He looked toward the sky. *How can the sun shine so bright on a sad day like this*? He opened a door and eight sobbing high school girls exploded past him to escape. Taking a deep breath he went in.

Flower arrangements, photographs, and weeping overwhelmed his senses while soulful organ music competed with whimpers and convulsive gasps. The Trinity football team dressed in their red-and-white jerseys stood in solidarity. *Mike was loved*. Unmistakably he had come a long way in a short time. Falcon found a seat against the wall. Pain washed over him like hot lava. He hadn't realized Mike made this many friends or touched so many lives. Miranda was nowhere to be seen. Rumors traveled at light speed in town. Some said Miranda was sedated and committed to a hospital. Others said she gave into sorrow and died. Whatever happened to the beautiful young girl, Falcon never saw her again.

A pastor spoke of the young passing too soon and the strength to carry on.

Girls continued to wail.

Normally Falcon hated when women cried. On this occasion though, he found their weeping comforting. They were crying for his friend, and then they were crying the tears Falcon did not want to shed. He sat stoically and stared at the casket. *How fast life could end. One day you're here, the next you're gone. Just like that.*

"Thank you for coming," said the pastor. "Clearly Michael was a special young man, and the love shown here today validates his life. We pray he is in the presence of our heavenly Father and give thanks to his being in our lives however short that time may have been. In Jesus' name we pray, amen."

"Amen," responded a murmur of voices.

Falcon watched motionless as the procession passed Mike for the last time.

The bawling, which had subsided, commenced again as students passed his casket, the football team touched Mike's helmet.

Once the room emptied the pastor walked deliberately in Falcon's direction.

Falcon felt numb. His eyes stayed fixated on the mahogany box.

The pastor stopped in front of the young man who sat quietly. "Are you Falcon Sane?"

Falcon lifted his head, and a lone tear rolled down his cheek. He didn't try to wipe it away. He didn't answer. He managed a slight nod.

The pastor put his hand on Falcon's shoulder and waited.

Everyone had gone but Falcon, the pastor and Mike.

"I have a message for you from Miranda."

Falcon stared at him blankly.

"I'm sure you can imagine the difficulty she is experiencing now, but before she left Weaverville I promised to give you her message."

Falcon blinked as another single tear traced the path down his cheek.

"She said Michael told her you were special, that you would do special things one day. Although it didn't make sense to her at the time, he said for the rest of your life, he'd be watching over you." The pastor paused for a minute to check a piece of paper in his pocket. "To be accurate, he said he'd always have your back."

Falcon stared at the pastor and wiped his cheek. "Thank you sir. Can I stay a minute with Mike, alone?"

"Certainly. Take all the time you need son."

"Thank you sir."

Finally alone in the room with Mike, Falcon walked toward the casket. He focused on an oversized picture of Mike in his football uniform. He had a genuine smile on his face, and Falcon forced himself to smile back.

"So, I hear you're going to be stalking me the rest of my life," he spoke to the picture. "It's not going to be much fun flipping you one-liners when you don't respond, how about one for the road?"

It almost appeared to Falcon that Mike's smile got a little brighter. He stepped closer to his friend's picture, bowed his head, and put his hand on Mike's shoulder.

"I'm gonna miss you brother," he whispered. "See you on the other side."

They say time heals all wounds, whoever *they* are. Falcon didn't buy that line. He believed in focusing on the positive and staying productive. As the weeks went by his heart lightened, and he stopped questioning God or the "Big Fella" as he liked to call him. Although never receiving an answer, Falcon accepted Mike's time on Earth was done, and he was needed elsewhere. He doubted that resolution would work for Miranda and whenever she crossed his mind, he prayed for her. After Mike's death, the soccer team lost their coach. Miranda was gone, and the parents of the other kids turned to the best player on the team, Falcon Sane and asked him to coach for the rest of the year. He agreed on the condition if Miranda returned, she would get her team back. The parents agreed, and he turned his energy toward the soccer team and finished out eighth grade. The team had five games left; they won four and lost one. Each game Falcon watched for Miranda but she never returned. Following the last game, they dedicated their season to Mike and Miranda by running three times around the field together — the way their coach would have wanted it.

Falcon and Deeter were sprouting like summer zucchini. Every morning at the breakfast table Rachel was certain they were bigger than the night before. Both towering over her, she no longer could kiss the top of their heads, but day and night her guys gave her man-sized hugs. However as their hormones kicked in, what too often started as fun, ended with someone getting hurt — once even Rachel.

Deeter had a wild streak in him, and when provoked he went out of his mind, literally.

Falcon being older, faster and stronger usually handled it, but as the boys grew, so did the injuries.

Rachel had some rules. The rule for Falcon was simple. No matter what your brother does, never hit him in the head. The rule for Deeter was simple. Don't use weapons. But the rules weren't working anymore. Deeter slashed Falcon one time across the chest with a screwdriver, cut Falcon's shirt, and left a long line of blood. The time after that, some neighbor kids teased Deeter, and he grabbed a Louisville Slugger, threw it 20 feet and knocked a kid to his knees. Falcon was there too, and when the gang headed for his brother, he stepped in to protect him. Deeter wasn't deterred. He stood behind Falcon already armed with a shovel.

"I warned you to leave him alone," Falcon said.

"He hit me in the knee," whined the kid who'd been calling Deeter names.

"So what, he stabbed me with a screwdriver two weeks ago. What's your point?"

The gang looked mystified by the two brothers.

"He's crazy," said the injured party.

Falcon laughed, "He is crazy, and you're pretty stupid. He just threw a bat at you and now has a shovel, but none of that matters."

"Why's that?"

"That shovel is the least of your worries, because you aren't getting through me."

The boys shook their heads, "You guys are nuts!"

Falcon shrugged as the kids walked off. An hour later they were all playing Wiffle Ball.

But the last straw for Rachel was a fistfight between her sons. How it started was a blur ...

Deeter closed his eyes and started swinging for the fence.

Falcon blocked his punches and followed the rules of not hitting him in the head.

Mitch was right behind them when the fracas broke out. He wrapped his arms around Falcon and ordered his sons to stop. With both of Falcon's arms pinned to his sides, Deeter punched him square in the nose.

Falcon's head bounced against his father's chest and the

normally calm child raged, "I followed the rules and you let him punch me? That's not fair!"

Mitch being a fair man let go of Falcon.

Falcon wound up, threw from the hip, and landed a crushing blow to the side of Deeter's head.

Deeter collapsed into a pile and cried. "He hit me in the head," he wailed. "He's not supposed to hit in the head."

Mitch rubbed his son's head. "I told you to stop, Deeter."

Immediately Falcon felt bad about hitting his little brother. "Sorry."

Deed kept whimpering while Falcon helped him up.

"Say you're sorry too Deeter," Mitch ordered.

"Sor-ry," Deeter said not meaning a word of it with his ears still ringing.

That was the final act of insanity for Rachel, and Falcon, Deeter and Mitch began to study Kenpo Karate.

Mitch located an instructor in Weaverville, a guy who had turned his small den into a dojo. It was a well-kept room with mirrors on the walls and an assortment of kick bags, gloves, staffs, and nun-chucks, which are two sticks connected by rope or chain.

Eleven-year-old Deeter loved the nun-chucks and wanted to learn kicks.

Falcon, now 13, wanted to throw punches — lots and lots of punches.

Mitch had fought plenty in his life and wanted his sons to learn self-protection.

Rachel prayed they'd find some self-control.

All three guys were decked out in Crest-white gis, warmed up, did exercises, and stretched.

"Ssst! Ssst! Ssst!" Fists whisked through the air as they threw alternating punches.

Roger, the Kenpo instructor, barked out direction.

"Get your punches lower Falcon. Deeter keep your hands higher. Good, good. Let's move to the horse position and work on blocks."

After 15 minutes of working on techniques, Falcon said, "This is boring. When do we get to spar?"

Mitch gave him a harsh look, and the training continued another 10 minutes.

Roger said, "Okay Falcon, put on the gloves, footpads and headgear."

Falcon hated the headgear. It turned too much and blocked his view. Besides, it wasn't real.

"Is it okay if I don't use the headgear?" Falcon asked Mitch.

"Ask Roger; it's his dojo."

"Roger, is it okay?"

Roger only had headgear for the kids; the adults didn't wear it. Although Falcon had only been with him a short while he was impressed at the speed of the young man's hands and willingness to compete.

"Fine by me."

"I'm not wearing it either then," said Deeter.

Roger smiled, "That's fine."

Mitch said, "Don't tell your mom."

The boys shook their heads in agreement.

Roger had been teaching Kenpo for 10 years but his new students were his favorite. The father, who was a beast, enjoyed mixing it up, and his kids were willing and able to do anything he put in front of them. He felt excited about taking his new students to Redding for tournaments.

"Tumo, come here and spar with Falcon."

Tumo was a year older than Falcon but a bit smaller. Nonetheless he wore a purple belt, several levels above Falcon's recently earned yellow belt.

He must be good, Falcon thought.

The two boys bowed to Roger and then to one another.

Roger gave the command to engage, "Fight!"

Falcon bounced forward and threw a controlled punch into Tumo's rib cage.

Tumo stepped away and winced.

Falcon shifted to his left side and threw a side-kick he'd been working on. The kick landed in his opponent's stomach, and Tumo gave ground.

Roger said, "Fight Tumo Fight!"

Falcon switched back to his right side and flipped a left jab toward Tumo's face.

Both of Tumo's hands went up.

Falcon hit him in the stomach with a straight right.

Tumo fell off balance and into the wall behind him in the small dojo.

"Break!" said Roger.

Falcon returned to his spot and waited.

"Falcon, take a break. Deeter you're next with Tumo."

The boys took their places.

Deeter's eyes widened as he assessed the older bigger boy.

Falcon shook his head and laughed silently as he watched his little brother. He'd just hit and kicked Tumo three times with relative ease. He wasn't trying to hurt him but he bet Tumo's ribs and stomach were sore right now. Watching the purple belt line up with Deeter, Falcon predicted it was going to get worse for Tumo.

Deeter was like a little spider monkey, all legs and arms. He didn't bother much with punches. He'd fallen in love with kicks. His legs were long and flexible and his first line of attack. As far as he was concerned, he was fighting for his life. Without control or aim, Deeter threw kicks as hard and fast as he could.

"Bow to me." Roger instructed. "Bow to each other. Fight!"

Tumo looked at the skinny, blond younger brother and breathed a sigh of relief. His stomach was burning from being hit and kicked, and his back hurt from smashing into the wall. *This little kid shouldn't be near as fast or strong.* He shuffled forward with that thought in mind and threw a small left-handed fake that he never got back.

The spider monkey spun on his back leg and threw a kick that whipped past the older boy's ear.

Falcon knew missing that first kick would send Deeter into panic mode. It did, and Deeter threw a vicious snap kick to Tumo's groin.

The protective cup popped and Tumo went down in a pile.

"Break!" Roger yelled, and helped the purple belt to his feet and into the living room.

Falcon rolled his eyes at his dad.

"Deeter," Mitch said, "you can't kick people in the balls."

"Sorry Dad, it just happened. I didn't even control it."

Falcon said, "Yeah we saw."

Roger returned to the dojo and wore a disconcerting expression. He approached Deeter who shrunk a bit. "Deeter, you're here to learn control. Your kicks are getting better, but as you can see without control they hurt people."

"I don't know what happened," Deeter said with that crazy glaze in his eyes.

"You need to know, and watch where your kicks are going."

"Okay Roger."

The glaze was replaced by a slaphappy grin when he realized there would be no punishment.

Roger said, "There's a tournament coming up, and I want the three of you to attend. But all of you have to be under control.

Mitch, you hit like a Mack truck. The last time we sparred you left me with welts. Control is the key if you want to compete. Let's finish with katas and call it a night."

After dinner that evening Rachel asked how class went.

Deeter grinned, "It was great mom, hiya!" He kicked the air. "I beat a purple belt."

Falcon laughed at his brother, kissed his mom goodnight, and walked back to his room. Karate was done for the day. Tomorrow was the Brain Drain.

The Brain Drain was a group version of *Jeopardy*, which gave the small schools up and down the river an opportunity to compete. Weaverville Elementary was slated to match Junction City tomorrow. Although Falcon engaged in competition through Little League and the soccer team, he'd only been involved in one other school versus school match. A school from Lewiston traveled to Junction City to play flag football. While Falcon and Deeter were the most talented kids on the field they couldn't be everywhere. After the opening play when Falcon threw a perfect spiral over Deeter's shoulder for a touchdown, they never scored again. The Lewiston team was well-coached with blocking assignments, plays and substitutions. Falcon drew the only plays Junction City had on the fly in the dirt. Finally out of desperation Falcon started throwing the ball to Deeter every time as he was the only one ever open *and* could catch. The 49 to seven beating still stung Falcon, and he welcomed a new opportunity to compete, this time using his mind. He'd fallen asleep last night as he did most nights with a book on his bed as he had tried to cram as much information in as possible. Another 49 to seven whipping was not to be tolerated.

The next morning Falcon was raring to go. He dressed, ate breakfast, and hustled Deeter out the door to catch their ride at the corner.

"Good morning gentlemen." Mrs. Winn was a neighbor and teacher's aide at Junction City. She liked the Sane boys and admired Rachel for transferring her sons out of Cox Bar and driving them 120-miles every day when they lived down river.

"Good morning Mrs. Winn," they answered in unison.

"All ready for the Brain Drain Falcon?"

"Yes ma'am."

"Good. We're counting on you. Can't let it be like Lewiston again."

"No way, this is different. It's school versus school, but it's only five on five."

Both schools were allowed to choose their top five students to compete. Whoever answered the most questions won the match.

Mrs. Winn scrutinized the young man who sat beside her. She was pleased to see a smile on his face again. She didn't know Mike or his connection to Falcon, but the boy had taken an earnest hit to the heart when his friend died. It was nice to have him back. He was driven, polite, took responsibility for his actions regardless of the outcome, and rarely got in trouble. He was easy to understand. Establish and enforce the rules then get out of his way. The only problem she'd witnessed was when other people were out of line and suffered no consequences. Then he could turn into a verbal battering ram. Hypocrisy was a bitter pill for him to swallow. *Thank goodness he's only a few years away from adulthood.* The country was starting to slide away from its belief in personal responsibility. *We need more Falcon Sanes.* They pulled into Junction City and parked.

"Do you need me to carry anything, Mrs. Winn?" Falcon asked.

"Yes, please take that case of milk into the kitchen."

Falcon stacked his books on the case of milk. It wasn't the

brand his family sold. "You should talk to my dad. We sell milk. He'll make you a sweet deal and deliver it himself."

"That's a good idea, thanks."

"It feels wrong carrying the competition."

Mrs. Winn smiled. *What a loyal young man. Someday one lucky lady will eventually capture his heart and have him forever.*

Falcon stored the milk in the refrigerator and slid the case under the table in the kitchen. The bell was about to ring when the Weaverville school bus pulled into the parking lot. His heart revved as the competition neared. Falcon loved to compete and better yet, to win. Staring through the window as the bus stopped, he thought, *sure is a big bus for only five kids.*

The doors opened and the parade started. He counted, 38, 39, 40 students. *Wow!*

Mrs. Winn peered through the window too. She let out a whistle, "Looks like they brought a cheering section."

That was fine by Falcon: *the bigger the crowd the better.*

The Weaverville students filed through the front door while Falcon and Mrs. Winn sized them up.

Mrs. Winn looked at Falcon and smiled. He already had his game face on and was ready to go.

The bus doors closed and then suddenly opened again. Falcon watched as the prettiest girl he'd ever seen stepped off the bus.

Mrs. Winn checked Falcon's expression and knew they were in trouble. *The game face was gone.* Falcon had been struck by lightning.

"You okay?" She nudged him in the ribs.

His eyes were glued to the girl, and he answered in slow motion, "Yesss ma'am."

There goes the pennant. It's Lewiston all over again. Mrs. Winn chuckled.

The girl was a vision. Silky golden hair tickled her shoulders when she walked. A pure white blouse was tucked into snug Guess jeans and black slip-on shoes showed the tops of her feet. Her cheeks blushed pink and her full lips were wet with gloss. On each hand she wore white Madonna-type fingerless gloves.

Falcon watched mesmerized by the apparition that belonged in a movie.

She climbed the school stairs with deliberation, flipped her hair, and disappeared through the door with her classmates.

Falcon remembered he wasn't alone and glanced sheepishly at Mrs. Winn.

"You sure you're okay, Falcon?"

"Sure," he tried to sound casual. "Why wouldn't I be?"

"Just checking," Mrs. Winn grinned.

Falcon grabbed his books, left the kitchen, and headed for the room where the Brain Drain would take place. Competition was the farthest thing from his mind. He wanted to see her again. Weaving through people in the crowded room, he spotted the green-eyed beauty on stage where she sat in the captain's chair. He stopped and watched her pass out paddles to each of her teammates.

To answer questions the contestants used the paddles. The first paddle to be raised allowed that team the first chance to answer.

Falcon watched as she finished and sat back down in her spot.

Cassandra Ross sat in the captain's chair designated for Weaverville Elementary. Waiting for the crowd to settle she felt excited. Competition and winning were two of her favorite things. She was good at sports, but her true gift was her mind, and she enjoyed using it. As the crowd calmed she sensed she was being watched. A tall, athletic boy who stood in the back caught her attention. Boys looked at her all the time, but this was different. He wasn't ogling or leering; he seemed focused on her face, looked directly into her eyes. She looked away then quickly back again.

His blue eyes sparkled, and he nodded to her with the smallest hint of a smile, like they were sharing a treasured secret.

She wanted to stop staring but couldn't help herself. *He's handsome.* Her face got warm.

They continued to gaze at each other until the room full of people faded.

"Ahem," came a voice from behind Falcon. Mrs. Winn reached out and squeezed his hand briefly. "You should probably take your seat on the stage."

"Oh, okay," Falcon answered in a trance as he headed for the stage with a new purpose.

Cassandra watched him cross the room. As he walked, he'd look away and then glance at her again. Her cheeks flushed each time, and she realized she had held her breath. When he stepped onto the stage she exhaled.

The stage held 10 chairs, five for each school with a small gap between the team captains. Six feet away a panel of judges faced the teams.

Falcon climbed the stairs purposefully and walked in front of the Weaverville team. He hoped to get as close to her as possible.

Aware of his every move, she sat motionless.

He paused in front of her and smiled, "Hi."

"Hello," she returned his facial expression.

Falcon smelled her perfume and his knees almost buckled as he continued toward his seat.

He's not handsome ... he's beautiful. Cassandra fought the urge to reach out and touch his hand.

A judge introduced the contestants.

"Our captains are Cassandra Ross from Weaverville Elementary ..."

Cassandra Ross, Falcon repeated the lyrical name in his head.

"... and Falcon Sane from Junction City Elementary."

Cassandra smiled. *We've only just begun Falcon Sane.*

For Falcon, the rest of the competition became an irrelevant blur. The Brain Drain completed the school year with Weaverville winning on the last answer given by Cassandra. It was the first time Falcon lost at something and didn't care.

The Weaverville teachers began to hustle their charges aboard the waiting bus.

"Congratulations," Falcon extended his hand.

She answered shyly, "Thank you."

A jolt shot through her body as their hands touched.

"Let's go Cassandra," a teacher ordered oblivious to the romantic interlude taking place.

"I have to go," she said.

"I know."

Still they continued to hold hands.

"Falcon," Mrs. Winn broke in gently, "please help me put the chairs away."

Falcon nodded and released his grip.

Cassandra hung on, gave his hand a soft squeeze, and walked away.

Falcon's feet were cemented to the stage.

Cassandra reached the door, and glanced over her shoulder.

"Goodbye Falcon Sane."

Falcon watched helplessly as the girl of his dreams disappeared into the bus and out of his life. She had turned his world upside down, and it felt as if the Earth was crushing his heart.

He couldn't shake the feeling all summer. His only reprieve was sports and work, which helped to make his body tired and quiet his mind. Although they lived in the same town, a 13-year-old boy had no wheels, and Falcon sadly lacked the blood-hound gene. In Del Loma, he would've found her and quick, but Weaverville had 2,500 people, and Falcon couldn't stand on a corner hoping for her to pass by — he had responsibilities.

Then Rachel's brother, Charles came for a visit. Chip, as he preferred to be called, was a wannabe Hollywood star in-between gigs. He needed a job and a home. Rachel split the master bedroom in half for the boys, leaving the third room for Chip. Mitch gave him work on the dairy route along with Falcon and Deeter. Three times a week Mitch would crank up the semi at two in the morning, hook up the refrigerated trailers, and head out with a set of doubles. Rachel always woke up too and prayed for the safety of the four people she loved most in this world. They worked a long, hot summer logging hundreds of miles on Highway 299; but business was seasonal and the money made selling ice carried them through the thin months.

Chip wasn't the most responsible person in the world, but he was a lot of fun. Over the summer he and Falcon talked quite a bit. One Friday night Falcon wanted to go to the movies. He was too old to go with his parents — that wouldn't be cool. Deeter wouldn't work either. Falcon might look like he was babysitting. Chip would fit the bill. His model looks and easy laugh made for a perfect friend to hang out with. Falcon didn't care about the movie. He was hoping to spot Cassandra.

"Hey Chip you want to go to the movies with me tonight?"

"Sure, but I'm a little short on cash."

It wasn't lost on Falcon his uncle made a lot more money than he did and lived for free in their house. Because Falcon always earned and saved, traits he learned from his parents, he was free to spend his time and money as he pleased.

"It's on me Chip."

Chip assessed the young boy he'd always been close to. *What a great kid*. No, not a kid anymore, Falcon was taller than him now. "You're a good man Falcon, what are we going to see?"

"I don't care."

Chip stopped, "You don't care?"

"Nope, hanging out with you is fun."

Besides if he saw Cassandra he might need a wing man.

"Let the party begin," teased Chip.

"Yep. Let's go. I want to get there early."

The movie theater was located on Main Street and the primary attraction on Friday and Saturday night. The rest of the week you could walk down the middle of Main after eight o'clock and not see a soul. The whole of Trinity County didn't have even one streetlight. The theater was an easy three-mile walk from their house, and the two bachelors talked and enjoyed the warmth of the summer night.

"So, how goes it with the ladies?" Chip asked.

Falcon thought about Cassandra. Being a private person, he hadn't told anyone about her.

"Nothing at the moment."

"What about all the girls at Junction City? A smart, good-looking jock such as yourself, well, your mom says they're hot and heavy after you."

Falcon shrugged. Popularity with girls wasn't new to him, but his shyness was often misinterpreted as arrogance. He battled the same insecurities every other teenager did and like most men, suffered from misunderstanding female signals. He thought about Cassandra but wasn't ready to talk about her so he changed the subject. "What about you?"

Although they'd never discussed it, Falcon was aware Chip was gay, and Chip knew it. "You know I'm gay right?"

Falcon wasn't sure how he knew, he just did. It wasn't a

big deal to him. "Yeah I know. I was always curious about that, I mean, come on man, girls are beautiful."

Chip laughed his natural easy way and winked at his nephew. "Yes sir they are."

"Have you ever kissed a girl before?" Falcon asked.

"I have. Many times. I've even had sex with women a few times."

"Really?"

"Really."

That surprised Falcon. He hadn't had sex yet but it was definitely on his mind lately. "Did you like it?"

"Not really," said Chip.

"Why not?"

"It isn't what I am attracted to."

Falcon could not imagine this. "Is that how you knew you were gay?"

"It was part of it. You know when you look at a pretty girl how it makes you feel?"

The expression on Falcon's face told Chip he got that. "Yeah."

"I feel the same when I look at an attractive man."

Falcon tried to wrap his adolescent mind around this idea. "I believe you, but I just can't see that."

"Of course you can't," said Chip. "You aren't gay."

"Why do you think you think like that?"

"I don't think that I think like that, it's just the way I feel. Believe me, it'd be a lot easier being straight. Most of the world isn't gay and some people hate homosexuals."

"Why?'

"For some people it's too different from themselves. For others it's a religious thing. There are some people out there who hate homosexuals who are gay themselves."

"That doesn't seem right."

"It isn't about right or wrong. They just have to figure themselves out."

"Still, if you're gay and saying you hate other gay people ... that's just wrong."

"That's why you're special," said Chip. "You don't suffer hypocrites, gay or straight."

Falcon grew silent as they continued to walk.

Chip could tell his nephew was struggling with something. It was easy to forget Falcon had just finished eighth grade. "Do you understand what I mean?"

"No. What to do you mean by suffer?"

"It means you don't like people who say one thing and do another. It's just a different way to use the word suffer. You should look it up in the dictionary."

"I will."

They walked along quietly with their own thoughts before Falcon jumped back in the conversation. "Do you think you'll ever like women?"

His uncle laughed, "Not in a sexual way."

The young man shook his head. "I just can't imagine that."

"I'm sure you can't." Chip winked, "Not a woman-lover like you. So dare I ask again, you got a special lady?"

Falcon wanted to talk about Cassandra, but ... "Is this conversation between you and me?"

"Of course."

"Swear to God?"

Chip roared. He'd been raised Catholic along with Rachel, he'd even been an altar boy. God was a whole other discussion. But it was interesting that Falcon used this terminology since the boys weren't raised with a religious background. Rachel and Mitch decided the boys could choose for themselves.

"Okay!" Chip crossed himself." I swear to God. "Man this girl must be something."

Falcon hesitated.

"Come on." Chip nudged Falcon's shoulder. "I promise I won't tell a soul. Not even your mom."

Falcon took a deep breath and blurted out the story.

Once he finished Chip grinned, "It doesn't surprise me."

"What doesn't surprise you?"

"That you chose the prettiest, smartest girl in the room."

Falcon reddened a little under his summer tan. "Thanks."

"You are very welcome." Chip lifted his sunglasses and flashed his brilliant smile. "Are we hoping to see her at the theater?"

Reluctantly Falcon nodded.

"That's cool. I just need to know my part. Do I have any lines?"

"Come on man." Falcon gave Chip a slight punch in the arm.

They both laughed and headed to town.

The theater loomed in front of them. *Superman Three* was spelled out by the placards over the top of the theater as lights twinkled in the night. Falcon and Chip stood in line scouting out the scene.

"What's she look like?" asked Chip.

"She's maybe five eight, blonde hair, green eyes ... beautiful."

Chip scanned for girls fitting that description. Zip. But a couple of brunettes in their early twenties were checking him out. "There's two brunettes behind me that are pretty cute."

Falcon didn't bother to turn around; he wanted Cassandra. "No thanks."

"A one-woman man, huh? You're a rarity."

Falcon was an optimist, Chip said once. It was one of his best assets.

That positive attitude wasn't working tonight though. The

line moved without a sighting of Cassandra, and Falcon peered through the circular window, ordered two adult tickets, and handed the young cashier a $20.

"Two adults are 10 dollars out of 20," she said aloud, and then put the $20 in the drawer.

Falcon had made change hundreds of times in the Del Loma store. Repeating the amount he'd given her was correct, but she should have left the $20 out in case there was a discrepancy over the change made.

"Here are your tickets and change." The girl handed Falcon two tickets, two fives and a 10.

Even though Chip wasn't paying, he caught the error immediately and reveled in them scoring free passes.

Falcon counted the money in his head. Not wanting to embarrass her he slid the $10 back over the counter. "I gave you a $20," he said quietly. "I'm only supposed to get back $10."

Her face froze as she realized her mistake and quickly stuffed the $10 into the register. "Thank you so much. It's my first night. If the count had been off they might think I stole it. Thank you," she mouthed silently.

"You're welcome." Falcon got into the snack line.

"I saw that," said Chip. "You had free tickets!"

"She made a mistake. It would've been wrong to take the tickets."

"A lot of people would have."

"That doesn't make it right."

Chip looked at his nephew and nodded. "You learned that from your parents."

It was their turn at the refreshment counter and with Cassandra nowhere in sight Falcon soothed his soul with food. "One large popcorn, two large Cokes, and a bag of peanut M&M's please."

5

The road from Weaverville to Redding forced drivers to slow down. The tight turns and blind curves could be punishing to the reckless and irresponsible. For Falcon the road was an enemy since motion sickness was a part of his life. This particular adversary was known as Buckhorn Summit.

"How are you doing?" Rachel asked.

Falcon tried to focus on the road, "Okay."

"If you need to pull over say so," said Mitch. "I don't want to wear your lunch again."

Rachel and Deeter smiled quietly to themselves as they remembered the last time.

"Mom?" Deeter leaned against his door and hoped to get as far away from Falcon as possible. "He's not looking good."

Falcon didn't know why he suffered from motion sickness. He'd experienced three concussions earlier in life and suffered from debilitating headaches occasionally, but the doctors couldn't find anything wrong with him. "Maybe you should pull over Dad."

Mitch stopped at the nearest turnout.

Falcon bolted over Deeter and just cleared the car when his breakfast came up.

Rachel said, "Maybe we should slow down a little Mitch."

"If we go any slower we might as well walk."

"I know, but he'll be feeling bad all day now."

"Blech!" Deeter rolled up his window. "That smell is making me want to puke."

"Deed, sit on the other side in case we need to pull over again," said Rachel.

She handed Falcon a towel and some water. Falcon wiped his mouth, swished and spit a little water out to remove the puke taste, and got back in the car.

"Only 20 more miles, buddy. Keep your eyes on the road."

Falcon mumbled, "Okay Dad," then tracked the winding pavement all the way to Redding.

Today was a Kenpo Karate tournament. Falcon and Deeter had previously entered two loosely judged beginner tournaments where points weren't counted and matches didn't have a winner or loser.

Falcon thought this was ridiculous and said so, "I'm here to win not participate." He complained to his parents and instructor following the second event. "If there isn't real competition at these tournaments I'd rather just fight in the dojo."

The fights in the dojo had begun taking on intensity as Falcon started sparring with adults. He couldn't match their power, but his hand speed kept most of them at bay as he gave as good as he got with the exception of his father. He sparred with his dad but knew his dad just toyed with him. Still it was great experience and as close to a real fight as you could get.

"There's a tournament coming up," Roger had announced one evening in class. "I'd like all three of you to enter. It's time for you to take the next step."

Falcon couldn't agree more.

Roger said, "Deeter you still have a ways to go, but I believe you are ready for real competition." He smiled at Mitch. "You've come quite a distance in controlling your temper. I believe you're ready too." Looking at Falcon stoically he said. "And you Falcon, it is time to see how good you really are."

Falcon thrived on competition and counted the days down to the tournament in Redding as if it were Christmas. *Now if I can only survive the car ride.* After stopping one last time to dry heave on the side of Highway 299 they finally arrived at their destination.

The basketball gymnasium at Theodore Roosevelt High School was transformed into dozens of fighting squares. Each square sat 15 by 15 feet, marked off by blue tape that established the boundaries. Hundreds of combatants dressed in black or white gis strutted around as they sized up the competition. Different colored belts, which resembled a starter box of Crayola crayons, represented every level. Some wore bands or scarves wrapped around their foreheads and bare feet slapped the wooden floor of the gym.

Falcon's growling stomach reminded him of the drive, but as he roamed the gym infused with testosterone and sweat, his adrenaline kicked in. He stood in line with his age group and surveyed the scene. His dad was bunched with the rest of the adults matched by weight. Falcon spotted his little brother in line.

Deeter already had a little of that crazy look going but grinned when he saw his big brother checking him out. Deeter was grouped with the 10- to 12-year olds, and this seemed right since he was eleven. One kid looked to be several inches taller than Falcon and easily out-weighed Deeter by 50 pounds, Falcon gauged protectively. *He's huge*! *He should at least be in my division.* Falcon being 13 lined up with the 13- to 16-year olds. In the middle of the pack, as far as size was concerned, he looked forward to battling the older kids. He considered slipping in line with the 17- and 18-year olds, but the size difference would've been too much. He wanted to compete and win at the top level he could handle, not get his ass kicked.

With the signups complete the matches throughout the huge gym started.

Falcon was the first called into the arena. His competitor, who was a bit taller, sported a purple intermediate belt to Falcon's lesser yellow beginner belt. They squared off in the ring.

The black belt who refereed their match commanded, "Bow to me, bow to each other, fight!"

Falcon danced left.

The purple belt took one quick step and threw an axe kick.

Falcon tilted his head. The purple belt's foot whistled passed his ear and crunched down on his neck and shoulder. Pain was immediate and intense. For a second he thought his collarbone was broken.

"Break!" yelled the black belt. Addressing the three judges who circled the ring for confirmation, his right hand shot up and pointed to the purple belt. All three judges nodded.

He shouted, "Point purple! Axe kick. Bow to each other," he commanded again.

Falcon shook his right arm around trying to get the feeling back. *This purple belt certainly isn't Tumo*! Falcon bowed to his opponent, as fear and embarrassment turned to anger. His anger fueled by the realization that *controlled aggression*, the supposed mantra of this tournament, might be out the window. The axe kick that maimed his shoulder was meant for the top of his head and face and would have broken his nose.

At the same time Falcon dodged kicks, Deeter's name was called.

He trotted to his spot on the floor and visually measured the huge guy across from him. It was the same one Falcon had seen earlier. *Give me a break, no way is this kid 12.*

The honor system was used in signups, and Deeter's much larger 14-year-old opponent cheated using it to his advantage and the detriment of all others. Clearly the match was unequal, even to the judges, yet they ignored what their eyes told them and allowed the lie to stand.

Rachel had seen the blow Falcon took and even with her inexperience of the art, knew it should've been called. Now with her little Deeter, matched against a gorilla, she wanted to run out and pull him off the floor.

"Bow to me!" yelled the judge. "Bow to each other!"

Deeter evaluated the giant in front of him and trembled slightly, but got into his stance. His little yellow belt wrapped twice around his skinny waist quivered.

"Practice control Deeter!" he heard Roger's voice over the crowd.

"Fight!"

Deeter took a small step forward as the orange belt charged. He tried to move out of the way, but the height and weight difference was too much. The monster threw a wide haymaker that slammed into the side of Deeter's face. He flew through the air sprawled on his back and slid into an adjoining fighting square. Multiple hands scooped Deeter up and set him back in place. The little guy blinked twice and stared at the behemoth who just attacked him.

Rachel was beside herself.

The referee raised his hand and pointed to the orange belt, and the three surrounding judges agreed.

"Point orange, roundhouse punch. Bow to each other. Fight!"

As the welt below Deeter's eye began to swell Mitch's name was called. He entered the square and prepared to bow.

"Remember gentlemen, controlled aggression. Only light contact to the face, bow."

Mitch evaluated his competition. The man stood six two, probably 230 pounds. He wore a green belt, a half step below brown; advanced. Mitch shorter and lighter, who wore a yellow beginner belt like his sons, readied to begin.

"Fight!"

Mitch slid to his left looking for an opening.

The two combatants traded a couple of jabs in the air when suddenly the referee jumped in.

"Break!" he commanded.

As Mitch stopped his opponent delivered a left hook to the side of his face.

"Break! Break! Break!" yelled the referee as Mitch charged toward the antagonist. "Back to your positions!"

Mitch glared at the man and the referee. He believed in order and following the rules, but he didn't believe in getting abused. *I'll give them a chance.* He returned to his spot.

The referee pointed to the man who had sucker punched Mitch and to the judges. "Point green!"

Mitch said, "He hit me after you stopped us."

"Back to your spot!" yelled the referee. "Bow. Fight!"

Mitch gave a head fake and threw a clean, controlled punch into green's ribcage.

"Break!" the referee pointed to Mitch.

The three judges turned their thumbs down.

The ref nodded, "Point green. Too much contact by yellow."

"Too much contact! He just punched me in the face!" said Mitch.

"Places! Bow. Fight!"

Mitch's jaw ached from the sucker punch, and the judges just robbed him of a point for a clean shot. Down two to nothing the fight would end with the first one to three. He'd had enough. If they weren't going to enforce the rules then everything was fair game. He didn't even draw upon the karate techniques. He'd been in too many fights to bother. He took a rocker step forward and threw a right-handed uppercut to the green belt's wide-open chin, followed by a left cross that missed, because his target was already on his way to the floor and knocked out cold.

Holding onto the back of Mitch's gi, the black belt yelled, "Break! Break!"

Mitch spun like a caged lion and the ref jumped back out of range.

He backed closer to the judges for support and yelled, "You are disqualified!"

Mitch's chest was heaving. He stood in the middle, pointed his gloved hand at the judges, and said, "This is on you! Enforce the rules fairly for everyone!"

The judges and referee bunched together. Their belts weren't going to protect them from Mitch's rage.

"Roger!" One of the judges said, "Come get your student."

"He's right," Roger backed up Mitch. "I was right here."

"He's still disqualified and needs to leave."

"I have two other students in competition right now, his sons. We'll leave when they're finished."

"Fine but he has to sit in the bleachers."

Roger and Mitch headed toward Falcon's fighting square.

Falcon danced around looking for angles as the purple belt continued to throw kicks with both legs. They were good kicks thrown with full force and had they landed would've hurt. Falcon expected the referee to warn the purple about control, but none came. When another axe kick whipped by his ear he decided enough was enough and set his trap.

Purple could kick all day but he never used his hands.

Falcon noticed he kicked in a pattern. Left snap kick, right snap kick, left axe kick. He'd done it three times in a row. Falcon dodged the left- and right-snap kicks and waited for the axe to drop. *There it is, on its way up!* Falcon dropped almost to one knee and threw a vicious right punch into the solar plexus right under purple's ribcage. The punch felt like it went out his opponent's back as all his weight came forward to deliver the axe kick. Instantly, five hundred fans, competitors and onlookers roared as they watched the kicking whirling dervish land on his back and curl into a ball as he sucked in air.

"Break!" The referee jumped in to keep Falcon from attacking.

It wasn't necessary. Falcon calmly moved back to his spot in the square and watched purple spasm on the floor as he tried to breathe. Scanning the crowd, he saw his father and Roger a few steps away. His dad had a red mark under his eye and looked pissed, but Roger looked rather pleased. Falcon's attention snapped back to the referee in his match.

"Due to your competitor's inability to step back into the square you are deemed the winner. Please move to the left outside the square and await your next fight. Bow to me."

Falcon bowed to the referee who shook and raised his right hand in the air for all to see.

"Hell of a punch son. Keep it up."

"Thank you sir."

Falcon joined the winner's side while he slowly massaged his right shoulder.

Roger and his father approached.

"That guy almost broke my shoulder." Falcon said

Roger said, "Good job Falcon. You stayed under control and delivered a punch within the rules."

Mitch regarded Roger with a bit of disgust. "Give me a break."

"I'm not saying you were wrong Mitch, just outside the rules."

"If I'm the only one following the rules Roger then there are no rules."

"Fair enough," Roger smiled. His students were doing quite well.

Falcon said, "Dad, what happened to your face—?"

Falcon's question was cut off as a murderous banshee scream filled the gym — Deeter.

Although the welt over Deeter's eye was growing it didn't bother him at all, in fact he didn't even feel it. After being carried back to his fighting square, nearly all control disappeared. He managed to wait for the referee to give the command to fight, something he would try and get credit for with Roger later. But unlike his brother, Deeter didn't care about winning or losing. Deed just wanted to have fun. However under stress his fall-back position was always attack. The yellow belt still hanging loose around his narrow waist had stopped quivering. His opponent thought he had the little guy on the run but failed to notice Deeter wasn't trembling anymore.

"Fight!" yelled the referee.

As soon as the letter F left his lips, the spider monkey sprung. Deeter leaped onto the big cheater like he was diving into a pool. He harnessed the monster in a headlock, and they tumbled to the floor with Deeter on top. The banshee screamed again, and the crowd let out an approving roar. Little yellow's arms were like an out-of-control windmill, throwing left, right and lefts again; he smashed the big kid's face.

The teenager screamed as if an animal was attacking him, which was fair, because one was.

The referee tried to break up the fight to no avail.

Falcon's father raced over with Roger behind him. Reaching down with one arm, Mitch snatched Deeter by the back of his yellow belt and lifted him off.

Deeter hung in the air with his eyes shut tight as he wailed away like an airplane propeller, and because his legs were now free, he started kicking too.

Mitch strode away as he carried his younger son like a lunchbox.

"He's disqualified!" the referee yelled.

"Why?" asked Roger

Exasperated the ref said, "We can't have kids attacking each other, Roger."

"Look at the size difference," Roger said. "Do you really think you should have allowed a teenager in with younger kids?"

"He said he was 12."

"And you believed him?"

The referee didn't answer.

"Shame on you. This is supposed to be about teaching an art, maintaining control, and following rules."

"He's done. Don't enter him in anything else."

Roger said, "Why would I? You might have him fighting adult black belts next."

The referee huffed away.

Roger approached Rachel who'd just returned from checking on her husband and son outside.

"How is Deeter?" he asked.

"He'll be fine," she paused and then stared him in the eye. "This isn't going very well Roger."

"Oh I completely disagree. I think it's going very well."

"How's that? Two of them have welts on their faces and have been disqualified."

"Life gives us lemons. We make lemonade. Did you see Falcon?"

"Yes. I thought the guy was going to kill him."

"But he didn't. Falcon stayed under control and won."

"I'm not interested in my family being hurt so they can win a karate match Roger."

"I understand, but this isn't about winning. Well maybe for Falcon it is, but it's much deeper than that. It's about survival. The world is changing and frankly not for the better. Your family is learning how to survive when rules don't apply."

"You may be right, but even God wouldn't expect a mother and wife watch her family be abused."

Roger understood, but she'd feel differently when real life came knocking at the door.

Falcon laughed as his father carried Deeter outside with one hand like a loaf of bread. A path cleared for his dad and the little spider monkey, while nods of understanding showered upon them. Falcon's name was called and he stepped back into the ring. Across from him was an orange belt with two stripes, second level intermediate.

"Bow! Fight!"

Falcon's right shoulder still hurt but was moving well. The orange belt was older and bigger but clumsy. Two right hands to his ribs and a controlled back fist to his nose and the referee raised Falcon's hand again in victory. Falcon went back to his place outside the square and waited for his next opponent. Ten minutes later back in the square he faced a blue belt, skilled and several levels above Falcon. Blue was shorter than Falcon but older and stronger. The winner of this match would fight for the tournament championship.

The order was given to fight.

Blue had studied Falcon moving through his opponents. He'd never seen the tall yellow belt before and was surprised when his one punch took out Kevin the "Kick Master," as Kevin liked to call himself. He also noticed Falcon didn't throw a lot of kicks and thought he may be able to take advantage of that.

Three lightning punches later, taking two to his stomach and one to his nose; blue's match was over.

Falcon moved into the finals.

Deeter and Mitch returned to the gym and joined Rachel.

"Falcon's going to win!" exclaimed Deeter.

"We shall see," Roger smiled.

Falcon was summoned back to the square.

"Congratulations gentlemen," said the ref. "You have earned the right to fight for the title. The first fighter to score three is the winner and champion. Good luck!"

Falcon nodded to the referee and looked across at his opponent. He was taller, a bit heavier, and just turned 16. Falcon heard him say so while he registered. He wore a purple belt with a blue stripe, two levels above Falcon. Falcon had watched him fight three times, and he was good. He preferred kicking over punching while Falcon was the other way around. He'd learned the closer you could get to someone who liked to kick, the harder it was for them to kick you. Punching was the exact opposite. The closer you were the easier it was to hit your target. Falcon could throw kicks and had been working on a spinning-reverse kick that targeted the lower ribcage and stomach but was more comfortable using his hands.

The commands were given, "Fight!"

Falcon felt at ease inside the square. He understood the boundary and how to use it. As the blue belt moved cautiously Falcon threw two kicks as cover and pinned his rival into the corner.

Blue knew he couldn't step back and, as a cornered animal will do, attacked.

Falcon was waiting for it and slid behind the first kick then delivered a back fist to blue's nose and danced back to his original spot.

"Break!" yelled the referee.

Pointing to Falcon, he looked at the three judges for confirmation. Three thumbs up.

"Point yellow. Back fist! Bow! Fight!"

Blue skimmed his glove across his nose and wiped away sweat. *This guy's quick.*

Falcon bounced in front of blue as he knew he would have to be ready. Blue was good, bigger and older and definitely wanted to win. He moved closer and watched for any opening

Blue suddenly pivoted and kicked.

Falcon dropped his elbow enough to block most of the kick but the foot had gotten through to his side.

"Break!" the ref yelled and pointed to blue and scanned the judges.

Falcon already knew their decision.

Three thumbs pointed to the sky.

"Point Blue! Side kick! One Yellow, one Blue! Bow to each other!"

The combatants bowed and measured each other.

The blue belt wanted to win.

Falcon wanted to win too, but his stronger desire was his pure hatred for losing. He narrowed his eyes and searched for an opening.

Both fighters were now very respectful of the other's talents. The blue belt didn't want one of those lightning-quick hands to hit him in the nose again, and Falcon knew blue's kicks were too strong to be allowed to hit their targets repeatedly.

Falcon circled and waited for his shot.

Blue threw a snap kick, leaped into the air and threw a right cross.

Falcon blocked the kick with his knee and ducked under the right cross. Using his head as a battering ram, he exploded into blue's exposed stomach and knocked him to the ground. It wasn't a Kenpo move. It was survival.

"Break!" The ref pointed toward Falcon. All three judges pointed their thumbs down. The referee agreed and gave a quick explanation. "You can't use your head as a weapon in here. That isn't a taught technique." *Pretty sweet move though kid.*

Falcon nodded.

"Two blue, one yellow. Bow to each other."

A little panic welled up inside of Falcon as he knew he was one point away from losing. He bowed quickly and decided to attack.

"Fight!"

Falcon sprang like a cat throwing two front snap kicks and followed with a left jab to the head.

Blue raised his arms to counter, which opened up his midsection.

The crowd gasped when Falcon dropped nearly to one knee and prepared to deliver the same punch that knocked his first opponent from the tournament. It was the same punch, but Blue was fighting with control and Falcon wasn't trying to deliver a message, he just wanted the point. The lightning right struck Blue's unguarded midsection with enough force to make him gasp but with enough control to not knock him down.

"Break!"

The referee pointed to Falcon. Three thumbs up.

"Two Yellow, two Blue! Next point wins. Good luck gentlemen! Bow to me!"

They did.

"Touch gloves and bow to each other."

Falcon tapped gloves with the blue belt and bowed.

"Fight!"

Blue flew out of his spot and threw right and left kicks.

Falcon guessed this was coming and darted left. The kicks hit nothing but air.

Out of position Blue panicked and threw an illegal blind-spinning back fist.

Falcon darted left, which put him in a good position, but his foot slipped as he tried to push off. This was a savior, as the spinning back fist whipped over his head. Falcon regained his balance. *That's a move I need to learn.*

The referee knew the spinning back fist was illegal, but the punch had missed so he let it go. He didn't want the match determined on a penalty. Besides he had a hunch the yellow belt had a surprise in store.

Falcon squared up the blue belt and decided it was time to take a chance. With his left foot forward he flicked his left hand out with a tiny jab intended to stop blue from advancing. It did. Then he rocked forward onto his left foot and pivoted, while throwing what appeared to be an out-of-control right roundhouse. As he did this he hopped onto his right foot, spun in a tight circle, and threw a vicious left-reverse donkey kick.

As the wild right roundhouse buzzed through the air, Blue's eyes lit up because Falcon's back was exposed to him for a millisecond. *I'm going to win.* Lunging forward with a left jab and right cross, he strained to punch the yellow belt in the back of the head. As his punch left, warning bells went off. *Move! Move! Move!* His body screamed, but it was too late. The wild roundhouse was the bait, and Blue felt the championship slip away as the crushing pain of the reverse-donkey kick landed in his stomach and launched him backward and out of the square.

The thundering crowd said it all.

"Break!" the referee yelled before Blue even hit the ground and stepped in front of Falcon just in case he was moving in for the kill.

He wasn't. The blue belt fought within the rules and Falcon appreciated that.

The referee offered a hand to Blue, which was accepted, and pulled the fighter back into the square. Facing each other the referee went through the preliminary although everyone in the building knew the outcome. The referee pointed to Falcon — and all three judges gave thumbs up.

"Three Yellow, two Blue. Yellow winner." The ref took Falcon's right arm and raised it above his head. "Congratulations young man. Hell of a kick. Bow to me. Bow to each other."

Falcon slapped gloves with the blue belt.

"Great kick," his opponent said.

"Thanks. I had no choice. You were all over me."

Blue smiled, "Apparently not enough!"

Falcon collected his trophy and joined his family.

Excited, Deeter bounced around his brother. "Good job Fal!"

"Thanks buddy. You were pretty good out there too."

"I showed that big gorilla, I just gave him one of these."

Deed squeezed his eyes shut and imitated his earlier exhibition.

Falcon laughed and grabbed him around the neck. "Calm down you crazy spider monkey before you put me out of commission."

Deeter grinned.

Falcon wasn't wound up anymore, just excited, tired and hungry. He'd left his breakfast on the side of the road four hours ago.

Rachel rubbed her son's back. "How's your shoulder honey?"

Mitch said, "Aw, he's not feeling it now Mom, are you buddy?"

Falcon shook his head.

"Let's load up and go home," said Mitch.

"Can we stop and eat first Dad, I'm starving?" Deeter begged, clearly over the attack of the wild banshee.

"I think I'll eat when we get home," Falcon said not wanting another test of wills with Buckhorn Summit.

"Good idea honey," Rachel agreed as they began to leave.

"Hey Falcon!" Roger was beaming. "Congratulations son, you did a mighty fine job."

"Thanks Roger."

Falcon stopped, and then handed Roger the gleaming four-foot trophy.

"This is for you, for the dojo."

Overcome by emotion, Roger couldn't speak. He simply nodded.

Falcon headed for the door, scooped up some trash from the floor, and tossed it into a nearby bin. He glanced back at Roger who hadn't moved.

Roger lifted the trophy in the air as if to say thanks.

Falcon nodded and walked out.

"That's a special kid," Roger said out loud to no one. "No, he's a special young man."

Summer flew by filled with water skiing and swimming at the lake, the Fourth of July celebration, working on the route, and athletics. Falcon's search for Cassandra went unfulfilled. Unbeknownst to him her family went to the Bay Area in the summer after the Fourth of July every year. As the smoldering days faded and the leaves changed colors, high school arrived.

After dropping Deeter at Weaverville Elementary, Rachel and Falcon pulled up in front of Trinity High School.

"Make it a great first day," Rachel said.

"I will Mom."

Falcon jumped from the still-rolling car.

Rachel worried about her number-one son. Extremely sensitive and shy, Falcon had hated the first day of school ever since she could remember. That morning he had passed on breakfast, French toast, his favorite. She had sensed he was nervous.

She lowered the passenger window, "I love you."

Falcon turned on a dime and headed back to the car.

Poking his head in he said, "I love you too."

Then he hurried away. She meant well, but this was high school. He couldn't have his "Mommy" proclaiming her love every morning at the curb.

Trinity was his third school in the last five years. High school provided the great American tale of beginning dreams and glory days too soon gone. Falcon planned to make the most of it. He located his locker and carefully turned the knob on the combo. Thankfully it worked the first time. Nothing screamed freshman more than a kid who struggled with the combination. He stowed his lunch and headed off to find his first-period class, freshman English. Although he recognized a few faces from Junction City, all girls, they were sophomores and not about to recognize him in public until he established himself. It was an unspoken rule in high school, and Falcon got it. He found his room and wasn't surprised to be the first student to arrive. He didn't tolerate tardiness.

The English teacher didn't even bother to look up. She pointed to a stack of books. "Grab the text and find a desk."

"Thank you."

He followed her instructions, and like cowboys of old, chose an aisle seat in the rear to achieve the best view of the room.

As students filed in, the teacher pointed and repeated her line. A little chunky, she managed to squeeze herself into a blouse and skirt a size too small. Some student had nicknamed her "Rosie" and the rumor was she had a rose tattoo on her breast.

Falcon didn't want to imagine how a student would know that. But during summer vacation he'd witnessed "Rosie" on the back of a Harley Davidson letting it all hang out. The story seemed to fit. Falcon stretched his long legs in preparation for the opening speech barely aware of the ocean of kids flowing into the room until … his dream girl appeared. He shook his head and blinked twice as his senses came alive. Sitting up tall he watched Cassandra Ross hurry to the last seat available in the back, three desks away. English had just become his favorite period.

The bell rang and the teacher talked.

Falcon didn't listen. The girl he'd been yearning for all summer sat barely 10 feet away; besides, he could pass English in his sleep. He tried to shift his body to view Cassandra without staring.

Rosie was taking roll, "Cassandra Ross?"

"Present."

Present … Falcon sighed. It was the sweetest sound Falcon had heard in his whole life. *I wonder if she saw me?*

Cassandra had noticed Falcon the second she had walked into the room. She couldn't believe her good luck to have the boy of her dreams in her class, and her misfortune of having to wear braces.

Falcon had been watching her when she answered to her name and noticed she didn't open her mouth very wide. A buzz in Falcon's ear awakened him.

Rosie called, "Falcon Sane? Falcon Sane?"

"Right here." A little embarrassed he raised his hand.

Rosie stared down her nose at him. "Glad you could join us Mr. Sane."

He turned his winning smile on Cassandra, "My pleasure."

The teacher paused and tried to decide if he was a smart ass. Surprisingly he appeared happy, even genuinely excited. She continued to call names. Falcon's warmth made Cassandra forget her braces, and she smiled back — only to instantly clamp her lips together and look away. *He saw them. Now he thinks I'm ugly!*

Falcon's heart quickened from the recognition. *She's prettier than I remembered. Why did she turn away?*

Rosie droned on while Falcon drifted in thoughts of Cassandra: holding her hand, smelling her perfume, and kissing those tantalizing lips. The bell rang much too quickly for the love-struck teenager. Students raced for the doors and hoped to find their next class without getting lost, as his Cassandra disappeared in the wave.

The next period getting dressed for P.E. in the locker room Cassandra complained to Lacey, her best friend since grade school. "I hate my braces!"

"I know but they'll be off soon," said the cute brunette.

"Soon. Are you crazy, I'll have them at least a year!"

"Yeah but it's already been two months. What's the big deal now?"

"Remember the boy I told you about at the Brain Drain?"

"Uh-huh?" Lacey tied her hair in a ponytail.

"Well he's in my English class!" said Cassandra.

"Shut up!" laughed Lacey.

"I know!"

"No way!"

"Seriously." Cassandra plopped down on the bench.

"Is he still cute?"

"Is he? Too cute for a girl with dumb braces."

Lacey tried to console her friend as they dressed for gym.

Falcon mulled over Cassandra's behavior on his way to P.E. A novice where girls were concerned, he wondered if she still liked him. Carrying the required shorts and t-shirt in one hand he bounced down the stairs to the men's locker room. Fifty other freshman boys packed into the dressing area and tried to change in a privacy that didn't exist. Falcon changed, stored his clothes in the temporary P.E. locker, and followed the herd to the gymnasium.

The boy's physical education teacher barked out orders, "Boys to the left of me, in five lines of 10, arm's length from each other, let's go! This isn't home ec!"

The band of boys snapped to it and began jumping jacks.

Twenty feet away the girl's physical education teacher rallied her freshman charges.

"Let's go ladies! Put the makeup away! Yes, I know the boys are over there! This is P.E! Physical Education, and I guarantee you will be tired after this class!"

"Gentleman!" yelled the boy's teacher. "I know the girls are right next to you but you have six other periods to try and score their numbers! In here you're mine! Hit the ground; it's push-up time!"

This continued for 40 minutes, running in place, sit-ups, lunges, and moves even Jack Lalanne would have approved of.

Drenched in sweat, Falcon and the other boys trudged toward the locker room where they hoped to revive themselves with 60-second showers. En route he caught Cassandra's eye.

She looked away.

A brunette beside her gave Falcon a big smile and tiny wave.

He checked around to see whom she was waving to, but no one responded. He shrugged. *Girls.* The bell rang for third period as Falcon struggled to pull his socks over damp feet. He slipped into his shoes and took off since he knew he could tie the strings in class. *This is crazy. I need to come up with a better system.*

Except for history, the rest of Falcon's day was uneventful. He didn't have Cassandra in any other classes, but his American History class was amazing.

Mr. Albert Jacobsen stood at the front of the classroom and

spoke passionately about freedom. The six-foot, 175-pound hardened physique of liberty with a crew cut, piercing grey eyes and jaw line etched from granite lectured on the Constitution and its importance, specifically the First Amendment. Mr. Jacobsen fought in World War II under Patton. He was adamant about the freedom of speech and the responsibility of the free press, a *responsibility* his teacher felt the press was abdicating. The 55-minute class flashed by as Falcon consumed the patriotism and genuine love of freedom that emanated from his *teacher* whose life provided an example to follow.

"Remember this, my young patriots, freedom of speech is listed first in the Amendments because it is the most important." Pausing to let that sink in he continued. "And the Second Amendment, the right to bear arms, provides insurance to the first."

The bell rang, and day one of high school was over.

Freshman English and American History kept Falcon interested, and after a few weeks he acclimated to his new school. During week one he'd used his lunch break to locate the baseball diamond. Barely a 60-second walk from campus, the entire field sat above and away from the rest of the school. Cut out of a large hill and flattened by a bulldozer, hundreds of trees that surrounded the field provided a green serenity, which was cordoned off by a chain-linked fence. This architecture created a Roman Coliseum view for the fans who looked down on the combatants. Each lunchtime he sought out his sanctuary and sat in the dugout. Gazing over the field, he ate and dreamed of great plays and greater days ahead. Isolated from the noise and cradled safely in the arms of the diamond, Falcon felt at home. He loved the dirt and smell of fresh-cut grass. He imagined his future in the big leagues, Cassandra Ross, and the one time he held her hand and dreamed of doing so again. This became his routine until Junior Varsity basketball tryouts in November pulled him out of the shadows and into the light.

"Okay everyone listen up!" said Bernie Model the head JV basketball coach. "There are 30 of you and we're only keeping 12. Tryouts last one week, and then I'll post the names of who made the team. Any questions? Good! Get on the baseline!"

Twenty nine players scrambled to the baseline.

Falcon froze.

"Whataya doing kid?" the coach yelled. "Get on the baseline!"

He'd marked Falcon as soon as he saw him in the group, six feet, strong and moved like a cat when he walked.

Falcon hated anyone screaming at him. He faced the coach, angry and embarrassed. "I didn't know what a baseline was," he said honestly and followed the group.

The coach shouted, "Whataya mean you don't know what a baseline is! Haven't you ever played basketball?"

"No … not really," Falcon said, feeling self-conscious and getting angrier.

The coach scrutinized the young man who was taller than himself and then motioned him over. "You've never played basketball?"

Falcon answered quietly, "Not like this. We had a hoop growing up but we played on the dirt."

The coach was surprised. He'd have pegged him for an athlete.

"Okay — that's the baseline." He pointed. "Stand with the others and do what they do."

"Yes sir," Falcon said, relieved to be out of the spotlight so that he could turn his focus on competing.

The week blew by for Falcon who for the first time experienced basketball shoes and blisters; pushing a dry mop head while running liners; and the realization he couldn't dribble or shoot with his left hand. He was definitely right-hand dominant. He realized, almost immediately, he was in better shape than most, quicker than everyone his size or larger, and just as fast as the little guys. What he lacked in experience he made up for with athleticism and hustle. Rebounding better than anyone, except his new friend Jerry, he played balls-to-the-walls defense — that's where his strengths abandoned him. Timid of shooting, only a right-handed dribbler while his head was down, basketball wasn't baseball (something he could roll out of bed and play) or karate, something he now had some experience with. Basketball was a whole other animal.

Coach Model continued to holler at Falcon when he was out of position.

Falcon hated being yelled at, or worse, told what to do, but he listened and sucked it up all week. Monday morning 12 names would be posted on the wall outside the gym, Falcon was determined one would be his. While waiting for his ride home, Falcon felt a slap on the back. He turned.

"Hey Fal," Jerry smiled, "good job today."

Jerry was all arms and legs, tall, strong, and filled out like a man. Perfectly built for basketball, which probably explained why he didn't play any other sports. He was the only freshman everyone knew would make the team and likely start. He was also a nice guy, and the two teenagers hit it off during tryouts.

He was Falcon's one and only friend.

"Thanks. I hope I make the team. If I could shoot like you I know I would." Falcon smiled.

"Yeah and if I was as fast as you I could play point guard. Don't worry. You'll make it. I heard coach talking to the varsity coach. They like how aggressive and fast you are. They kept saying natural-born athlete."

Falcon had never heard that phrase before. "Isn't the varsity basketball coach the varsity baseball coach too?"

"Yep."

"Who's the JV baseball coach?"

"There isn't one."

"Why not?"

"Because we don't have a JV baseball team."

Falcon's heart sank.

Jerry said, "Here you either play varsity or you don't play at all."

"Seriously?"

"Uh-huh."

That meant Falcon would have to compete against juniors and seniors. He'd played one year of senior league, ages 13 through 15 and did pretty well. The bases were 90 feet instead of 60 feet in little league. Against 15-year olds he'd been fine, 16- and 18-year olds would be interesting. Falcon practiced his baseball skills every day, year-round, and figured he was ready for some real competition.

"I just have to make it work," he said aloud but more to himself.

"Don't worry. The varsity coach likes you." Jerry raised his hands in the air to make a quote sign and said, "He's the one who called you 'the natural-born athlete.'"

Falcon smiled, "Nice."

Rachel drove up.

"Jerry, do you need a ride? My mom's here."

"Nah, I live over that hill." He pointed west through the forest. "I'll be home before you will."

"Okay. See you Monday."

"You bet," said Jerry.

As Falcon drove home, Cassandra sprawled on her bed and tried to focus on her French homework. Lacey was making this impossible.

"You want me to go talk to him, you know I will," her best friend offered.

"What I would like is to finish our homework so we aren't trying to get this done Sunday night."

Lacey twirled her pretty dark hair around a finger and thought about what to say next, while *Alphaville's Forever Young* soulfully ached in the cassette player on Cassandra's desk. "I love this song, it's so true. Life flashes by so fast."

Cassandra rolled her eyes. "We're only freshmen in high school."

Lacey flipped her workbook open again and absently filled in a verb conjugation. "We'll be in college before you know it and then married with a mortgage after that ... at least that's what my dad says. You know his favorite line, 'living in the moment.'"

"He means it in a positive way not like those hippies who tuned in, turned on, and dropped out in his generation."

"I know ... that's what I'm saying. You need to live in the *Falcon* moment before the moment is gone."

The weekend passed and basketball season began. Jerry was right. Falcon made the team and improved so much he even started a few games. His defense and rebounding helped the team to a little better than .500 record. His lunchtime activities also changed — now he ate lunch with Jerry, the star of the team, and a few other teammates. English was still his favorite class because of Cassandra but aside from an occasional tight-lipped smile their relationship seemed to live only in Falcon's hopeful mind. Before basketball wound down, he'd become popular with the freshman class and even knew a couple of Cassandra's friends, although not well enough to share his feelings about her. Nor would it have mattered. Some of her *so-called friends* made it clear they'd jump at the chance to go out with him if he asked. He didn't. Cassandra was his first real crush and although there were plenty of pretty girls, the romantic he was, he waited for her.

Mr. Jacobsen, Falcon's favorite teacher, brought history alive with riveting stories about World War II and opinions on the Soviet Union. Captivated by the information, Falcon digested the differences between the freedom of America and the lives of people living in oppressed nations.

Mr. J was on a roll today. "Our national press flap their gums about the Soviet Union and communism. We've all heard the saying 'better dead than red.' Some reporters write about Hitler and his Nazi Socialist party. The reporters or media are getting this all wrong. Hitler and Stalin weren't communist or socialist. They tried to hide behind the idea of an equal or communal society. Humans like those two want us to think they are creating some type of social or equal way to live. They aren't. They were thugs willing to do anything including murder and rape to stay in power. I know. I saw it. The term that should be used to explain this type of behavior is fascism. For tonight's homework look up the definition of fascism and where it is found in the world today."

A few students let out a groan, typical of teenagers who heard a homework assignment moments before the bell would spring them free.

Mr. Jacobsen paused for a moment and then continued.

"Let me be clear. Anyone calling themselves a socialist or a communist or tries to tell you the United States of America is a democracy is unbelievably misguided, a danger to free people and violently ill-informed."

"What are we then, Mr. Jacobsen?" a student in the back asked.

"We are the greatest country on the planet!" He turned and saluted the American Flag next to his desk.

As the information sunk in, heads nodded in agreement

with their teacher.

Darn right, thought Falcon.

"But to answer your question accurately we are a Constitutional Republic. The Constitution gives us our rights as Americans. Rights many Americans have died for; rights that cannot be taken from you unless you allow it."

One girl said, "My mom said we are a democracy."

"No she is incorrect. We practice democracy although not well these days, in my opinion. But we are by definition a Constitutional Republic. Homework item number two!"

The groans became louder.

"Get out your *Encyclopedia Britannicas* and bring in three paragraphs on the United States being a Constitutional Republic."

Falcon's brain was clicking as he copied the assignments. He knew one thing for sure. *America needs a lot more Mr. Jacobsens and a lot less pot-smoking, fat, welfare hippies, having too many kids.* The bell rang and Falcon gathered up his books.

Mr. Jacobsen walked toward Falcon's desk and smiled at his young student. *This kid is impressive, always early to class, polite, and incredibly bright.* He liked the quiet, thoughtful young man who soaked up and shared his teacher's love for freedom. They also shared another passion, baseball.

"I hear you are quite an athlete young man."

"Basketball has been interesting, but my real sport is coming up next week." Falcon answered.

"Yes, that's what I wanted to talk to you about. Do you know Coach Pluto?"

"No, I've only seen him on basketball trips or at games."

"I know him quite well. He mentioned you yesterday in the lounge. The rumor is you are a shortstop."

"Yes sir."

"Well he's looking forward to you coming out next week and

wanted to make sure you were."

"Oh yes sir. I'll be there."

"Good. You address me as sir quite frequently, Falcon. Did your father serve our great country?"

"Yes sir. He was an Army medic in Korea, but mainly my parents taught me to be polite to my elders. Except my mom says unless you're southern don't call women ma'am, it makes them feel old."

Mr. Jacobsen laughed, "Well, she should know. Carry on soldier."

"Yes sir."

Falcon floated out the door. *Mr. Jacobsen is a great man. Too bad my other teachers don't have his enthusiasm and love for teaching ... and America.*

Baseball and basketball tryouts had one thing in common — lots of running.

Coach Gary Pluto addressed the 50 male students who hoped to make the baseball team.

"For the next five days don't bother bringing your glove or your bat. You won't be using them. There will be no baseball drills whatsoever. You're a hefty group, but we will only be keeping 18, and only 14 of you will be given a uniform. This isn't Little League and I ain't your momma. If you don't like it there's the gate. Don't let it hitcha where the good lord splitcha! We don't play games here. This is Varsity Baseball — Trinity Varsity Baseball. I don't care what you think you know or who your daddy is. This is my team, and I'm here to win. If you can help me win then you will make the team. If you can't you won't. I'm not a camp counselor. Don't come crying to me if you're sore or tired. Don't care. Don't come to me about missing a practice. If you miss practice, don't bother coming back. This is big-boy baseball," he hocked and spit. "Welcome aboard."

Falcon stood next to some of his basketball buddies in the large group. There were only 300 kids in the entire school and more than half of them were girls. Over one third of the boys attending Trinity High School came out for the varsity baseball team.

Pluto continued, "Before I forget, by tomorrow some of you need to get a haircut. No ponytails or hair in your face. Don't care if you don't like it. It looks bad and can be unsafe, and no earrings either. If you come back tomorrow without a haircut or wearing earrings I'll cut you on the spot. Don't waste my time. Now line it up on the right field foul line."

There would be no replay of basketball tryouts for Falcon. He knew everything there was to know about a baseball field. Lining up on the foul lines meant one thing, sprints.

Coach Pluto strutted out 20 paces beyond second base halfway to center field. "Watch my hand. When it goes down you bust your ass as fast as you can through me."

Falcon tensed waiting for the hand to drop. He didn't wait long.

"Go!" Pluto screamed as his hand dropped.

Falcon bolted as if shot out of a cannon and sprinted as fast as he could. Out of the corners of his eyes he could see only one other player ahead of him. He strained to catch him but came up a step short as they passed Pluto.

"Good job Bobby," Pluto said to the winner.

Bobby Burke could fly. He was also a junior and Pluto's shortstop last year.

"Line it up next to me gentlemen. We're going the other way. Get your hands off your hips and stand up straight," he bellowed.

Falcon was already on the line, wanting another shot at Bobby. He got another shot and then some.

At sprint 15, six guys grabbed their gloves and bats and

walked off together. "This isn't baseball," one muttered. "I didn't come out here to run track."

"Thanks for coming out guys!" yelled Pluto.

His job just got easier. By the time they reached 40 sprints only 25 players remained. Bobby won most of the sprints, but Falcon managed to win a couple when Bobby tired. By the time they were done they'd rolled off 50 sprints.

"Okay good job gentlemen! Get into lines of five. It's push-up and sit-up time!"

Falcon was exhausted as he got into his line.

"Okay listen up! Get in push-up position and hold it. No up and down, just hold it. Go!"

Falcon pushed his body up and held the position while his legs started shaking.

Pluto shouted, "On your backs! Legs straight out, six inches off the ground. Don't give me two inches or three feet! Six inches off the ground! Go!"

Falcon flopped onto his back and raised his legs six inches. This duo of exercises went on for 30 minutes. He knew he would never quit but wasn't sure how much longer his arms would push his body up.

Nobody was at six inches anymore.

Pluto watched the entire group and knew they were tired. They'd been at it for almost 90 minutes. "Okay everyone on their feet and to me!"

Twenty-five exhausted players moved as fast as they could toward the coach.

"Four laps around the entire field and we'll call it a day. See you tomorrow."

As promised, this practice schedule continued through Friday. The soreness the players felt after the first four days intertwined with a certain pride of surviving this athletic insanity.

Juniors and seniors who didn't know Falcon or the three other freshman rookies left standing started talking to them as equals. In the hallways nods of affirmation and even friendship were bestowed on the freshmen from the upper classmen.

Respect earned respect given.

Pluto gathered his troops around him at the end of Friday's non-baseball workout. There were 20 left.

"Congratulations men. That was a hell of a week. As you know there were almost 50 in the beginning. Now we have 20. I told you we are only keeping 18 and only dressing 14. The 20 of you who are left have officially made the team. Congrats. You've earned it. But to get a Varsity letter you've got to be on the roster. Only 14 jerseys will be passed out. Those jerseys will only go to the players who can help me win. Bring your gloves and bats on Monday. We have two weeks to see who can help me win before we play our first game. See you Monday!"

That evening Falcon leaned against his shower wall as hot water cascaded over his sore muscles. Oblivious to the pain, he formed his plan. Although he practiced baseball year-round it was time to really pick it up. Saturday and Sunday mornings were packed. Extra batting practice and more grounders than he could count, his dad smoked one-hop bullets at his feet or yanked him back and forth with ground balls in the hole or up the middle. Falcon added a pair of ankle weights and took ground balls and hoped it would help his range — it did.

For two weeks Falcon battled Bobby Burke as he tried to earn what he knew was his. The competition was fierce as the junior refused to lose his spot, especially to a freshman.

But the greater the competition grew it became clear to one man who his shortstop would be.

The night before the first game and announcement of the starting lineup, Mitch asked Falcon how it was going.

"Eight guys went out for shortstop Dad, and they moved all of them into different spots except me and a junior."

"How is he?"

"Pretty good. He doesn't have my range but he's a little faster and has a better arm ... right now."

Mitch smiled at the "right-now" comment. He knew his son hated admitting someone was better than him at anything. "Have you talked to the coach?"

"No, I just keep going out to short when he calls my name."

"And they haven't put you anywhere else?"

"No sir."

"Maybe you should check with the coach. Tell him what you told me last night."

Falcon said, "You think I should?" He didn't talk to Pluto very much.

"Couldn't hurt."

"Okay. I'll do it tomorrow."

Falcon considered his father's advice the next day as he laced up his cleats.

Pluto, who was still in his office, hadn't gone out to the field yet.

"Coach, can I talk to you for a minute?" asked Falcon.

Pluto searched the firebrand standing in his doorway and tried not to smile. *If I had nine kids like this one I'd win every damn game. He doesn't say much, but on the field his talent speaks volumes.* Pluto had a feeling as soon as he relaxed into his role he'd take over the game athletically, and more importantly, as a leader. "Sure Falcon, come on in."

"Thanks coach." He entered the office. "I know you're going to name the starters, and I wanted you to know I'll play anywhere you want. I just want to play."

Coach Pluto restrained a grin, "You know Falcon I've been

thinking. Why don't you just stay at short."

Falcon lit up like a kid on Christmas morning. "Yeah?"

"Yeah, and I don't care if you don't hit either. Just keep making every play for me."

"Oh, I'll hit, coach," said Falcon.

"I'm sure you will, but I don't want you stressing about it. Play short for me and give me everything you got." It was music to Falcon's ears. *I believe in you. Go play as hard as you can for me.*

"Thank you Pluto. Thanks Coach, I won't let you down."

It was the seriousness in Falcon's voice that caught Pluto off guard, and he stopped and studied his 14-year-old warrior. "I know you won't son. I'm counting on you."

Falcon stood straight as an arrow. Pluto couldn't have chosen better words. He craved responsibility. Falcon nodded and headed for the field. *It's the beginning of the 1985 Varsity Baseball season.* Falcon played the announcement in his head. *And starting for Trinity High School at shortstop: Falcon Sane. "Ahhh!" the crowd goes wild as Falcon steps onto the diamond.* Lifting his arms, he gestured like Rocky Balboa and danced in a circle.

"Oh say can you see by the dawn's early light what so proudly we hailed by the twilight's last gleaming ..."

Falcon stood on the first-base foul line with the rest of his teammates. Holding his brand-new hat over his heart, he listened to a tape of the *Star Spangled Banner.*

On the third-base foul line stood their competition and hated rival, Hayfork.

"And the rockets' red glare ... the bombs bursting in air, gave proof through the night that our flag was still there ..."

Cassandra and Lacey were in the bleachers and stood with hands over hearts along with the other 75 fans from both towns.

Mr. Albert Jacobsen stood at attention with a crisp salute.

A spring breeze carried the smell of freshly cut grass, which blanketed the wonderful drama of high school athletics and freedom. For one brief moment there was no Trinity or Hayfork. In that moment they were all Americans.

"O'er the land of the free ... and the home of the brave."

The audience clapped and settled in along with Cassandra and Lacey.

Mr. Jacobsen leaned on the fence next to his home team.

"Give 'em hell Trinity!" he called to the Wolves as they came together in a tight circle outside their dugout.

Bobby Burke in the middle of the pack pumped up his team. "What are we here to do?"

"Win!" roared the deep male voices.

"How are we going to do it?"

"Together!" thundered the Wolf Pack as the Trinity starters sprinted onto the field amid the applause of their fans and took their positions.

In a full sprint, ran number 13, Falcon Sane, who pulled up and settled into his favorite place in the world, shortstop.

Mitch and Rachel smiled at each other and shared the moment. They would have a happy boy at home tonight.

Falcon scooped up a couple of ground balls from his first baseman and fired them over. Someone in the crowd's boom box played John Cougar's "Jack and Diane". *I love that song.* He hummed along with the words as he paced back and forth waiting for the game to begin. He watched his pitcher warm up and checked the rest of his team to make sure they were in the right positions. He scanned the crowd, found his parents, and smiled to himself. *It's good to be loved.* He took another quick glance and spotted Cassandra. *This might be the best day of my life. I wish I could stay here forever.*

Pluto watched his young shortstop quite pleased with

himself. He'd been right. Giving Falcon responsibility and the freedom to achieve greatness transformed the young man into a hungry lion who paced back and forth as he waited to be fed. Pluto smiled. He was going to feed every team on the schedule to this kid for the next four years. It was time to be a champion, and his shortstop was going to lead him there. Pluto glared through his sunglasses at the other team that waited to hit. *I fucking hate Hayfork. They've been a pain in my side for years. Now it's our time — Trinity time.* It was time for a lion named Falcon to roar.

The umpire brushed off home plate and claimed his spot behind the Trinity catcher. He nodded slightly and barked the words everyone was waiting for, "Play Ball!"

The first game of the season against Hayfork was a battle as the ferocity of the hated rivals reached new heights. Trinity had a team this year, and a new shortstop who never seemed to shut up.

Pitch after pitch Falcon coached from his position as he roamed back and forth, never still.

Inning after inning, the two teams hammered away and as the sun set the game was called. No one celebrated the official score: four to four. It was a precursor for Trinity. They finally had some talent, and more importantly, desire.

Falcon had been joined by another freshman, a pitcher. Between the two of them Pluto envisioned championships in the coming years as he watched his freshman shortstop battle, make mistakes, and learn every day. Good as his word Falcon made plays for Pluto — some plays Pluto was still in awe of. He also hit as he said he would and began to garner attention from roaming major league scouts. Battling on week after week, enjoying the wins and hating the losses, the baseball year ended too quickly for Falcon as his team ran out of games. Trinity finished third in their league, unfortunately out of the playoffs. Although not happy with the ending it had been a tremendous jump from the cellar where they'd dwelled in past years, and Pluto was pleased with the early returns. His team was young and he knew they would be a force for the next three years.

The year ended on a personal high note as Falcon hit a bullet over the left field fence in his last at bat of the year for his first home run. As he glided around the bases, he could almost hear John Fogerty singing "Centerfield" and couldn't contain his smile.

Life was good.

Falcon's freshman year ended, and his excitement for summer was dampened only by the thought of not seeing Cassandra every morning — not that their communication had improved. It hadn't. But his shyness and her seeming disinterest did not squelch his feelings. Falcon, "the hopeless romantic," as his mom called him, fantasized of one day holding Cassandra's hand again and kissing her lips.

Summer was delivering more baseball, occasional sleeping in, and working long hours for Falcon and Deeter with their father. On the weekends the boys traipsed all over the town with their friends or headed out to the lake to swim or ski. The big deal during the summer was The Fourth of July celebration in Weaverville. Tourists flocked to the event and stretched the small town of 2,500 people to the seams. Young and old enjoyed the entertainment from an era gone by and the locals reveled in the excitement of their usually sleepy village. At 6:00 a.m. Fourth of July officially started with the firing of the anvil and continuing booming throughout the day. In days gone by, the firing of an anvil, which culminated in packing gunpowder into its hole and lighting in on fire, was used as a warning to the citizens something bad had occurred like a mine collapsing or a forest fire. Now the firing of the anvil marked the beginning of the festivities.

The Sanes lived only a mile from the firing in the local park, and Falcon smiled each time he heard the explosion. The only downside was how frightened their Australian Shepherds Amber and Bootes became as the dogs spent the day hunkered down under the bed and whined. The Lion's Club hosted a pancake breakfast, and if you weren't planning to make an appearance in the parade, which anyone could, folks camped out early along Main Street to get a good seat. The best spot for catching the goodies the clowns threw to the crowd was in front of the theater. There were art and craft booths, the famous Trinity Congregational Church ladies' ice cream social, a crash-up derby, a carnival, and a live theater where the audience partook of hissing and booing the nasty villain. Red, white and blue streamers decorated columns, American flags hung at every corner, and families picnicked in the lush park. The Fourth of July was an innocent affair that seemingly turned back the hands of time.

Falcon skipped the 6:30 a.m. breakfast. Not an early riser, especially on his days off, he needed only venture to his mom's kitchen for the best grub in the world. But he always made the ice cream social. Fresh-baked pies, cakes, and plenty of hand-churned, homemade ice cream was right up his alley.

Falcon and two of his friends, Ricky and Lloyd, waited in line Saturday morning to sample the church ladies' wares.

"If church was more like this," said Lloyd, "I'd go every day."

The women fawned over the young, handsome athletes and loaded the plates of their local sports heroes with extra servings.

The boys ate it up, literally and figuratively. Licking their plates clean, the three friends started up the street in search of vendors, the parade and girls.

Lloyd and Ricky had only one thing in common — Falcon.

Lloyd, a slick-talking, soon-to-be sophomore played with Falcon on the JV basketball team. He loved rap music, making jokes, and admiring the ladies.

Ricky, the polar opposite, a soon-to-be-junior focused on his studies and baseball. Falcon and Ricky met during baseball season. Ricky was coming into his own and aiming to be the starting catcher next year. His passion for baseball and his personal ethics matched Falcon's perfectly.

Maturity cemented Falcon and Ricky's friendship.

Lloyd made Falcon laugh.

After a couple hours cruising Main Street, the boys claimed a spot to watch the parade.

The Weaverville Parade had it all. Fire engines spraying water on the sweating audience, crash-up derby cars, sexy cheerleaders, and two marching bands with gleaming tubas and big bass drums. A massive Budweiser beer truck, clowns on unicycles or stuffed into little cars, fancy horseback riders, and homemade floats passed through the street. The entire caravan took over an hour to complete and made it worth every second.

Always on the prowl, Lloyd pointed to one of the floats. "Hey isn't that Cassandra?"

Falcon snapped to attention and sprung to life.

Cassandra, all dressed in white, waved one gloved hand, while she held a paper-mache torch in the other. She was the Statue of Liberty.

In a daze Falcon followed her so closely he almost became a part of the procession.

Cassandra saw Falcon, fluttered her lashes, and blew him a kiss as the float continued down the hill.

Grinning and glued to the pavement, Falcon watched as she disappeared around the bend on Main Street.

Ricky said, "Man, I think she blew you a kiss!"

Lloyd punched Falcon in the arm. "Dude, you've got it bad."

Falcon didn't seem to notice.

"Did you hear what I said?" Lloyd repeated, "You got it bad, dude!" He punched Falcon in the arm again a little harder.

The second punch annoyed Falcon, and he spun around. He didn't like being touched, and he hated being teased, especially about Cassandra.

Lloyd jumped back and laughed, "Whoa tiger! Don't take it out on me man just because you're in looove."

Falcon lowered his voice, "Don't touch me again, Lloyd."

"I was just trying to wake you up." He snapped his fingers in the air. "Don't get all Karate Joe on me."

Lloyd was one of the few people who knew Falcon studied Kenpo. Falcon had mentioned it once to see if Lloyd was interested. He wasn't but he liked to tease Falcon. Falcon asked Lloyd to keep it between them. It wasn't anyone's business what he was learning nor did he want to sound like a braggart. Besides, sometimes Lloyd flapped his gums at the wrong time.

Ricky wasn't a Lloyd fan but tolerated him because of Falcon, the best friend he'd ever known. He could tell Falcon was getting hot. "Hey buddy, he didn't mean anything by it. Did you Lloyd?"

"Nah, you know I didn't. I was just playing, besides Ricky's right. She blew you a kiss, bro!"

Falcon's anger subsided as quickly as it surfaced. Staying mad at Lloyd was like staying mad at Deeter, almost impossible. Falcon could be moody at times, but he didn't want to be angry. He was having too much fun. "Yeah she did, didn't she?" He imagined her kiss on his lips as the '80s hit, the "Summer of 69" came from the next float. Falcon agreed — these were the best days of his life so far.

Lloyd interrupted Bryan Adams. "You know I have a friend who knows her a little bit."

Wrenched back to reality, Falcon's musical dream evaporated into the air.

Ricky warned, "Leave it alone, Lloyd."

"Just trying to help the big guy out."

"Does he look like he needs help?" asked Ricky.

Both friends focused on poor love-sick Falcon and nodded to each other.

Lloyd shrugged. "Fine, can't say I didn't try."

Falcon and his pals wandered toward the town square across from the courthouse. As they approached he had a clear recollection of the courthouse those many years ago. Falcon's heart stopped for a second as the reminder took him back to his childhood and Mike. It amazed him how one tiny thought had so much power. He smiled as he remembered Mike's message from the preacher. The words reverberated through his head: *"You will do special things. For the rest of your life I will be watching over you. I got your back."* He blinked twice and swallowed away the emotion building in his chest and eyes.

Ricky looked at the courthouse and then back at his friend. "What's up?"

Falcon shook his head. "Everything's great, just saying hello to an old friend.

Ricky and Lloyd shared a quizzical expression.

Lloyd said, "Whataya mean? We're standing right here."

Falcon patted Lloyd on the back and smiled, "Yes you are. Come on, I see Mr. Jacobsen over there."

Dozens of flags encompassed the Square. With the parade officially over, people gathered around the next opportunity for entertainment. Mr. Jacobsen stood on the platform dressed in his WWII uniform. Displayed behind him waved a yellow flag with a coiled rattlesnake, ready to strike, imprinted with the words, "Don't Tread on Me". A lady decked out in the American colors spoke into a microphone.

"Happy Independence Day to everyone! Please rise and

recite with me the Pledge of Allegiance."

Falcon and Ricky removed their Trinity baseball caps and covered their hearts with their right hands.

Lloyd was making a move on an out of town brunette.

Falcon kicked him. "Come on man."

"Sorry, she's cute."

The pledge finished without any further drama.

"I am pleased to introduce," said the woman, "our own Albert Jacobsen, a WWII Veteran and fantastic teacher at Trinity High."

Falcon and Ricky whooped and clapped with the crowd as Mr. Jacobsen advanced to the podium.

Lloyd went back to the brunette.

Albert Jacobsen stood splendidly in his Army dress uniform although the shine that came off his shoes could not compete with the glow that emanated from his chest. The medals seemed to take up half of his body. Among his many decorations were a Silver Star, two Bronze Stars, and three Purple Hearts.

Falcon couldn't help but admire the fact his uniform, decades old, still fit perfectly and although a huge crowd waited to hear him speak, he behaved exactly as he did in class.

Clothes don't make the man.

"Thank you for allowing me this platform today. It's an honor to be gathered here in celebration of our independence! I've been asked many times if I could live my life differently would I do so. My answer is always the same, 'no'. I've been blessed with two great loves. The first has graced me with her presence for the last 30 years."

The crowd cheered as he pointed to his wife a few steps away. "I love you sweetheart."

She mouthed the words back to him.

The crowd cheered even louder.

"Nice," Lloyd chimed in. "Mr. J is smooth."

Falcon and Ricky ignored him.

"My second love has been with me a little longer, in fact my entire life. My second love protects the weak, emboldens the brave, and cherishes the greatest thing of all, freedom."

The crowd hushed and hung on his words of wisdom. Heads nodded solemnly when he spoke of the bravery of those gone before us, and sacrifices made for the good of mankind. No doubt some hearts swelled with pride and eyes filled with tears as Mr. Jacobsen spoke of the greatest nation to ever exist, the United States of America.

This is what ethical leadership can do, Falcon thought. Guide people to do kind things as his parents did. But more importantly, through sharing his beliefs, create in others an appreciation for the American way of life. It was a paramount juncture for Falcon, one he would remember the rest of his life.

6

Cassandra returned with her family from the Bay Area the day before school began. She was a sophomore now and headed toward her first class of the year with Lacey. "Have you seen him?"

"Just this morning out front with Lloyd and Ricky," Lacey answered.

"Seriously?"

"Seriously."

Cassandra had mooned over Falcon all summer in the Bay Area. Falcon in his shy way tried to talk to her throughout the school year many times, but she always kept it short or acted as though she didn't see him. By the time she finally got used to having braces and was determined to come out of her self-imposed shell, baseball season had taken off and Falcon had become a mini celebrity. As older girls began fawning all over him, Cassandra grew insecure, faded into the shadows, and back into her shell.

Lacey said, "What are you gonna do if you see him?"

"I don't know. Is he going with anyone?" She prayed the answer was still no.

"I don't think so, but I saw some juniors and a couple of seniors talking to him this morning."

Cassandra's heart sank. *How can I compete with juniors and seniors? Braces would be the least of my problems.*

Lacey felt bad for her friend. She was pretty sure Falcon was interested and had mentioned it to Lloyd over the summer at the lake. Lloyd just kind of shrugged and said his buddy had lots of choices.

"Why don't you walk up to him and tell him you like him?"

"I can't do that. What if he just laughs?"

"Falcon would never laugh at you," assured Lacey.

"How do you know?"

"He's too nice and has manners. If he didn't like you he would try and let you down easy."

"Let's stop talking about this."

Cassandra and Lacey disappeared into French class.

Falcon was hustling to his first class too with one eye on his watch and the other scouting for Cassandra. Mr. Jacobsen's door was still open. The history teacher was big on punctuality, so was Falcon. He let out a sigh of relief and shifted his backpack when, wham! Another late sophomore banged into him.

"Hey! Slow down!" Falcon tried to catch his backpack.

"Fuck you!" The guy kept going.

Falcon started after him when the first bell rang. He vacillated between his anger and respect for Mr. Jacobsen. Mr. J won.

Mark Waiters shuffled on. Mark was a slightly disheveled sophomore with pockmarks and thick eyebrows. He was the same height as Falcon, but a combination of extra weight and a slouch gave him the appearance of a fat, grubby hyena.

A few minutes later he bragged to his friend Dave, "Guess who I bumped into and told to fuck off?"

"Who?"

"Falcon Sane."

"Seriously?"

He nodded, "You bet."

"Why?"

"I told you before he thinks he's better than us."

Dave didn't know Falcon well, but knew his friend had a hard-on for him. "What's your problem with him?"

"Remember I told you I was sitting in P.E. when the football coach practically begged him to come out for the team, and the asshole told him no thanks — that he's going to get a baseball scholarship and couldn't risk having one of his knees blown out."

"You mean like what happened to Steve in practice last week?"

"That's not the point, man. Whose fucking friend are you?"

"Yours, but what's that got to do with you?"

Mark said, "He just thinks he's better than everyone else."

"I've talked to him a couple of times. He seems okay."

"Man, shut the fuck up!" He shoulder-bumped Dave. "He's a dick. You know I heard Jenny likes him."

Dave finally got the picture. Mark was in love with Jenny. She went out with him once and then gave him the dreaded "let's-just-be-friends" routine. "He's not going after Jenny."

"Why not? Mister Superstar baseball player has the pick of the litter."

"Maybe, but rumor is he's in love with Cassandra, although that's not working out. It looks like Kelly is getting interested."

"Seriously?" questioned Mark. "She's a fucking junior and the hottest girl in school. What a prick."

"So see, he isn't interested in Jenny," said Dave.

"I don't care. He's a prick anyway."

Dave let it go as woodshop started. He didn't agree with Mark, but they were friends. And though Mark was bigger than Falcon, he'd heard a few whispers about the baseball player. *It might be better to leave him alone.*

Football season came and went. Falcon continued year-round baseball training taking a little time off for JV basketball.

He knew his sophomore year would be better.

Pluto coached varsity basketball and offered Falcon a spot on the varsity.

"I really appreciate it Pluto but I'm still learning. I'm going to start down here. Will I start up there?"

"No you won't start. You've improved but you're not ready to start."

"That's what I'm saying. At JV, I'll start and play most of the game."

"I get it," said his coach.

"Thanks anyway."

Although Falcon stayed with the JV and started every game as a guard, he also hung around and practiced with the varsity. His dribbling improved along with his court vision which allowed him to feed the shooters on the team. His defense and rebounding were important, but his ability to be steps ahead of the defense became his gift as he put the ball in the right place play after play. No one was more shocked than he when he was named All-Tourney at the Trinity Invitational later that year.

Kelly Baker missed none of this. The junior with flowing blonde hair and crystal blue eyes fit the idea of California dreaming to a tee. Smart, funny and physically endowed made it easy to understand why everyone considered her the most popular girl in school. She'd noticed Falcon last year. All of her friends did, but dating a freshman wasn't cool. Falcon wasn't a freshman anymore. Baseball season had arrived. He was a star.

Kelly's friend Kim asked, "Have you ever dated someone younger?"

"No, but he's so cute. Mmm, mmm. I just want to grab his tight, little ass!"

"He is cute Kelly, but you could have anyone in school. You could even date some of the men in town. I know because you did."

She smiled coyly, "Just once."

"Bad girl," Kim laughed. "I heard Falcon has a thing for another sophomore?"

"Yeah, I heard that too." She flipped her hair, "Cassandra Ross. You know Cassandra, smart, braces."

"He likes her?" said Kim.

"I don't know. I've never seen them together."

"What if they were? Would you still go for it?"

"I don't know," Kelly shrugged. "But they're not, so it doesn't matter."

"How are you going to do it?"

"Easy, he's in one of my classes."

Kim said, "No way."

"Seriously. Falcon and his friend Lloyd are the only guys in the class."

"I know Lloyd. He's a dork."

"Yeah but I'm not interested in Lloyd."

"What's the class?"

"Typing. Falcon said he needed an elective, and it was the only one open."

"You talked to him already?"

"Sure last week," said Kelly. "He's got a great smile."

Kim said, "I thought that class was for juniors and seniors?"

"Guess not. He sits at the other end of the room. I can see him perfectly."

"I'll bet you can."

"I'm going to his baseball game today after school."

"Then what?"

"We'll see," said Kelly. "I know some people think he's stuck-up, but I think he's just really shy."

"So you're going to make a man out of him?"

"Oh, he's already a man. I'm going to make him my man."

Kim shook her head and laughed, "Look out Falcon Sane."

During basketball season his guidance counselor informed Falcon he would need to take a foreign language for college prep. He'd have to squeeze it into the final quarter of the year, which was scheduled during baseball. He thought the Big Fella was lending a hand as he knew Cassandra had taken French earlier in the year, and he hoped they might be in the same class together. Freshman English had been their only class together in two years and seemed so long ago. Falcon enthusiastically signed up for French. Unfortunately his enthusiasm was short-lived. Cassandra was in a different class, and for the first time in his life he was struggling with a subject. Night after night after baseball practice, and on the road after away games, he struggled with the conjugation of the most common verbs, etre and avoir.

The French teacher established an "honor system" regarding homework.

"I do not check or grade your homework," she said. "You are young adults and will be treated as such. We will have a weekly vocabulary test, midterm, and final, which are all equal in points. The other 25 percent will be your homework. Each day I will circulate a clipboard, initial next to your name if you've completed the homework assignment."

A month into the class Falcon was drowning.

The girls sitting around him noticed he never signed the sheet.

"Why don't you sign your initials?" one friend asked.

"Yeah," said another girl trying to help. "She never checks."

"No," he said, "it wouldn't be right."

"Who cares? None of us do the homework."

"I do the homework," said Falcon. "It's just all wrong."

"So what? You just have to do it — it doesn't have to be right. I'll write it in for you."

"Nah." Falcon passed the clipboard along. "I appreciate your help but just leave it alone."

"Okay your funeral."

A second monster was about to rear its ugly head in Driver's Education. A class of all boys, the room was packed with sweat, chewing tobacco and testosterone. Although the class was a breeze, the instructor Mr. Frump was half deaf and out of touch with the students, which made it a real snore-fest. Falcon sat next to his buddy Jerry while Jerry chewed Copenhagen and spit it into a cup on his desk. From time to time he missed and hit the carpet.

Mr. Frump appeared clueless.

Other than that Falcon was flying high. He'd hit a game-winning home run against Fall River the day before, and Kelly Baker was now his girlfriend. He still thought of Cassandra every day, and even chanced one last opportunity a couple of weeks before and asked her to a dance. She said she couldn't go and walked away. Kelly had been flirting with him for a month, and although Falcon's feelings hadn't changed, apparently Cassandra wasn't interested. Kelly and Falcon went to the movies a week later. The movie was a bomb, but it didn't matter. They weren't there to watch the movie.

Monday, sitting in Driver's Ed., Falcon replayed their date in his head when he was jerked back to the present.

"Hey asshole," hissed Mark Waiters. "Give me my pen back!"- Falcon considered the voice that so rudely interrupted the rerun of his hot-and-heavy theater evening.

"I said, give me my pen!"

Falcon focused on a pen near his foot and glanced at Mr. Frump.

Mr. Frump said, "Now, gentlemen, the importance of highway warning signs."

Mark said, "What are you deaf like Frump? Give me my fucking pen."

Falcon turned his foot and flipped the pen forward. It slid to the front of the class almost at Frump's feet. "I'm not your slave, get it yourself."

Jerry spit into his cup, leaned around Falcon to check out Mark and his buddy Dave seated beside him. "What's up, Fal?"

"Have no idea."

"Didn't Mark slam into you at the beginning of the year?"

"Yep. Told me to fuck off too. After that he always went the other way so I let it go."

"Sounds like he's got a problem," said Jerry.

Frump switched from signs to traffic lights.

Mark was about to launch another round when Dave jumped in.

"What're you messing with Sane for?"

Mark couldn't explain his problem with Falcon Sane; he wouldn't even want to try. Insecurity, jealousy or spite isn't usually something explainable by the person with the problem. Deep down they're simply miserable, and misery loves company. Mark ignored Dave and started in again. "I'm going to kick your ass."

Falcon turned completely around and stared at Mark. He didn't know what Mark's problem was; but he knew Mark had one now. "Go for it."

Shocked, Mark gaped at Falcon for a second, and then regrouped.

"I'm going to."

"I'm waiting."

Mark said, "I will."

"I heard you the first time. Go for it," Falcon said louder.

Mr. Frump paused for a second as the students in the front

spun around to watch the show.

"I'm going to beat your ass after class," said Mark.

Falcon lowered his voice, "Why wait? I'm right here."

"No, after class behind the gym."

"I'm not meeting you anywhere. Stop being a pussy and make your move."

Mr. Frump appeared to be listening.

Mark wanted to jump on Falcon, but couldn't move. Not knowing what else to do he slumped back in his chair.

Falcon's temper flared as he studied Mark.

"That's what I thought," growled Falcon. "Now shut the fuck up and get your own pen."

Mark muttered to himself, "I'll meet you behind the gym."

Mr. Frump bent down, picked up the pen, and put it on Mark's desk. "So who can tell me what the legal alcohol limit is?" Their "quality" education continued.

The meeting behind the gym never took place. In the right setting Mark was willing to fight, but Falcon's dare to go for it in the middle of the classroom confused him. Later in woodshop, Mark told his friend Darrell Port all about it. "He told me to go for it."

"What'd you do?" Darrel asked.

"Nothing. I never heard of anyone fighting in the classroom before. Maybe he's crazy?"

"He ain't crazy. He just called your bluff."

"I would've fought him behind the gym."

"Maybe, maybe not. Doesn't matter. He was ready you weren't."

"Now what do I do?"

"Nothing," said Darrell. "You want me to handle it?"

What Mark wouldn't give to see Darrell mess up that pretty boy Sane.

"Would you?"

"Sure. Show off baseball player parading Kelly around campus. It's about time he's put back in his place. He'll know he's been in a fight when I get done with him."

A seventeen-year-old junior, Darrell wore cowboy boots and a hat every day. A can of Skoal imbedded a permanent circle on the back pocket of his Wranglers. Mark was bigger than Falcon, and Darrell was bigger than Mark. Where Mark was fat, Darrell was lean from riding horses and working livestock. He was older, bigger and stronger than Falcon, and he still went looking for trouble.

Falcon on the other hand hit another game-winning home run against Burney and was actively exploring his older girlfriend. They were a good-looking young couple, but looks were deceiving. Kelly was a 17-year-old young woman who'd already experienced an adult relationship. Although Falcon looked and talked like a mature male he was still young and inexperienced. While Kelly was looking to be led, Falcon was trying to figure out which way to go. Her patience was beginning to slip.

Fighting wasn't on Falcon's mind; love was his nemesis. But he was with the wrong girl. Kelly was pretty, smart and wildly popular, but she didn't touch his heart the way Cassandra Ross did. What he sought in Cassandra was not fueled by the testosterone of an adolescent male. Falcon was a hopeless romantic who dreamed of caressing her hand and walking her to class. Holding Kelly's hand didn't feel the way he thought it should.

Kelly was also disengaging from their short relationship. Over Easter break she'd run into an old flame who wasn't a high school boy anymore. Nothing had happened (yet) but it was only a matter of time.

With baseball season humming, Trinity was in first place. The talent and leadership Pluto recognized in Falcon as a freshman came to life. Combined with Bobby Burke and sophomore pitcher Jimmy Brock, Pluto was enjoying the ride of the best team he'd ever coached. His only concerns lay with his starting shortstop. He'd heard rumors about a big chain company moving in on the Sane's family business. There was a good chance they'd sell while they had something to barter with, which meant leaving the area. He also heard of a problem Falcon was having with some older students. He called Falcon into his office prior to the double header the team had today.

Pluto leaned back in his chair, feet crossed on the desk. "How's everything going, Falcon?"

"Good. French is a little tough."

"What are you taking French for?"

"Thought it would be a good elective," smiled Falcon. There was no way he'd ever admit the truth.

"So what's the problem? You're a bright kid."

"I don't know. It hasn't been quite what I was expecting." *Isn't that the truth?*

Pluto nodded, "Anything else?"

"Like what?"

Pluto wasn't touching the story about his parent's business right before a game. Falcon was a wonderful young man but very sensitive.

"I heard about some problems with Darrell Port and his crew."

Falcon shrugged. He had no idea why Darrell and his group had started harassing some of his friends in the hallway and had been making snide comments to Falcon. No one touched Falcon, but the bullying and mouthing off was wearing his patience thin. "Nothing I can't handle."

"Are you sure? Stan Tunstell is a pretty big guy."

Calling Stan Tunstell a pretty big guy was a joke. Six four

and an easy 250 pounds the eighteen-year-old senior sported a full beard. He was a friend and enforcer for Darrell, one who could pass for a grizzly bear. He didn't say much, but kids and teachers alike gave him a wide berth.

"It's okay," said Falcon. "It's under control."

"That's not what I'm hearing."

Falcon didn't respond.

"Are you sure? I can have a little chat with him."

Falcon pushed his baseball cap up. "Absolutely not. I've got it under control."

Pluto could almost see the smoke pour out of Falcon's ears. "Okay, see you on the field."

"Yes sir." Falcon walked to the locker room to dress. It was a big day today, a double header. He'd worry about this garbage later.

It wasn't Pluto's intention to pump Falcon up but he did.

The Baseball Gods smiled on Falcon as golden sunshine and freshly mowed grass created perfect playing conditions. The young shortstop attacked both ends of the double header with a vengeance, blistering the field and his opponents, on offense and defense. He was taking no prisoners. Falcon was in the zone.

"Attababy!" Pluto slapped Falcon five as he rounded third after hitting his sixth homerun of the year, locking up the second game, and giving them the league championship.

Falcon touched home and was mobbed by his teammates. They laughed and pounded him on the back all the way to the dugout. He whipped off his helmet, sat on the bench, and watched his pals continue to pile on more runs. *This is awesome. I never want it to end.* Childhood dreams were being fulfilled.

Ricky hit a double off the wall.

"Go baby go!" Falcon jumped up cheering for his friend.

Ricky stood at second base and pointed back to the dugout.

Bobby Burke yelled, "You gotta love Trinity baseball!"

"Yes, you do baby." Falcon jumped on Bobby's back.

Another line drive up the middle and the dugout sprinted for home plate as Ricky came into score, which ended the drubbing on account of the 10-run rule. They tackled Ricky, and the pile of red-and-white uniforms morphed into a blur of hands and cleats.

"We're league champions!" the mass hooted and hollered.

Smashed on the bottom Ricky reveled in the euphoria.

Ten minutes later Pluto addressed his team.

"Great job guys. Couldn't be more proud. This was our last home game of the year. Let's clean up the field and get on home. We have class and practice tomorrow. Playoffs start in a week on the road. Let's be ready to win the section!" Pluto walked over to Falcon who grabbed a rake and started out to the field. He extended his hand to his young shortstop.

"Couldn't have done it without you, son."

"Thanks for believing in me as a freshman coach."

"Like I had a choice," Pluto laughed. "You would've driven me nuts if you weren't on the field."

Falcon grinned, "Yeah probably."

The two stood quietly for a second. Coach and player viewed the field as excited as champions could be, and then a bit of sadness crept in.

Pluto said softly, "I hear you're moving?"

He heard the catch in the young man's breath.

"Yeah," Falcon said softly in return.

The coach regarded his star and nodded. "Anything I can do?"

"Probably not," said Falcon who knew there was no probably about it.

Pluto stared off into the mountains that surrounded every view in Weaverville. "There's room at my house if you want to stay ... already talked to the wife."

"I appreciate it Coach. I really do, but I've got to stay with my family."

"Yeah I figured. Just wanted you to know you had options. If you change your mind the door is always open."

"Thanks."

"No sweat." Pluto left him to his solitude.

Falcon began raking shortstop, chucking rocks off the field into the bushes, and preparing his position for one of the few practices he figured he had left. He took his time. Inherently he knew he'd just played his last game on his field. The play-offs would all be on the road, and unless a miracle happened he would be moving at the end of summer. The rest of his team-mates already started down the hill back to the locker room while Falcon continued raking his position over and over.

"Thank you," he whispered, "for all the good hops and great plays. I won't forget you."

He did one more loop around shortstop and headed back to the dugout.

Ricky sat on the bench and waited for his best friend.

Lloyd stood outside the gate and waited for them both.

Falcon turned one last time and surveyed the field, his home field; the place where he belonged. A small breeze ruffled his hair as though the field was saying goodbye too, and it was done.

"Thanks for waiting," he told Ricky.

"Anytime brother."

Lloyd opened the gate for his friends. "Where's Kelly?"

"We broke up."

"Wow, sorry."

"Thanks. It's okay. It wasn't working anyway."

The three friends walked down the slope toward the locker room. The school grounds appeared empty.

"It's amazing how fast people clear out of here," Lloyd said to no one in particular.

Falcon still in full uniform, including cleats and protective cup, walked with his friends. Thirty yards away he spotted three bodies heading for the exit that led to the parking lot. He knew he wouldn't reach them before they got to the door.

Lloyd followed Falcon's stare. "Uh-oh," he said under his breath.

"Just relax," Falcon replied. "I got this."

Darrell Port, his girlfriend Hillary, and Stan Tunstell crossed the court ahead of the three friends who were headed in the opposite direction, which was fine with Lloyd and Ricky.

Although young, Falcon finally understood most things in life were about timing. His mind flashed back years ago to Cox Bar and his Gandhi-like approach to violence when he removed himself peacefully from the equation. This time he knew that approach would not work. It would only put off the inevitable. Today was slated for Patton, Old Guts and Glory, and that time was now.

Falcon yelled at the two behemoths, "How ya doing!"

Lloyd muttered, "Are you nuts?"

"Relax buddy, it's under control."

Ricky tensed, "Falcon ..."

Falcon ignored his friends. He didn't know Stan and couldn't remember what started the trouble with Darrell, not that it mattered. "This isn't going away until I deal with it," he said aloud to himself.

Ricky said, "What's that buddy?"

He was Falcon's friend and would back him to the end, but he knew he couldn't handle Stan Tunstell. Who could?

Falcon's mind was made up. He was in the moment, and the moment was happening right now. He continued to stride toward the bullying upperclassmen.

"How ya doing!" he challenged Darrell again.

They stopped and both faced the shortstop.

Falcon swallowed hard. He knew he was *willing* to take on the gigantic bearded senior, but was *hoping not to*. Darrell was the problem, and he hoped to deal with him.

Darrell and Stan had a side conversation Falcon couldn't hear.

"What's that?" Falcon yelled. "What'd he say?"

The senior turned and postured. "He said fuck you!"

"Why don't you tell him to come over here and say that to my face?"

Falcon's friends froze too stunned to move.

"Are you fucking crazy?" Lloyd mumbled.

Falcon observed the situation as his mind moved through a mental checklist, while his heart pounded, adrenaline kicked in, and both hands shook uncontrollably. This had gone on for too long — he just wanted to get it over with. Time elapsed in slow motion, and he couldn't wait much longer.

Darrell kissed his girlfriend goodbye and pointed toward the exit as if he was heading off to war.

"Drama queens," Falcon said to no one in particular.

Lloyd panicked, "You've lost your mind!"

Darrell turned and began to tromp toward Falcon with Stan at his side.

Falcon counted the steps as he waited for the two bears to arrive. One, two, three, four, five …

Darrell screamed, "I'm gonna kick your fucking ass!"

Eight, nine, ten …

"I'm gonna fuck you up you cocky little prick!"

Twelve, thirteen, fourteen, fifteen … move! A trigger fired in Falcon's brain as Darrell reached out and pushed him. Falcon stepped forward and his fists became a blur as he landed eight consecutive punches squarely on Darrell's face.

Blood and chewing tobacco sprayed through the air as Darrell's neck snapped back and forth like a rubber band that held onto his head.

"Holy shit!" said Lloyd.

Falcon continued to throw punches while Darrell's face kept eating them. As suddenly as he started, Falcon stopped. His brain told him to keep throwing but his arms felt like mush. Gassed and covered in blood, he stood there and stared at Darrell, his arms punched out.

Although Darrell's face was a bloody mess and starting to swell, his lower lip splayed and hanging by threads, he still had plenty of fight left in him. He grabbed Falcon by the waist and took him to the ground, and they wrestled briefly — each trying to get the better of the other one.

Finally the shock wore off of the bystanders, and they leapt in and separated the two combatants.

Falcon quick to his feet stood tall and watched the two bears lumber off.

"That's it!" yelled the shortstop. "It's over!" he declared but knew full well it wasn't.

"Fuck you!" the junior mumbled over his shoulder through his swollen lips. "It ain't over!"

Falcon examined his baseball jersey soaked red with blood. He touched his face searching for cuts. "Ricky, am I bleeding?"

"I don't think so. Let me look."

"You ain't bleeding," Lloyd crowed. "You beat the shit out of him. That's all his blood! I've never seen anything like that! Did you know you were gonna do that?"

"Shut up Lloyd," Falcon ordered as the adrenaline started to work its way down.

Ricky said, "You weren't too chatty before the fight, Lloyd." He checked over his friend. "I think you're okay. Maybe some blood coming from your nose but it could be his."

"Okay thanks buddy."

Lloyd three feet away, shadowboxed and mimicked Muhammad Ali. "Float like a butterfly sting like a bee!" He danced around throwing rights and lefts.

Falcon shook his head and picked up his baseball gear. His body started checking in with him. His nose did hurt, and his groin was sore. He mentioned this to Ricky while Lloyd kept dancing.

"Yeah, he kicked you in the balls in the beginning then you started hitting him. After you stopped hitting him I think he head-butted you when you guys were wrestling around. Good thing you still had your cup on. Those cowboy boots could've done some serious damage."

Falcon turned toward the locker room and told his friends he would be out in a minute. After checking to make sure he was alone he slowly pulled the blood-soaked jersey off his body and stared into the bathroom mirror. His eyes said it all.

Late Bird lay down no more.

Darrell Port wasn't a bully by nature. He came from a good home with a family who cared about him. After he cleaned his face up, his older sister, a college sophomore asked what happened. It didn't go well for him. She knew Falcon and liked him. She'd also been friends with Miranda and remembered Falcon stepping in to coach her soccer team. Even after Miranda disappeared from Weaverville, he always referred to it as Miranda's team and his sister reminded her brother of this. Darrell wasn't the only one having issues.

Upon arriving home after the fight Falcon had to explain all the blood. "Relax Mom, it's not mine."

Falcon told the story to his parents. Once he finished his mother went into the kitchen and called the local doctor.

"Are you all right?" his father asked him.

"I'm fine."

"Did you start it?"

"No, it's been coming for a while."

"And you're sure you're all right?"

"Yes sir."

"Okay. Great games today."

"Thanks Dad."

Falcon had forgotten all about the league championship and breaking up with Kelly.

Mitch said, "Kelly bring you home?"

"No, Ricky's mom; Kelly and I broke up."

"Boy you've had quite a day," said Mitch. "And I don't think it's over."

Rachel hung up the phone. "Okay get in the car. We're going to the doctor."

The drive was quiet other than Falcon telling his mother twice he was fine.

The doctor examined Falcon's nose and asked what happened.

Falcon couldn't say, "I think it was a head-butt, maybe a fist."

"And where did this happen?"

"At the high school."

"With whom?"

"Another guy. Does it matter?"

The doctor looked at Falcon and carefully pinched the bridge of his nose.

"Does that hurt?"

"Not too much."

"Well it looks like you have a small fracture on the bridge.

Nothing I can do about it. Welcome to your new nose."

"Thanks."

"You should probably take it easy for a few days maybe a week."

Falcon almost laughed out loud.

"Thank you doctor," said Rachel. "I'll make sure he does."

As they walked to the car Falcon said, "I am *not* taking off a few days. Forget about a week."

"That's what the doctor said."

"It's not happening, Mom. Look, we have to move. I have six weeks of school left with my friends, and I'm sure not missing baseball."

Rachel took stock of her son. He was practically a grown man. The days of telling him what to do were over. She tried a different approach.

"Honey I just want you to be safe. What if you sit out tomorrow, then you can resume practice the next day?"

Falcon considered it. His head was pounding, and he didn't want to make matters worse and get a migraine. "Okay, I'll talk to Pluto."

"Thank you sweetheart. I only want what's best for you."

He wanted to say, then why are we moving? *But it's not Mom's fault, why make her feel any worse.* Falcon gingerly touched his nose.

"Do you think my eyes will turn black because of my nose? I don't want anyone to think that guy got a punch in."

Rachel said, "If you let me pack you in ice all night, it'll be our secret."

"Really Mom?"

Rachel smiled. "Trust Mommy, you'll look as handsome as ever."

Falcon wasn't worried about being handsome. He just didn't want it to look like he'd had his ass kicked.

7

The next day in school Mark said to Darrell, "Whoa man, what happened to your face?"

"What's it look like happened. I got my ass kicked."

"By who?"

"Falcon Sane."

"Fuck you!"

"Shut up Mark. I'm more than willing to beat the shit out of you right now."

"Sorry. I just can't fucking believe it."

"Believe it."

"Should we do something about it?" Mark asked.

"Like what?"

"I don't know. I got friends. We could jump him."

Not being much of an athlete, Darrell hung out with Mark and Stan. Neither one was respected, but even the teachers feared Stan.

"Just leave it alone, Mark," said Darrell.

"What are you some kind of pussy?"

The last 24 hours had not been fun for Darrell. He'd gotten his ass beat by a sophomore in front of witnesses, been reamed by his sister, looked like shit, and had a pounding headache. Darrell wasn't a coward; he just wasn't making good decisions.

Mark shook his head, "What a pussy."

Darrell grabbed Mark by his neck and slammed him into the lockers. "Shut up!" He squeezed harder.

"Let gooo…" wheezed Mark. "I can't breathe".

Darrell kept squeezing until Stan pulled him off.

Mark fell to the ground and gasped for air.

"You trying to kill him?" asked Stan.

"He just pissed me off."

"Why?"

"He called me a pussy."

Stan said, "Man you need to get a grip. You got your ass kicked by a punk, and if you don't do something about it everyone's going to think you're scared."

And there it was — the reason most fights and wars begin, someone having to prove how tough he is to someone else.

Darrell took the bait and spread the word. In two days the word swept like the plague. The message was clear: Falcon and his friends were going to get jumped. One guy upped the ante and mentioned stabbing. The halls at Trinity High School grew very uncomfortable.

The next day in French class, Falcon sat mulling over what to say to Pluto when a monitor popped in with a hall pass. The teacher called Falcon's name and gave him a sour look as she handed the pass to him. For whatever reason, she seemed to hate athletes. She'd given him grief about an assignment a few weeks ago when he traveled for baseball. Pluto and the principal had to get involved in order to make it happen. Falcon strode down the hallways and into Pluto's office. "Hey coach."

"Come on in and have a seat."

Falcon settled into the chair across from his coach's desk.

Pluto carefully eyed Falcon, "You look the same to me."

Surprised by his comment he said, "Should I look different?"

"Well on my way to the locker room this morning I saw a

trail of blood."

Falcon's back stiffened slightly.

"After I saw the blood I asked around and found out you had a little problem after the game. But looking at you now it doesn't look like it was your blood."

Falcon smiled inside. *Ice! Mom was right.* "No sir it wasn't."

"Are you okay?"

"Yes sir."

"Anything you want to tell me?"

"Not really, but my mom wants me to sit out practice today to make sure I'm all right."

"I think that's a good idea."

Falcon shrugged

"You don't agree?"

"I don't need to sit out. There's nothing wrong with me, but I told my mom I would talk to you."

Pluto chuckled, "Sometimes we have to humor the women in our lives son, you may as well learn that early. So let's have you watch practice today."

Falcon agreed and returned to French class. The second his seat hit the chair the bell rang. He handed the hallway pass to the teacher, she responded with a dirty look. *What is her problem?* Falcon traipsed out the door and onto Mr. Jacobsen for history. He noticed Mark and a few of his cronies crowded in the hallway next to the door Falcon needed to pass through to reach class on time. *It never ends.*

Mark noticed the cocky baseball player, and they locked eyes.

Falcon stayed focused on Mark. He was the problem, and if he made him the target the rest of the group would probably fade away. Falcon was right, the group started to back off as he stared Mark down. *Three steps to go*

Mark blinked and moved aside.

Once Falcon cleared the door he heard the coward say: "We'll get you later pussy!"

He didn't bother responding. It seemed Mark always wanted to fight, *later.* Never right now. Having made good time, Falcon reached history a little early.

"Good morning my fellow American," Mr. Jacobsen motioned Falcon to come to his desk.

Being a teenager, Mr. J occasionally struck Falcon as being a little corny; but he respected the man so much, he'd come to enjoy even that side of him.

"Good morning sir."

"Are you actively pursuing happiness?"

"I'm sure trying."

"Don't try my young friend. Succeed. You're a successful student and athlete. I've heard you're top drawer with the ladies too." He winked.

Falcon smiled: *If you only knew.*

"I hear you've added boxing to your repertoire and quite good at defending yourself."

Falcon tilted his head and took stock of his mentor. "I don't know about that."

"And humble too," said Mr. Jacobsen. "I'm bringing this up because the halls are whispering. You did what you felt you needed to do, and I applaud your willingness and courage. Now is the time to lead with a purpose. Violence is the easy way out son, the non-thinking way. Trust me I know. You're bright. Use your intellect to find a solution that will protect you, your friends and others. You used the hammer. The nail is in the coffin. A wise carpenter wouldn't have to hit the nail a second time."

Falcon sat in class mulling over his teacher's words as he tried to decipher his code until the bell rang. He grabbed his books and walked by his teacher's desk. Mr. Jacobsen smiled and tapped his finger against his temple.

"Here lies your greatest gift and most powerful weapon. Use it wisely."

Watching Falcon walk out the door, Mr. Jacobsen decided it was time to pay the principal a visit. The path Falcon was following required little guidance, his feet firmly planted in righteousness and his leadership skills well honed. But the boy was young and should not be forced to stand alone. Part of his responsibility as a teacher was to ensure the safety of all the students. After all, bloodshed did not belong in school. This was an educational institution, not a war zone.

Baseball practice was uneventful for Falcon as he watched his team prepare for the playoffs. It galled him to see someone else in his position. He knew he wasn't going to be Wally Pipped by another player, but it left him irritated and in a dark mood.

His teammates didn't say much.

One of the seniors was quieter than normal around him. Ritchie Cherub was a no-nonsense tough guy who played middle linebacker on the football team. He'd battled cancer and won but had a permanently bald head as a reminder. Sports can open doors to many things, and the young athletic sophomore became friends with his hard-nosed senior teammate as the season progressed. Ritchie called Falcon "Casanova," because girls flocked around him during school, after school, or on the coed bus trips when their teams traveled together. Their friendship was solid. Ritchie also knew Darrell and was friendly with his sister and their family. Two friends fighting wasn't his idea of a good time. His normally brilliant smile was absent throughout practice, and everyone breathed a sigh of relief when the session ended.

Falcon skipped a ride home. His mind full, he needed time to work through his thoughts. He worried about Lloyd, Ricky and his other pals being threatened now because they were his friends. He believed *he* could deal with almost anything including more fighting, but his friends couldn't. Besides he didn't want them to have to. The answer was in Mr. Jacobsen's riddle. *A wise carpenter wouldn't have to hit the nail a second time.* Falcon sensed the solution in that line, but what was it? Repeating it over and over, he took larger steps until half a mile from home his brain engaged. He started walking faster and finally running until his long legs carried him home. He bounded up the stairs onto the deck and inside the house.

"Mom?" He found her in the kitchen baking. "Anyone on the phone?"

"I don't think so."

"Great!" He kissed her and snagged two cookies from the cooling rack. "I need to make a call. I might be a few minutes."

"Okay," Rachel was accustomed to seeing the long phone cord stretched down the hall when Falcon disappeared into his room as he tried to find privacy to call Kelly, but he never announced it. "Who are you calling?"

"Kelly, I need somebody's number."

"Whose number?"

Falcon grabbed the phone off the counter. "Darrell Port."

Rachel paused, "The guy you were in the fight with?"

"Yep."

"Oh honey, is that a good idea?"

"Well ... we'll see." He grinned, "Depends on the kind of carpenter I am."

"What?"

He gave her a hug and winked, "I'll tell you later pretty lady."

She watched him evaporate behind his bedroom door with the phone. She wasn't sure about his carpentry skills, but he was one exceptional son.

Kelly and Falcon had parted as friends. She hoped he was okay, said she'd miss him when he moved, and gladly gave him Darrell's number.

Falcon took a deep breath and dialed.

Darrell's older sister answered, "Hello?"

"Hi, it's Falcon Sane. I'm calling to talk to Darrell."

She paused. She liked Falcon, but her brother was her brother.

"What about?"

"Things are getting ... out of control at school. I thought we could talk about it."

She exhaled, "I think that's a great idea Falcon, let me get him."

Falcon waited.

"Hello?"

"Hey Darrell. It's Falcon."

"Yeah that's what my sister said. What's up?" he said brusquely.

"Like I told her, things are getting a little out of control at school. I thought we could talk about it and see if we could work things out."

"Work 'em out, how?"

"I don't know," said Falcon. "I don't even know you. I'm not sure how we got here ..."

Both guys remained quiet as reality set in.

Falcon continued, "We don't have to be friends or anything, but we don't have to be enemies either. People talking about someone getting stabbed are making this worse. I can talk to my friends, you talk to yours, and we can be done with this."

"What about Lloyd?" asked Darrell. "He keeps running his mouth."

"I'll take care of Lloyd. I'll make sure he stops that."

Darrell wondered if this was a trap, but he was tired of this crap too and could care less what Stan thought anymore.

Falcon tried another angle.

"Do you really want to fight again? I don't. Like I said, we don't have to be friends, but we don't have to be enemies either." Falcon imagined Darrell wanted to agree but something was holding him back. *A good carpenter doesn't have to hit the nail twice.* "Look Darrell. We fought. There are no cowards *in* a fight. Cowards talk too much and then run away or stand on the sideline and yell at other people to fight. You didn't run away. We fought. You were there. I didn't head-butt myself in the face or kick myself in the balls."

Darrell said, "Yeah, sorry about the balls."

"Thanks," Falcon laughed mildly. "Good thing I had my cup on."

"Yeah probably," Darrell laughed a little as well.

Sensing some momentum Falcon pressed, "All right, so we're good?"

"Yeah we're good, but what about everyone else?"

"I have an idea," Falcon said, explaining his thoughts.

A few minutes later Darrell hung up the phone and let out a deep sigh.

His sister leaned into the room. "How'd it go?"

"Good. We worked it out. We're going to meet at the 'rock' tomorrow."

"Glad to hear it. You guys going to be friends?"

"Nah, I don't think so but we don't have to be enemies either."

She said, "That's a pretty mature thing to say."

Proudly Darrell said, "Yeah well, you know me."

He smiled and then winced as he felt Falcon's fists all over his face again. He stood and looked in the mirror. *I can borrow the guy's lines, I paid for them.*

Falcon smiled as he hung up the phone and stood quietly for

a second in his room. *Good job. You'll be a carpenter yet.* He slept like a baby that night.

As he sat in French the next day a note came from the office. His French teacher rolled her eyes and handed him the hall pass.

"It appears you have friends in high places. Now the principal wants to see you," she said. "I've had about enough of this."

What is her problem? He took the pass and headed for the principal. *It's probably about the fight. It's common knowledge now.*

Outside the principal's office sat Darrell Port.

"You too?" Darrell asked

"Yep," said Falcon, "looks like they didn't hear about our talk; but everything is still the same, right? We're good?"

"Everything's good."

"All right then. I'm going to try and head this off before it gets any bigger."

"How you going to do that?" asked Darrell.

"Depends on what he says. Just follow my lead."

"Okay, I hope you know what you're doing."

Falcon's stomach churned, "Me too."

Darrell opened the door and motioned for Falcon to enter.

Falcon went in first. *It's kind of funny we're working together all of a sudden.*

"We're here to see the principal," Falcon announced to the secretary.

"Sit down gentlemen. He'll be with you shortly."

Falcon and Darrell sat next to each other and waited a long five minutes. Finally the secretary waved them in.

"Have a seat, boys." They looked at the chairs, and then chose to sit right beside each other on a small couch across from the principal.

"I hear we have a problem."

A little late jackass, thought Darrell.

Where've you been? wondered Falcon. Falcon tried to act casual and surprised. "No sir, no problem here, right Darrell?"

"Nope," Darrell's timing was perfect as he'd followed Falcon's lead and sat beside him like old friends. "No problem at all."

"That's not what I heard. I was told you two had quite a fight — left a trail of blood."

"Things that happen in the past are in the past," Falcon said, hoping to keep the inquisition short. "Everything's good now."

"Is he right, Darrell?"

"Right as rain."

"Well good. Glad to hear it. I'd hate to have to expel you both."

Falcon winced. *I can't be expelled. The playoffs are next week.*

The principal paused and looked at his desk.

Falcon took the opportunity to wrap it up and stood. "Anything else sir?"

Darrell, a quick study jumped to his feet.

"No I guess that's it. Let's make sure you two aren't in here again."

"Absolutely not," Falcon answered.

"Never again," Darrell said with a bit of biting humor.

The two new allies walked out of the office.

Darrell was impressed. "You're a pretty fast-talker."

Falcon laughed, "Thanks, when you said never again, I thought he was going to choke."

"Yeah, these guys think they can deal with stuff after the fact. If we had more supervision a lot of this crap wouldn't happen. I was in three fights my freshman year alone."

"No kidding?" asked Falcon.

"Yeah, fucking seniors think it's funny to trash can freshman or give wedgies and crap like that. Pissed me off. I knocked three teeth out of one guy's mouth, never got called into the office though. Somebody must have said something."

"I think you're right. Somebody must have." Falcon thought about Mr. Jacobsen.

The two teenagers walked along quiet with their own thoughts.

"I'm going this way," Darrel said. "See you at 'the rock' after third period."

"You bet."

Falcon returned to class amid glares from his teacher and curious stares from his classmates. The bell rang 20 minutes later, and the thundering herd of students roared through the hallways in search of their next class.

Third period was next, and Falcon mulled over his plan to seal the deal with Darrell. He'd chosen the 'rock' fountain as the stage for several reasons. The enormous water fountain stood directly in front of the school cafeteria. It had multiple drinking spigots surrounded by benches cemented into the ground. Two captivating 50-year-old redwoods provided shade, and lush grass circled the enchanted setting. It was the hub for the cool kids and although an open area, an unspoken rule required an invitation. But wanting to be a part of the elite group, most students hung around the periphery and dreamed of one day becoming a part of the in-crowd.

Falcon had been welcomed at the rock as baseball unfolded his freshman year, but it wasn't his style. He was considered popular, but being shy and preferring solitude as opposed to large groups, he spent little time there. This was yet another reason he'd chosen the rock fountain, a perfect location to send a message. Rumors and gossip spread like wildfire through high school, but if everyone witnessed it firsthand, it would hopefully put an end to the trouble.

Falcon approached the rock.

Sitting there by himself was Darrell Port.

Falcon was surprised no one else claimed the inner circle when it dawned on him everyone wanted a spectator seat *safely* on the outside lane.

Upholding his word at every turn, Darrell was rapidly earning Falcon's respect. He seemed open to growth and change. A skill many of the current onlookers weren't willing to learn.

As half the school watched, the drama unfolded.

Falcon strode over to the fountain and sat right next to Darrell.

Darrell cracked, "We've gotta stop meeting like this."

"No kidding." Falcon grinned, "People are going to say we're dating."

Darrell laughed and scanned their audience. "How long you think they'll hover around watching us?"

Falcon shrugged, "Until they think it's safe."

"Maybe we should give them a show."

"Oh yeah? Darrell, you're not my type."

Darrell laughed.

Falcon said, "What kind of show you have in mind?"

"I don't know. I'm just tired of all the stares."

"Yep me too. How about we stand up and shake hands? That should finish this."

"Yeah ... I like that."

"Okay," said Falcon, "On three. One, two, three."

Falcon and Darrell stood and turned toward each other.

The crowd hushed as they sensed something was about to happen.

The two young men extended their right arms and shook hands.

"I think that should do it. Catch you later, the fountain is all yours," Falcon said.

"Yep, show's over. Thanks Falcon. See you around."

Falcon nodded and headed to the cafeteria. Stress made some people eat. He was the exact opposite. Now that everything was back to normal, he was starving. Two breakfast burritos, milk and a chocolate chip cookie later he was ready for a nap. *No time for napping though.* It was time for his next class. Turning a corner in the hallway he ran right into Mr. Jacobsen who motioned with his head for Falcon to join him away from the herd of students.

"Mr. Sane, my sources tell me we had a collaborative meeting of the minds today?"

Falcon looked at his favorite teacher. *Wow gossip does travel fast.* "Yes sir. I thought about what you said and tried to be a better carpenter."

"Ah yes. You know Jesus was a carpenter."

"So I've heard. I didn't know you were a Christian?"

"I'm not. I do follow the Ten Commandments to the best of my ability. No I am not a Christian, but I do believe in the greatness of Jesus."

"What do you mean?"

"Well as the story goes we have a human being who travels far and wide preaching love for his fellow man. His words are so wonderful those in charge become afraid, frightened they may lose their power. So they hammer him to a cross and murder him. As Jesus is suffering this incredible amount of pain and his life is slipping away, he asks God to forgive *them*."

"'Forgive them Father for they know not what they do,'" Falcon chimed in.

"Exactly. I don't need to call myself a Christian or hear any more stories about this man. This one story tells me all I need to know about the greatness of Jesus. Are you familiar with the Buddha?"

"No ... other than a Buddha belly."

Mr. Jacobsen smiled at Falcon, "Maybe we will get into the Buddha next time. Back to my original question, things are back to normal?"

"Yes sir."

"You know why I used the nail metaphor?"

Falcon didn't and shook his head.

"I used it because it fits perfectly. Once a nail is imbedded in the wood there is no longer a need to hit the nail. If you continue to bang on the nail you damage the wood around it leaving it bruised or cracked. This causes long-term damage to the wood and eventually the nail. Every action has a reaction, so says Sir Isaac Newton. In this case more violence, or banging the nail, was only going to cause more violence. The need to hit the nail once ... unfortunately was required. But hitting it multiple times weakens the first time. As with most things in life, less is more. Capisce?"

"Capeesh?"

"Yes. Capisce. It means 'do you understand?' in Italian."

Falcon shook his head, "How do you know all this stuff?"

"I read every day, books, newspapers, magazines, whatever I lay my hands on. I read opinions from people I agree with as well as people I don't. I'll admit the people I don't agree with are becoming more difficult to stomach every day."

"Why is that?"

"Too many people do not appreciate our freedoms. They have allowed the insecurities, which we all have to a certain degree, to control their lives rather than challenging themselves to be better and serve their fellow man. Ethical and physical laziness are already challenges in our great country. These two things are leading us down a road of guilt and apathy. It will be up to your generation to turn things around. Otherwise the combination of those who are chemically dependent and the greed from warmongers of the M*e* Generation will cause a lot of pain for Uncle Sam."

Falcon listened intently. He wasn't clear on the warmongers, but he'd seen plenty of druggies in Del Loma. The more he heard the more he knew he needed information. Although he loved to read, he always read for pleasure or school. It was time he began to read with a purpose. He wanted to be able to speak knowledgeably on subjects like Mr. Jacobsen.

"Now off to your next class."

Falcon nodded and started for the door.

"Falcon?"

"Yes sir?"

"I'm extremely pleased with the way you handled this situation."

Falcon felt warm inside. "Thank you Mr. Jacobsen."

"Do you know why I didn't say proud?"

"No sir."

"First of all I believe that is something only said by one's parents, but most importantly is because pride goeth before the fall."

Falcon cocked his head. "Not sure if I understand?"

"You will one day my young friend. Now off you go, you know how I abhor tardiness!"

8

aseball practice encompassed an extra intensity as Falcon did every drill at hyper speed. His one-day hiatus created a backlog of energy, and he took it out on the horsehide as he smacked line drive after line drive.

Ricky smiled as he watched his friend hit the next batting practice pitch over the fence. "Good to have you back."

"Good to be back," Falcon said, as he hammered the next pitch off the chain-link fence in left field.

"Save some for the playoffs," Ricky said.

"I've got plenty for them too."

He drove an outside pitch to right field; one hopped the fence. "One more and I'm good."

The BP pitcher added a little extra and tried zipping a fastball inside.

Falcon flicked his wrists, and the ball took flight, soared over the left-field fence, and landed on the soccer field below. He'd forgotten how many swings of a bat he'd taken in his lifetime. *Too many to count.* It was as natural to him as breathing and just as important. He took his turn as he ran from base to base and ran back into the dugout to grab his glove.

Ritchie Cherub sat putting his cleats on when Falcon took a seat beside him.

"You do make it look easy," Ritchie said.

"Thanks. I love to hit, could do it all day."

"Yeah, I believe it. Hey, I heard you called Darrell last night. Is that true?"

"Yeah it's true."

"I thought so." Ritchie studied the sophomore he'd nicknamed Casanova and shook his head. Falcon was smart, athletic, popular and unbeknownst to everyone, apparently knew how to fight. He'd won the fight. He didn't have to make that call. The big senior finished tying his laces and stood up in front of Falcon.

"Pretty impressive Falcon. I am very impressed with you."

"Thanks. That means a lot coming from you."

Pluto interrupted them and called out, "Hey Falcon come on over here a minute."

Falcon grabbed his glove and ran over to his coach who was standing with the principal. *Two times in one day ... come on.*

"Hey Pluto, what's up?"

Pluto was upset and looked at his boss to explain.

The principal appeared uncomfortable and returned Pluto's gaze. Falcon was confused. "Coach, what's up coach?"

Pluto said, "Midterm grade checks were just finished. How's it going in French?"

"We've had three tests so far. I've gotten two C plusses and a C minus."

"Anything else?" said the coach.

"I have A's or B's in the rest of my classes if that's what you mean. I think my GPA is at least a 3.0. What's the problem?"

Pluto stared at the principal.

The principal shook his head.

Falcon was getting a bad feeling. "You only need a 2.0 to be eligible. I'm way above that."

Pluto glared at the principal and said, "Yes, you are but according to the powers that be if an athlete has an F on his midterm report, he is ineligible."

"What are you talking about?" asked Falcon. "I don't have any F's. I've never had an F in my life!"

"According to your French teacher you didn't complete the homework assignments." Pluto continued staring at his boss.

"Yes I did, I just didn't think they were right so I didn't want to take credit for it. I have the workbook. I can show you. I'm pretty sure the answers are all wrong, but I did all of the assignments. She called it the honor system, and I didn't think it was right taking credit for something I was pretty sure was wrong." Falcon was talking fast trying to save his life.

Pluto regarded his boss and said, "Makes perfect sense to me. The kid should be commended for having ethics." *Or maybe the teacher should get off her lazy ass and make sure the kids were learning something by checking their work.*

Falcon felt the panic squeezing his chest. He lived for baseball. He had to talk his way through this somehow.

"I've gotten three C's on the tests. How am I getting an F? Even with an F I'm still way above the 2.0 limit. I took French as an elective. I didn't have to take it. I could have taken all kinds of other things."

He was running down every argument trying to win his case.

The principal said, "I'll talk to the teacher and see if she made a mistake, but as of right now you cannot practice and are ineligible."

Pluto threw his cap on the ground. "This is bullshit!"

The principal ignored them both, turned, and headed down the hill.

"I'm not missing the playoffs. No way!" Falcon directed his anger toward the principal.

Coach and player watched until the principal disappeared.

Falcon grabbed his glove and started back to the dugout.

"Where you going?"

"I'm going to talk to her. She's out of her mind. How do you get an F out of three C's? The homework would have to count twice as much as all the tests, and I know it doesn't. Even if you weighted them all the same I'd have a D not an F. She's crazy!"

"Just wait," the coach said. "Give me a chance to talk to her first and see what I can do."

Falcon was fuming. *It couldn't hurt. Maybe he knew her well enough to talk some reason into her.*

"Go on home and I'll call you tonight."

"What about practice?"

"You can't practice right now. Technically you're ineligible. If I let you practice it could come back and hurt the team. It's not like you're some guy off the bench, Falcon."

He certainly wasn't going to put his team and teammates in that position. Grabbing his gear, he hustled to the locker room where he changed and headed to the front of the school. Normally he would walk home but today he needed some help. He slipped a quarter into the pay phone.

"Hello?" answered his mother.

"Mom, can you come get me?"

Rachel could hear the tension in his voice.

"Is practice over?"

"No."

"Are you okay?"

Falcon felt like crying and blurted out, "No Mom. The principal came up to practice and told me I was ineligible because my French teacher gave me an F halfway through the semester and ..."

"Hang on honey. I'll be there in a few minutes. Just try and calm down. I'm sure this is a mistake."

Falcon let out a heavy sigh, "Okay. See you in a little bit."

Rachel couldn't believe what Falcon told her. How in the world could there be such a big mistake? He never had problems with school. It was a godsend it was so easy for him. She felt like crying as she drove to school. *Falcon's been through enough drama this week Lord. His French teacher better have a good excuse. An F! The woman must be insane.*

Pluto wrapped up practice early to hopefully catch Falcon's French teacher. He didn't know her well. She wasn't actively involved in the school and never attended sporting events or supervised school functions like dances or drama. *What's the best way to get this fixed?* He knocked on her classroom door and stepped into the room.

Pluto smiled, "Good evening."

"Hello Mr. Pluto. Our boss just left. I'll tell you the same thing I told him. Athletes don't get special treatment in here."

"I'm not looking for special treatment, just fairness."

"Fairness? Between you and our boss, Mr. Sane spends more time walking the halls than in my class."

"I'm not sure I understand?"

She rolled her eyes and said flatly, "The hall passes. Between you and the principal he wanders the halls like a nomad. Always in the middle of *my* class! Then he's gone for athletics at least once a week. He's supposed to be a student not a traveling football player."

"Falcon is not a football player."

"Who cares?"

"I care. He plays baseball for me. Did you see the blood in the corridor on the way to the gym a couple of days ago?"

"What's that have to do with it?"

"I sent for him because he'd been in a fight defending himself, and I wanted to make sure he was all right. You know he went to the doctor, right?"

Her sour expression left her face long enough for Pluto to think she was considering this information. He was wrong.

"So he's a troublemaker too," she replied sarcastically. "I'm not surprised."

Wow, this lady needs to get a grip. "Not only is Falcon not a troublemaker, he's one of the most polite kids you'll ever meet, which you should know. He's also a leader on the team and cares about his teammates."

"As I stated before, athletes are not special. Someone needs to remind all of you jock people that the students are here to be educated not run around playing stupid games."

Pluto knew his face was giving away his frustration. *If this old bitch was a man, I'd knock her out.* "Listen lady we don't run around playing stupid games. These young men learn things on the field that will benefit them for the rest of their lives! And for the record, because of baseball, Falcon has a great chance at a college scholarship where I guarantee he will be educated and not majoring in French!"

"I don't appreciate your tone."

"And I don't appreciate you taking your prejudices out on one of my players. How did you come up with an F anyway? He's got three C's!"

"I don't have to explain myself to you. My decision is final. It will be a good lesson for him."

"A lesson? The only lesson I see here is you can't do math. Three C's do not equal an F! You don't give an F to a student who shows up to class every day, works hard, and passes three of your tests! Even with your F he still has a 3.0 grade average. What's the lesson here?"

She glared at Pluto as she tried to think of a comeback. The news about the fight was new to her — that would explain his face being a little red in class that day. She just thought he was out late partying like all prima-donna athletes. He was a very polite young man … maybe … no, her mind was made up. If she caved she'd have no credibility. *This is my red line.* She had to enforce it whether it was right or not. "I don't think we have anything left to talk about. I'm not changing my mind. You will have to find someone else to play quarterback."

He didn't bother correcting her. She was too far gone. She didn't care about the students, her issue was control, and she wasn't going to give it up. "Ma'am, life has a way of righting wrongs and you're *so* wrong, I pity the moment you are righted."

Pluto opened the door and returned to his office. He dialed Falcon's home number and his heart winced when he heard him answer.

"Hello?"

"Hey Falcon, it's Pluto."

Falcon heard the disappointment in his voice. "Didn't go so well, huh?"

"No son, I'm afraid not. The principal and I both talked to her but she's not budging."

Falcon's voice sounded tight, "What's her problem?"

"She thinks we need to learn a lesson."

"What's that?"

"That athletes aren't special."

"I never said I was."

"I know. It goes deeper than you. You're just the target."

"So let me get this straight. If I'd filled out the clipboard that I did the homework I'd be eligible. But because I didn't feel it was right I now have an F in a class, where I could flunk the final, and still get a D? There's something wrong with this Pluto."

Pluto listened to Falcon's rational thinking and could find no argument with his statement or his math. "I don't know what to say son. I agree. This is wrong. Unfortunately there's nothing I can do about it."

Those last words, *there's nothing I can do about it* felt like a mountainside falling down on him. He was done. No playoffs. No last practice with his teammates. His days playing baseball for Trinity were over. Falcon couldn't even breathe as that reality set in.

"I'm so sorry son."

"Uh-huh," was the only sound he could manage.

"I'll see you in school tomorrow."

Pluto knew his former star was about to breakdown. He'd seen it once when Falcon was a freshman after a tough loss. He found him in the equipment closet desperate for privacy as he choked down his disappointment.

"See you tomorrow," Coach repeated and hung up the phone.

Falcon hung up and sprinted past his parents.

"What did the coach say?" asked Mitch.

Falcon shook his head and escaped into his room.

Rachel pressed her body against his door and called softly, "Falcon?"

"Mom," came an anguished reply, "please leave me alone."

His parents respected his privacy. Rachel bolted to her own room to cry, and Mitch returned to the living room and raised the volume on the TV. But the house shook with suffering as the hacking sobs of a heartbroken soul could be heard through the paneling walls.

Trinity won their first two games in the playoffs and found themselves in the Section Championship. Those games were played during school hours. Falcon struggled on those days the most as he watched the clock and knew his team was playing while he was held prisoner in class. The complex emotions of excitement for his teammates and the gnawing pain of not being a part of it devoured him. He hid his torment the next week isolated at the field in the dugout at lunch. It was the only way he could think of to stay connected and keep his sanity.

Pluto climbed up to the field one day at lunch to collect equipment, but stopped and turned around when he heard Falcon talking to the field. Falcon needed to grieve and time to heal. Sitting in his office the day before the Section Championship, Pluto knew he couldn't leave things as they were. He sent a call slip to Falcon … in French class.

To Falcon's credit, he continued to be polite to his French teacher and continued to not take credit for the homework he knew was wrong.

At first his teacher thought it was an act of rebellion, but after a few days realized she'd been wrong. But being wrong and apologizing for it were two different things. She did give him more attention but the die had been cast. She couldn't wait for the year to be over. The guilt only mounted as Falcon continued to be polite and the team continued to win. When the call slip came her excitement said it all.

"Take as much time as you need," she gushed and handed him the pass.

Falcon's mouth said "thank you" but his eyes burned into her as he could not hide his contempt for hypocrisy. He moved with a purpose to Pluto's office. He wasn't sure why he sent for him, but he held no hope that anything had changed.

Pluto said, "Falcon come on in." He motioned to a chair.

"Thanks Coach."

"I've been thinking about the Section. It's our last game win or lose."

"Let's go with win," Falcon said and breathed a small prayer of gratitude to the Big Fella upstairs it would be the final game one way or the other.

"I couldn't agree more. I also know we wouldn't be here without you."

Falcon sat motionless. He appreciated the words but the wound was still hemorrhaging. He didn't want to breakdown in Pluto's office.

"You guys are doing fine without me." He attempted a smile but felt like he might puke.

Pluto didn't want to make this hard on him but felt some things needed to be said: "We won the league by two games. You hit game-winning homeruns in two games alone. Without you Falcon, we wouldn't be here, just wanted you to know."

Falcon nodded feeling his chest tighten.

"You should be on the field but I can't put you there."

His chest tightened further.

"I shouldn't be doing this either but I want you in the dug-out with us tomorrow during warm-ups. You can't stay once the game starts, but you've earned the right to be there. I know how you feel about the field. Once the game starts you can sit in the bleachers."

Falcon took a deep breath before he spoke, "What about class?"

"It's all been worked out. Just leave after your second period."

"I appreciate it. I'll talk to my parents."

"No problem. I know you can't ride with us on the bus but please tell your parents I hope to see you all there."

"I will."

Falcon left Pluto's office as the bell rang and bumped right into Cassandra.

"Hi," she said shyly.

The sight of her made him temporarily forget his problems.

"Hi."

"I heard about your fight. Are you okay?"

He subconsciously touched his finger to his nose.

"Yeah, I'm fine. How are you?"

"I'm fine ... I just ..."

Falcon waited.

"I heard," she said. "You're moving too?" She hoped it wasn't true.

"Yeah, selling our business, new start, blah, blah, blah."

Cassandra gazed at Falcon. *He's matured since the first time I saw him in eighth grade. He's thicker in all the right places. His face has hardened a bit but his eyes are still full of innocence, excitement and love. He's looking at me now the same way he did two years ago.*

Students started filling the halls, and their private chat wasn't private anymore.

She said, "I want to tell you something."

"Sure," he said and waited for her. He'd wait for her as long as it took.

Cassandra glanced down at the ground as more kids flew by. She began to blush and her heart started racing.

"I just wanted to say I ..."

Falcon stepped closer to her and shielded her from the crowd. "Yeah?"

"I just wanted to say I ..."

Falcon leaned forward, lifted her chin slowly, and melted into her green eyes.

"I just wanted to say I lo—"

"Cassandra! Let's go we're going to be late for French!" a classmate grabbed her arm and whisked her away.

Falcon froze in utter disbelief as he watched her friend practically drag Cassandra to class and away from him.

Cassandra looked back twice and then disappeared.

Falcon shook his head. A few months ago a relative had told him one of the first descendants in his family tree was from France. *I'm having a hard time believing that. France doesn't seem to be any friend of mine.*

After school Falcon walked home, deep in thought.

Lloyd came up beside him and jabbered about some rapper named Kurtis Blow and his new song about basketball and women.

Falcon interrupted Lloyd's verbal onslaught, "You pretty tight with Lacey?"

"Not as tight as I want to be."

Falcon ignored the comment and continued, "Maybe you could check for me what's going on with Cassandra."

"Like what?"

"We were talking today ..."

Lloyd perked up, "Really? Where?"

"In the hallway between classes. Why?"

"Just curious."

"Anyway she was trying to tell me something but then got ripped away to class."

"Sure I can check. What about Kelly?"

"What about her?"

"Permission to speak freely Bruce Lee?" Lloyd saluted Falcon.

The question and salute was Lloyd's smart aleck way of checking out Falcon's mood before he said anything stupid. Falcon had come down hard on him when the Darrell drama was in high gear. Lloyd would not stop running his mouth.

Falcon had finally grabbed him by the shoulders and said, "I can't protect you from all these guys. You've got to stop thinking you're safe and telling everyone I'm going to kick their asses because we're friends. The next time you pop off, I'm going to step aside and let them do whatever they want."

Now it was a common joke. Lloyd would give a salute and ask to speak freely.

Falcon shook his head, "You never stop. Yes speak freely."

"Kelly's practically a woman and quite a woman at that. I know you've got it bad ... I know you like Cassandra, but come on already. Kelly? Cassandra? It's not even close man."

"Don't say that."

"Sorry. Okay seriously bro. The whole school can see Kelly is trying to get back into your picture. What's up with that?"

While Kelly and Falcon went their separate ways they'd still remained friends. It might have been the only real mutual break-up in the history of breakups.

Kelly'd had an itch she'd scratched and she'd found out older didn't mean better.

Falcon was still trying to figure out Cassandra. He walked on quietly thinking.

"Is it complicated?" Lloyd asked.

"I've told you a million times there's nothing complicated about life. You either have the guts to speak your mind and do the right thing or you don't. Nothing complicated about it."

"Okay then what's the deal?"

"I want to be with Cassandra."

"That's not new news, bro."

"But we can't seem to have more than a conversation every three weeks in the hall for 30 seconds."

"So if Cassandra isn't available then it's Kelly time."

"Don't talk about them like that. They're not chess pieces I trade back and forth."

"What's wrong with that? There are plenty of guys who'd love to take your place."

"Enough, stop talking."

"Hey Bruce Lee, I asked for permission. You can't get mad at me."

"Stop calling me Bruce Lee you freaking idiot."

"Touchy, touchy, touchy. I know my rights. I asked permission first."

Falcon glared at Lloyd, then started laughing. "It's a good thing you make people laugh because I guarantee you're going to need those skills in the future."

"Nah I'll just call you."

"You're high. I'm not showing up at some woman's house because her husband caught you in the wrong place at the wrong time. You're on your own, pal."

"Oh dare to dream. I can't wait for those kinds of problems."

Falcon shook his head and laughed as they arrived at Lloyd's house.

"See you tomorrow lover boy," Falcon said.

"Look who's talking *Casanova.*"

Falcon was still laughing when he trotted down his driveway. His father was out changing the oil in their semi.

"Hey Dad."

"Hey Buddy. How was school?"

"It was good. Pluto called me into his office today, said I can't be on the field when the game starts, but he wants me in the dugout during warm-ups. He was hoping you guys could bring me."

"Do you want to go?"

"I didn't want to at first, but yeah, it might be a good idea. What do you think?"

The last two months for Mitch had been rough. He was working 12-hour weekdays and sometimes eight on the weekend as he prepared for their business to be sold. Their house was for sale too as the Sane family made plans to move south and re-establish themselves financially. The current situation began to weigh on Mitch as his life felt like it was splitting at its seams. A week ago Falcon saw his father cry for the first time in his life. He'd been sitting on the edge of Falcon's bed talking, when Falcon asked if he was okay. It appeared useless to try and hold back a flood of tears. He told Falcon he loved him three times and hugged him tight. Falcon always respected and feared his father, but on that night their bond reached a new level as his dad allowed him to see even the strong need help sometimes.

"I think you should go. It will be important for you to be there."

"It's tomorrow. Can you take the time off?"

Mitch couldn't afford to take it off but knew he was going to anyway. "This is why you always want to work for yourself. To be able to do what you want and not check with someone else. Financial freedom. We've worked hard over the years, we've earned that right. Go ask your mom if she wants to come along."

"Okay Dad. Thanks." Falcon walked into the house.

Rachel was suffering through homework with Deeter.

Deeter was in eighth grade and like Falcon, good looking, popular, and a basketball star, but a bit of a hell-raiser. Rachel had found a specialist nine months before who had diagnosed Deeter's dyslexia correctly, and he was finally starting to read. Unfortunately too many years of struggling left Deeter more interested in entertaining his classmates than studying. He had one last chance to pass the U.S. Constitution test or he wouldn't graduate eighth grade. Of the two people who sat at the dining-room table, only one cared if he accomplished that feat, and it wasn't him.

Falcon waited until his mother and brother finished and asked her opinion about him going to the game.

"You know Mom, I can see you have a lot to do right now what with planning the move, doing the books, and trying to teach this yahoo about the Amendments. If you'd rather not go, I understand."

Rachel knew her son well. His statement was code for, "I don't want to hurt your feelings Mom, but I'd rather go with Dad alone." She did want to go. Her son had suffered so much lately, and like most mothers Rachel wanted to spare him any more pain. But throughout her children's lives she also knew when to let go, even when it broke her heart.

"You know honey that might be a good idea if you and Dad went by yourselves. I do have a great deal on my plate, and I appreciate you being so understanding."

Falcon was hoping she would say that. He breathed a sigh of relief.

"Be sure Dad takes a cooler of milk and juice for the team. Show the guys their team Mom is there in spirit."

"Sure Mom, we will."

It would give him a chance to spend quality time alone with his father, something he'd had his whole life with his mom.

"Thanks Mom." He hugged her, "I love you."

"I love you too baby, besides someone's got to keep an eye on your brother." She winked at her oldest son.

Mitch picked Falcon up at school after second period the next day and drove to Biggs, California. The little town nestled in the middle of nowhere was the perfect site for the Section Championship. The grass was perfectly manicured, and Falcon leaned against the fence in the dugout as he watched the two teams warm up. Easier to keep his distance from the agony, he focused on the competition. At least that's what he told himself until the equipment manager began chalking the foul lines. Waves of nostalgic pain crashed down on him. He forced his eyes to narrow. Clenching his jaw, he held his emotions at bay. A hand landed on his shoulder.

"Glad you could make it, son," said Pluto.

"Thanks Coach." He swallowed. "Appreciate the invite."

"The pleasure is mine. You know, I can't let you on the field but that doesn't mean I can't do this." He held out a red and white Trinity jersey.

Falcon peered at his coach and slowly accepted his jersey. It had killed him to turn it in, but the principal insisted. Cradling it in his hands, he felt the imprint of his number 13. He noticed a faded blood stain left from the fight with Darrell, which seemed a hundred years ago.

"Are you sure Coach?"

"You can't wear it here, but it's yours to keep. It just didn't seem right that someone else would wear it ... so no one else will." Pluto cleared his throat. "You earned it. But you didn't get it from me." He smiled at his own joke.

Falcon knew he if he tried to speak he wouldn't be able to hold back the tears. He just nodded.

Pluto nodded in return as he felt his emotions swelling. He cleared his throat again, "I gotta get back on the field, but Falcon, stay here as long as you want. Screw 'em!"

"Thanks, but my dad's here. I'll sit with him."

"I understand." Pluto reached out and shook Falcon's hand. "It's been an honor son. You're a helluva ball player, and I have no doubt I'll see you on TV one day."

Falcon gritted his teeth and narrowed his eyes to stay under control.

Pluto realized the young man was barely hanging on, as was he.

"God bless son. My door is always open."

Pluto let go of Falcon's hand and strode swiftly onto the field where he barked out commands behind his sunglasses. He had to do something. The tears were starting to flow.

Falcon returned to the bleachers and sat next to his father.

"How'd it go?"

"Good."

"Are you hungry?"

"Not really."

"You want to sit here a bit and watch the game?"

"Yeah if you don't mind."

"Don't mind at all. I'm very proud of you Falcon."

"Thanks Dad. Thanks for coming with me."

Father and son sat through seven innings of highly competitive championship baseball when Trinity succumbed at the end, four to three. It wasn't lost on Falcon or Pluto that the last out was made by the number two hitter in the lineup. Falcon had hit in that position all year, and both he and Pluto would have given a kidney to have been able to have him in there with the Section Championship on the line.

The drive home was broken up by a dinner stop before they faced the trip over Falcon's old nemesis, Buckhorn Summit. With food still in his stomach at the end of the long-winding mountain road, a battle had been won — boy over mountain. *Maybe this is a sign of good things to come.*

The few remaining weeks raced by for Falcon as almost all impediments were out of his way. Darrell and Falcon remained true to their word. They didn't become friends but stopped being enemies. Kelly and Falcon shared a little time outside of school, but the expiration date on that relationship had passed. Falcon finished French with a C and a smile, and his integrity intact. Not once did he sign his initials to the homework, and the only French phrase that stuck with him after a quarter of French was appropriate. Je ne sais pas ... *I don't know.*

On the last day of school only two things remained on his checklist: saying goodbye to Mr. Jacobsen and asking Cassandra to sign his yearbook.

The day was filled with hugs, laughter and some tears for the seniors. Classes were over as Trinity students floated from room to room sharing stories with each other and the teachers they liked. Some kids didn't go to class at all. Instead they hung out by the rock fountain and attempted to capture memories one last time.

Falcon caught up with Mr. Jacobsen who was informally holding class all day. Not surprisingly his room was decorated in red, white and blue. The American flag stood on one side of the room and waved proudly, caught in the breeze of an oscillating fan. Holding down the other side of the room was a yellow flag with a coiled rattlesnake and the words "Don't Tread on Me". A cassette tape squealed in a boom box on a loop and filled the background with "The Star Spangled Banner," "God Bless America," and Lee Greenwood's "God Bless the U.S.A." Students were given handshakes, hugs, and each one a memorable token, a small American flag. Falcon waited in the back until the room emptied and approached his teacher and mentor.

"Ah my favorite student coming to say goodbye?"

"Unfortunately yes sir."

"Never be unfortunate. But for the grace of God go I, and you my young friend have been graced. However before I get all sentimental it appeared you were about to ask me a question."

"Yes sir. I've seen the yellow flag with the rattlesnake before, but I'm not sure what it means?"

"Good question. If you don't have the answers, ask! It's called a Gadsen flag named for General Christopher Gadsen. He designed it in 1775 before our official Declaration of Independence. The rattlesnake apparently was quite common among the original 13 colonies, and as we all know living in Northern California can be deadly if provoked or 'tread on'. The infamous snake was first used by Benjamin Franklin as an answer to England sending their criminals to America. Franklin published a paper saying America should send rattlesnakes to England in return. It grew from there."

"One day Mr. Jacobsen I hope to have your knowledge."

Albert Jacobsen smiled, "You will surpass me by leaps and bounds, Falcon. But if you've learned anything from me let it be this: don't hope for things. Make them happen. Don't wish for change, make change happen for the betterment of all those choosing to be assertive and positive."

"What about negative people?"

"You require that behavior to stop. First by example, second by enforcement of law, and if that fails you implement your free will. Something I know you understand already."

"You make it sound so easy."

"Leading by example should always be easy. It's called doing the right thing. Enforcement of law is getting harder with an overabundance of attorneys. But if the time comes when someone thinks their free will is more important than yours that is the time to assert yourself in any way necessary to protect your free will and the free will of others."

"Do you mean free will or freedom?"

"Freedom is an agreement among citizens. There are plenty of countries on the planet not practicing freedom. Free will is God-given. There is no agreement. You have it. How you use it is up to you."

Falcon listened intently. Mr. Jacobsen was unlike any of his other teachers. He was alive, passionate and spoke truth.

Albert Jacobsen joyfully observed his favorite student absorb the information. His generation or "Generation X" as they'd been labeled was being fed intellectual garbage through TV, radio and the press and nutritional garbage in the grocery stores.

If America was going to thrive and not succumb to Roman lore, ethical leadership must rise to the top. He'd already witnessed this young man lead ethically. With certainty Falcon would rise again when needed. Albert knew Falcon was moving, and this would be the last time he would have him in his class. He also knew about Cassandra Ross.

"I'm going to miss you son. Your love for our country always warmed this old man's heart." He patted his chest. "But enough of this mushy stuff, it appears my next group of students has arrived and ..." He cleared his throat, "I believe a Ms. Ross is waiting for you outside the door."

Falcon's head snapped like a trip hammer at the mention of Cassandra's name. He peered at the door but didn't see anyone.

Albert Jacobsen smiled a knowing smile and lowered his voice so only Falcon could hear, "Trust me Casanova, she's right outside. Godspeed my fellow American and please come back over the years and say hi. I'll watch for you in the papers."

Falcon sprung forward and gave Mr. Jacobsen a huge hug who returned his embrace in kind.

"Thank you for everything Mr. Jacobsen. I know it was you who went to the principal."

Mr. Jacobsen smiled. *This kid didn't miss much.* He finished hugging him and fired off a salute. "Be bold, be brave, be kind my fellow American."

"Yes sir!" Falcon returned his salute and marched toward the door.

As always, Mr. Jacobsen was right. Cassandra was standing next to his locker waiting for him. Just the sight of her took his breath away.

"I didn't want to interrupt you and Mr. Jacobsen, but I wasn't sure when I would see you again today. Do you have your yearbook?"

"Sure, right here." He handed it to her.

"Can I take it to my next class and give it to you afterward?" she asked. *No way can I write two years' worth of feelings in five minutes.*

"Okay. Can I take yours with me?"

She sighed, "I don't have it right now. Lacey does, but I can give it to you later."

"That sounds good; then I'll get to see you again."

Mr. Jacobsen observed from a safe distance as the two shy almost-lovers stood close to each other. The glow on their faces reminded him of his feelings for his wife, then and now. *America's got a chance with kids like that.*

"Okay, eyes on me," he said to the new batch of kids filing in. "I pledge allegiance to the flag of the United States of America ..."

Cassandra's next class was biology. Since she'd already received her A, she headed to the one place she could be alone, the library. Settled into a small cubicle, she flipped through Falcon's yearbook and looked for the perfect spot. She needed a full page. Page after page was filled with messages from friends, teammates and virtually every girl in school! There seemed to be hundreds of "I'll miss you," "You're the best guy ever," "Wish you'd asked me out," — all with phone numbers attached. Some girl named Sara said she wanted to marry him, which made Cassandra's nose wrinkle in jealousy. Lloyd's message perked her up because he referred to Falcon doing something about "the one you have it so bad for." She knew Lloyd was talking about her. Then she came across Kelly's pretty handwriting and signature at the bottom. She turned it quickly to ignore it. A couple of seconds later she flipped back and read Kelly's message to Falcon. It punched her in the stomach and made her heart ache. After reading it twice, she knew she had to tell him how she felt. *Don't be chicken. Don't hold anything back.*

The pen had no eraser, she had no Wite-Out. Once it was on the page it would be there for all eternity and everyone to see, especially Falcon. She dove in and wrote line after line with no thought of repercussions. Her flowing penmanship only added to the depth of emotion, and a small tear turned into many as she tore down the self-made walls and filled the page with love. Her love for him. She finished with a flourish and signed her name. Closing his yearbook she wiped her eyes and sat quietly. A tremendous weight had been lifted. After two years he would know how she truly felt. The first time she'd ever seen him, watching him play baseball, and choking on his dating Kelly. Finally he would know. But the euphoria wore off, and the realization of him knowing exactly how she felt about him was suddenly replaced with the same fear and panic that had kept them apart for so long. *What if he doesn't feel the same? I can't give this to him myself. What if he reads it in front of me?* Her mind began to swirl. *What if he gives this to someone else to sign? They're going to see what I wrote. I can't let that happen.* Panicked, she contemplated throwing his yearbook in the trash.

"There you are," Lacey approached Cassandra. "What's wrong? You look scared to death."

Cassandra started rambling, "I have his yearbook, and I wrote in it, but I can't give it back to him now."

"Who?"

She snapped, "Who else, Falcon!"

"Oh … let me see." Lacey reached excitedly for his yearbook.

"No!"

"What did you say?"

"Girls, shush," said the librarian.

Lacy pulled up a chair. "Come on. Let me see. Maybe it's fine. I promise I won't say anything. I'll just read it."

Cassandra hesitated. Lacey was her best friend. "All right,

but no comments."

"I promise."

Lacey shook with anticipation as she took the yearbook. She'd been hearing about Falcon Sane for two years and thought she knew exactly how Cassandra felt. She smoothed out the page.

Cassandra wandered in and out of the bookracks to sneak peeks at her friend.

Lacey took her time, read it twice, and closed the book.

Cassandra covered her eyes with her hands. "Well?"

"Wow."

"Wow good or wow bad?"

"Just wow. All this time listening to you, I never really got it until right now."

"What do think he'll think?"

Lacey smiled, "Only one way to find out."

"I don't think I can give it to him."

"Sure you can."

"I don't think so. Can you do it for me?"

"You don't think he's going to come looking for you?"

"Yeah … I don't …" Her hands turned to ice as her face grew hot.

"You know he will."

"Just give it to him, please? I'm leaving early today anyway."

"Why?"

She moaned, "Family vacation. We're leaving for San Francisco today. This is my last period."

"You guys don't normally go until after the Fourth of July?"

"Mom and Dad changed their minds."

"For how long?"

"Most of the summer."

"Wow."

"Just give it to him for me, please?" she pleaded.

"Sure."

"Thank you," Cassandra gushed. Gathering her things, she prepared to leave school. No doubt her parents and older sister were already waiting in the parking lot.

"Here's your yearbook." Lacey handed it to her.

"Thanks."

Lacey said, "Call me when you get a chance."

"I will." She hugged Lacey.

"Do you want me to say anything to him?"

"No, I think I said it all."

Lacey shook her head as her friend disappeared, then bolted off to find Falcon. She spotted Lloyd first.

"Lloyd, have you seen Falcon?"

"Yeah he's by the cafeteria. Why?"

"Cassandra wants me to give him his yearbook back."

Lloyd's eyes widened. "Did she write in it?"

"Oh yeah."

He reached for the yearbook. "Let me see."

"No!" she hugged it to her chest. "You'll have to ask Falcon."

He grinned, "That good, huh?"

"She definitely did not hold back."

"Why are you giving it to him?"

"She had to leave early today."

"Today? Why would you leave early today? This is the best day ever."

"Parents made her. Family vacation."

"When's she coming back?"

"End of summer."

"She knows he's leaving right?" asked Lloyd.

Lacy grimaced, "She knows."

"This is like the worst romance novel ever. He never gets the girl."

"What about Kelly?"

Lloyd said, "You know that was because he wasn't with Cassandra."

"Yeah I know."

"Come on let me take a quick peek at it."

"Go ahead, but then I'm going to tell Falcon you read it before he did."

It didn't take Lloyd a second to change his mind. "Fine, I'm sure he'll show me anyway."

"I doubt it," said Lacey.

"You want me to call him over here?"

"Don't bother, I see him."

Lacey walked toward Falcon with Lloyd a step behind.

"I think I'll come with you," said Lloyd.

Falcon saw them coming.

Lacey was all smiles as she handed him his yearbook.

"Cassandra asked me to give this to you. She had to leave early today. Her parents just picked her up."

Falcon immediately scanned the parking lot for her. *She was gone*? The look on his face almost made Lacey cry. She tapped his yearbook with her finger. "She wrote you a letter inside. It pretty much says it all."

His expression looked stern. "You read it?"

She answered quickly, "She asked me to."

Lloyd was instantly grateful Lacey hadn't let him read it.

"All right," Falcon sighed. "Thanks Lacey."

"You're welcome ... I ... uh ... she ..."

Lacey considered her next words. Maybe she shouldn't tell him Cassandra was gone for the summer.

Lloyd jumped in. "Well, talk to you later Lacey."

He guessed what she was about to say and telling Falcon she was gone for the summer would not go over well — no matter what was inside that yearbook.

Grateful to Lloyd, Lacey walked away with her heart still pounding. "See you guys later."

"Man I do enjoy watching her walk away," Lloyd said.

Falcon barely heard him. Torn between excitement about Cassandra's letter and the pain of not seeing her again today, he decided to focus on the letter. "I'll be back."

"Where you going?"

"Some place quiet."

"I'll come with you."

"That's okay."

"It'll be my pleasure."

"No, not this time."

"We both know you're going to the baseball field," said Lloyd.

"Yes we do, and we both know I'm going alone."

"Whatever."

"Don't pout. I'll catch up with you later." Falcon hurried toward his second home.

"It's a lot more fun watching Lacey walk away." Lloyd called after him.

Falcon laughed over his shoulder, "I sure hope so."

He moved past the gymnasium and the outer corridor toward the field. Adrenaline rushed through his body and forced him into sprinting up the hill. His favorite place on school grounds was quiet as usual. He sat in his home dugout and began flipping the pages. He hadn't read anything in his yearbook yet but rushed past everything until he saw her signature below her letter. She'd chosen a page with a smiling picture of herself and Lacey in French class.

My Beautiful Falcon,

I cannot believe the year is over so soon and yet we are still so far away from each other. I remember the first time "ever I saw your face" and the first time you held my hand in Junction City. I've dreamed about that moment every night hoping one day to replace it with a better memory of you and me. Our first year together in Rosie's English class was amazing as I got to see you every morning. I am truly sorry I've made it so hard for you to talk to me. You are amazing! Every time you are close to me my heart pounds so fast I can't breathe and I lose my ability to tell you how I really feel. I know you don't care about my braces but I do. I am so sorry if you thought I was ignoring you. I would never ignore my number 13. You probably don't know this but I've watched every single one of your home baseball games. Even when you started dating Kelly I continued to come ... because I wanted to be near you. When you smile at me in the hallways you fill me with joy and break my heart at the same time because you are close but so far away. I dream of holding your hand, being your girl, and kissing you. I know you don't listen to Madonna but her song 'Crazy for You' says exactly how I feel about you. I know us not being together is all my fault and now you are moving away forever. I would beg you to stay if I thought it would help but ... please don't go! Please stay here with me, Falcon. Nothing will ever be the same without you, and we have so much to do together if only you'll stay. I know I've blown the last two years but I am ready now. Please don't leave me my beautiful number 13. I have to go now as I'm starting to cry. Sorry for my tears on the page. I'm trying to dry them off. If you have to go, please come back for me. I will wait for you. I will always be yours forever.

Je t'aime,
Cassandra

Falcon read her words over and over. Finally closing the yearbook, he sprinted down the hill to look for Lacey. *What does Je t'aime mean?* He found her by the fountain with some friends.

Lacey saw him coming. *I told her he would come looking for her.*

Hey Lacey," he said a little out of breath.

"Hi Falcon, so, you read it, right?"

"Yeah." Falcon thought about his next question.

Lacey bit her lip. She'd never spent any time alone talking with him. Her heart started to race as she felt the energy and intensity emanating from him. She hoped someday a guy like this would feel that strongly about her.

"I need to talk to her ... now," said Falcon.

Lacey did not want to wreck Falcon with the news. "She's gone with her parents."

There was something about the way Lacey said *"gone"* that made Falcon hold his breath. "What do you mean 'gone'?"

"They left for their summer vacation. Every year they go to San Francisco for the summer."

"The entire summer?"

Lacey nodded, "Pretty much; she's supposed to call me."

"When?"

"I don't know she could call anytime or in a month."

Falcon almost crumbled. "You have got to be kidding me," he said aloud, but more to himself than anyone else.

"I'm so sorry Falcon." Lacey wanted to hug him he looked so devastated but she didn't dare. First because of her loyalty to Cassandra and second she didn't think Falcon would let her.

He stared off into space. *Even if I think about this all day there isn't anything I could do about it.* "Can you tell her I'm leaving at the end of the summer?"

Lacey felt like crying. "She knows Falcon ... but I'll tell her if she calls."

"Thanks," he walked away toward nothing.

"Good luck Casanova," she whispered, "may all your dreams come true."

Falcon's only remedy for this kind of agony was staying busy and thankfully the summer was providing that. Senior league baseball, all stars, working with his father on the route, and prepping to move; he packed his days with lots of physical labor as he tried to outrun the misery. As the months passed, his anger toward leaving behind everything he treasured started to harden into a type of armor. He smiled and laughed when the gnawing pain disappeared for brief moments, mostly time spent on the field competing or hanging out with Lloyd and Ricky. Lloyd's family was moving too, and their commiseration made them both feel a little better. Ricky vowed to make Falcon's last days in Weaverville the best ever, and at times it worked. Both Ricky and Lloyd, and Cassandra for that matter, had their driver's licenses. Although Falcon had taken the classes and completed driver training he was still months away from turning 16; but Ricky took advantage of having his license and chauffeured Falcon around town and to the lake. Eventually summer wound down and the last weekend of August arrived.

It was Friday night and Falcon's family was scheduled to leave Sunday morning.

Ricky felt certain he would never see his friend again.

"What do you want to do tomorrow, buddy? Anything you say. We could go to the lake. Lots of people are heading out for the last party of the year before school starts." Ricky hated seeing his best friend suffer. "Who knows, maybe she'll be there?"

Falcon had yet to connect with Cassandra all summer. He'd seen Lacey at a few parties, but she didn't have any new information. "I doubt it but the lake sounds good." He knew Cassandra didn't care for parties. Like him, she wasn't a drinker or partier. He only went this summer because he hoped to find her. Every single one had been a major letdown.

Cassandra Ross was experiencing the worst summer vacation of her life. Her parents tried everything to make her feel better but nothing worked. Finally after months of anguish and arguing with their normally-sweet-natured daughter, they agreed to cut their vacation a couple days short and head back to Weaverville. Cassandra told her parents she was going for a walk and called Lacey from a payphone.

"Hello?"

"Hey it's me!"

"Finally! Are you back?"

"No, I've got them talked into coming back tomorrow morning. Is he still there?"

"Yeah he's still here and looking fine. He's all tan and still searching for you."

"You've seen him?"

"Yep, he's been showing up with Ricky at some of the parties. He doesn't drink anything, just talks to people and looks for you."

"How do you know he's looking for me?"

Lacey said, "Pahleeeze. He asks everyone he sees if they've seen you! It's pitiful."

"He's not with Kelly?"

"No sweetie he's not with Kelly. He's been waiting for you. You've got one more day... and then he's gone."

Cassandra's chest tightened and tears began to form.

"Are you there?" asked Lacey.

"Uh-huh."

"I'm sorry sweetie ... it's just ... I know how you feel about him and I know how he feels about you. It's crazy that you two haven't happened. Lloyd was right. This is the worst love story ever. I think my heart is broken just knowing about it."

Cassandra sobbed as she listened to her best friend. "What, what should I do?"

Lacey thought a moment. "Falcon will probably be at the lake party tomorrow, and if I know him, he'll stay out there as late as he can hoping for a chance to see you before he's gone forever. What time do you think you'll be getting back Saturday?"

"Maybe two ... depending on traffic."

"That should work. I'll wait for you until you get here, and then we can drive out together."

"What if he's not there?" Cassandra moaned.

"I'll go out in the morning. If he's not there, well, I'll figure something out. "

Cassandra wiped her eyes. "Thanks Lace."

"Sure sweetie. We've gotta do something. I might give up on love forever if you two can't figure it out."

Saturday morning Cassandra rode in the backseat of her parent's car as she stared out the window. She smiled remembering her talk with Lacey and felt convinced they would make it home to Weaverville in plenty of time to see Falcon.

Her mother noticed the small smile from her youngest daughter.

"Haven't seen a smile on your face in months Miss Gloom and Doom, it's nice to see it back."

"Thanks Mom. Glad to be going home."

"And why is that?" asked her father.

Cassandra shrugged.

Her older sister said, "Doesn't have anything to do with a certain baseball star who happens to be moving does it?"

Surprised, Cassandra's father looked into the rearview mirror.

Her mother said, "Is that what the problem has been all summer?"

"I don't want to talk about it," Cassandra said.

"We're a family," her mother said. "We talk about everything. You know the rules."

Cassandra gazed out the window as tears rolled down her face. "Please can we not talk about this ... please Mom?"

"What's wrong honey?" her mother asked concerned.

Cassandra tried to hold it in but the burden was too great. Her emotions exploded and she told the whole two year story of herself and Falcon Sane.

Before she finished her sister and mother were crying too.

Her father said, "Is this the boy I keep reading about in the newspaper, the shortstop?"

"Yes Dad," she said.

"Apparently he's pretty good."

"He is."

Her mother began connecting the dots. "That's why you went to all those baseball games?"

"Uh-huh."

"Why didn't you tell me?"

Cassandra shrugged and looked back out the window through bleary eyes.

"And he's leaving tomorrow?" her mother asked.

Cassandra began to sob.

Her mother glanced at her husband and placed her hand on his arm.

"I think we need to get our girl home. I'd hate to think I wouldn't be able to see you one last time if you were leaving forever."

"I was just thinking the same thing." He pushed the gas pedal down.

Cassandra's parents couldn't fix the traffic though. As they reached Redding the traffic came to a stop. There'd been an accident on Buckhorn Summit.

Falcon and Ricky arrived at Trinity Lake as they tried to enjoy Falcon's last day. Falcon knew this day was coming but managed to ignore the reality until it stared him in the face. Most of his peers were swimming, getting some sun, and drinking wine coolers and beer while Falcon stood at the edge of the lake throwing rocks in the water.

Bobby Burke snuck up behind Falcon and grabbed him around the waist and lifted him off the ground. "I'm throwing you in the water you sober son of a bitch!"

Falcon smiled and went with it. Bobby was his friend, and it was his way of saying goodbye.

When Falcon didn't struggle Bobby let go and stood beside his friend. "You need a beer."

"It's eleven o'clock in the morning."

"Scotch?" said Bobby.

Falcon smiled, "You do make you laugh."

"Yeah man just trying to lighten you up."

"I know," said Falcon. "Thanks."

"Anytime, hey listen this isn't really my thing, but it's been good knowing you."

Falcon turned toward his teammate and friend. "Thanks, you too."

Bobby said, "I remember the first day I saw you at baseball. I'd been hearing about this cocky freshman who could do just about anything on the field. I have to admit I hated your guts for about a month, especially after you took my job, but playing centerfield ended up all right."

Falcon just nodded.

"But after a few games I realized you hated to lose more

than I did, which is saying something. I mean you're the only guy I've ever seen cry after losing a game."

Falcon stepped away from his friend. "You're high. You didn't see that."

"Well I didn't see it, but I knew what you were doing in the equipment room. Don't kid a kidder, besides it's a compliment. I wish everyone cared about winning as much as you did ... do."

Bobby's small slip of the tongue brought Falcon back to the present. And the present was slipping away from him minute by minute as the sun headed westward.

Bobby dug through a cooler for another beer.

Falcon dove into the water and swam out to one of the buoys marked to keep the boats away.

Lacey arrived at the lake, parked her car, grabbed a small towel, and walked down to the shore. The beach was packed as she scanned the area for Falcon. *There's Bobby and Ricky ... where's Falcon? What if he isn't here?* Her heart skipped a beat. She'd told Cassandra she'd figure something out but that was just to make her feel better. She expected him to be here. Heading for Ricky, she roamed between coolers, towels, half-naked bodies, and inner tubes as she searched for Falcon.

Lacey called, "Hey Ricky where's your buddy?"

Ricky turned and pointed to one of the buoys out in the water.

Lacey breathed a sigh of relief. She'd done her job and located him. Now Cassandra had to do hers and get home.

"How long you guys gonna be out here tonight?" Lacey inquired

"Probably until dark, it's his last day you know?"

"Oh I know."

"What's that mean?" Ricky asked.

"Nothing. Everyone knows he's moving, right?"

Ricky looked at Lacey. He didn't know her very well, but he was picking up something from her. "Yeah I guess everyone knows."

"Well... see you later."

Lacey walked away leaving Ricky with a quizzical look on his face. *Wonder what that was all about?*

The traffic on Buckhorn Summit finally started to move. Cassandra, now beside herself, at one point thought about walking. The slow-winding mountain road from Redding to Weaverville took forever as she tracked the second hand on her watch that stole away her last chance of seeing him. She pressed her fists into her aching eyes as the four o'clock hour passed.

Her mother reached back and patted her leg. "It'll be okay honey. We'll make it."

"I don't even know where he is," she said and rested her head on her folded arms.

"These things always have a way of working out. We'll be home soon. You can use your sister's car as long as you prom-ise to be safe. I'm sure Lacey is trying to track him down as we speak, right?"

Cassandra looked at her mother with surprise.

"Don't look so surprised honey. I was your age once too you know."

"She was beautiful too ... still is," her husband chimed in.

"Were you high school sweethearts?" Cassandra's sister asked.

"No, I didn't meet your father until after college."

"Then how do you know she was beautiful, Dad?"

"She was born beautiful ... just like my daughters."

"Blah!" said her sister. "Enough already. I can't take much more of this! Here's the keys to my car." She tossed them to Cassandra. "Take it when we get home, just don't crash it!"

Lacey hung around for twenty minutes then left when Falcon started to swim in. She then drove home and waited for Cassandra to call like she promised. At two o'clock she started to worry. At three it turned into panic, now almost six a nightmare was unfolding. *Where are you?* she wondered after calling Cassandra's house multiple times. *It's got to be traffic.* Grabbing her keys, she headed out the door as the clock struck six. *I'll go back to the beach ... maybe I can stall him.*

Falcon watched the sun begin to set and bowed his head in surrender as the day started to close. Most of the partiers were gone. He and Ricky sat in the shade of a Redwood, silence having the last word.

"I'll stay here all night with you if you want?" Ricky offered.

"Thanks. I doubt it'll matter how long we stay here ... I think this is it."

"I'm still willing to stay if you want to."

Falcon smiled, "Nope, I think it's time to call it a day. Long drive tomorrow."

Ricky nodded as they grabbed their shirts and towels and headed back to the car. The sun began to disappear behind the mountain showing Falcon no mercy as the clock in the car registered 7:13.

Cassandra and her family finally arrived home at a quarter after seven. Jumping out of the car she ran to her sister's Honda Accord. The reliable little car started up and Cassandra took off down the road toward Lacey's. Five minutes later Lacey was nowhere to be found, and Cassandra started to panic. *She said the lake. Please God let him still be there.*

Ten miles away Lacey screeched her car to a stop and jumped out running toward the beach. Seven thirty arrived as she surveyed the deserted area — the sun almost down.

She called frantically, "Anybody here?" Silence greeted her

as the orange circle in the sky slowly disappeared behind the mountain. "This is so not right!" she yelled into the darkness.

Three miles away Ricky leaned on his car at the only gas station by the lake as he tried to stall Father Time.

Falcon left the little store with a couple of Cokes, an Eskimo Pie, and a Tony's Pizza. They stood there eating in the glow of neon beer lights as bugs were zapped to their deaths in the early night.

"I guess this is it my man," Falcon said acquiescing.

Ricky nodded, "What about ..."

"Nah ... I think it's time to face the facts. I'm out of time."

"What about Cassandra?" Ricky asked.

Falcon shrugged and watched another bug perish.

Ricky shook his head, "You know I can't believe I'm going to say this, but Lloyd was right. This is the worst love story ever."

"Can't argue with you there."

Two miles away completely ignoring her sister's warning, Cassandra flew down the road. *Almost there ... almost there... please be there.* Turning onto the lake road a car hurtled toward her. Both stopped in the middle of the road with their headlights on.

"Cassandra?"

"Lacey?"

The two girls jumped out of their cars and hugged each other.

"Where have you been?" said Lacey.

"Traffic was horrible!"

"I'm glad you're back."

"Me too, is he here?"

"He was here all day today, but there's no one down there now. I waited as long as I could for you and then came out here hoping to find him."

"He's not here?" she asked and almost started crying again.

A horn blared and a car pulled up as it tried to pass the two girls.

"Hey!" Bobby Burke yelled. "Will you two get your cars out of the road?"

Lacey yelled, "Sorry" and then recognized him. "Hey Bobby do you know where Falcon Sane is?"

Bobby squinted at the girl who yelled at him. He'd known Lacey since grade school. He got out of his car, walked toward them, and stared directly at Cassandra. "There's only one Falcon, you don't need to use his last name. You're Cassandra Ross, right?"

"Yes?"

"I thought so. You're the girl who's been breaking my buddy's heart all year aren't you? Now you want to know where he is on his last night? Talk about taking your time."

Cassandra's eyes began to fill with tears.

Protecting her fragile best friend, Lacey snapped, "Do you know where he is or not?"

"Easy little lady," said Bobby, "I'm just playing. Sure I do."

The silence was killing Cassandra as Bobby stood there smiling.

The two girls blurted "Well???"

"Oh sorry. You want me to tell you where he is?"

"Bobby I swear to God ..." Lacey threatened.

Bobby chuckled, "He and Ricky just left the store on the corner headed home."

"Seriously?" Cassandra cried.

"As the day is long. Drove right by them myself." He signaled with one finger in the air and pointed in Falcon's direction.

"Go! Go! Go!" yelled Lacey.

Cassandra leapt into her car, and as the car pulled away it sprayed gravel all over the road.

Bobby eyed Lacey and grinned. "So, what are you doing tonight?"

Lacey laughed and crossed her arms across her chest. "Don't you wish Bobby Burke."

Cassandra floored her sister's car and bounced back onto the paved highway headed for town. *Please God please let me catch him*! She flew around the first turn.

Up the road a piece the radio played in Ricky's car as they drove slowly toward Falcon's house. Madonna's "Crazy For You" echoed through the speakers as it appeared to Falcon the world was purposely torturing him. "Can you turn the channel?"

"Yeah sure ... isn't that the song she wrote about in your yearboo—?" Ricky let the last part drop.

Falcon groaned, "Yeah. Freaking unbelievable."

"Definitely strange, maybe even surreal."

"Surreal huh? You been reading the dictionary again," Falcon teased.

"No I heard Mr. Jacobsen use it," said Ricky. "I like the way it sounds, and it seems to fit here I might add."

"Don't I know it."

Ricky turned the knob a couple of times and settled on a DJ talking. The talking only lasted for a second as the familiar wail of an electric guitar opened up and the melancholic words of Don Henley's "Boys of Summer" purred through. Falcon shook his head as the former Eagle sang about summer's end and un-requited love which captured Falcon's pain perfectly with each verse.

"Wow! Buddy, that's brutal. Sorry." Ricky reached for the radio dial again.

"Just leave it." Falcon stared into the night.

Ricky drove along in silence as the lyrics reminded Falcon again and again of the last two years.

Falcon stared out the window and clenched his jaw as tight as he could as he attempted to grind out the despair. After the song's last gasping plea for *her* love Falcon sighed. *I guess I'm the 'boy of summer' because I'm long, long, gone.*

Ricky checked his rearview mirror as headlights of a car seemed to be careening through space toward them. He glanced at his speedometer. He was doing the speed limit. "Someone behind us is in a big hurry."

Falcon checked the side mirror as the lights barreled down on them. Then the lights started flashing on and off, on and off.

Ricky said, "This guy's crazy."

"Maybe he needs help or something," said Falcon. "Pull over and let him go by."

Ricky slowed down and veered to the shoulder as an out-of-control Honda pulled up beside them turning on its interior light.

Falcon and Ricky stared into the car as it passed.

The driver pulled in front of them and flashed its right-turn signal.

Shocked, Ricky said, "I think that's a girl."

Falcon didn't get a good look at first but as the car hovered his eyes locked on her face. *Are you kidding me? That's impossible ... thank-you-Lord!*

The car in front of them pulled over and came to a stop.

Ricky pulled in behind and looked at his friend who appeared to be in shock. He wasn't.

The car still rolling, Falcon yanked the door open and jumped out. "Wait here buddy."

Falcon scanned the little Honda and strode toward the driver's side. Bending over, he put both hands on the car door, peered through the rolled- down window, and smiled. "Been looking for you all summer."

Cassandra smiled in return. "I've been trying to get back to you all summer too."

He shook his head, "Not hard enough."

"I'm sorry," she whispered.

Falcon studied her beautiful face and knew this would be the last time.

"I'm leaving tomorrow."

She shared the pain of his words, "I know."

"I read your letter in my yearbook. Did you mean it?"

"Yes, every word." She faced him as he leaned in the window and stared into his magnetic blue eyes.

His face inches from hers, he whispered. Can I ask you a question?"

"Yes?"

"What does Je t'aime mean?"

She blushed, "It means I love you."

"And do you?"

"Yes," she sighed.

His voice grew husky, "Then tell me."

"I love you Falcon Sane."

The sweet taste of their lips closed the distance between them as their world slowed to a crawl. Tomorrow could wait on their sorrow for this night two hearts became one.

9

*T*he scent of her perfume still lingered on Falcon's skin as he climbed into the driver's seat of his dad's pickup that Sunday morning. Mitch sat shotgun since he had agreed to his son's request to drive now that he possessed his permit. The town was still asleep as the two-vehicle caravan gradually left their past lives. New opportunities lay ahead for the family yet too many regrets for Falcon lay behind. Keeping his eyes riveted on the deserted road, his former adversary, Buckhorn Summit, seemed to sense his turmoil. The curvaceous road showed him mercy and appeared to straighten in the early morning shadows. Falcon guided the truck away from past dreams toward an uncertain future, as his mind reeled with a loop of memories, Lloyd, Ricky, Mr. Jacobsen, Roger, Pluto, Bobby, and of course Cassandra. Every mile pulled him further from what could have been and closer to what would be.

Son and father drove in silence; both were physically spent and lost in their own thoughts. Falcon had not spoken to God for some time. He found himself asking why was this happening? A memory dragged him back to a moment when he peered off a cliff in Del Loma and gazed at the Trinity. Only 12 at the time, he threw questions at the water like pennies into a fountain. Why am I here? When will I find her? And other deep uncertainties too advanced for a child. He felt confused because he'd thought *he had found her*, but like the ever-changing current, today he was swept away in a different direction. *Do you really know what you're doing God?* The past years flipped through his mind like a Rolodex. Mr. Jacobsen on the Fourth of July; Lloyd shadowboxing and chasing skirts; and Ricky's sensitivity and loyalty, which was a gift Falcon would cherish forever. Mike crossed his heart and he realized why. Mike had learned from Falcon that given a chance people could change. Falcon had learned from Mike how fleeting life could be. He whispered a prayer for Miranda, thanked the Big Fella for Mrs. Winn, and the Brain Drain that led him once again to Cassandra and his questioning of God's plan.

The sun came into full view as the beauty of the Northern California forest disappeared behind him. Falcon stayed close behind his mother and brother in the car ahead as Highway 299 came to an end. With a head nod Falcon said goodbye to the highway he'd shared so much of his childhood with. *You take care 299.*

They slipped through Redding and headed south as powerful I-5 beckoned, and Falcon guided the truck onto the freeway.

The growth of a Late Bird was complete.

It was time for a Falcon to spread his wings and fly.

Part 2

1

*R*eporters from the alphabet of networks and newspapers packed the room, as they drooled over the thought of tearing into Falcon. Thirty years had passed, and everything that had happened following his departure from Weaverville led to the kickoff of his first live press conference scheduled this evening on November 7, 2015. While not surprised at the position he found himself in, Falcon had always hoped this moment would never come. He'd prayed the corruption of America would stop. He had waited patiently for someone with a calm mind and brave heart to put an end to the madness; an individual who shared his own beliefs who would challenge the corruption from above and laziness from below; one unwilling to take campaign contributions or a salary; and one solely dedicated in service to America. The responsibility lay heavy on Falcon's mind, and his heart no longer allowed him to expect such a leader to appear.

"Hey Boss! They're ready to go out there," Tommy announced to Falcon. "I swear, I think some of them are panting."

Tommy laughed at the subtext that captured his thoughts. *And some of the women are making me pant!* An attitude he knew his boss would not appreciate. Tommy Perry, a six-two, fit, boyishly handsome 50-year-old former Army Ranger, had an eventful lifestyle that trailed behind him. With enough Cherokee blood filling his veins, he inherently knew to stay away from booze. Tommy's drama lay in his insatiable lust for women. All shapes, sizes, skin or hair color, were irrelevant to Tommy. Relationship status didn't matter. He craved what many American men and women of his generation desired: sex. Because of his hunger, physique and charm, he rarely spent a night alone. His skill with the ladies transferred to the workplace, specifically sales; the man could sell water to a well. Blessed with a disarming smile and soft heart, Tommy easily breezed through life. Over a decade ago an advertisement for a sales position at FUKEN Manufacturing led him to be hired by Falcon Sane – and changed his life forever.

"Is it a full house?" Falcon asked his employee and friend in regard to the rabid room of people who awaited him.

"Like a tin of sardines," Tommy grinned.

The craze to interview Falcon began after his novel sold 20 million copies in the first month. Each refusal to promote his book left the media circling like sharks. Falcon wasn't interested in fame. And being taped and edited down to a few sound bites that might inaccurately depict his true feelings and thoughts made refusal of the requests a no-brainer. However, the public appetite hungered for the man responsible for a story many readers prayed would spring to life.

Falcon strode out the door of his office at R&R, the successful Responsible Recycling business he had begun in Sacramento well over a decade ago. Straightening his tie, he smiled at his notion to appear tonight in a t-shirt, shorts and running shoes, his usual attire. But with 52 Friday night press conferences ahead of him, he realized the importance of a first impression. He planned to impart excitement in most, fear in a few, and energy for all, and needed the costume of influence. He settled into his jacket and ran his fingers thoughtfully down his necktie. The tie, a gift from an old friend long passed, was fashioned after the American flag. Simply touching the silky material ripped Falcon back in time and the words of his friend, Matthew Bettie, reverberated through his mind.

"My father gave me this tie." Matthew stroked the garment that hung loosely around his neck. "It was revered by him because he fought in World War II on Iwo Jima. I carried it every day in Vietnam. You can imagine what it means to me. I haven't any children Falcon, and my time is running short." Matthew coughed, and wiped a streak of blood from his mouth. "Life isn't a box of chocolates, son. You do know what you're gonna get. My country asked me to defend our freedom in a foreign land, and I did. I did things in war …" He paused, and with a somber face shook his head. "I did things that I'll no doubt have to answer for soon." With every hacking cough, Matthew's handkerchief tinted a deeper shade of red before Falcon's eyes. "My government thanked me with an honorable discharge and cancerous tumors. I lived as a good American, worked hard, paid my taxes. Paid off my mortgage early and continued to work. I work, because I need to belong. That's why a lot of us end up in the military. We need to belong. Problem is the backbone of this country is being used by politicians to do unspeakable things. It's got to stop." He struggled for air. "Most of these jack-off politicians never served a day in their lives, or if they did, they didn't see any real combat. They've made a mess of our country." Matthew stood up from his desk, turned his back to Falcon, and stared out the window. "How is it …" he seemed to be speaking to the air, "I was able to survive the Vietcong but not my own government spraying chemicals all over the place? Didn't they realize me and my guys had to walk through those fields?" Coughing again he faced Falcon and squared his shoulders. "I heard somewhere that Henry Kissinger called foot soldiers like me dumb, stupid animals to be used as pawns."

Falcon's jaw tightened at the memory.

"One day when you get the chance, you tell Kissinger I'll see him after." Physically depleted, Matthew crumpled into his chair. He removed the tie from his neck and said, "I've been saving this, waiting for the good Lord to guide me. I believe it's meant for you, son."

Falcon gently clasped the treasure Matthew presented to him.

"All right enough of all this complaining." Matthew wiped blood away from his mouth. "It's time to go to work."

Falcon sighed at the memory, progressed down the hall, entered the warehouse, and stepped onto the stage. Chatter from the audience continued until Falcon ensconced himself behind the podium, then the reporters hushed.

Every chair and square foot of the warehouse was filled. Curious eyes focused on Falcon Sane, the man who refused their phone calls, dismissed million-dollar interview offers, and when threatened by producers and reporters who wanted to scrutinize his past, challenged them to have at it. He had nothing to hide. Besides, his life, although enjoyable, was no longer his primary concern. His duty fell toward freedom, his desire to rebuild the nation, and the rebirth of America.

Falcon perused the crowd.

"My name is Falcon Sane, and I'm offering my services to the American people as their next President of these United States."

The room filled with voices that exploded and demanded, "Why won't you give interviews?"

"What makes you think you can win?"

A British voice hollered, "Why do you shave your head?"

Falcon raised a hand for silence. The electric energy felt amazing, but was wasted. "Please stop yelling."

A month after his book had skyrocketed, the Independent Party asked Falcon to consider being their nominee. After somber consideration, he had filled out the proper paperwork, paid the fee from his own pocket, and allowed his name to be entered into the presidential election in November 2016. Although the Independent Party had a primary, Falcon wasn't worried; as long as he did his job he would be on the ballot. He intended to do his job.

"Every Friday until the election," he said. "I will make myself available to you. Each of you may ask one question, and I will cover as many as possible. Outbursts will disqualify those parties from receiving a thorough answer to their question." He stared across the mob of reporters. "Follow-up questions will roll over to the next week unless you choose to work together and use our time productively. Before your questions begin, let me share with you the five principles I believe will put our country back on the path to prosperity, safety, and ultimately recapture our freedom. These are the five goals that will be obtained if I'm elected President."

"If or when?" said a loud voice.

"Although I am planning on being elected, I'll never be so presumptuous as to assume the will of the people. I am offering to serve, and that, sir, is your one question."

He signaled to Tommy to begin the PowerPoint presentation. It took 60 seconds for them to fall in line. They wanted leadership. They wanted to be safe. They wanted to belong. America needed a leader. Falcon knew he needed the people in this room. If they grasped the power and energy behind assisting others, America would be inundated with positive words. Falcon felt confident he could achieve that surge early on. He also knew it was unsustainable.

"The first thing to go into effect will be a consumption tax," said Falcon. "Federal income tax and corporate taxes will no longer exist. There will be no loopholes or write-offs. Some economists think by implementing a consumption tax more revenue will be produced. More revenue for the federal government is not a good thing. American money needs to be in American pockets, not sitting in accounts where politicians play shell games or funnel it back to their political donors. If more revenue is created for the federal government the consumption tax rate will be reduced. We're stronger with our money in our community banks and when we spend locally.

"Number Two. All campaign contributions made to any politician will be against the law. Once sworn into office I'll advise the House and Senate to construct a law to be passed in my first 30 days. The law will have criminal repercussions as well as civil fines. Any politician or politician- elect will forfeit the opportunity to run for office and or, be removed from office immediately. In addition they will be fined double the amount of monies accepted and serve a prison sentence no shorter than two years. Furthermore any person, corporation or other entity providing or attempting to impart money to any running or elected politician or government official in any capacity will be imprisoned for a year and a day, and be fined double the amount they attempted to, or did deliver. Bribery is against the law folks. It is time for it to be enforced.

"Number Three. Congressional Term Limits. We have a term limit for the presidency, if two terms are good enough for the top job then two terms will be the limit for Congress as well. Furthermore, there will be no lifetime retirement pay or medical benefits for past members of Congress or the presidency, and that will be retroactive."

Falcon felt hopeful as heads nodded like undulating waves across the room. America had changed. The powerful at the top continued to make money, but failed to understand that by motivating new ideas, occupations and better pay, more revenue would be created. The bottom of the spectrum, ingrained in welfare, food programs, prison, drugs, alcohol and obesity, stayed the course as generations blamed others for their failures, while they expected a monthly check. Self-esteem was in the toilet. The rich were just better at hiding it behind mansions, Lamborghinis, maids, bulimia and colonics.

"Number Four: The American-Mexican border will be secured with a wall, manned by US military 24 hours a day, 365 days a year. All attempts to illegally cross our border will be seen as hostile acts against America and stopped by any means necessary. I shouldn't have to tell you, people, a drug and gang war is occurring on our border right now and is stretching its tentacles throughout the entire United States. Once the drug lords have been vanquished on U.S. soil, and trust me they will be, the Mexican drug gangs will be no match for our Marines, then our country can begin to heal."

The reporters stirred.

"Yes, I said Marines. I don't want to hear about Posse Comitatus. We are under attack, and the security of the United States border is a federal issue. We can no longer close our eyes to a war happening on American soil. Our military will put an end to the border atrocity because they will be given authority to vanquish the opponent. I believe in giving and sharing. I also believe in right and wrong. Evil lurks where good people do nothing. We will have law and order.

"Number Five: The Affordable Care Act or aptly named ObamaCare will be repealed immediately, and all federal government programs will be audited for fraud and abuse. Right now in America we have an obesity crisis yet 50 million people are on food stamps. It is unacceptable to be obese on welfare, and sign up for government medical care for type II diabetes medication, heart medication or Levitra. If you want to eat irresponsibly and abuse your body that is unfortunate, but part of free will. The American taxpayer will not be paying for that decision anymore."

Falcon gestured toward a crew of cameramen placed in key positions around the room. "My staff will be filming everything. I understand some editing on your part must take place in order to fit your timeslot. However if your editing should create a slant, positive or negative, you will not be invited back. I'm volunteering my time and covering all expenses. Ask whatever you like, but present the information accurately."

Having to be patient and remain quiet throughout the

introduction undoubtedly felt foreign to the reporters. When Falcon acknowledged the first person, the woman in the front row popped up and the question came quickly.

"C. Allie, Wolf News. Why are you doing this?"

"Because someone who actually cares about the upcoming generations of Americans has to step up and lead by example." His focus fell on her. "We get the government we deserve."

The next reporter followed the set protocol. "Can you give an example of this leadership from your own life?"

Full of examples of the benefits of helping others, Falcon nodded. A born team player, helping others had always been his primary motivation. He flipped through his memory and landed quickly in the Pacific Northwest. "Let me tell you about my experience in the mountains of Coeur D'Alene, Idaho."

Coeur D'Alene, or the Heart of an Awl, was truly touched by God's hand. Majestic mountains, massive forests and pristine lakes surrounded the lightly populated town. Winter wore the personality of a bad-tempered bear, but the overall landscape provided year-round breathtaking beauty. Twenty-three-year-old Falcon landed amongst this blessing in the middle of winter. His Ford Ranger pickup gripped the sanded highway at sunrise. Man and truck did not fear the weather. After a trek across America, including frigid stops in Minnesota and Maine, they'd made peace with Mother Nature.

 Falcon affectionately patted the truck's console. "Deeter's going to be excited to see us."

The Ranger appeared to accelerate at his words, as both seemed primed for a break from travel. They'd been on the road for almost a year. He seemed to be constantly on the move after leaving Weaverville. Baseball continued to open doors for him, and at 17 his childhood dream of a college baseball scholarship became a reality.

Unlike many athletes, he took advantage of the educational opportunity. Loading up each quarter as many units as the university allowed, he graduated with a bachelor's degree in psychology.

Psychology fascinated Falcon's curious mind. Once introduced to Abraham Maslow's hierarchy of needs (water, food, shelter and belongingness that culminated in self-actualization), it changed his perception of the world forever. He recognized this as a new tool in understanding others and more importantly, himself. As luck would have it Maslow's Theory presented itself to him early in his career during one of his more memorable games. After going five for five with two home runs, his team cruised to a win in their first conference game of the year. Home runs were great, and winning never got old, but the pinnacle of the game was his coach Jim Parnell, who extended his hand afterward.

"Falcon Sane, damn glad you're here son," which was a brief but powerful statement for Falcon. Like Pluto at Trinity High, Coach Parnell opened the door to belongingness, and Falcon gratefully stepped through. Although he'd been successful at many stops along the way, this was the first time he intrinsically felt he belonged since he left Weaverville and the diamond of Trinity High.

After graduation he took off to see the world. He ate chicken piccata in New Mexico, drove through a blizzard in Indiana, enjoyed late-night dancing in a bowling alley in Kentucky, and sipped moonshine in Virginia. He finally reached New Jersey where he boarded a Virgin Atlantic flight to London. His European tour via legs, thumb and a Eurorail pass dazzled him with White Cliffs in Dover, a windy climb of the Eiffel Tower, a spectacular vision of the Champs Elysees at dusk, and an all-night train ride to Spain in the company of two French beauties who didn't speak a word of English. Grateful to be back on U.S. soil, Falcon drove across the greatest nation on the planet, from Newark, N.J. to Coeur D'Alene, Idaho. Falcon's next destination was the home of his brother Deeter,

Deeter's wife and their three-month-old son. He'd missed the Spider Monkey. The Ranger crunched to a stop in a pile of snow out in front of his brother's house.

A typical California boy, Deeter tromped onto his deck wearing shorts, a t-shirt and snow boots. "Look what dropped out of the sky!" Deeter grinned and gave his brother a crushing hug.

Falcon smiled at his kid brother who'd grown up and filled out. He wasn't a Spider Monkey anymore. "You're looking good man, must be the water up here."

Deeter flexed his bicep. "That's right baby, 100 percent all natural – natural light beer, that is."

Falcon laughed and gave his 100-percent-hilarious brother another squeeze. "So where is your little red-headed twerp?"

"Come see for yourself. But I'm warning you, cute as he is, he can raise a ruckus and spew more stuff out than Linda Blair in The Exorcist."

The two men chuckled, embraced again, and went inside.

The next morning Falcon dug through the skimpy want ads and an advertisement for an outdoor wilderness counselor caught his attention. He shivered at the thought, but decided it could be interesting and punched in the phone number.

"Second Chance for Children, how may I direct your call?"

"Hello, I saw your ad in the pa—"

"Please hold."

The sound of a connecting phone clicked.

"Second Chance this is Ross."

"Hi Ross, my name's Falcon Sane. I saw your ad in the paper for—"

"Hang on a sec."

Sitting on hold, Falcon questioned working for a place that rudely cut him off twice.

"Sorry about that," said Ross. "I was on the other line. We're settling into a new office, and the phones are a work in progress. So you saw our ad?"

"Yes sir."

"Good. Tell me about yourself."

"Sure." Falcon backstroked through baseball and his college years. "I planned to enlist in the military, but they were downsizing, so I worked a year with severely emotionally disturbed youths and saved my money."

"And where was all this?"

"In the Sacramento area."

"California — what are you doing up here?"

Falcon welcomed the question as it segued for the travel gap in his employment record. "My brother moved here while I was traveling."

"Where'd you travel?"

Falcon wrapped the phone cord mindlessly around his wrist. "Across America and parts of Europe."

"There are a lot of Californians moving to Idaho," said Ross.

Falcon read an article about that. The writer referred to it as "White Flight," the Caucasian population leaving in droves because of crime and increasing tax burdens, as if black or brown Californians enjoyed those pressures. "I'm aware of that. It sure isn't for the weather."

Ross laughed at the joke. "No that's for damn sure. How long you planning on staying?"

"Permanently, if I find the right situation."

"Do you know what we do here?"

"Only what the ad said, working with troubled youths."

"Yep," said Ross, "that's what we do. Do you have a pen?"

"I'm ready, go ahead."

"We're on Ruby Creek a few clicks from Ruby Ridge." He gave him the address. "Come tomorrow at nine, and we can do a formal interview. Bring a resume if you have one and any documentation."

Falcon finished writing and repeated the information to confirm its accuracy.

"That's it. See you tomorrow."

"Yes sir. I appreciate the opportunity."

The next day Falcon drove from Coeur D'Alene, through Sandpoint to Bonners Ferry and still had not reached his destination. Fortunately Deeter had suggested he should leave early. Turning off the main highway, he continued onto a snow-lined frozen dirt road and headed five miles out into the middle of nowhere toward Ruby Creek. The white drifts and sun shining on untouched mountains took one's breath away, but the bone-crushing temperature grabbed his attention, and Falcon cranked the heater to high.

His interview with Ross lasted 30 minutes, and Falcon sat in a waiting room while his references were checked.

Bob Phillips, a former supervisor and friend of Falcon's, told Ross everything he needed to hear.

"The kid's like a pied piper," said Bob. "He hikes the group for hours and talks with them at night. They feel safe when he's around since he handles his business or theirs if needed. He isn't on a power trip, he really cares, which is why they love him so much. Even the hardcore kids respect him."

Motioning for Falcon to step back into his office, Ross said, "If you're half of what I just heard, this should work out great."

Falcon nodded at the compliment.

Ross asked, "Do you have any questions for me?"

The presidential candidate paused briefly with his story to recall the original question? *Give an example from my life demonstrating concern for upcoming generations through leadership. The reporters appear engaged. I must be on the right track.* He took a sip of water and resumed the tale.

Falcon said, "Questions, yes... Ross, can you tell me about the kids and your procedures?"

"Sure. They're from every part of the country, mostly private placement. We aren't a government program. Sadly, plenty of wealthy people for whatever reason have teenagers at risk. Most kids don't come voluntarily. The parents, I use that term loosely, grant us temporary conservatorship. We do the pick-up, usually at their homes; some come from the street — drunk, high, even having prostituted themselves. It can get a little harried at times. Right now we do have one who is a ward of the court. His tab is being picked up by a municipality."

Falcon nodded.

"They're lost. A good portion already committed crimes mainly misdemeanors. Most were physically and or sexually assaulted, and we have to turn them around during an eight-week crash course in reality. Step one, strip-searched for contraband."

"What if they refuse?"

"Their parents sign their rights over to us. Safety first, they can't be carrying weapons or drugs. If they refuse the procedure, we do it for them."

Ross watched the young man for signs of discomfort, but Falcon remained unemotional.

"The girls must keep their hair in a secured ponytail or cut it. The boy's heads are shaved whether they like it or not. You've dealt with kids like this before. Your job was to keep them from sexually acting out and killing each other, right?"

"Pretty much."

"How'd you handle that?" asked Ross.

"Most trouble begins with a comment or a look. Pay attention to the small things and deal with it before it grows. Mainly they want someone to care. If they know you do, and you'll stop anyone else from hurting them, they learn to trust you."

"What about sexually acting out?"

"It can be harder to spot, but my strategy is to wear them out during the day so they're too tired to do anything but sleep at night. Besides, if adults are doing their jobs, none of the kids should ever be alone with each other."

"True," said Ross. "Are you going to have a problem with a 17-year old punching, screaming or threatening to kill you?"

"If I'm doing my job, that shouldn't happen often, but in a word … no."

The conversation finished with a handshake, commenced again in the morning with a job offer over the phone, and Falcon happily began the next day.

Falcon matched his new supervisor stride for stride on the three-mile trek through the Idaho forest to Base Camp. Snow coated the Sorel sub-zero boots he'd borrowed from Deeter; grateful they shared the same size.

Supervisor Noel Chacha stood six three and moved pretty well for a guy who could afford to drop 70 pounds. A full beard didn't quite cover his double chin, but his overalls almost camouflaged the excess bulk. He had incredibly straight teeth and a smile that hint-ed something dark lay behind it. He spoke rapidly, like a machine gun firing word after word. "I've heard good things about you Sane. Make sure it stays that way."

Falcon's jaw clenched as he attempted to hold his ginger tem-per in check.

"Did you hear what I said?"

"I'm standing right here, what do you think?"

Noel sniggered and continued walking. "I like redheads. They always come with fire."

"You like fire, huh? How much can you handle?"

Noel stopped abruptly.

Falcon squared off, dropped his chin and swiftly brought his hands in front of his face like he was praying. He wasn't. He appeared non-confrontational but with his chin tucked, elbows guarding his ribs, and his hands protecting his face, he could punch repeatedly if need be. *There's always another job. I'm not taking crap from this idiot.*

Noel scrutinized Falcon. In seconds the guy had transformed from tall, relaxed, and smiling to a dangerous animal ready to attack or defend.

Noel grinned, "Very good Sane. That was a little test. Sometimes they send me pussies out here, and it makes my job harder."

He hocked and spat, debasing the pristine snow. "We have eight weeks to get these punks back on the straight and narrow. They keep sending harder kids and softer counselors. I'm the man that keeps all of you in line. You'll do just fine." He extended his gloved hand to Falcon.

Falcon paused, shook his hand, and made a mental note to keep an eye on this guy. They continued in silence and arrived at Base Camp in good time.

Dense blue spruce speckled with untouched snow swallowed up the camp. Two skyward-bound canvas teepees that appeared to brush the clouds were bolted to wooden decks to provide shelter for the children. In front of the decks a large hole in the ground consumed a constant flow of firewood. The fire pit seemed almost negligible to Falcon as the surrounding icy air swallowed the heat from the wood as soon as it attempted to escape. The outhouse or potty sat in the shadows, and the acrid odors pierced the freezing cold air and kept visits to a minimum. The mess hall consisted of a large 50-by-50-foot redwood platform with canvas walls designed to roll up or down and latch to the flooring. Inside the mess hall, eight wooden picnic benches surrounded an enormous woodstove, which sat in the middle of the room. A makeshift kitchen existed but was only used to cook oatmeal in the mornings. The other meals were prepared outside the camp, miles away in the office building where Falcon had interviewed. As if fetching royalty, handpicked residents transported the meals and used a two-man cart balanced upon their shoulders. The comparison appeared appropriate to Falcon, since food was that important in this desolate, challenging wilderness. Across from the mess hall stood a small cabin for the counselors primarily used to store personal gear. The structures encircled a small open space known as the perimeter that completed the camp.

In the perimeter, Falcon scrutinized three pitiful, forlorn teenagers crouched close to the ground. Their genders were impossible to make out. White powder concealed their parkas and made them appear to be obscure snow goblins, as they teetered on various size cut logs referred to as "stumps". Stumps were saved for the punks, Noel informed him, who didn't want to get with the program. The rest of the punks, as Falcon's new supervisor labeled them, huddled in two groups according to gender. As they waited their turns outside the potty, several kids held their breath while wisps of body heat escaped and hovered in clouds above them. This sight led Falcon to determine it might be well under 10 degrees. Not that he needed an example. He was freezing. His thermals and 501 jeans did their best, but after an hour it didn't matter. He was numb from head to toe. *Thank goodness for Deeter's Sorel's, otherwise the next fourteen hours might have cost me a few toes.* But even his feet couldn't be called warm by any stretch of the imagination.

Noel said, "Listen up! This is our new counselor. His name is Falcon and if you know anything about the actual bird you know it is a hunter. I'm telling you right now, any of you punks challenge the new guy, he'll eat you for lunch with my permission!"

While Noel continued on a tirade, a fit, clean-shaven counselor with a ruddy complexion approached the new guy.

"Hi," he extended his arm. "I'm Jon. Try to ignore Noel. It's just his way."

Falcon shook Jon's hand. "Maybe it's time for a change."

Jon's face brightened under a wide grin. "I've dreamed of that moment." A nice guy, Jon Marker's soft-spoken way and slowness to anger left him a target. He was intimidated by Noel, as it turned out were most of the staff and kids. His job had become a love-hate relationship; he loved working with the kids, hated working with Noel. Originally from Arizona, Jon had trekked to northern Idaho with his girlfriend after graduating college with an outdoor education degree. As the day progressed, Falcon and Jon swapped stories.

Jon said, "Yeah my uncle gave me an old Caddy. On my first day here I drove up the mountain spewing exhaust and backfiring. I jerked into the gravel parking lot and ran right over Noel's lunch."

Envisioning that sight, Falcon laughed, "What? What did he say?"

"After I said I was sorry, he called me a tourist, which is kind of bizarre considering he's from New York. But I was still in my car," Jon grinned, "so I rolled over it again!"

Falcon laughed hard.

"Accidentally of course," finished Jon.

"Of course!"

That clinched Jon and Falcon's friendship, and as luck would have it their shifts were the same – 14-hours long, three days on and four off. With plenty of work at Base Camp, physical and emotional, Falcon dove into his job with everything he had — daily (PT) physical training, hauling and sawing logs, and keeping guard as kids endlessly sat on stumps. Most kids exhausted quickly and broke in a couple of days. Once the crying started, the healing process could begin. Falcon understood the theory behind tough love and even agreed with most of it. Love without discipline provided no love at all. It enabled negative behavior.

As the first year went by Falcon and Noel came to a mutual understanding; they didn't like each other and that wasn't going to change. Falcon could not respect a man who screamed, ridiculed and literally spit on kids. In Falcon's mind Noel was probably not too different from the parents who spawned these kids. To make matters worse, the supervisor appeared to enjoy his techniques. After 18 months of working at Base Camp, things grew dramatically worse. Counselors ignored rules, and the overall attitude of the place became dreary.

One summer morning as they rode in Jon's Caddy, Falcon and Jon rolled into the parking lot. Falcon noticed Noel and Ross talking. He loaded his backpack and headed for camp.

Jon started toward the office to complete a report.

Ross smiled, "Good morning Falcon."

"Good morning," he said and passed the two men.

Noel asked his boss, "Are we done here?"

Ross nodded.

"Good. I'll walk out with Falcon."

Falcon didn't acknowledge him. They had a silent agreement to maintain a distance, which he had no desire to break. He continued his hike.

Noel called, "Hey wait up!"

Falcon slowed his pace and adjusted his pack just in case he'd need to dump it quickly.

Huffing slightly Noel said, "Thanks. We got a new kid coming in. Not really a kid, he's almost 18, about your size, six feet and maybe 190, supposed to be pretty tough. The report says he likes to fight. Mostly his dad, some teachers, and even knocked a guy out in a street brawl."

Falcon listened as they continued through the forest.

"He'll be here soon. You, me, Fred, and the two guys bringing him in will meet at the office to check him in." Noel's eyes lit up. "I think it's going to be a battle. Afterward we'll march him to camp, and I'm gonna put him on the smallest stump I can find. At camp he's all yours." Noel smirked. "You two should be perfect for each other."

"Why's that?"

"Because you think you're pretty tough too."

Falcon laughed at the comment, "I know I don't get my rocks off spitting on people."

"You're just an asshole, aren't you?"

Falcon spun and flipped his backpack a few feet away to avoid becoming entangled in it.

Noel stepped back and glared.

"It's just you and me out here you fat prick. Go ahead and spit in my face and you'll find out how tough I am."

"You could get fired for this," said Noel.

"Like I care. Then you, me and Ross can have a little sit down and discuss your management skills. But don't change the subject pussy. You opened the door by calling me an asshole. This ain't my party you fat prick, it's yours, and I guarantee you'll cry if I want you to."

Noel cautiously regarded the snarling beast in front of him. He had a decision to make. Change tactics or fight.

"Okay good," he forced a smile. "You're ready for war. Just save that heat for the kid, he's gonna be a battle." He extended his hand.

"Are you kidding me?" Falcon dismissed Noel with a wave. "Get away from me. You're either stupid or crazy."

Noel laughed as his eyes danced. "Maybe some of both."

The two men took visual measure of each other, as the other animals in the forest remained motionless, curious to see the outcome.

"The kid's name is Flint." Noel crunched forward in the snow again as if nothing had happened.

Falcon grabbed his backpack and stayed two paces behind.

Noel blathered on over his shoulder. "If you can't handle him let me know, but once he's at Base Camp he's your responsibility. And keep him on the stump until I say so."

"Sounds like you're in charge of him then."

Noel spun around. "That's right! I'm in charge of everything out here, including you."

Falcon snorted, "That'll be the day."

They finally arrived at Base Camp, and Noel couldn't help but drive his point home. "You'll see that I run this show. I'm not crazy enough to take on a wild animal like you in the middle of nowhere that might cost me my job, but as long as you work here I'm your boss, like it or not. Be ready for this kid."

Falcon ignored the statement completely and secured his belongings in the counselors' cabin. His adrenaline still speeding, he took a drink of water, as he tried to calm down. *Why does it have to be like this? Bullies in school, steroid freaks in college; every job I've had so far had a jerk in charge of something. Maybe it's me. Maybe I'm the problem. How much easier would it be if I ignored the abuse and bullying like most people do? Just go with the flow?* Instinctively he knew he couldn't. It wasn't who he was. As he was flushing those thoughts out, the door to the cabin popped open.

Noel leaned inside the room as he kept his feet outside. "He's here." He grinned, "Shooow time."

Falcon zipped up his bag and stuffed a Snickers bar into his back pocket. It already felt like a long day.

Flint McCracken glared at the five men in front of him. Only 12 hours ago, in the middle of the night, his lying asshole father had said the two men in his bedroom were taking him to a summer camp to hike, swim, kayak and enjoy the serenity of the mountains. The mountain part appeared true, but he hadn't seen any lakes yet.

Besides I can still see snow in the mountains. It's freaking summer… *what kind of place still has snow in the summer?* One red-eye flight and hours of driving did not leave him feeling serene. *My dad is such a prick!* Flint knew his life was out of control, and he probably needed help, but he doubted having his head shaved and being strip-searched would achieve that goal.

Standing on the side of the room that went five men deep, Noel challenged the scared teenager. "Are we gonna have a problem, punk?"

Falcon observed the kid mentally flip through his options only to realize he had none. His jet-black hair grazed his shoulders and gave him a slight bad-boy look, and he was big! But he didn't appear stupid.

"Who you calling a punk you fat prick!"

Falcon's expression stayed frozen but inside he smiled. *Well, he's not a coward and doesn't like being called a punk.*

Noel let out a huge fake belly laugh. "Looks like it's gonna be the hard way."

Falcon intervened, "Look buddy, this is going to happen, one way or another. You look like a smart kid. Use your head."

Noel said, "Looks like a punk to me."

Falcon straight-armed Flint to stop, turned and glared Noel down.

Noel shrugged and backed off.

What appeared to be good cop bad cop was really good guy… total dick.

Falcon said, "Sit on the stool, and we'll get this over with."

Flint hesitated. "Can I do it myself?"

Normally they allowed kids to buzz their own heads, but Falcon wasn't sure about this one.

Noel said, "Go ahead, let Nancy shave her own head. But swear to God punk, you're getting slammed to the floor if you do anything

I don't like."

The men surrounded Flint as he sat on the stool while his next-to-last speck of individuality fell to the floor.

Falcon held the year-round required camp attire under his arm: wool pants, a cotton t-shirt, wool cap, boots, long johns, wool socks and an REI parka. Even though it was summer, the nights still got cold, besides the clothes weren't meant for comfort.

"Take off your clothes."

Flint couldn't believe his ears.

"Right here?"

Noel motioned for Fred and Falcon to take him behind the curtain. "Make sure you check him for weapons and drugs too."

Flint undressed quickly, and Fred kicked his clothes out under the curtain.

"Raise your arms, turn around, squat and cough," Falcon said. "Stand back up. Look at me. Do you have anything on you?"

"No."

Flint stood humiliated and naked in front of the two men; but unwilling to give them the satisfaction of knowing that, he puffed up his chest and refused to cover his genitals.

Falcon finished, "Open your mouth and stick out your tongue. Okay, here are your new clothes. Hurry up and put 'em on, we got a hike ahead of us."

Flint dressed in record time, and the three of them stepped out into the room.

"Sleeping bag, water bottle, and gloves." Noel dropped them on the floor. "Pick 'em up and let's go."

Flint put on the gloves and grabbed the rest. As they stepped from the building his two original escorts disappeared. *Three on one now – there is no way the two porky fuckers are catching me if I run.* He glanced at the lean red-headed dude who'd been decent. *It's like walking with two fat bears and a mountain lion.*

Falcon led the way, and Flint followed with Noel and Fred directly behind him. As they headed into the forest the gravel road disappeared.

Flint appeared calm but his heart raced like a deer being hunted. He watched for a chance to escape as the forest multiplied and the thin path twisted and turned around rocks and fallen trees. The mountain lion in front of Flint moved deftly through the woods as the two bears behind him plodded along. He watched the red-headed guy leap nimbly over a fallen tree. *That's the spot.* Arriving he jumped it too, spun and threw the sleeping bag and water bottle at the two men behind him. He backtracked over the fallen tree as the forest opened in front of him. Flint sprinted down the trail and almost screamed in delight at his freedom.

When Falcon heard the scuffle, he turned and witnessed the new kid throw his gear and hit Noel in the face with the water bottle. Using this as a diversion, he split the men and sailed past like a running back through two linebackers. Within seconds he watched the kid fly down the path, and he pulled away.

Noel and Fred regained their balance and took off to give chase.

Falcon, many yards behind, sprinted to catch up. Leaping over the fallen tree, he pulled behind the two men who were gamely plugging along, but wholeheartedly left in Flint's dust. The deer path wasn't wide enough for three, so Falcon swung into the brush and blew past Fred and Noel. Back onto the path Falcon instantly gained ground on Flint.

Flint didn't hear anything and guessed he'd left them all behind. Beginning to tire, he took a quick peek to see if anyone was following. "Ugh!"

The red-headed mountain lion plastered him against the ground. Falcon commanded, "Stay down or it's going to get ugly."

Flint obeyed.

As they sucked in air, Noel and Fred caught up.

"Good catch," Noel wheezed.

Falcon ignored him and pulled Flint to his feet. "You're pretty quick."

Still breathing hard, Flint remained silent. *Don't try and buddy up to me; I'm done talking to you assholes.*

With a man on each arm, Noel made Flint gather his things.

Falcon followed behind and didn't give the kid a second chance to run.

"You're going to be on a stump for a month!" Noel blurted out, embarrassed that the teenager had gotten the best of him.

Flint didn't answer. *On a stump for a month? Whatever... good luck you fat prick. You don't own me.*

The three men and Flint reached camp without any further drama. Ross, the camp supervisor, stood on the platform between the teepees and observed their arrival. *The kid doesn't appear to be fighting, but Noel's yanking him around mighty hard.*

Noel yelled to a staff member, "Grab a small stump."

A large log landed inside the perimeter of Base Camp.

"Too big! I want the smallest you've got."

Falcon watched as a piece of wood the size of a rolled-up newspaper tumbled toward Noel, who kicked it at Flint. "There's your new best friend! Have a seat," he laughed at his own joke.

Flint remained motionless.

"I said sit down!" The decimal level of Noel's voice literally rocked the boy back on his heels.

The teenager attempted to sit on the tiny cut limb as he balanced on one butt cheek, but the wood slipped, and he fell to the ground.

Noel cackled, and then spoke so only Flint could hear him, "Get used to it punk. Welcome to hell." Then he shouted, "Get back on that stump boy!"

Ross watched the kid waver like a newborn fawn as he tried to maneuver on the stump, then turned his gaze to Falcon. Falcon was poised with his hands pressed together at chin level, elbows tucked. He looked to be in prayer except for the hatred in his eyes focused on Noel.

Noel leaned in inches from Flint. Sucking in his cheeks, he filled his mouth with saliva, flashed his perfect teeth, and fired, "Should've stayed in Seattle sucker!"

With each deliberate "S" Flint's face became drenched in spit, never mind the fact he'd never been to Seattle.

The boy flinched repeatedly, turned his head to the side, and wiped the back of his hand across his face in a futile effort to remove the slime.

Noel smirked and shouted to Falcon, "He's all yours," and pranced over to Ross.

Falcon's chest tightened as he studied the bowed, poorly shaved head in front of him. Walking to one of the water receptacles Falcon filled a Dixie cup with water and tore off a paper towel. He approached the boy cautiously and stopped three feet away, not concerned with being attacked, just didn't want to frighten the child.

Flint heard a noise and looked up.

Falcon offered the water and towel.

The boy cleaned his face, drank, and then stared at Falcon through eyes of complete unadulterated humiliation.

Falcon recognized the emotion immediately.

Like staring into a mirror, he was looking at … Late Bird.

Noel sauntered by Flint. "I'll be back tomorrow pretty boy." He pursed his lips and made a kissing sound. "Then it's just you and me." He motioned Falcon to follow him.

"You're off the next three days starting tomorrow, so you only have him tonight. Make his life a living hell." He pronounced the word "hell" like a raging Santa Ana wind.

Falcon ground his teeth. *How about I break your fucking jaw?* "I know what my job is."

Noel knew he should be careful with Ross standing by, but he couldn't help himself. "Did you hear what I said? A living hell! You'd better be spittin' on that piece of shit all night."

Falcon shook his head. "Not gonna happen."

"What do you mean?"

"I mean I won't do it. I won't spit on this kid or any kid for that matter."

Noel puffed his chest and postured over the smaller man. "I should've kicked your ass the first time we met."

Falcon's steel blue eyes flashed as he met Noel's challenge. "Go for it."

Time froze, as did the two men.

Noel huffed and stepped back to put some distance between them. He knew a better way to get to Falcon. "If you don't come down on him tonight, I'll crush him the next three days and it'll be all your fault, because you wouldn't do your job. If I lose control or something bad should happen to your new buddy." He hocked and spit, "I guess it'll be on your head." As he turned toward the boy he said, "See you tomorrow Flinty." He winked twice and left Base Camp.

Falcon waited for Noel to leave, then approached his boss.

Surrounded by a group of kids who shared their experiences with marijuana and alcohol, Ross caught one glimpse of Falcon, stepped out of the circle, and signaled the young man to join him by the teepees. "What's up?"

Falcon exhaled heavily. He liked Ross for the most part. Pleasant enough, he communicated well, and his background in philosophy added a different slant to their occasional discussions. But to allow Noel on staff was ludicrous and asinine. "You know about Noel spitting on the kids, right?"

Ross cringed mentally, but had no intention of discussing the issue. "Everyone comes with a different skill set, Falcon."

"Spitting on people is not a skill set, Ross."

"You know what I'm saying."

"I do, and it's bullshit."

"We all have opinions."

"Opinions! Look at that kid." He pointed to Flint who teetered on the stick with his face buried in his hands. "Does it look like we're helping him?"

"Again, we all have opinions and technique—"

"That's crap, and you know it!"

Ross pulled up to his full height. "Enough. You may not agree, but you do have to follow orders. And you need to get your temper in check young man."

Falcon bit the insides of his cheeks. *Stay calm. Violence won't fix this*. As he presented a wide, disarming smile, he nodded and coolly strolled away.

Ross' heart rate returned to normal as the distance between the two men grew. *Noel may have unconventional methods; his childhood in foster homes and teen years on the street give him an edge Falcon could never understand or relate to. Noel can be ... raw at times, but he gets results. If a cocky college kid thinks I'm willing to rock the boat to make my cushy job harder or jeopardize a fat paycheck, he'd better think again. Falcon's problem is he cares too much. Kids today need to learn respect for their elders.*

Noel tramped toward his truck and could care less whether Falcon respected him or not. He wanted Falcon and all the other counselors to fear him. Over the past year and a half he'd noticed the way many of the counselors, especially the ones close to Falcon, looked at him. Before Falcon showed up, he'd lorded over the camp but now with that punk who undercut him at every turn he'd lost the fear factor needed to run things. *All these namby-pamby whiny bitches know nothing about life. I learned about life – the hard way.* As he reached the parking lot the sun shone high in the sky, but Noel noticed none of its beauty nor the brilliance of the mountains. He tossed his stuff in the back of his worn-out Chevy and looked around for Falcon's truck. Not seeing it, he put two and two together and figured he'd ridden in with Jon. He grabbed a piece of paper and a pen out of his bag, composed a special note for Falcon, and tucked it under Jon's windshield wiper. Smirking, he loaded up and drove away. *Let's see how that little bitch likes that.*

Falcon and Jon walked to the parking lot – their three-day shift completed that evening. Arriving at Jon's Caddy, they found a paper clamped under the wiper blade. Falcon freed it from the windshield, opened it, and read it to himself.

Jon watched as his friend's face turned deep purple with rage.

Falcon folded it in half and stared at the sky.

Jon asked quietly, "Do you mind if I take a look?"

Continuing to scan the sky, Falcon's arm shot out.

Jon took the note and read it aloud: "Falcon, I doubt you did what I told you to do. Remember, you work for me. I'm your boss! Because of your laziness I'm going to have to make that punk's life hell. Whatever happens now is all your fault. I hope your next four days off suck, just like you."

Falcon climbed into his friend's Caddy, and he sat in silence as they traveled toward Jon's house.

Jon glanced at his friend from time to time. He could practically hear the inner ticking of the time bomb inside Falcon ready to erupt.

Falcon couldn't erase the picture of Flint who had wobbled in pain on his stump, and while his heart ached for the kid his temper boiled about the note. He had pressed the boy hard, but he'd only had him for the day before the night guard arrived and all the kids climbed into their sleeping bags inside the teepees. Years of abuse weren't going to go away in one day. Tomorrow Noel would return and hammer the kid.

"This is bullshit!" Falcon blurted to no one in particular.

"Yeah Noel's a prick, but he's here to stay."

"The whole thing is crazy. I'm all for making kids toe the line and be respectful but he's an idiot. He likes spitting on them and calling them names. How is that helpful? It's not. Hell the moron even picks on the staff."

"Not you." Jon turned on the heater.

"That's because I stand up to him Jon, but he still pisses me off."

"Not much we can do but quit."

"Why not? This isn't Russia. We have laws here. That guy's a piece of crap, and the way the kids are being treated has gotten out of control! How the hell did this place even get started?"

Jon shrugged. "Maybe it was God's idea; He works in mysterious ways you know."

"God?" Falcon made a fist and punched his bag.

Startled, Jon jumped.

Falcon hammered on, "Pahleeese. What kind of God allows shitty parents to abuse their kids, let's them off the hook because they slam down a couple of G's only to send them away so another asshole can pick up where they left off? What kind of God is that?"

Falcon pounded the dash with both fists. "Where are you God? How the hell can you allow it?"

Jon's eyes widened, and he remained focused on the road as he hoped his buddy might calm down.

Falcon shook his head. "Almighty my ass! Kids burned, beaten, sold for crack by prostitute mothers, and raped every day by fucking predators. I'm sick of this bullshit. If we're supposed to give you the glory God then you get the fucking blame too! All mighty? Yeah right. I'm probably better off without you," Falcon said sarcastically.

"Hey it's okay," said Jon. "I didn't mean anything by it."

Uncommon as it was for Falcon to be oblivious, he completely missed his friend's discomfort and went after God again. "I've seen enough. Maybe you should come get me right now." He rolled down his window and shouted toward the sky, "I dare you. I fucking dare you! If this is the best world you've got, Big Fella, I'm done with it. Come get me right now!"

Jon clenched the steering wheel and looked up through the windshield nervously. He sighed and tried to relax his shoulders when a thought crossed his mind. "Falcon, you don't think God could mistake the two of us right now, do you? I mean we're about the same height, and well I'm pretty good looking, and you are sitting right beside me."

Jon's intentional humor brought Falcon back to reality and his fatigue replaced rage. "Nah, I think you're good … well, maybe not. Your vanity might trump my righteous indignation." He chuckled then turned both palms up and raised his hands in a gesture as if to say who knows. "He could take you and leave me. That would be classic!"

"That's not funny!" Jon laughed nervously.

Gradually returning to Earth Falcon smiled at his friend. "I've never done that before."

"Done what?" asked Jon.

"Challenged God. I've pleaded, thanked Him, asked questions, but never flatly called Him out before." He thought a minute, "Have you?"

Jon almost levitated in the driver's seat. "Are you freaking crazy? I'm not going after God. I can't even handle Noel!"

They drove in silence as Falcon entertained the consequences of handling Noel. *What's the worst that could happen? I get fired, beat up?* His mind rolled through the possibilities, and he realized he didn't care about the outcome. Rules and laws were fast becoming a joke in America. Rich and poor alike abused their kids and passed the responsibility off. Society looked the other way. Politicians didn't care. Children couldn't vote. The breakdown of America was in plain sight, and Falcon hated the view. *Lord, help me understand; I'm not asking for myself. I just can't watch this bullshit anymore. Give me a sign or get me the fuck out of here.*

The car stopped at Jon's condo. Falcon stepped out into the cloudy night and from force of habit perused the area. He narrowed his eyes, and stared hard at the rooftop of a farmhouse in the distance. Blood drained from his face, and he staggered slightly.

Jon said, "What's wrong, you all right?"

Falcon formed his lips to respond, but no sound escaped. He tried again. "Do…" His voice was low and gravelly. He cleared his throat then whispered, "Do you see that?"

Jon followed Falcon's gaze. "What? I don't see anything."

Falcon didn't blink as he continued to stare. "Come here."

Jon did.

"Stand right behind me." Falcon lifted his arm and pointed. "Look down my arm like a scope."

Jon crouched behind his friend. He could see Falcon's arm trembling. "I don't see anything."

"Are you looking down my arm?"

"Yes."

"Okay, track my finger as I point." Falcon moved his arm about a foot.

"I don't…whoa! What the hell is that?"

"You tell me. What do you see?"

"I don't know, some kind of smiling … no, leering … creepy face?"

"Anything else?"

"Yeah, a bright, glowing green light around it."

Falcon dropped his arm. "I'm going over there. Maybe it's some kind of old Halloween thing. Stay here. I want a witness in case something happens."

"Oh that's a great plan." Jon didn't think much of Falcon's idea, but he would watch his friend's back from a distance.

Falcon started toward the farmhouse, through the gravel parking lot, and jumped a rotting fence. The face grew with intensity, and Falcon wanted nothing more than to turn and run. His heart banged against his ribs as his adrenaline started to work on overdrive, but he ignored his body's signals, swallowed the taste of fear, and pushed onward. The image seemed to gain energy with each step, and it pulled him closer almost against his will. Coal-black eyes flashed, somehow piercing the darkness as the pulsating glow encompassing the face kept perfect rhythm with the beat of Falcon's heart. The image bore an evil smile, that which might have descended from the bloodline of hell. One hundred feet, 50 feet, and when Falcon stood just 10 paces away, the blinding apparition was clear. Mesmerized and unable to move, Falcon knew he'd seen it before. It was the portrait of his dead uncle, Chip, which Rachel had shown him on his last visit home. Chip's lifestyle had caught up with him, and he'd passed away from complications of A.I.D.S a few years ago. Rachel's younger brother had painted it as a tribute, not realizing he had captured a very dark side. Rachel felt it possessed the essence of Dorian Grey, the fictional character who traded his soul for youth, and she refused to hang it on her wall. The presence radiated a low hum that drew Falcon closer to an answer he wasn't sure he was ready for. He held his breath as the menacing power captured his mind and baited him to challenge again as if saying, *"Take a good look son. This is life ... without God."*

It was easy to rant, but what if God decided to rant back? "Get a grip," he muttered as he remembered how much his uncle loved him. *God would never use Chip to hurt me, would he?*

Only 10 feet separated Falcon from the hideous likeness, and then as if someone flipped a switch the face faded into the darkness. Falcon blinked, and then studied the remnants left behind. Three different tree limbs illuminated by an old street lamp 20 feet away could possibly explain the shape of the face. And by stretching his imagination he rationalized the branches into a smirk. But the farm-house was still hundreds of yards off, and hard as he tried he could not logically explain what he had witnessed, particularly the eyes and the neon-green throbbing glow. Nothing pulsated now, and the yellow street lamp did not possess a hint of green.

A warm breeze passed over and left Falcon quiet and in peace … and then it was gone. "I'm sorry Father," he whispered. "It won't happen again."

Relieved, Jon sighed as his friend made it back, and they both took one last look in the direction of the farmhouse.

"I don't see it anymore do you?" Jon asked.

Falcon searched the sky and shook his head. "I think it's gone."

"What was it?"

"A message."

"From who? About what?"

How could Falcon explain his dead uncle's portrait and God's warning? For the first time in his life he didn't have the words. He shoved his hands into his pockets and stared into the night. "Like you said brother, God works in mysterious ways."

2

The reporters in the room sat in stunned silence. Falcon turned to the next one in the row and nodded.

The female reporter waited, and then almost in a whisper asked, "So you think God was sending you a message?" Her voice cracked like a 12-year-old boy on the word "message".

Falcon thought about the question; it was a fair one. If you weren't there it was difficult to believe. He answered it like he did everything else – honestly. "I'm not speaking for God. I'm just telling you what I said and what I saw."

The next reporter in line followed up. "So what did you do after this?"

Falcon laughed, "I stopped challenging the Big Fella upstairs and went back to work!"

The reporters laughed nervously and tried to wrap their arms around what they'd just heard. *Entertaining, and a little freaky if true, but what is his point?*

Falcon stood at the podium and waited for the next question. Not done with his story he hoped this little break would elicit the question he wanted to talk about right now. *Religion.* He didn't wait long.

"So then are you a Christian?" asked a male reporter in the back. *There we go.*

"No sir I am not. I'm not Christian or Catholic, Muslim, Jewish, Mormon, or an atheist. I'm a human being, as I believe God intended."

Many heads in the room began to nod, no doubt refreshed to not get bogged down in the religion debate.

Falcon continued, "I am a firm believer in the separation of church and state. I do not equate God as being for or against any religion. As a wonderful World War II veteran and teacher of mine told me many years ago, God gives us all free will at birth. What we do with it is up to us. Next question please."

Susan Matsumoto, a reporter from NBS was next. "I'm sure I'm not alone with this question. Can you explain a little more about sitting on a stump?"

Falcon felt his heart stir as he remembered Flint McCracken.

"A stump is a piece of wood. Living in that type of environment required cutting and stacking firewood. I don't know who initiated the idea of placing kids in the perimeter, perched like birds on the small rounds, but it served as a punishment. The smaller the stump the longer it felt, minutes like hours and hours like weeks. Fortunately for Flint it was July, but it regularly dropped into the forties at night and even snowed up there that year on the Fourth of July. I returned four days later early at 6:30 in the morning and saw the boy still on a stump. I asked one of the night staff why so early?"

The presidential candidate slipped back into the past.

The guard shrugged. "Noel's orders before he left last night."

Falcon looked at Flint and noticed his sleeping bag two feet away on the ground. Certain he knew the answer to his next question Falcon gritted his teeth. "Why's his bag out there with him?"

"Because he slept there too."

Falcon dropped his head and inhaled deeply. "Still not talking?"

"Not a word since he arrived at Base Camp." Perplexed, the guard asked, "Why are you nodding?"

"Because he's showing strength. Most kids who try that tactic start blabbing in the first hour. His head's got to be swimming right now. You try not talking for one day, let alone four."

A second night guard broke in, "His wife would love that."

Falcon tried to enjoy the brief humor then took a closer look at the stump Flint currently resided on. It appeared about four inches in diameter, as thick as a rolled-up newspaper, and maybe twice as tall. *The poor kid's been sitting on a two-foot Seven Eleven Slurpee cup. Freaking Noel!*

Exhausted and glum, Flint's whole body ached but nothing compared to the agony he suffered in his butt. The stump wasn't big enough for both cheeks so he shifted back and forth from one to the other. When he'd used his hands for balance, Noel threatened to slam him to the ground if he did it again. After his third day on the stump, taking Noel on didn't feel that risky. That hadn't gone well.

One of the counselors took Falcon aside to fill him in on what had been going down with the kid.

"Flint tried to appear bored when Noel and four other men closed in on him," began the night counselor. "'I'm the law here so get used to it,' Noel had said. Then saving up the spit in his mouth, he got face to face with the boy, and stressing the P barked, 'You're nothing but a wannabe punk,' baptizing Flint in spit." The group of men knotted tighter. "'That's right pretty boy,' continued Noel, 'I'm in your face and there's nothing you can do about it pussy.' When Noel leaned on the P for the third time the kid lost it. He jumped on Noel and tried to claw his eyes out. Sounds, not words, more like a screaming animal came out of the kid. It was eerie. Then Noel started screaming, 'Get this fucker off me.' So we all jumped the kid."

Falcon could picture the poor abused young man buried under a thousand pounds of human flesh.

The night watch added, "The kid ended up with bruises on his arms and legs, a cut below his nose, and a black eye."

Falcon held up his hand, "That's enough."

He didn't want to hear anymore. He was too familiar with No-el's M.O. *That prick deserves more than a good ass-kicking just for leaving that kid out all night. I don't see the justice here God.*

When Flint saw the red-headed mountain lion walk into camp and talk to the overnight guards his plan to run evaporated. *Even at full strength I can't outrun that guy.* He heaved a heavy sigh and struggled to find a less painful position on the stump.

Falcon approached the boy. "Get back in your bag."

Flint rolled his eyes, but said nothing.

"Now."

The boy studied Falcon. *Is it a trick? He's not being friendly, but he's not being a dick either. Besides he didn't come over with a crowd like that fat fucker did. It might be better to do what he says. For now.* He painfully straightened to his feet.

"Okay man," Flint mumbled. "Whatever."

Falcon sprung to life, his voice low and threatening, "Stop right there and look at me young man!"

Flint realized his mistake and froze.

Falcon had closed the space between them in a single stride and in a quiet, hair-raising tone said, "I am not your man, this isn't what-ever, and you better get that hard look off your face. We both know you can't handle me. You're here because you need help. I'm here to provide it. Get it? Got it? Good. GET IN THE BAG!"

Flint was startled, shot into the bag and lay still. *Geez must be some kind of head trip. These guys are idiots. They're never gonna break me.*

Falcon's eyes shined. The kid had spoken. *It shouldn't be too much longer now.* "I'm putting my gear away, Flint. You'll be out of my sight for a few minutes. I'm telling you, do not move an inch."

Falcon strolled off. It was a test. For Flint to break down he needed to experience trust. His file was too typical: abusive father, enabling mother, and zero positive discipline. When guilt got the best of them they offered only material things, not hugs, trust or love. Falcon watched from behind a tree.

The kid lay still.

It was important to show Flint, he could be trusted. The tougher they were the more they wanted trust. The tougher they were the more they needed a hug. *Noel's approach is idiotic. The faster we break 'em the faster we make 'em. That fool thinks he's the reason every kid breaks. Au contraire you fat prick, that approach slows the process. Spitting on and degrading these poor kids. They've suffered enough of that already. It's why they're here in the first place asshole!* Falcon didn't coddle the kids, and when they got physically out of control, he took them to the ground to keep everyone safe; including themselves. *No, Noel's way only makes the process harder and more painful – just another bully hungry for power.*

"Hey!" Noel hollered at the guards as he approached camp. "What's this piece of crap doing in his bag? I told you guys before I left to—"

Falcon's head jerked around. *What the hell is he doing here? It's supposed to be one of his days off.*

"Don't yell at them!" Falcon bound from behind the tree. "I told him to get in the bag! You said he's mine while I'm here." He stopped just inches from Noel. "Well, I'm right here."

Caught off guard, Noel flinched and jerked back. *I'd like to beat your fucking head in. I should've done it in the woods!* He knew if he opened that door he better be able to close it. That lingering doubt made him even madder.

Flint scarcely shifted his bag and peeked at the bear and the lion.

The two combatants staked their grounds as the entire camp watched mesmerized.

One of the night guards whispered to his buddy, "I hope that kid beats his ass."

"Me too; Noel's such a dick. I'd pay to see that. You think Falcon can take him?"

"I don't know," answered the counselor, "But he doesn't look scared that's for sure."

Flint edged his bag open a sliver more to get a better view. He couldn't hear the argument, but it couldn't be good.

Noel lowered his voice. "What the hell are you doing? You're undermining me in front of the kids and staff."

"No I'm not. I'm following orders. You said he was mine when I'm here."

"Do you know how hard it's going to be to get that punk to crack now?"

Falcon said, "I know spitting in his face isn't working."

Noel's anger got the best of him, and he leaned forward.

Falcon closed the gap and nodded, "Go for it."

"Good morning gentlemen," came a voice from thin air. Ross approached the two men in conflict. "Do we have a problem here?"

Noel rocked backward and flashed his straight teeth. "No sir boss, no problem."

Falcon stayed his course, "We're about to."

"Falcon," Ross said. "Would you give me a minute? Noel, meet me back at my office. I'll be along shortly."

Noel sneered at his heated opponent, turned and grinned at Ross. "Sure boss whatever you say."

Flint studied the new scenario and wondered how the outcome might affect him.

The night guards turned back toward the teepees to focus on the rest of the kids still sleeping.

"What's the problem?" Ross asked as the two men put some distance away from Flint.

Still feeling hot, Falcon repeated, "Problem?"

Ross regarded Falcon, "I can't have staff fighting out here."

Falcon asked sarcastically, "Okay, where would you like it?"

Ross shook his head and almost laughed. "You really do lock onto every word don't you?"

Falcon exhaled a deep sigh, "Actually, I pay more attention to actions. People say all kinds of things. Words they don't mean or even think twice about, for example." Falcon waved his hand toward the camp. "Probably each of these kids has heard I love you from their parents, more times than I can count. Yet here they are with emotional, physical and sexual trauma. Now they're acting out, and in trouble, but where are the parents? They wash their hands of them, give up, or ship them off. All words, no action. It's a joke."

Ross didn't disagree. Clearly his generation set Falcon's up for failure. *The only way to turn things around is for young people like Falcon to take charge, which is virtually impossible.* Ross' generation dwarfed Falcon's. *Things will get worse before they get better. What did that singer say? 'That's just the way it is ... some things will never change.'* Still he had a job to do. "Back to business Falcon, you've met Flint, right?"

"Briefly."

"We're in a tight situation here."

"How's that?" asked Falcon.

"He's going to be 18 shortly. We need to get through to him soon. Otherwise he'll just walk right out of here."

Falcon questioned, "What about his parents?"

"They're only coming back if we've 'fixed' him. Their words not mine. Otherwise I've got a bus ticket and $200 on his 18th birthday in about five weeks.

"Happy birthday." Falcon shook his head, "That's rough."

"Yes it is. We need to get through to him. This is his fifth day here, and we're getting nowhere. I'm going to keep you and Noel on different shifts, Noel for three days, then you. Your primary job is to get through to this kid."

"Not sure that's the best idea."

Ross said, "Why?"

"Well, let's just say Noel and I have different styles."

"I'm actually counting on it. We're running out of time."

Falcon paused, "You know, often less is more."

Ross lowered his voice, "I'm aware Noel isn't popular with you guys. I've heard a few complaints lately. I'm planning to address it today. You just do your part." He headed for his office and Noel.

Damn right I'll do my part. I always do. Falcon walked over to Flint's bag. "All right hero out of the bag and back on the stump. We need to chat."

Flint stretched his arms and arched his back.

"This isn't yoga pretty boy, get out of the bag! Now!"

The boy scampered out, grabbed his stump, and sat. "Oooh!" He sucked air.

"There you go," said Falcon. "Where do you think you are, summer camp? I read your file. Just because the ladies think you're so cute doesn't mean you can waste my time."

Flint's eyes narrowed at the mention of a file. *I wonder what he knows about me?*

Falcon imagined the internal conversation running through the kid's head. There was nothing in the file about females except Flint's mom and sister. He had supposedly knocked his mom down and grabbed his younger sister by her arm. Both stories held one brief line added at the bottom of the page. Falcon selected a much larger stump and sat down about a yard away.

"So you've been sitting on that twig for almost four days give or take a few hours when you were sleeping in your bag. Looks like you've got a black eye too. How's your butt?"

Flint stared at him.

"That's it? You're just going to stare at me?"

Shoeless, slouched, and four days without shaving, Flint looked more the part of a miserable homeless person and less a tough guy.

"You know you probably don't know my name. It's Falcon. I'm the guy who ran you down like you were standing still."

Flint raised his eyes.

"Oh, I see you do remember. Yep that was me. Twenty yards behind you and brought you down easy as a lame deer. I expected more from a guy who rolls drunks. Why don't we talk about why you're here, so we both know where we stand, or should say sit, as that stump will soon feel like you sprouted a third leg. Let's see …"

Falcon rubbed his chin in a thoughtful way and counted off Flint's offenses on his fingers.

"Your file says you punched your daddy, beat your momma, sold drugs, skipped school and robbed houses. All that, and my hand comes up empty. Any comment?"

Flint ignored him.

"No? Okay buddy, I love this. I can talk all day long. I have plenty to say, and I get paid to do it. We'll skip your problems for now and chat about something else; for example did you know America is having an obesity crisis? No wait. You might not know what obesity is. It means fat. Anything? Bueller? Bueller? Anybody?"

Falcon began singing the "Star Spangled Banner".

Flint watched in disbelief. *This guy's freaking crazy.*

"And the home of the brave. Play ball!" Falcon prattled away.

The other counselors rustled the camp out of their bags, and the rest of the kids moved on with their chores, PT, cutting wood, dragging logs, and the specifics required to survive in the wilderness.

Breakfast, lunch and dinner disappeared over the next 10 hours as Falcon verbally charged on, pausing only to eat the delivered meals, or occasionally stand to stretch as he and Flint sat in the perimeter. It was now 5:00 p.m. and Falcon's jaw was sore from his talk-a-thon.

"Do you know what a filibuster is Flint?" Falcon asked. "No? That's really sad. I mean you're going to be 18 soon and able to vote. Do you know what voting is? No? Wow! Let's try something new. Four score and seven years ago our fathers brought forth on this continent a new nation, conceived in liberty and dedicated to the proposition that all men are created equal. Not a Lincoln fan, huh?" Falcon shook his head. "What are they teaching you kids in school these days? You know I had a graduate student for a professor one time who wanted to overthrow the government. He was one crazy dude, probably in prison now. Hey, maybe you'll meet him some-day. I mean with your attitude you're going to prison eventually. You can't beat women and children forever. Even here in America we don't usually let you beat a woman more than three times, although you'd be surprised at how much you can do to children and get away with it … oh wait I forgot who I was talking to. You got caught, huh? Maybe being a tough guy isn't in the cards for you slick. Maybe you oughta get a real job, maybe a car. Yeah, get a car; that way you won't get tackled from behind by someone like me. You know what, have you ever heard of Nathan Hale?" Falcon babbled on like a nev-er-ending stream as he looked for cracks in Flint's armor.

Slowly the bedraggled Flint lifted his head and stared at the crazy man in front of him. Through glazed eyes he watched the lips of the mountain lion move. "Do you ever shut the fuck up?"

Falcon, sensing a change, increased his pace. "Nathan Hale was an American patriot who said he regretted that he only had one life to give for his country. He was then executed by the—"

"I wish you'd join him, asshole."

Falcon continued to press the young man, gauging the explo-sion was near. "Hey welcome to the party! I'm so glad to hear you're enjoying our great country's history. Did you know our country was founded on freedom from every form of tyranny known to man? Another word for tyranny is fascism. Most people don't understand this kind of stuff you know, back to our school system again, but I'm thrilled you want to hear more! Fascism is socialism on steroids. Let me clarify that. Socialism is a label used by fascists the same way they use the label communists. Now the commies, that's quite a story. They like to tell people they believe in community, but really they're just dictators or fascists like Hitler, Mussolini and Stalin."

Falcon appeared relaxed and animated but behind his sunglasses, Flint was under a microscope.

Every cell in Flint McCracken's body screamed in excruciating pain. He'd lost track of the days as he'd sat on a stump and had slept on the ground, which filled every 24 hours. Round and round the hours went – stump, sleep, stump, sleep, stump. Now his head ached from the nonstop blathering of this maniac in front of him. *Socialism? Fascism? Botulism? Who the fuck cares? I'm going to lose my mind.*

"So as I was saying we all have to be personally responsible for our own lives. I had an amazing teacher, Mr. Jacobsen — what a wonderful man. He believed in our great country because we have freedom. Now I know you believe in beating women and that would make you a fascist in my book; some others might just call you a piece of crap, but when you start beating the helpless, you're practicing fascist behavior. Did you know that fascists don't like ice cream?" Falcon raised his arms up in disbelief. "Who doesn't like ice cream? Some stupid fascist who probably beat his mother, just like you."

Flint gaped at the constantly moving hole in front of his eyes. His head buzzed, his teeth ached. He felt so much pain, even the little hair he had left hurt. *I can't take any more of this! I've got to get out of here!* He measured Falcon through rabid eyes.

Falcon leaned forward and shifted his weight onto the balls of his feet.

"As I was saying about ice cream, how does a man not like ice cream? You have vanilla, chocolate, straw—" he shook his head.

"Nah, I don't really like strawberry either. I wonder if that makes me a—"

"If you don't shut the fuck up—" Flint growled.

Falcon continued talking casually waving away three of the counselors who heard Flint's threats.

"I believe in capitalism with a twist. See here son, I believe in ethical capitalism. I also believe in belongingness, sitting back on a curve ball, crushing fastballs, and finding true love. I really do. True love is a beautiful thing, but now that I've said it out loud what's the alternative, false love? I don't think so. I think it's really very easy. One day I'll find the woman of my dreams and then … maybe I'll run for president. You'd vote for me wouldn't you tiger? Do you like tigers? Bengal? Or is it Tigger? Do you like Winnie the Pooh? I do."

As he was blinking through his red-rimmed eyes, Flint was trying to ignore the noise, but words kept shooting out the hole like angry bees escaping a stirred-up hive.

Falcon went on, "Pooh does love honey, although I think I'd prefer a cold Coke over honey, but then again I'm not a Pooh. What is a Pooh? Do you have any idea how much money a Pooh makes? I don't. It must be quite a bit though and I'm sure he …"

Flint's entire body trembled as his mind collapsed. He panned left, then right, and bolted for the woods. A scream trailed behind him and hung like streamers in the air, "Fuuuuuuuuck yooooooooou!"

Falcon was midway through his Three Stooges routine when Flint jumped. *It's about freaking time kid!* He took three steps and spear tackled the boy under his right armpit.

Flint lost his footing and landed hard on his face. The lion was on his back – again.

Falcon heaved all his weight onto the boy and covered him like a blanket, then locked Flint's arms and legs with his own.

"Fuck yooooooooooou!" Flint struggled to get free.

"Relax."

"Fuck yoooou!"

"Relax buddy. I'm here to help you."

Flint sucked air. "You don't give a shit about me! Nobody does!"

"Actually," Falcon said softly, "I do. Just relax."

Flint stopped moving. "Nobody cares about me."

"It's okay little brother. I'm here to help you."

"No-no-body …" Flint's voice muffled as the tears began.

Falcon shifted off Flint's back but remained sitting on his legs, which allowed the kid to breathe, and more importantly, to cry. He waved off the other counselors who'd come to help. Relieved and exhausted, Falcon waited quietly, as the young man who lay spread-eagled on the the ground released deep painful hacking sounds. It was heart-wrenching to watch, but Falcon knew the process of healing had finally begun.

"Trust is a two-way street," Falcon spoke at last. "I'm going to trust that you'll stay laying there while I get off your legs. Nod if I can trust you."

Flint nodded.

Falcon released him.

The boy lay on the ground and sobbed until eventually the sorrow decreased and the tears ebbed.

Falcon snagged two waters from a staff member and set one next to the kid. "Drink up. You can stand when you're ready."

"Thanks." Flint followed the directions and slowly got to his feet.

"My pleasure young man."

They both drained the bottles.

Falcon ambled in a small circle, stretched his long legs, and rubbed his rear. "I can't believe you sat on that stump for almost a week."

Flint grimaced, "Yeah, but the stump was nothing compared to listening to you go on about fascists."

Falcon laughed, "I can't stand them either buddy." He rested a hand on Flint's shoulder. "Look me in the eye son. I know you didn't beat your mother; you were only trying to protect her and your sister from your father.

Flint lowered his head.

"Look at me, Flint."

He lifted his chin and tears spilled over his cheeks.

Falcon paused. "We're here to help you Flint. Take advantage of it and your life can get better."

He nodded, heaved a deep sigh, and smeared sweat, dust and tears with the back of his hand.

"I understand. That's enough for now. You have a week of PT to make up for," Falcon informed him.

"PT?"

"Physical Training. I want 20 laps around the perimeter, and at the end of each lap you owe me 25 pushups. Here's your shoes buddy, let's go."

Flint acted surprised. "Are you doing them with me?"

"Get real," Falcon winked. "You can't keep up with me."

Days passed into weeks as Flint worked hard along with the other kids. Hours of manual labor broken up by 30-minute breaks for group chats encouraged trust among the children, and most of the staff. Rumor had it Ross mandated Noel take a four-week vacation as he decided his long-time enforcer had burned out. No one missed him.

When Ross heard of Flint's progress he made time to speak with Falcon in his office. "Good job. I hear the kid is coming around. The psychiatrist said he's pretty bright."

"He is. He still has garbage inside that's going to take a while to flush out. It's not all going to disappear in a few weeks."

"Yeah that's what the doc said. Our job is to get them back

on track."

"Then throw them back to the wolves?"

"It's not a perfect system, Falcon, I'll grant you that. We do the best we can with what we have."

"I have to say Ross, I'm real tired of hearing that excuse from the top. It's a copout. If this is the best your generation's got, then step aside."

"I'm not arguing with you."

Ross did not want another confrontation with Falcon. He gently flipped the topic. "I'd hate to lose you, but maybe you should set your sights higher."

"Like what?" said Falcon

"I don't know." Ross smiled, "You got a lot of opinions. How about politics?"

Falcon practically snarled at the word, "Yeah right."

"You don't like politics?"

"I don't like politicians. A teacher once broke the word down for me. 'Poli' means the people, and 'tician' means being lied to. The word says it all. They're like ticks, blood-sucking parasites."

"Sounds as if your teacher knew some Latin," Ross said as he tried to keep the conversation amiable.

"He knew lots of things, and people like him are the reason America still exists and the French aren't goose-stepping."

Becoming annoyed at Falcon's perceived implication about him, he changed subjects again. "How'd you get the kid to start talking?"

"Everyone has a breaking point, and most people who are suffering want help. They just have to believe someone cares."

"And how did you do that?"

"I set boundaries, and he knew as long as I was present, he was safe. After that it's simply pushing the right buttons."

"He told the doctor you were talking about Winnie the Pooh,

ice cream and fascism."

Falcon nodded, "His power was silence. I took that away from him. Once he started losing control it was only a matter of time, although he hung in there longer than I expected. He's a strong kid."

"What's this about fascists not liking ice cream?"

Falcon laughed at that memory and shrugged. "I don't know. I was just connecting each thought to the next. I'm sure there are plenty of fascists who like ice cream. Ask Noel."

Ross raised his eyebrows. "You think Noel's a fascist?"

"Oh yeah, all bullies are fascist. He just doesn't have control over millions of people, thank goodness, but the behavior is the same."

"I've never thought of it like that."

"That's the problem, most people don't. People get bullied or allow it of others by ignoring it. If it's not happening to them then ... it's why this place is in business."

"How so?"

Falcon appeared surprised. "We're here because of child abuse, Ross. Parents blame bad behavior on kids, but seriously, where did they learn it? From their parents. It's like never letting the dog outside and then punishing it for peeing on the carpet."

"Perhaps accurate but maybe a little crass."

"I'll take crass over burning kids with cigarettes, sexually assaulting them, beating them, and sometimes what feels even worse – simply ignoring them. We have a whole generation of abused and ignored children. We even labeled them. We call them 'latch-key kids'."

Ross knew this was true, but over the years he had slipped into the "if-it's-not-happening-to-me" camp. "You're sure full of information."

"I live in the real world, and I read everything I can get my hands on. I used to bring books to the dining-room table."

"I can see that."

"So did my mom. She made a rule, no books, so I read the milk carton. Pretty soon that disappeared too." He laughed and shifted in his chair. "Ross, I'm going to be leaving in a few weeks, once Flint's group ceremony is complete."

Ross was disappointed but not surprised. Falcon was aptly named. "Why the change?"

"Sometimes it's just time."

"You're going to be missed around here, especially by Jon and the people on your shift."

"Jon is leaving too."

"Jon's leaving?" Ross' heart did a flip as he realized he would now need two new counselors.

Falcon nodded, "He gave me permission to tell you so you'd have more than two weeks to find replacements."

Ross collapsed into his chair.

"Well," Falcon shrugged, "Noel burns people out. The positive attitude in camp while he was gone showed a perfect example of that."

The boss felt the beginning of a migraine. He didn't want to ask, but "Anybody else?"

Falcon looked at Ross with sadness. *He's not a bad guy.* Three more counselors planned to leave within the month, but Falcon wasn't at liberty to say so. His loyalty was to them not the man who invited the fox into the hen house. "I'm not speaking for anyone else, but Noel isn't popular. His behavior is abusive, your staff hates his guts, and the kids fear him. This job is hard enough, Ross. Noel makes it torture." Falcon paused, "You're the boss. You can make change or suffer the consequences."

Ross leaned forward a bit irritated and felt like Falcon was holding back. "I'm just asking for a heads-up."

Falcon leaned forward too, eyes sharpened. "Here's a heads-up.

If you get rid of Noel, Jon will stay and keep working for you. I'm guessing some others will too."

"That doesn't seem very democratic of them."

"Actually it's very democratic; majority rules. If you'll remove the bully my guess is the majority will stay. Healthy people with other options aren't going to be pushed around forever."

"Wouldn't have picked you for a Democrat."

"I'm not. I'm an American."

"You know what I'm saying."

"I do, and you're wrong. Man, didn't anyone in your generation pay attention in civics, or were you all too busy smoking pot and burning your bras?"

Ross rolled his eyes at Falcon's question. "What's that supposed to mean?"

"Democracy by definition is the ruling of the majority, or majority rules as we've all heard a million times. It's also referred to as mob rules, but that's a conversation for a different time. Our country isn't a democracy; it's a constitutional republic. Democracy allows for the majority to dictate to the minority. Republics give protections to the individual by constitutionally guaranteeing equal rights to each citizen. What you've done here is hire a tyrant to supervise your workers. That might work in a democracy if you can get enough tyrants on your side, but in a constitutional republic the workers have the same rights as the tyrant. And as one of those workers, I'm exercising my right to work somewhere else in better conditions."

"I thought it was just time. Isn't that what you said? Sometimes it's *just time*."

Falcon waved his hand. "It is for me. I'm giving you an example."

"So if I get rid of Noel then you'll stay?"

"No, not me personally but you might have a better chance with the others. They need their jobs and love living here and working with the kids. But like I said before, when you bully people who have options they exercise those options. What you should be looking into are the people who aren't leaving and get rid of them."

"Why is that?"

"Any person willing to be bullied will eventually join the tyrant. Simply out of survival. Many Germans and half of Europe demonstrated that. Abuse is heinous in any job, but when your job is to help children it's counterproductive, deplorable, and quite possibly illegal."

"What do you mean by that?"

"Simple; go into town right now and spit in somebody's face and see what happens to you."

Ross grimaced slightly at his words, stood up, and extended his hand. He'd heard enough. "Point taken, I hope you find whatever it is you're searching for."

"I appreciate that. I will eventually."

"I have no doubt."

Falcon paused for a sip of water as he stood at the podium and shared the tale of Flint McCracken.

The reporters listened solemnly and with circumspection. The topic of child abuse had been written about endlessly but little ever changed. This candidate just put a spotlight on the negligence of the political world and the generational breakdown of the American family.

Falcon set his water down, stretched his lower back, and continued …

The day of Flint's graduation ceremony arrived quickly, only a few days before his 18th birthday, which was a present well-deserved.

Originally based in Native American philosophy as a rite of passage, most of the symbolism of the ritual had long disappeared. But surviving Base Camp was a monumental achievement – an experience most would speak about for the rest of their lives. The sense of belongingness was a first for the majority of kids; and through the nurturing staff, trust and growth developed. Flint's growth allowed the rest of his peer group to view him as a leader. With his anger disarmed, he spent hours sharing with staff and peers about problems others could relate to. He listened, he learned, and earned a second chance. That second chance would arrive soon.

The night before the big event Falcon and Flint gathered in the glow of the campfire.

"My parents are coming tomorrow," said the teenager.

"I heard."

"I'm not sure what to say."

"What do you want to say?" Falcon asked.

Flint mulled this over. "My sister is easy, but my mom ... well, I love her, but I'm sick of her covering for my dad."

Silent and motionless Falcon listened.

"She should stand up to him, but I know he'll beat her if she does," Flint sighed. "I'm still mad at my dad," he said gruffly. "But one thing I've learned, there's nothing I can do about other people's behavior."

"That does include your mother," Falcon reminded him.

Flint exhaled heavily, "Yeah ... I know."

The tranquility of the forest and crackling fire filled the gap in conversation.

Flint broke the silence, "It's so peaceful here."

"Yes it is, little brother."

A slow, wide grin crept across Flint's face.

"You know, the first time you called me that it sounded weird, but now," he tilted his head toward Falcon, "I like it."

Falcon faced the young man and placed his hand on his shoulder, just as he'd done to a boy weeks ago.

"You have a special heart Flint, and with it come responsibilities. I have faith in you and expect greatness from your life, but what you make of it is your decision alone. Greatness isn't measured by things, money or even power. It's measured by the number of people whose lives you enhance. Never doubt that greatness lives within you, demonstrated through patience and forgiveness. We afford others patience by showing them grace, and when we forgive, well, the most important person let off the hook is us. Most people are unaware when they've done us wrong, and the rest plain don't care." Falcon shook his head. "Loving your neighbor as yourself can be a tough task, but very rewarding. Understand?"

Flint hesitated, "It's an awful lot to think about."

Falcon smiled, "Yes sir, it is. Lucky for you, you have the brains and the time to do so. Use both wisely, little brother."

Tomorrow came and with it the beginning of the ceremony. At Flint's request, Falcon would facilitate. The circle consisted of both his parents, his 14-year-old sister Meghan, four peers Flint had grown close to, and Jon.

Flint entered the center of the perimeter.

Falcon began, "The circle is synonymous with completion. Ever-flowing energy without a beginning or end, it is believed to continue forever providing its own sustenance. The circle provides warmth from the sun, movement of water from the moon, and life from Mother Earth. Flint has entered his circle of life; a sacred place each of you has been invited to join. It is a source where joy and responsibility are shared, where his happiness is your happiness, his pain is your pain. Please close your eyes and bow your heads. Anyone unwilling to embrace Flint's circle in this manner is asked to leave now without guilt, shame or malice."

Falcon silently counted to 10 and raised his head. No one had left.

"You may open your eyes. Every ring is named specifically for the individual. As Flint requested I facilitate today, that responsibility falls to me. From this day on Flint McCracken's ring of life will be 'The Circle of Greatness'."

Flint and Falcon locked eyes, smiled and shared their special definition of greatness.

"Let his Circle of Greatness begin."

Flint faced his sister. "The six weeks I've been here I've missed you so much. I apologize for not being there for you. I'm your big brother. It's my responsibility to watch out for you. I ... I didn't realize that before."

Tears pooled in the young girl's eyes.

"I'm truly sorry Meghan," Flint struggled to speak. "Can you ever forgive me?"

Meghan addressed Falcon, "Is it okay if I hug him?"

Falcon smiled and nodded.

The brother and sister met halfway and embraced.

In a choked whisper Meghan bleated, "I love you."

Flint held her close. "I love you too."

When they returned to their places Falcon asked Meghan, "Is there anything you want to say?"

She stole a glance at her father and nodded to Falcon. "Flint, I am so proud of you. You're like a superhero."

Many in the group chuckled or smiled at her comment.

Falcon surmised Meghan was finished and acknowledged the next person. This procedure continued as Jon, and a few of the kids Flint selected, spoke about his growth and their time together.

When it came to his mother's turn, the well-groomed woman's face appeared ravaged, crimson and puffy from crying, mascara streaks stained her cheeks. The wait became more than she could bear. "Please, may I hug my son?"

Falcon agreed and mother and son repeated the scenario that

took place between brother and sister.

"I am so sorry honey for not being a better mother." She sobbed, and then gently cradled her son's head and kissed his cheek.

"It's okay Mom," Flint's voice cracked. "You did your best."

Although the scene turned into a touching display Falcon's primary job was safety. As mother and son hugged, he kept close watch on McCracken senior.

The man easily, six four and pushing 250 pounds, carried himself the way some men of his generation did, uncomfortable with physical intimacy and emotions, stiff, and sporting a tough guy mask. Many hated their jobs, drank too much, and abused their wives and children.

Jon followed Falcon's gaze and took heed of the man as well. He appeared uncomfortable but not aggressive.

Flint and his mother returned to their spots.

"Mom I love you, and I'm sorry for everything. I really am."

She wept uncontrollably as she listened to her baby boy.

He continued, "I've learned the best part of life is helping others, and from now on that's what I plan to do."

Between whimpers, she managed to speak, "I'm so sorry, I let you down. I know you're going to be a great young man. I can see you already are. I love you Flint with all my heart." She hopelessly tried to dry her eyes.

Flint turned and faced his father, and everything he'd learned over the last six weeks began to slip away. As he confronted the man who abused him, thoughts of his sister and mother filled his mind with memories, bad memories, and ignited a raging fire in his belly. He wanted to forgive him, but was he really ready? Father and son stared at each other as Flint searched for the words.

Jon glanced at Falcon, now on high alert, chin lowered, hands to his chest, slowly flexing his knees.

Falcon gently guided the young man by using his voice. "Do

you have anything to say, Flint?"

Flint continued to stare at his father. Then as if seeing the man for the first time he thought, *he looks old, tired and beaten down.* Flint's anger dissipated and he stepped into the moment. "Since coming here, I feel much better, but I know I still have a ways to go. I think I'll just say this. Thanks for coming Joe."

Joe? Uh-oh. Falcon's adrenaline began pulsating through his body.

The man frowned, displeased by the use of his name, but as he studied his son he recognized some changes. The scared mouthy teenager had been replaced with a strong, handsome young man, who appeared confident. He peered past his son's shoulder at the man who ran the ceremony. Then closing his eyes he inhaled, as the sweet pine and solitude of the mountains calmed him. *I'm tired. Tired of the noise, the pressure of life, the drinking, just plain tired.* He asked for permission to speak.

Falcon nodded.

"Flint, I've tried my best …" He paused, knowing that wasn't true. An attempt to swallow was futile, his mouth felt parched from guilt. "I look at you now, well, I'm damn proud. I failed you son. I'm so damn sorry."

He felt the words brush his soul. His body crumpled taking him to one knee, and he hid tears of shame behind massive hands.

Flint watched in awe; he'd never seen his dad cry. Stunned, he almost missed the apology. The mountain of a man who'd terrorized him as long as he could remember convulsed with deep, racking sobs. Flint blinked several times and looked to Falcon for help.

Falcon appeared pleased, and mouthed the word "greatness".

Flint approached the crushed man and placed his hand on his head.

His father reached up, they locked fingers and Flint helped him to his feet.

The two men studied each other momentarily then Flint opened his arms wide. Wrapped in his son's embrace, the huge man cried harder.

Silent tears baptized Flint's face. "It's okay Dad. I know."

Caught in the emotion, the two men hugged as never before, which quite possibly they never had. Those in the circle showed signs of weepiness too, and Falcon signaled Flint's mom and sister to join their family. "If you so choose."

They sprinted into the center disappearing into a mass of arms, catapulting the father into another crying jag.

Falcon, Jon, and those in the circle smiled. *This is how family should be.*

The time to complete the ceremony had arrived. With everyone back in place, Flint returned to the center alone to face Falcon. The two young men, only six years apart in age, smiled at one another.

It was Flint's turn to speak.

"The first time I saw you, I thought of you like a mountain lion. You ran me down as if it was nothing, although I had a huge lead. When you pulled me to my feet you said I was pretty quick," he chuckled. "But then you started talking, and talking ..." Flint shook his head. "... about crazy stuff like ice cream, fascists and Winnie the Pooh."

The staff and kids in the circle laughed; they'd heard Falcon too.

"But when I tried to run again, you stopped me, held me, and called me your little brother." Flint's jaw tightened as he attempted to suppress tears. "I'll never be able to thank you enough. I've never met anyone like you, Falcon. You really care about people. I'm honored to be your little brother." Although he smiled, his eyes brimmed over with tears and gave way to the deep sentiment.

Falcon blinked several times. Usually stoic at the ceremonies he could feel his emotions betray him. He blinked again, but it didn't work. A long, slow drop found its way down his kind face.

Falcon met him in the middle, and they hugged.

"I'll never forget you, and I hope you won't forget me. You saved my life, Falcon."

"Thank you, little brother." Falcon looked him in the eye. "You made mine better."

Falcon returned to his spot, cleared his throat quickly, and wiped his eyes.

"From the moment you stepped onto this mountain your potential to make the world a better place increased. You are a special human being, Flint McCracken, and today you have recaptured your freedom. As you pass through life remember you are never alone. You are surrounded by love, compassion, integrity and courage. Your Circle of Greatness is complete and as a fellow citizen of the greatest country on Earth your greatness is expected. Continue to be the gift, my friend, the gift of you."

With the completion of the story the reporters sat hushed, as perhaps some thought of their parents, children or even childhoods. A few tears were visible, and a woman softly crying could be heard from the back.

Falcon took a gulp of air and swallowed. As he remembered Flint, moisture began to form in his eyes, and he tried to blink it away. *Get your emotions under control!* But he realized that voice in his head was wrong. It was time for real emotion. No more lying smiles of Bill Clinton or good ole boy smirks from George W. Bush, and enough "Eeyorish" depression from the wet-blanket Barack Obama. It was time for sincerity, and American excitement! American greatness! It was high time to make a positive difference in America, and the group in front of him possessed the power to fulfill that vision.

3

C losing the conference with the last reporter, Falcon made a beeline for the open arms of his wife Avery.

Avery Sane flashed a smile at her husband. She was an irrefutable beauty inside and out, with iridescent green eyes, long silky blonde tresses, and angel kisses dusting her cheeks. She possessed sexy, tan legs that many women would die for, and most men fantasized about. Forty-four and fit, she still emulated the perfect description of a "California Girl," which was appropriate, as she'd grown up 50 miles south of the Sacramento Valley in the Delta. Possessing charm, heart and an IQ of 130 almost seemed unfair, but blessed with true grace the adoration heaped on her by all was well-earned. A bit of a grinder, at 20 she had enlisted in the U.S. Air Force and had become a load master. She had volunteered for Desert Shield/Desert Storm and when asked why she felt a need to go, her answer was purely American: "I'm proud of my country and believe it is my duty." *Duty.* The same word she had used only months before when Falcon had first brought up offering his services to the American people.

It was his "duty".

"You sure are pretty," he told her.

No matter how many times Falcon had complimented her over the last 15 years Avery always blushed.

"Thank you baby," she said. *Time is racing by, and now my*

sweet love is running for president. She corrected herself. *We are running for president.* From the beginning, he had made sure she understood what they were undertaking. Months of discussion ensued while he dissected every scenario they might have to deal with. *This is really happening.*

"You were great tonight," she cooed.

"Thanks sweetheart." He pulled her close. "Just telling stories, hopefully they're picking up what I'm putting down."

She melted into his body. "I have no doubt whatsoever."

Falcon lifted her chin. Hidden in the shadows of the fading spotlights, he kissed her lightly. *I hope she's right.*

Tommy held the door as the reporters filed by. He smiled bright, flashing perfect teeth. "Have a good night folks, and thanks for coming."

Still on door detail Tommy more thoroughly checked out the attractive female reporters. Instinctively he felt eyes upon him and glanced around.

Falcon raised his eyebrows.

Tommy smiled and shrugged his apology.

Falcon shook his head. *Will he ever learn?*

Tommy knew Falcon's mind well. *I'm trying.*

Avery said, "Time for Lilli to go out." She escorted their five-year-old toy Bishon-Poodle outdoors.

The place empty of press, Tommy flipped the lock. "Quite a night boss man!"

"Just getting started hero, time to make a difference."

"Yes sir!"

Falcon checked the room. "Where's Maya?"

A female voice floated from around the corner, "Here Chief."

In walked Maya Fiero, 42, wickedly smart, loyal, and Falcon's right hand. Her parents and both sets of grandparents had worked in the fields of California their entire lives. They were grateful to

America for the opportunity to escape the disease, corruption and death in Mexico. Hard-working people, they'd set a great example for Maya. One of her grandfathers frequently said, "Usted puede respirar en America mi niña. *You can breathe in America my girl. America is filled with opportunity and dreams. God Bless the United States.*" Maya steered clear of trouble and went to church and college. She genuinely believed in the American dream. Over a decade ago she had answered an advertisement for a sales position and was hired by Falcon Sane. That day her life truly began to blossom.

"You were great Chief!" Maya smiled. "I heard a couple of them say they'd vote for you right now."

Tommy added, "We sure are a long way from FUKEN Manufacturing."

Falcon laughed, "That's a bit of an understatement. You guys ever miss those days?"

"NO!" they belted out in unison.

Avery came back inside with Lilli and joined the group. "What's going on?"

Tommy and Maya looked at Falcon, "I asked them if they ever missed FUKEN Manufacturing."

"I don't think any of us miss those times," she said.

"I'm with the boss lady; I'm glad those days are in our dust," Tommy said emphatically.

"I agree with Avery," Maya added. "I've tried to erase them from my memory tapes."

Falcon studied the three of them as his mind flashed to the past. *Had it been that bad?*

Located in Sacramento, California FUKEN Manufacturing needed a warehouse supervisor. The position didn't pay much, but 29-year-old Falcon thought it a great opportunity to get management experience. His first day was an eye-opener. The small branch, recently thrown together by the parent nationwide corporation, was a mess. His management job consisted of ordering product and sorting and organizing a warehouse covered with scattered merchandise on broken pallets surrounded by four cement walls. He was his only employee.

The current general manager (GM) was a fair salesman but incompetent in dealing with people and unethical with his accounting. The GM's flaws however, gave Falcon several opportunities to problem solve. Six months later Falcon was the one the entire branch came to for help, and sales skyrocketed. The GM soaked up all the attention and credit from the big boys upstairs, and as business was running smoothly he rarely came into the office. But he showed up just often enough to gum up the works and make sales drop one month. Mass confusion ensued and a mini revolt began amongst the employees. After three letters of resignation the GM called Falcon into his office.

"What's up?" said Falcon.

"My company work at home has taken a backseat now that I'm here so much. Unless there is something important to be attended to, I won't be coming in."

Falcon almost laughed aloud, "By important, you mean running the place?"

The GM wanted to verbally cuff Falcon, but knew he could very easily lose him, which would undoubtedly cost him his own job. He handed Falcon three letters of resignation. "Can you fix this and bring sales back to where they were?"

Falcon perused the resignations. One he was glad to see go. The other two he'd hired personally. "As long as you stop getting in my way this place will be back on track by tomorrow."

With the GM absent Falcon was free to run the show and sales returned, but it was the employees who made this happen. Two of those people were incredible workers and Falcon hires. Their names: Tommy Perry and Maya Fiero.

Thirty-four-year old Tommy Perry was a born salesman. Divorced, living paycheck to paycheck in a studio apartment, he rarely spent a night alone. But his true calling came when he arrived at work. Because the rest of his life was challenging, Tommy found sanity in the presence of his relationship with Falcon, who immediately became the one person he could count on. Because of that, he never wanted to let his new boss down.

Falcon gave Tommy two rules when he hired him.

"Number One. No excuses. Number Two. Never be late or call in sick. I don't believe in being sick. If you're tired ask for a day off; being successful is all about a positive attitude and motivation. Motivation is why no one is ever sick on Christmas."

Twenty-seven-year old Maya Fiero was the complete opposite of Tommy. Driven, determined and in need of very little direction, she embraced the opportunity given to her by her new boss. She adopted Falcon's motto of sweating the small stuff so the big stuff never happened.

Under Falcon's keen eye, one year later Maya and Tommy's careers had flourished.

Tommy grew into the top salesman in the company. His name led every FUKEN Manufacturing newsletter across the nation. He still chased women, but in the business world he had matured.

Maya became Falcon's second-in-command and ran the place with ease.

Falcon, on the other hand, was struggling with his supervisor. Cavalier about Falcon's age and salary, their conversations were always short and fruitless.

"You're the youngest GM in the nation. You've got plenty of time to make money," his boss said.

Falcon was incredulous. "You're promoting me to GM, but

cutting my pay?"

"Yes, you have to pay your dues."

"I've paid my dues. The problem is you're taking my money."

"Just be patient," his boss promised that day.

Falcon's branch soared to number one in the country. Assured a raise three times in 12 months, each time it arrived he was denied. The first time his boss and the vice president stated it was an oversight that could not be fixed until the following quarter.

The second time the excuse was again because of his age. Being the youngest GM in the country he needed to be patient. Again he swallowed his anger as the vice president flew in from Cincinnati and promised Falcon would be taken care of next quarter. When the next quarter passed without the raise promised to him almost a year ago, Falcon gave his notice. They thought they could lie to him forever. With Falcon's two-week notice the vice president called and asked him why he was leaving.

"I'm leaving because you won't give me the raise you guys promised me a year ago," Falcon stated.

"I can walk down the hall right now and get you your raise. Is that all it will take?"

"Yes, I want the raise you promised," answered Falcon.

"Then it's done. I'll call you back in 30 minutes."

"I'll be right here, like I always am."

After a half an hour the vice-president finally kept his word. His tune however had changed. "I think you're making a mistake, Falcon."

Falcon almost laughed. He had zero respect for liars especially ones in positions of power. "How's that?"

"You are willing to quit a job when the economy appears to be getting tough."

Now Falcon did laugh, "I'm sure I'll be fine. But if you are so worried about me, why don't you just give me my raise?"

"I spoke with your boss. He's against it"

"The same guy we both know committed fraud?" Falcon asked rhetorically as he knew he wouldn't get a response. He knew this to be true because he'd reported the information to the vice president himself. Falcon tried a different approach.

"He works for you, right?" Falcon asked.

"Yes he does."

"You just said you could walk down the hall and get my raise. I run your most profitable branch. You personally promised me the last time I saw you I would be given my raise. The raise I earned. I have been more than patient. The only person keeping their word here is me. You have my two-week notice in front of you. I guarantee if I don't receive my three-time promised raise today, I will continue to keep my word and be finished working here."

Silence crept over the phone until the vice president finally spoke.

"I'll say it again. I believe you are making a mistake."

Falcon's temper finally flared. "The advice of a liar is worthless — not to mention, I didn't ask for it."

He hung up. It took him 12 months to establish his business, Responsible Recycling, and to make it profitable enough to afford employees. It took 12 months because he did not borrow a cent. He didn't believe in debt.

Unfortunately only three months had passed when Tommy became the first FUKEN casualty. Too much for the new rag-tag management team to handle, they'd fired him.

"You're really letting me go, huh?" he asked the new inexperienced GM.

"Yeah, uh, it's nothing personal, but I, uh, we, don't think this is a, uh, a good match."

Tommy shook his head, took his two-week severance check, and walked out the front door for good.

The GM, who was trying to make time with one of the female secretaries, watched as Tommy left. He was relieved it didn't involve a confrontation. "I thought he might go ballistic. I heard he's crazy."

She nodded and laughed on the inside. She knew Tommy well. Too well. He was lucky Tommy had left without grabbing him by the throat.

Tommy's first phone call was to Falcon Sane with five simple words: "They let me go, boss."

Falcon gripped his cell phone tight and tried not to lose his cool. Not ready for employees yet, he knew he couldn't leave Tommy out in the cold. He did some quick math in his head and knew he had to take the chance. He couldn't tell him no.

"We've got to work hard brother. No excuses, no nothing, 12-hour days, Monday through Friday. You can ride with me. I'll pay you commission on what you sell as well as what I sell. We're a team."

Three months went by as they cold-called every inch of the Sacramento region to pick up clients.

Avery and Falcon had been together for six months and decided it was time to live together. Avery rented her condo out and moved in with Falcon into a small apartment in the Sacramento area, which made it easier for him to build his company. It made her commute a little longer to work, but they wanted to be together. When Falcon explained Tommy's situation, Avery smiled and told him everything would be okay.

Tommy cut almost all his expenses and rented a room from a female friend. It was hard, stressful work, but through it, their bond grew even tighter.

Maya got the ax next. FUKEN knew she was close to Falcon and began harassing her. Demoting her after Falcon left, she was thrust back into sales. She worked as hard as ever and was the top salesperson in the branch for six straight months. As a reward they cut her pay and took away half of her customer base. Still she continued on until they followed her home from work one night and questioned her about her sales and loyalty to Falcon in front of her house. She gave her notice on the spot and called Falcon that night. "I had to quit Chief. They followed me home."

"You did the right thing."

She didn't want to ask because she knew if he was ready, he would've already called.

They both sat in silence for a few seconds then Falcon spoke, "You ready to rock and roll sister?"

Relieved, Maya exhaled. She understood his code. "Yes sir. I've got my cold-calling shoes on right now."

"See you tomorrow. Seven a.m."

Maya's eyes watered. "Thank you Falcon."

"It's my pleasure my friend."

Hanging up his phone, he knew he wasn't financially ready for her either, but ... He was now back to making less money than his employees. At least this time it was his company.

Falcon's thoughts were interrupted by Avery's infectious laughter. She, Tommy and Maya filled his office and were running through humorous events of their first press conference. *Tommy is right. We have come a long way.*

4

*T*he new week arrived and disappeared as fast as it came. Round two with the reporters was on tap today after work. As Falcon cruised down the hall to his office, Tommy tackled him.

"Easy buddy." The two men steadied themselves. "I only have one dance partner, and it isn't you."

They both laughed.

"What's up?"

"Two things boss. Bob Phillips called and left a message on my private cell phone. He said yours was full."

"Bob called?"

"Yes sir, good guy, smart man. I always enjoy talking with him."

"Me too. What's the second thing?" said Falcon.

"Well, your announcement really stirred the pot. My voicemail has been slammed with what I am guessing are reporters wanting one-on-one interviews." Tommy paused and envisioned the possible names that sat in his voicemail. "I haven't checked it yet but it might be easier if I throw some names at you, and you tell me yes or no – that way if I come across them I can delete or save. Just stop me if anyone is a yes."

Falcon thought about his request briefly then nodded. "Go for it."

Tommy fired away from a list he'd written down.

"Hardball, Fox and Friends, Meet the Press, Fox News Sunday, CBS This Morning, 60 Minutes, Good Morning America, that show with Stephanopoulos, *Time*, *Wall Street Journal*, *The Economizer*—"

Falcon interrupted, "*The Economizer*?"

"Yep, *New York Times, LA Times*, Yahoo, Drudge, Bill O'Reilly, Jon Stewart, Stephen Colbert, James Lipton, Rob Ritchie, *The Enquirer*, Perez Hilton, Neil Cavuto, Joel Osteen, the Catholic Church, and my personal favorite … drum roll please. *Playboy*!" Tommy grinned.

"That's all?" Falcon laughed. "Anyone else?"

"Oh yeah, I have an entire list." Tommy waved multiple pages in the air. "It would be quicker to tell you who probably isn't in my voicemail."

"Who probably isn't in your voicemail?"

"Your mom."

Falcon smiled, "Mom has my direct line."

Tommy said, "So what's the plan?"

"Okay. No one-on-one interviews for anyone. As I've said before, less is more—"

"Unless we're talking about Kate Upton, right?"

Falcon shook his head. "I want the reporters hungry every Friday night and more importantly, I want the American population to start thinking of our press conferences as must-see TV. It's the only way we can dish out uncensored thoughts and ideas." Falcon paused, "Do me a favor, call Bob back. Tell him I'm available anytime. The chemo is taking its toll, and it's getting rough on him. Last week he looked exhausted. Working 14-hour days at the ranch with the kids would wear a healthy man down."

"Bob works in the hills with the juvenile delinquents?"

"Severely emotionally disturbed youths, and yes. Bob said it's the best way to get through the treatments, one day at time, turning kids lives around. It's his best means of survival."

"That's something coming from Bob. Wasn't he in Vietnam?" asked Tommy.

Falcon's entire demeanor changed. His eyes tightened into a hard stare focused at Tommy. To be accurate it wasn't at Tommy; it was through him. Falcon's mind left the present.

Tommy instinctively lowered his eyes. To outsiders it might appear Tommy had crossed a line. He hadn't. He'd simply forgotten about the deep connection between Bob and Falcon, and their close friendship with Matthew Bettie, a former Army paratrooper who'd served with Bob in Vietnam, and passed after succumbing to cancer. A cancer derived from the chemicals both Matthew and Bob were exposed to in Vietnam.

Decades ago Bob had hired Falcon as a counselor and assigned Falcon to Matthew's group of kids. Matthew had taken Falcon under his wing, and his friendship had been very meaningful to Falcon. Only after their relationship was cemented and Matthew was dying did Matthew share some of his experiences with Falcon. With Matthew's death, Bob and Falcon, who were already close, became family.

Tommy didn't know the whole story behind Falcon's silk necktie; only that his boss planned to wear it at every press conference the rest of the year. He waited a few seconds for his boss' eyes to stop smoldering and gingerly waded in. "If the Boomer culture was more like Bob, Matthew and your father, we wouldn't be in this mess right now."

"True, but with great problems come even greater learning."

Tommy sighed. *He's back.* "Always the optimist boss."

"That's right, brother. The glass around here isn't half-full, it's brimming over. In fact, we don't have glasses. We have water pitchers!"

Tommy appreciated the kind of energy Falcon brought to the table and fed off it, as did everyone in his presence.

"If Joel Osteen calls let me know. I'd like to sit down with him privately. I caught him once on television when I was channel surfing for a basketball game. Long story short, his message was 'Asking for God-Size Prayers'. I did." Falcon smiled, "And here we are."

"You asked to be President of the United States?"

Falcon laughed and shook his head. "No, I asked the Big Fella for the largest platform available to make a positive difference in people's lives."

Tommy nodded, "I'd say He was listening."

"We shall see brother, we shall see."

"Okay, Mr. Osteen it is." Tommy wrote himself a note. "You were surprised about *The Economizer*? Should I call them, too?"

"No. I wrote them an in-depth letter when I canceled my subscription years ago. They should know how I feel."

"What happened?"

"They endorsed Obama. When they chose the policies of Bush and Obama over Romney, I was done with them."

"You really liked Romney, didn't you?"

"Respect is a better word. I respect a life lived responsibly, and the man created jobs. Something we need more of. More jobs, less welfare. More jobs, less taxes. More jobs, more freedom."

Tommy listened intently. It'd been a long time since he'd been without a job but he remembered how it felt to be fired from FUKEN Manufacturing like it was yesterday. *Unbelievable despair.* "I don't understand guys who don't want to work."

"You know what buddy, I don't either, although I do think most people want to work. We've just made it too easy for some of them not to. You know the saying, 'Give a man a fish and he may eat for a day. Teach a man to fish he may eat for a month, but require a man to fish and he will eat for a lifetime.'"

"I've never heard that last part."

"Yeah I added that."

Tommy laughed, "Of course you did. I remember when you first hired me." Tommy tried on his best Falcon voice. "'Tommy, I see great things here for you but no excuses and never be sick. No one is ever sick on Christmas!'"

Falcon roared at his friend's mimicry. "That's right, but you left out an important part. Do not date your fellow employees!"

Tommy started to protest then stopped. Falcon knew virtually everything that happened under his supervision. Besides, he would never lie to his boss. "Yeah what can I say. You have to admit though, I am getting better."

Falcon chuckled along with Tommy. "Yes you are. Any other questions?"

Tommy looked at his notepad. He had an entire list of things deemed important: Climate change, the ever-increasing debt, too-big-to-fail banks, the ruining of American neighborhoods through government loans, bankrupt cities, and the list when on and on. *How are we going to fix all of this?*

Falcon knowingly watched Tommy's brow furrow. "I know buddy. It's a mess. Just take it one at a time. That's why we're here."

"It almost seems impossible," Tommy said.

"It is for just you and me. Well I'll never say impossible. Nothing is impossible. But for just the two of us it's improbable that we'll fix every single thing. That's why we introduce new ideas and systems and free the American people to fix their own problems and neighborhoods. And that my friend is something we can do."

Tommy thought for a second. "We're going to need a lot of votes, boss."

"We'll get them. The Republican Party is just as much to blame for this mess as the Democratic Party. The conservatives still refuse to call George Bush what he really is, a lesser version of Obama. They won't admit Bush policies are exactly the reason Obama was elected. They just rail on about Obama expanding our debt. Bush did it first. They worry about Obama becoming a dictator. Where do you think the Patriot Act came from? Is Obama taking things to greater extremes? Absolutely. But it's difficult to complain credibly about Obama while ignoring the behavior Obama is modeling. This is also where the liberals have zero credibility. They excoriated Bush but encourage, or quietly allow, all Bush policies under Obama. It's like a disease. I call it 'Boomeritis'. I have a cure for Boomeritis. I call it responsible behavior. I'll never be a conservative or a liberal. I'll always be a responsible American who values freedom over everything else. The American people regardless of party have had enough. They just need an alternative, which we are happily providing."

"We should have recorded that. You could have given this as a speech one day."

Falcon smiled at Tommy. "I can give that speech every day without notes or teleprompters. Ethics are easy to remember. They never change."

Falcon noticed Maya coming toward them. "Anything else?" he asked Tommy.

"No sir, I think that's it"

"Okay buzz if you need me." Turning to Maya he asked, "What's up?"

"You know Margaret Thatcher was right. The problem with socialism is you eventually run out of other people's money."

Falcon laughed, "Okay?"

Although normally calm and collected, a fire burned inside Maya few others could handle well. Every once in a while the flame burst through her cool demeanor. This was one of those times. "I was listening to the radio this morning on the way to work. The host was saying he could see a race war coming in America. A listener called in and said he was an idiot. He said there was no way you would ever get Americans to kill their neighbors, friends or family members because of the color of their skin."

"True."

"Then the host said if that didn't happen we would have a revolution of the poor against the rich. The caller laughed and asked the host if he'd seen any poor people lately. Poor people were poor in America for a reason. They were poor because they weren't willing to bust their asses. He said *If you're poor in America that's a YOU problem*. Besides, most of America's poor lived pretty well for not having a job! Air Conditioning, free food, free housing, free cell phones, give me a break! Go to Tijuana. Those are poor people, and they're poor because they aren't willing to bust their asses and put it on the line either. We know there are plenty of Mexicans willing to bust their humps. We know this because they're here in America working! Did he really think poor people were going to riot in the streets because they were poorer? Please. Besides did he really think all the fatties had enough energy to fight? Most of them couldn't run a hundred yards without puking their guts out!"

"Wow," said Falcon.

"Oh he wasn't done. He gave an entire explanation about welfare, prison, tattoos, drugs, backward hats, his right to the Second Amendment, and the dumb punks whose pants are too big they have to grab their crotch with both hands to cross the street. He said geriatrics with walkers cross the streets faster!"

"I've seen that a few times myself," Falcon added.

"Me too," said Maya.

"Do you know where the pants hanging off their backsides came from?

Maya closed her eyes, nodding. "It's prison dating, right?'

"Well that's one way to put it."

"Do you think these kids know by hanging their pants low they're telling other males they are ready and willing?" Maya asked.

"I doubt it." Falcon shook his head.

They both sat quietly in their own thoughts.

"There's a lot of fear out there right now. Fear eventually turns to anger," Falcon stated.

Maya looked at her boss. They were both thinking the same thing. *How bad can this get?* She wondered.

"You know how they say we're kicking the can down the road?"

"Yes," Maya answered.

"The can is gone. There is no road. Our politicians are out of control."

"Lovely. What do we do?"

Falcon gave her a serious look. "We win."

"Yes sir."

Tommy's phone rang constantly as he attempted to juggle a bagel, notepad, computer and cell phone. As he unloaded everything on his desk, he stared at the invasive phone. He couldn't keep up with the voicemail as hundreds of people vied for his boss' time. The enormity of the task they were attempting hit him hard again. *Relax. Boss man said to take them one at a time.* Tommy inhaled, held it, and released. *Besides he's the one with the really hard job.*

Being the vice president of a nationwide travel agency, Avery arranged her schedule to be present at her husband's second press conference. Even though her business took a hit, as online bookings became the norm, the offices she managed grew due to hard work and excellent customer service. Client numbers shrank, but the wealthy still possessed plenty of money and happily parted with it for quality service from her elite concierge branches. Avery parked her truck and bounced through the doors of Responsible Recycling. She found Tommy, who sat at his desk, deep in thought. "Hi Tommy."

He lifted his head and shot her a beaming smile. "Hey Boss Lady."

"Please," she laughed, "call me Avery."

"Sorry can't do that. Falcon's my boss and you're his lady."

Avery smiled. She loved the loyalty and respect shown to her husband – he earned it and deserved it.

"Tommy?" Falcon headed down the hall toward the voices. "Are you flirting with my wife?"

Mortified he said, "Never boss. Not in a million years."

Falcon embraced and kissed Avery. "I have to keep an eye on this one. He's quite the player."

Avery tried to help Tommy. "He's always been respectful to me."

"Thank you, Boss Lady," Tommy exhaled.

Falcon chuckled, "Easy Luca Brasi, I'm just teasing you."

Tommy disappeared back into his work.

Falcon escorted Avery to his office. "You almost gave the poor guy a heart attack."

"Poor guy! I love him to death but what a player. I keep warning him that thing has an expiration date, I hope it doesn't fall off some day."

"Falcon!" Avery nudged him away.

He grinned, "I'm just saying. Come here." He held her face in his hands. "Did I tell you today how beautiful you are?"

Avery blushed, which made Falcon love her even more if possible.

"Do you have time for lunch before tonight's death match with the reporters?"

"You crack yourself up don't you?" He swallowed a laugh.

She smiled sweetly. "Yes."

Falcon checked his watch. It might be tight, but Avery was his first priority. The biggest drawback in wanting to make a difference in America was how it ate up their alone time. They were both displeased with it shrinking, but someone needed to stand for America, and if Falcon didn't try he wouldn't be able to live with himself. He joked with her often. *I'm only one stupid comment away from the circus folding and leaving town.*

Avery knew better. America was in so much pain they might be ready to give one of their own a chance to lead them.

Lunch was short, but they enjoyed every second, cuddled close, held hands, and laughed. They appeared to be a couple on a fifth date, not seasoned veterans of a 15-year marriage.

Avery said, "That Death by Chocolate cake on the menu looks amazing."

"Uh-huh, I know where this is going."

"I'll bet you'd like some for dessert, wouldn't you baby?" Avery batted her lashes.

Falcon leaned in and whispered in her ear, "The only dessert I want is sitting at this table."

Avery turned crimson. "Falcon, you are so bad."

He chuckled low and throaty, "Yep, that's one of the things you like about me best. If my baby wants cake, let's have cake."

Avery sparkled like a little girl on her birthday and gave Falcon a peck on the cheek.

"I'm going to expect a lot more than that later little lady."

Oblivious of the crowd around them, they fed each other cake and squeezed every bit of sweetness out of their brief time together.

The couple returned to the office, and Tommy said, "Ready for round two, boss?"

"Yes superstar, it's time to shine," Falcon winked.

"Do you get nervous up there?"

"No, it's kind of fun. Long as I don't take anything personally it's fine."

"Well, they've had a week to dig, plot, scam, and commiserate. What kind of questions do you think they'll be shooting tonight?" asked Tommy.

"Oh, probably my official view on abortion, social security, gay rights. Or they may surprise us." He glanced at Avery. "Are you sticking around sweetheart?"

"Of course!" She clapped her hands. "I love watching my man in action."

They walked back to his office where he kissed her again. "I am your man."

"You look tired," she said.

"A little bit. I need a good workout and some time alone with you."

"We can go to the gym tonight after you're done rolling with the reporters."

"And?"

"And what Baby-Cakes?" she asked unconvincingly innocent.

Falcon roared, "Oh that's the way we're going to play it, hmmm?"

She closed the office door, sat on his lap, and whispered her plans for him tonight after the gym.

Later that evening the second press conference began; Falcon took the first question.

"Jeff Laffer. In my research this week I found a story in the *Republic Reveal* newspaper connecting you to a Messmate County. What exactly happened?"

"In reference to what, Jeff?"

"It was an in-depth, lengthy story. If you could start at the beginning I believe we would all benefit and it might save time."

Falcon appreciated Jeff's ability to sidestep the one question rule. "Would you all care to hear that story?"

The majority nodded.

Falcon knew Messmate would surface. With Internet access everything in his life was bound to come up. Messmate County was not only his past, but also an appropriate microcosm of the damage done to America. His eyes flashed and he gripped the podium.

Avery caught the shift in her husband's demeanor. She'd seen that posture before. *Get ready America! Here comes Falcon Sane.*

Falcon began to unfold the tale, "I moved to Messmate County, 40 miles north of Sacramento in 1999, where I shared an apartment with my pal Charlie."

Charles Colt Edwards at 28 was a compact, 150-pound bundle of energy. Falcon and Charlie had met on a high school baseball diamond and had been best friends ever since. After a stellar baseball career at Nevada Union High School, Charlie earned an athletic scholarship to a private university in San Diego where he studied communications. He was smart, handsome, funny, and rubbed along with everyone. His most impressive attribute though, was loyalty. Charlie snagged the local paper and perused the daily betting lines while Falcon flipped the remote.

"Hello and Welcome to Channel Eleven News," said the anchor man. "Our top story tonight is the never-ending saga of impeached President Bill Clinton and the woman who brought him down, Monica Lewinsky."

Falcon groaned, "This guy's going to be the beginning of the end for America."

Charlie laughed, "What? A guy can't get a Lewinsky anymore? Nothing like being famous the rest of your life because you went down on a man old enough to be your father."

"He's married too. What a piece of crap."

"Falcon, he's not that bad. At least he didn't inhale."

"Not that bad? After his, 'I didn't have sexual relations with that woman speech,' some of the kids I work with told me the latest craze in high schools are girls giving blow jobs because the president said it isn't sex. One girl bragged she'd given Lewinskys to 20 different boys, but claimed she's still a virgin."

"Really?"

"Yeah. I'm not sure how much of this is true, but the kids are talking about it. Thanks Mr. President."

"What'd you do?"

"I reported it to my boss who said she'd look into it."

"Think she will?"

"I doubt it. She's a pencil-pusher, almost at her 20-year public retirement package. She's not rocking any boats. I checked into it, was told I didn't have the authority, and to stop. Can you believe that?"

Charlie shook his head and flipped to the want ads. "You need a new job."

"Tell me about it."

"I'm serious. Somewhere you have authority to stop this kind of stuff."

"I'm all-ears."

The television squawked, out of control crime in New York City, two murders locally …

Falcon exhaled heavily. *Man this stuff is depressing.*

Charlie's head stayed buried in the paper. "Hey this might work. Messmate County is looking for deputies. The Sheriff's Department is in Grassville. That's only a half-hour drive from here."

Falcon thought about the idea of law enforcement.

"This is right up your alley, buddy. Serve and Protect. You'll actually get paid to be yourself," Charlie grinned.

Channel 11 broke in again.

"The new language being taught to black children in Oakland called Ebonics has gathered some attention. Being hailed as the original language of the African slave trade it is now being called Black English."

Falcon clicked off the television. "Black English, White English, Pink with Purple Polka Dot English. If our country isn't careful we won't be able to talk to each other in 10 years, like Babel in the Bible."

Charlie looked at the ad again for the Sheriff's Department.

"I really think you should apply."

He folded the page over and handed it to Falcon.

At one time Grassville, California, located in Messmate County was a beautiful little town. Well-designed streets nestled between the Unknown Buttes and the Messmate River hosted famous Christmas festivals and 4th of July parades. But slowly Grassville succumbed to indifference followed soon by neglect, and those cousins wove their way through the community like weeds in a lawn. In short order the town gave way to the darkness of unemployment and crime, becoming known as the armpit of California; the once-charming city embraced methamphetamine as a way of life. Welfare became the norm, and ambivalence to broken windows and trash exacerbated their issues while it also attracted gang activity. The Peckerwoods, a White Supremacist gang, were predominant in the area, but plenty of trouble came from the Mexican and Asian gangs as well.

The Messmate County Sheriff, with the Grassville mayor's blessing, began importing criminals from outside agencies to house in the county jail … for a fee. The idea in the beginning was to funnel the extra funds to benefit the town. As with most politicians, once the money hit their hands it seemed to disappear into someone's pocket. The jail was already understaffed and its deputies poorly trained, in some cases no training was offered at all. Due to low pay, unsafe work conditions, and horrible morale, the Sheriff's Department ran a constant advertisement in the local paper in an attempt to fill positions caused by high turnover. The ad required law enforcement background or any four-year degree, as though a bachelor's degree in English literature would prepare someone to deal with felons; never mind sufficiently understanding the penal, health, safety or vehicle codes to book someone into jail legally. Legal standards with regard to operating a jail were set aside, and laws requiring deputies to undergo specific training were ignored.

As the greenbacks continued to flow, the elected officials initiated a housing program for INS detainees or illegal immigration holds. These holds were indefinite. Illegal immigrants from Cuba, Africa and Vietnam, guilty of major felonies like murder, drug trafficking and rape, were shipped to the Messmate County Jail. Already the proverbial bottom of the barrel, they'd somehow made it to America. Rather than showing gratitude and working hard, they were turning to crime. Now their lives entailed being locked down most of the day with no end in sight.

Into this mess jumped newly sworn Deputy #58, Falcon Sane.

Falcon's excitement grew as he drew closer to his destination. He was a cop, a police officer, part of law enforcement (technically) – a sheriff's deputy. The pride he felt kind of surprised him. Searching his memory for a similar feeling, he was coming up empty. *Probably the closest was signing my name to a Division One Baseball athletic scholarship.* Although that had been a proud moment and the culmination of a boyhood dream, this was different. This was a group of complete strangers who said he was good enough to join an elite part of society, law enforcement. He would be given a gun and a badge. The badge he looked forward to. Taking an oath to uphold the law and serve and protect the citizenry was as Charlie said, "Right up his alley." He'd been protecting people his entire life, stepping in-between classmates to stop fights, punching and being punched in defense of weaker people, and helping stranded drivers. Protecting others was right in his wheelhouse. The gun however, gave him pause. *The gun is going to be interesting.*

Growing up in the mountains of Northern California brought him up close and personal with weapons, and the responsibilities that went with them. Falcon learned early on he didn't like watching animals die, and purposely missed birds with his BB gun despite the ridicule of peers. He eventually got away from weapons completely. The thought of having one unleashed a tremendous amount of responsibility inside him. To tackle, restrain, punch or fight with hands and feet was not a problem. Pointing a gun at someone, however, was something he'd never done. He wasn't worried about hitting the target or being hurt. He wasn't worried about whether or not he would feel guilty or have trouble sleeping. He would only shoot if he had no other choice. His concern lay with the aftereffect. How the law would work, and being at the mercy of others to render a decision on whether he took appropriate action or not. Falcon believed weapons existed in two camps: as a potential protector of freedom and the potential to take freedom away, dependent upon who held the gun.

The damp, gloomy day seemed appropriate as he parked his truck in the dirt overflow lot assigned to the Sheriff's Department. As he stepped out of the truck, he grabbed only his keys and ID. No need for lunch. The adrenaline high would keep him from being hungry, and he'd learned to go without eating all day at the wilderness camp. With a large portion of excitement and a larger portion of trepidation he strode purposefully toward the discolored building. *I am going to jail.* He laughed at the drama building inside his head that produced stress throughout his body. *You signed up for this, buddy ... time to go to work.* He reached a solitary backdoor he'd been told to use marked JAIL, and pushed the intercom button.

A voice bellowed through the microphone, "What do you need?"

"My name is Falcon Sane. I was told to report here."

"Hang on."

One minute turned to two, then three. He pushed the button again.

"I said hang on!"

All trepidation melted away as a slow fire started to burn. Rudeness was something he rarely condoned. Coupled with his biggest hatred of all time, being told what to do, a verbal brawl, at a minimum, was about to take place. Pushing the button a third time he waited to hear the click of the mike; it came almost immediately. Not waiting for the voice to speak first, Falcon lowered his voice and commanded, "What's your name?" Tick, tick, tick, seconds clicked, and he could still hear the mike cued. A loud buzz sounded as the door in front of him unlocked. Pulling the door open, he entered the building.

The voice had disappeared.

He passed a break room and continued. The next door was unsecured; he pushed it open and walked down a corridor with rooms staggered on both sides. Easing his way into the jail, he passed a man dressed in orange sweeping the floor; undoubtedly a trustee. Falcon made a mental note about the lack of supervision and questioned why the department would allow an inmate access to rooms and offices closed to the public. What seemed like poor judgment and dangerous to the new deputy, later proved correct, as the trustees were part of gang activity that smuggled drugs, cell phones and weapons into the jail. He found the men's locker room he'd been told about the day he'd been sworn in, secured his personal belongings in one of the keyed community lockers available, and proceeded to the next secured door.

This time the voice was quiet as the heavy security door popped.

Falcon stepped inside. Once the door behind him secured the next door popped, and he was inside the jail. His first day on the job introduced him to his training officer; a non-verbal threat on his life, large quantities of unsecured prescription medications that ranged from Librium to Lithium to Darvocet, and the term FNG, or fucking new guy.

His training officer was a pasty-doughboy character with perfectly coiffed hair, a wife, and kids. Likable enough, he surmised his new trainee wouldn't need hand-holding, which was fine by him, freeing up more time to flirt with a female deputy he was having an affair with.

The training officer and Deputy Sane toured the jail and came upon three inmates who were working out in the common area of one of the pods.

One inmate stared up into the catwalk and spotted the JTO (Jail Training Officer) and new deputy who were watching them. He formed his hand into the shape of a gun and pretended to shoot the new deputy.

Trying to remain calm Deputy Sane asked his JTO, "Did you see that?" He was seething. *I wonder if grabbing that asshole by the throat would get me fired?*

"Yes, I did."

"He just threatened me. Aren't we going to do something about it?"

The JTO mulled it over. He didn't want to. The inmate was a jerk who always caused trouble. He scanned the new guy. His eyes were tight; face was a little red; he thought the new guy might be intimidated. Most trainees were. That's why he took them to the hardcore pods first. With a second glance at Falcon he realized he wasn't scared. *He's pissed.* He thought about it for a second and looked down at the inmate. *I don't want to deal with this idiot today.* The inmate always screamed racism. The "man" was holding him down. The "man" was the reason he'd spent 10 years in prison. He'd been written up for poor behavior, rules violations or criminal behavior, and always threatened a lawsuit. Most of the corporals and sergeants steered clear, so he and others continued the inappropriate behavior. The passive-permissive behavior put everyone in the jail at greater risk, deputies, nurses, doctors and even other inmates. Falcon's training officer looked back at his trainee. *He's looking at me like I'm a pussy.* "Okay, FNG. Let's go."

Four security doors and an elevator ride later Falcon stood eye-to-eye with the inmate.

The other inmates fanned out behind their leader and glared at the deputies.

As he stared at the punk who had pretended to shoot him, Falcon considered his options. His 60-second swearing-in last week in the sheriff's office had not produced a badge, handcuffs, pepper spray, baton, firearm, or law-enforcement training. That left only his hands, feet and head as weapons. But his most important skill lay in his ability or inability to take crap.

The inmate spoke with a drawl, "I see we got a new guy."

"Yes, we do," said the JTO. "Apparently you think it's okay to point your finger at him."

"I's just playing," said the inmate. The new deputy was bigger than he'd gauged from a distance. He didn't appear badge heavy and unable to do a sit-up. And he sure didn't look scared like all the newbies. *The way he's glaring at me... I think he's pissed.*

"You know making that gesture can be a felony," said the JTO.

"I's just messin' wich you man. Come on. It's cool, brotha."

He made a fist and extended it toward the new deputy.

Falcon had fist-bumped teammates for years on and off the field; it replaced handshakes or high fives. He fist-bumped the inmate and stared intently into his eyes. "Don't do it again."

"Just fuckin' around, aight? It's cool brotha, it's cool."

"Cool as the other side of the pillow brotha man." Falcon flashed the tiniest of amused smiles.

"And put your shirt back on," said the JTO as he found some new courage.

"Come on man, it's fuckin' hot."

"You know the rules," whined the JTO, his new courage faded fast.

"Man, fuck the rules!"

Falcon glared at the inmate, counting silently to five.

The inmate stared back, shook his head, and put his shirt on.

"Sheee-it, your new guy's fuckin' crazy."

Everyone in the jail would find out how crazy, in 48 hours.

Dressed in green polyester pants, a khaki shirt, combat boots and a utility belt, Falcon began his third day on the job. He'd finally been given a badge and possessed a reasonable grip on the radio, which was a relief since the radio and handcuffs were his only tools. He'd envisioned mace, a baton, a gun, and a bullet-proof vest. None were offered as none were used. He carried an overwhelmingly-massive key ring that held more metal than an armory, and he still lost his way in the four-story county jail. Fortunately no one realized that fact since he maintained a quick pace and called in jail checks wherever he found himself. Jail checks were an unpopular part of the job, so most deputies never bothered to ask why he did them constantly, they were just grateful. Rather than hanging out by the booking counter to gossip, Falcon became a walking, talking, jail check, as it took him multiple turns to find his destination. He didn't sweat being new. He'd pick up the lay of the land by moving around in it.

A hardened voice exploded from the radio.

"I need backup! F-Pod! There's a fight between a regular and a detainee. I need backup now!"

Falcon stared at his radio. Listening was easy. *Where the hell is F-Pod?*

The voice shouted again. "Right now, send backup to F-pod!"

Falcon knew F-pod was on the new side of the building by the elevators. As he rushed over, he faced the camera and waited for the doors to open. As expected they did, and he jumped on.

Deputy Dane Pullman's voice came through the intercom in the elevator. "Where's your help?"

"You asked for backup," Falcon said. "Here I am. Take me to F-Pod."

Pullman said, "There's a wicked fight up here, at least a dozen more inmates out of their cells. I'm locked in CRB and can't help you."

CRB or Control Room Bravo overlooked maximum security. The three pods held 40 inmates per section, typically 120 total. Pods D, E and F were locked down individually which didn't allow movement between pods. Encased in bulletproof glass the pods allowed protection and a full view from the catwalk inside the control room. An electronic panel allowed the deputy to open cell doors, intercom with the prisoners and staff, and control the elevators for disbursement of food and medication and performance of jail checks. The man in CRB had control of everything and yet nothing, because he couldn't leave the position unmanned, not even for a restroom break.

Upon receipt of his initial tour, Falcon had briefly stepped into CRB and thought it was a surreal experience being surrounded by murderers and rapists.

Still waiting at the elevators, Falcon said, "I can't do anything down here. Take me to F-Pod."

Pullman was a good man and an excellent deputy. He had a BS in business and also a POST-graduate degree. POST was the official academy all law enforcement must attend to be eligible for a sheriff's department, police or highway patrol in California. Pullman had worked the jail for six months. His goal was to be on the road, and he would be in 18 more months, for another county. Two years at Messmate had him brimming with enough stories to last the rest of his career. Sitting ringside to this horrific incident, Pullman couldn't take anymore.

"Okay Sane," he said. "Coming up."

The elevator clicked to level three, the doors opened, which reminded Falcon of the parting of the Red Sea. He exited and turned left. The first security door popped, he cleared it, and it slammed secure behind him. He heard screaming and shouting coming from the pod ahead. F-Pod consisted of two-man cells, tenfold, across two decks. The upper deck held a safety railing, but only four feet tall, it wouldn't deter someone from being thrown off. Falcon's heart rate quickened as he picked up his pace. As he reached the last security door, he glanced upward through the bulletproof glass and focused on the upper deck.

On the upper deck stood a six-four, 220-pound Somali who had been picked up by INS for cocaine trafficking. His fists poised like a boxer clearly weren't helping, as his blood-soaked face proved.

His opponent was a six-foot, 200-pound hardcore Norteño, Northern California Mexican gangbanger. Sweat poured off his body almost as fast as the blood gushed from his nose and eye. As he burrowed in, head down Joe Frazier style, he continued to throw wicked combinations.

Surrounding the combatants, a dozen screaming, frenzied spectators reveled as each punch landed. The vile mutilation was a conglomeration of the worst prison movies ever – except it was real.

They continued to dance – smack, pop, stick, fists connected with a face or body. The sickening stench of blood filled the air as it stained the cement platform.

Falcon waited at the electronic, impenetrable door maybe 10 seconds, but it felt like a lifetime. "Open it!"

Deputy Pullman studied Falcon. He'd met him briefly and heard two opinions through the grapevine. One guy whom he didn't like or respect had called him cocky and the other, his friend Ray Supplanter, had said the new guy worked hard. *He's the first to arrive. Cocky? Doesn't appear cocky, although he's screaming at me to open the door.*

Falcon's face expressed horror and fury.

Pullman understood. He'd been watching this blood bath for the last five minutes.

Falcon and Pullman would never speak of this incident, but

during those brief seconds they bonded and became friends, two good men who were watching a brutal fight and were feeling the exact same way. *The insanity of it all.*

Falcon screamed, "Open the fucking door!"

"I can't; you need backup. Where's your fucking backup?"

"I don't have any! Open the fucking door!"

Pullman yelled, "Hang on!"

Checking the elevator camera he saw two deputies, a male and female almost at level three. *Just five more seconds.* Pop! He released the lock.

Falcon pushed through as fast as he could and headed for the stairs that led to the upper deck.

"Move! Move! MOVE!" he screamed at the inmates gathered on the first deck fascinated by the fight.

Most jerked away as he steamrolled forward. Taking the stairs two at a time, he arrived on the top deck.

In full voice he shouted the only command he could think of, "Stop! STOP!"

"Lock down! Lock down!" Pullman screamed over the intercom.

His command was ignored as it had been since the fight broke out.

The ignorance continued as Deputy Sane landed on the second deck. Eight steps to go, time moved in slow motion for Falcon until he reached the actual fight. His shouts could not be heard over the crowd, so he grabbed the back of the Somali's drenched shirt. The Somali threw a nasty right hook at Falcon. Falcon ducked, pivoted behind the punch, wrapped his arms around the larger man, and slammed him to the ground. With his knee planted in the Somali's back he glanced up just in time.

Sporting a mean, glazed expression, the gangbanger headed toward Falcon.

"Back the fuck up!" Falcon yelled.

"Lock it down!" Pullman screamed repeatedly over the intercom.

Falcon warned again, "I said back the fuck up!"

Exhausted from battle and unable to move, the Somali covered his head with his hands and prayed the deputy on top of him would stop the oncoming attack.

The backup deputies still hustled up the stairs and weren't close enough to help as the banger drew closer.

Falcon's eyes blazed, and he started to stand. "Back off and get on the ground, or I'll fuck you up!"

The banger locked eyes with the deputy and his glazed expression from the heat of battle faded. As he stepped back, he smiled, lay face down, laced his fingers behind his head, and waited for the expected outcome.

Multiple deputies finally arrived on the scene one and two at a time, shouted incoherent commands, and fumbled with handcuffs.

Falcon eased off the Somali, knelt on one knee, and closely watched the banger as deputies flooded in, cuffed, and escorted the brawlers to the infirmary. He stood and exited F-Pod.

A corporal asked the new guy, "You okay?"

"Yes sir," said Falcon.

The corporal nodded approvingly. "Welcome to Messmate County Deputy Sane."

Falcon headed for the restroom, scrubbed his hands, arms and face and checked for damage. Miraculously, he didn't have a scratch on him. He glanced toward the ceiling. *Thanks Big Fella.*

Falcon paused and took a drink as he relived the moments and recounted the story to the press.

Everyone in the room was captivated, especially Maya and Tommy. They'd never heard of Messmate County.

Maya contemplated this new information about her boss and

mentor and perceived him with a wider view. *He's always so generous and peaceful.* Then again her grandfather had once said, "Good men will always fight when they have to."

Tommy's take was quite different. A former Army Ranger, he was no stranger to desperate situations. Although Falcon walked his talk about doing for others and giving without expectation, Tommy sensed the fire inside his friend. Messmate reinforced what he'd known all along. *I'd march through hell for Falcon Sane.*

Avery felt proud. She'd witnessed her husband disarm people with his warmth, willingness to listen, and charm. Messmate had happened before they'd met, but familiar with the story, she knew exactly where he was going. *Go get 'em baby.*

The next reporter asked if Jeff Laffer could continue with another Messmate question.

"That clears up the timeline," said Jeff. "But the *Republic Reveal* printed your interview regarding unsafe work conditions in the jail, and your support for a Georgia Blanco as a candidate for sheriff?"

Falcon stared at the reporter. He thought he'd made peace with that situation a long time ago. Anger began to swell. *Calm down and do your job.*

"What if I continue with the story? It should answer most things regarding Messmate County."

The reporters agreed.

Falcon shifted his feet and thought about Caitlin. *How would I describe her? Fit, hard-working and with a permanent smile.* He gazed into the past again.

Employed at the jail for many years, Deputy Caitlin Perly was highly regarded by her peers and inmates. She'd worked undercover, stayed calm under duress, and dished it back when prisoners flashed her. "If that's all you've got, put the mouse back in the house."

Once she'd even stepped in front of a rushing mob to cover Falcon's back while he restrained a guy. He could still hear her screaming at the control tower deputy. "Secure the door now!"

Although Caitlin didn't appear hardcore, in her case, looks were deceiving.

One day she hustled into the booking area and appeared flustered and flushed.

In the year Falcon and she had worked together, not once had he witnessed her upset.

"You okay?" Falcon went to her.

"Uh, yeah, I'm good."

He wasn't a mind reader, but clearly she wasn't. "Cat, what's wrong?"

"Hang on a second. I need to sit down." Her face paled; she appeared queasy.

This is strange. Once they'd observed a crazy INS detainee defecate into a toilet, pull out his own feces, and eat it. Falcon had gagged and almost vomited. Caitlin shook her head and laughed. She didn't rile easily, which concerned Falcon even more. He brought her a cup of water and waited.

She finally spoke, "You know that puke in solitary?"

"The rapist, right?"

"Yeah … what an asshole."

Falcon's heart banged against his ribs, as his anger gained momentum. "What happened?"

The cup of water trembled in her hand. She looked at her friend, her pupils dilated.

Words escaped her lips almost in a whisper, "He grabbed me."

"When?"

"Just now. There's no slot in the cell door, so I opened it to give him his food tray. He took the tray and grabbed my wrist with his other hand. Then he wrenched my arm and pressed up against me, put his face right up to mine, and said he was going to fuck me in my white ass with his big black cock." She paused and inhaled. "I told him to let me fucking go and tried to yank free, but I couldn't. Then he pushed me away, laughed, and told me to never forget he could've butt-fucked me right then if he wanted to." Caitlin's eyes watered and her voice cracked. "Falcon, he really could've."

Falcon's body shook with rage. Cuing his radio, he contacted a few of his buddies to meet in the booking area ASAP. Dane Pullman, Ray Supplanter and Patrick Traveller arrived and Falcon explained what had happened.

"What's the plan?" asked Deputy Traveller.

Patrick Traveller's sweet temperament contradicted the physic of a six-foot, 285-pound bull of a man. He and Falcon had started at Messmate the same day and immediately became friends.

"We're going to walk down and say hi," said Falcon

The rapist's cell was down a small hallway isolated from the general population and everyone else's vision. A single camera in the hall, manned from a locked control room on the other side of the jail provided the only view. With multiple duties and distractions, the deputy on duty could easily miss any action. The camera did not go into the cell, which created a blind spot in the cell. Had the rapist pulled Caitlin in she would've been off camera as she fought for her life against a huge male skilled in committing heinous crimes against women. One more wouldn't matter to him.

The closer the team got to the prisoner, the more anxious Caitlin became.

"Falcon," she said, "don't worry about it."

"Cat, if we don't handle this now ..."

He didn't want to say it to her. *If we don't handle this now he will rape you next time.*

Caitlin looked at him. She knew exactly what he was thinking.

She was thinking the same thing.

Falcon's anger turned to rage as he watched her fighting with herself because of someone else's behavior. *Calm down. You won't be helping her if you lose control and beat this guy to death.* "What if this happens to another female? Is it okay he grabbed you?"

"Hell no!"

"Then let's go. Do what I told you and say exactly what I told you to say."

Falcon told Caitlin to keep the door closed, but to key the lock so the door could be opened quickly and to talk to him through the window in the door.

"Tell him to never touch you again. Yell it at him. Tell him he better never touch you again," Falcon instructed.

The four deputies crowded together in the small hall and tried to be quiet.

Falcon mentally ran scenarios. *What if he apologizes? Possible, not likely ... what if...*

Caitlin silently keyed the door and stared through the window at the rapist. "Don't you ever touch me again."

The deputies crouched in the hallway.

"Did you hear me?" she spoke a bit more forcefully. "Don't you ever touch me again!"

"Bitch!" the inmate said, "I'll touch your fucking white cunt any time time I like! I'm gonna fuck you in the ass until you bleed, you cracker fucking bitch!"

Falcon's jaw tightened, and he motioned for Caitlin to open the door.

"That's right, bitch! I'll fuck you in the ass and cut your cracker ass, you motherfucking honky whore!"

With the door opened, Caitlin stepped aside as three male deputies piled in with Deputy Perly on their heels. Normally, Falcon was in the lead, but he trusted his friends and was the last one in.

"Get on the ground!" yelled Deputy Pullman.

"Get on the ground!" yelled Deputy Supplanter.

"Get on the ground!" yelled Deputy Traveller.

The rapist threw a punch at Pullman, who slid under the rapist's arm and slammed him against the wall.

"Fuck you, you fucking white faggot!" screamed the rapist. "I'll fuck all yous up!"

Deputies Pullman, Supplanter and Traveller restrained the inmate while Caitlin secured the hand and leg cuffs.

"Get off me you fucking crackers before I smoke alls you alls! You ain't nothing! It took a gang of you to handle this brother!"

"Shut up you freaking scumbag!" screamed Caitlin tightening the restraints.

Falcon stepped into the cell, leaned close to the rapist's ear, and whispered, "Can you hear me?"

The man quieted.

"Yeah, motherfucker, I can hear you," he wheezed.

"You know who I am, right?"

"Yeah I know."

"Good, because I want to be sure you understand. I don't like to repeat myself. I'm saying this one time." Falcon's voice was low and raspy. "This …was the easy way."

The prisoner panted as almost 800 pounds pressed on him.

Falcon lowered his voice further. "First let's hear you apologize to Deputy Perly."

"I … I'm sorry. I'm sorry," he stammered. His breathing was rough under the weight on him.

"Deputy Perly," Falcon growled.

"What?" the rapist gasped.

"You're sorry, Deputy Perly."

"I can't breathe, man!" moaned the rapist.

"Of course you can. You're still talking. Now let's try again."

He screamed, "I'm sorry, Deputy Perly!"

"Good. That wasn't so hard, was it?" Falcon hissed.

"No man, no," he gasped.

"Okay, we're going to booking," said Falcon. "Lucky you, get to hang out with us for a while. But the trip won't be pleasant. For your protection and ours we're carrying you, using your arms and legs as handles. You'll get a bird's eye view of the floor, and the pressure on your joints will probably hurt, just a little reminder that this went down the *easy way*, this time. Before we go I want to make sure you're very clear, are you listening to me?"

"Yeah, man, yeah, I'm listening."

Falcon got within an inch of the rapist's ear and whispered ever so slightly, "Touch her or any other female deputy again, and I'll be back all by myself. You understand what I'm saying you putrid piece of shit?"

"Yeah."

"Are you sure? I'd hate to think I wasn't clear."

He gasped, "I-I understand."

"You understand sir."

The inmate repeated, "I understand, sir."

The mentality that everyone was redeemable and deserved the right to be released after serving their time was growing amongst permissive Californians. No one person could stop savages like the rapist from being set free in the world again to torture and crush women's lives. If people understood how evil some of these twisted demons truly were, they wouldn't allow the state to let them out, ever. It was time for a change in California. It was time for a change in America. Falcon did not have the position or power to make those changes, but he could enforce control over the insanity caused by those animals while incarcerated at Messmate County.

After Falcon's shift he arrived home to find Charlie finishing a dinner of Pop Tarts, an egg sandwich, and a bowl of blueberries.

"Hey what's up hero?" Charlie said.

"You eat like you're still in college."

He grinned, "And yet I have six-pack abs."

Falcon chuckled, removed his recently authorized 9mm Beretta handgun, ironically not allowed in the jail, but required of him to bring to work, and dropped his backpack.

"How goes it with the convicts?"

"They're all still there."

"Any new pieces of crap?"

"Yep, remember the guy that allegedly murdered a little boy by cutting him up in little pieces with a serrated knife?"

Charlie grimaced, "Allegedly?"

"Uh-huh, that's the *manner* in which we're *mandated* to refer to it these days, to avoid hurting the bad guy's feelings."

"Give me a freaking break. Didn't that happen about a month ago?"

"Yeah, he's in protective custody now."

"What's that?"

"He gets a private room in the hotel because we're afraid the other 'guests' will kill him."

"Seriously?"

"As a heart attack."

Falcon picked up the Pop Tart box and read the label. "Can't even lock him in with the child molesters and the rapists, apparently even they have a code."

"What a place."

"Yeah I'd like to evacuate all the deputies and drop a bomb on it."

"Those guys are that bad?"

"You can't even imagine. I can guarantee, every piece of crap in there will commit another crime as soon as they get out. If California was smart it would be a one-strike state."

"Hey, not to change the subject."

Falcon decided against the Pop Tarts. "Be my guest."

"I've met someone."

Falcon focused on Charlie. "Whoa, whoa, whoa! Wait a minute. Are we talking about a female someone?" he teased.

"Yes we are. We've been seeing each other for about two months and–"

"Wait, you're just telling me now?"

"I didn't want to jinx it."

"You are the most superstitious person I've ever met," said Falcon. "Remember that week we bet on the Yankees every night, you wouldn't even change your socks."

Charlie offered Falcon some of his blueberries. "Hey, we kept winning, didn't we?"

"Not because of your freaking socks! So this must be serious?"

"Yeah I think so."

Falcon smiled, "Good for you brother, couldn't happen to a nicer guy."

"You're nicer than I am."

"I keep saying that," Falcon razzed his friend. "But who's getting the girl?"

Charlie said, "It'll happen."

"Oh please. Do not give me the, 'you'll-find-her' speech, after you just announced you'd found yours."

"One day you'll find her, and then go on to be the President of the United States."

"Oh really?"

"Yes really," said Charlie.

"Why's that?"

"Because this country needs someone who cares about children, justice, and knows the difference between right and wrong – that's you my friend."

"Can't argue with that."

"Of course you can't. I'm too rational to argue with."

Falcon roared, "Rational? Aren't you the same guy who kept your dream girl secret because you didn't want to jinx it? That's plenty rational."

Charlie tossed a berry at Falcon. "But who's getting the girl smart guy?"

"You want to play with fire, do you? I might let you hack me on the basketball court but that doesn't mean I won't come for you!" Falcon dove at his best friend.

Charlie nimbly jumped over the couch and wagged his finger at Falcon. "You big guys think you have it all figured out, all brawn, little brain."

Falcon laughed and fired a pillow that missed.

"How did you ever play shortstop with that kind of aim?"

Falcon flopped onto the couch. "Congratulations brother. When do I meet her?"

Charlie plopped next to him. "Tonight."

"Really?"

"Yep. She's coming to meet the famous Falcon Sane in an hour."

"That's not enough time to do my hair."

"Ha! Do what to it? If you buzz it any shorter, Head and Shoulders will go out of business."

"I don't have dandruff."

"You know what I'm saying."

Falcon smirked, "You are on fire tonight."

Charlie eyes appeared dreamy.

"Wait till you see her, Fal," he sighed.

He was pleased for his friend.

"I'm hitting the shower, got to be at my best when I meet Mrs. Edwards the Fourth."

Charlie was dazed. "Yeah … oh, I almost forgot. You have a

message on the machine."

"From who?"

"A woman named …" Charlie searched his memory. "Georgia something?"

"What'd she say?"

Charlie shrugged, "I didn't listen to the whole thing. She wants a meeting with you about the sheriff's position."

Falcon hit the button on the machine.

"Hello Mr. Sane. My name is Georgia Blanco. I am running for Sheriff of Messmate County in the upcoming election this year. I'm aware you were recently elected Vice President of the Deputy Sheriff's Association. I would like to sit down with you and explain why I am running. I can be reached at 969-3366. I look forward to meeting you. Thank you."

"The wannabes are coming at you already," said Charlie.

"Wonder how she got my number?"

"Politics is an ugly game my man. Where there's a will there's a way."

Falcon frowned, fiercely protective of his privacy and personal information. "People will do anything for power or money," he grumbled on his way up the stairs to wash the day off.

"Or both," Charlie called after him.

Feeling refreshed Falcon tread down the stairs just in time to hear the doorbell ring.

He purposefully said a little too loud, "Oooh she's here!"

Charlie's face paled at the joke. "Come on maaan."

"I'm just teasing," said Falcon. "She didn't hear me."

A female voice wafted through the door, "I did a little bit."

Falcon jumped over the couch, beat Charlie to the door, and waggled his finger. "See, big guys can move fast too."

He opened the door. "Hi," he flashed a sincere smile. "You must be Lara."

She extended her hand, "I am. Hello Falcon."

"Oh no Miss Lara." He waved her hand away. "This family hugs." He embraced her. "Come on in."

"Back off Casanova," Charlie teased, "Hi sweetie," he kissed Lara.

Falcon was pleased and smiled to see his friend so happy.

The trio visited for half an hour, and then Charlie walked Lara to her car.

"I was a little nervous to meet him," she said. "Now I understand why you guys are best friends."

"Yep, he's the hardest working, most loyal person you'll ever meet."

"Just like you."

Charlie smiled at the gorgeous brunette. "Call me when you get home."

"I will. Charlie?"

"Yes?" he brushed a wispy strand of hair away from her face.

"I think … I love you."

Charlie was surprised and smiled. He'd been thinking the same thing but superstition kept him silent. He sighed and kissed her through the open car window.

"I know I love you."

Her half of the delirious couple drove away, and his floated back to the apartment.

Falcon sat on the couch with the open newspaper held high in front of his face. He'd talk to Charlie in a minute, but only after he punished him for keeping a two-month secret.

Excited to hear what his best friend thought, Charlie paused in front of him.

Falcon raised the paper higher and bit the insides of his cheeks to keep from laughing.

Charlie exhaled and went into the kitchen and pretended to

wash his hands. He did a pirouette in the front room and stared at the newspaper that encompassed his friend.

Out of patience he blurted, "So what did you think?"

"Of?" was all Falcon managed to say without howling in laughter.

Charlie flicked the paper. "Are you kidding me?"

Falcon collapsed, "That's what you get for keeping me in the dark for two months!"

Realizing Falcon was playing a game, Charlie relaxed next to him on the sofa. "What'd you think of her?"

"What do you think of her?" Falcon asked.

"She's beautiful."

Falcon nodded, "She is brother. Yes she is. I guess I'll start working on my best-man speech."

Charlie sat dazed in a love-drunk stupor as the phone rang.

Falcon raised an eyebrow at his buddy. "Don't bother lover boy, I'll get it. Hello?"

"Hello. My name is Georgia Blanco. May I speak with Falcon Sane, please?"

"Speaking."

Exchanging typical pleasantries, Georgia continued, "We've never met, but I've heard some wonderful things about you and the job you're doing at Messmate County."

"Thank you."

"You are quite welcome. I've also heard you met with the sheriff to discuss specific safety concerns you have within the jail."

Falcon's senses went on full alert. "You appear to have good sources."

Pleased with herself, Georgia smirked, *if you only knew young man.* She was aware of the absence of food tray door slots, nearly nonexistent safety equipment for deputies, virtually no training in hand-to-hand combat, or in Falcon Sane's case, no training at all. He'd been at Messmate over a year and had never been sent to any academy of any kind, which was required by law. She doubted he would offer or corroborate this information, but as a leader and spokesperson for the deputies, she'd heard he'd made it clear the staff was fed up with the current sheriff. *If Falcon, and by proxy the deputies will endorse me, it will clinch the election.*

"I am as concerned with deputy safety as much as you are."

Falcon swallowed a laugh. *I doubt that. No way does she care as much as the person whose ass is on the line. Politicians – what a joke, say anything to get the job, do anything to keep it.* Her sources were spot-on though. He and the sheriff had discussed exactly those things. The incident with Caitlin brought about a meeting with Falcon's captain. Captain Writer felt the sheriff should be brought up to speed and arranged an appointment for Falcon. After dismissing the captain, the sheriff had wasted 20 minutes as he rocked in his squeaky chair and glared at Falcon over his huge belly. Didn't listen, didn't care, did nothing. Falcon refocused on his conversation with Georgia. "As the elected voice of the jail deputies, it is my responsibility to listen to any official candidate running for sheriff."

"Wonderful!" said Georgia. "My papers are in. I am indeed an official candidate."

"Okay. I'm doing a double-back working the graveyard shift tonight. Tomorrow I finish at zero 700. I can meet you after work."

"How about 7:30? There's a small coffee shop around the corner."

Falcon said, "Sounds good. I know it."

"Thank you so much Falcon. I appreciate you taking the time."

"You're welcome, see you tomorrow."

Georgia hung up. She glanced smugly at her husband. "He said he'd listen."

His voice was flat, "Yes I heard."

"What's wrong?"

Fred Blanco studied his wife. "You don't think the sheriff is going to find out about this?"

"Oh," she crooned. "I'll make sure he does."

"Georgia, if this young man is all you've said, he sounds like one in a million. Why he's wasting his time in Messmate, only Our Lord knows."

She rolled her eyes. *Not that religious crap again.*

Fred said, "Don't you think the sheriff will fire him on the spot if he finds out he met with you? He's not even off probation. They can let him go for no reason at all."

She crossed her legs and began to file her nails.

"He's a big boy." She shrugged, "he can figure it out."

Fred stared at the stranger who sat beside him. "Not sure what's happened to you in the last few months but there will be hell to pay if you start throwing people under the bus for your own ambitions." He clicked off the TV and stood over her. "You may not believe in the Lord, madam, but Karma is a bitch."

After talking with Georgia, Falcon called his friend Deputy Patrick Traveller.

Patrick answered in a sleepy voice, "Hey Falcon, what's going on?"

Falcon filled him in on the conversation and planned meeting.

"Mind if I tag along?" said Patrick. "It might be smart to take a witness. You know what I'm saying? I've heard things."

They agreed and reaffirmed their plans at work that evening.

Falcon walked the west side of the jail doing cell checks. Block after block he counted heads, then cued his radio and called in.

"West side secure and accounted for."

Patrick called in right behind him, "East side secure and accounted for."

Falcon started back toward the booking counter and past sleeping inmates. At the last cell block he cued his radio to request the pass-through door be opened when he heard a quiet voice. "Hey Deputy Sane?"

Falcon turned and found one inmate who leaned on the cell door, his arms wrapped around the bars. "Hey Jackson, what's up?"

Martin Jackson, a skinny dried-up meth head with stringy, colorless hair, tattoos on his forearms, and just enough teeth left to keep him from getting a full set of dentures answered.

"Can't sleep," he said. "It's tough sleeping in here you know?"

"I'm sure it is," said Falcon. "Maybe you should stop breaking the law and get a job."

"Yeah I know Deputy Sane. I wish I could. My life is, well … it's fucked up."

Jackson fell into the category of bad genes and worse decisions. His mother, a drunk herself, had him at 16. The first of nine children, she never told him his father's name because she honestly didn't know. He'd been in and out of so many foster homes even he'd lost count. Only 28 he looked 50, with a rap sheet longer than a roll of toilet paper: shoplifting, possession, DUI, drunk in public, urination in the park, burglary – an endless list of obtuse actions. He'd been in the county jail for six months and still collected welfare.

Falcon considered giving him a quick speech on personal responsibility, but what was the point? California politicians had come up with a better plan. Rather than require a guy like Jackson to be responsible, or lock him up forever, elected officials chose the worst of both worlds. Hand out free money to encourage abusive behavior to themselves and their community. When they got too far out of control, lock them down for a short period of time. Falcon called it shampoo enforcement: Wash, rinse, repeat.

"Can I ask you a question, deputy?" asked Jackson.

Falcon checked his watch. "Sure go ahead."

Jackson squinted and contorted his face concentrating on something.

"I know why I'm in here. We all know." he waved his hand indicating his sleeping cell mates, "why we're in here. But why are you here?" He paused, "We've talked about it and can't figure it out." He scratched his chin. "Most of the deputies we can figure out, but nobody gets why you're here. You should be in the FBI or CIA or, I don't know, President of the fucking United States." He shook his head, "But not here."

Falcon blinked a couple of times to absorb what the "tweaker" said.

"You know I'm right. I mean come on, you're the hardest working deputy, and you talk about the Constitution, freedom, and free will *all the time*. None of us understand what the hell you is talking about most of the time, but we appreciate that you talk to us, not down on us. You are better than we is, but you don't act that way, ya know, like some of the others. So, what the hell is you doing here, Deputy Sane?"

Falcon stared at Jackson. Aside from the urge to correct his grammar, he didn't know what to say.

Jackson waited as the man in front of him searched for a response. He didn't get one. "Sir let me tell you something. I am not a good man. The Lord knows that for sure. I'm not, but you is, and I swear to God you need to move on. You ain't doing no good being here. I know you care about kids and women. We all know what you did with the guy who grabbed Miss Perly. I'm telling you sir, you need to move on." The meth head watched Falcon as his radio squawked.

"All deputies report to booking. We have one in intake."

"I'll see you later Jackson." Falcon turned to leave.

"Remember what I said Deputy. It's the fullness of time for you."

Stunned, Falcon spun completely around and gaped at him. "What did you just say?"

"I said it's the fullness of time."

"Where'd you hear that?"

"You say it all the time. I thought it fit right here and maybe you'd listen to your own words."

Falcon stared at the tweaker one last time before heading to booking. Throughout his shift he couldn't help but think about Jackson's words. *What am I doing here? It feels like I'm a step behind on everything and now a meth head is telling me I should be doing more with my life.* Falcon recalled what his friend Jon said once, *"The Lord works in mysterious ways."* He glanced up. *Is this where you want me Big Fella? Is this what I'm supposed to be doing? If not, please give me a sign or move me along.*

Early the next morning Falcon and Patrick's shift finished. They drove to Uncle Bus' Coffee Shop around the corner, a quaint little place with good service and homemade "man-food".

Georgia Blanco, who waited in a booth, rose from her seat when the two deputies arrived. "Good morning gentlemen."

She extended a hand and appeared to be in her early 50s sporting a thickening midriff, glasses and a too-tight perm. The navy polyester pantsuit many women in law enforcement chose to wear clearly dated her, like an older version of the OJ Simpson prosecutor, Marcia Clark.

Introductions were made, the two men sat beside one another, ordered, and Falcon gestured with open hands for Georgia to begin.

Georgia began with a false slick of concern for the deputies' sleep deprivation and safety issues in the jail.

Patrick listened then asked, "Have you ever worked in the jail ma'am?"

In awe, Georgia examined the bull of a man who sat in front of her. His pleasant mannerisms did not match his massive frame.

Falcon enjoyed watching the woman mentally work through Patrick Traveller's presence. *She's intimidated by him – something to keep an eye on.* Patrick's sheer girth impressed people who seemed to have a penchant for doing the wrong thing. Inmates didn't know what to do with him as his physical being contra-indicated his peaceful nature.

"No Patrick, actually I have never worked in a jail. But I am willing to make necessary changes."

Georgia scanned Falcon when their food arrived. "Is there something that I can do for you guys?"

And here we go, thought Falcon. *I'm certainly not a fan of the current sheriff; the man is obese, lazy, and a poor communicator who allows his department to be run by cronyism and nepotism and doesn't care about his people in any way, shape or form. But this climber, Blanco, isn't any better. Just do your job as DSA Vice President and listen to what she has to say.*

"No, there's nothing you can do for us." Falcon peppered his eggs. "We serve the people of Messmate County as we swore an oath to. I'm here officially to listen to your ideas, report back to my brethren, and represent them to the best of my ability as I have sworn to do. Please, enlighten us."

Georgia labored for 30 minutes about safety, accountability and better pay. She closed as the waitress cleared their plates and placed a check for $25.42 on the table. "This one's on me boys. Thank you for your time."

Falcon held up a hand, reached into his pocket, removed two twenties and handed them to the waitress. "Appreciate the gesture but we cannot accept it."

Georgia said, "It's only breakfast."

"Actually it isn't," said Falcon. "It's called a slippery slope, and not one we're willing to slide down."

The deputies rose and shook hands with Georgia. Falcon closed with, "I'll share your comments with the other deputies. Concerning an endorsement, that's up to the members."

Georgia didn't give up easily. "Would you be willing to personally endorse me?"

"I don't know yet. I'll have to think about everything you said."

"Fair enough."

Falcon and Patrick started to exit when the waitress ran up with his change. "Sir, your change."

"That's for you." He nodded, "Excellent service."

Georgia and the waitress stared round-eyed at Falcon.

"That's almost 60 percent," she said to the waitress.

"Who was that?" the girl asked.

"That is Falcon Sane."

"Who is Falcon Sane?"

Good question young lady. Good question.

It was the same question being answered for Captain Frank Writer of Messmate County. After Falcon's election as Vice President of the Jail Division he had begun talking with Captain Writer regularly. Their relationship, although not close, consisted of mutual respect. Falcon appreciated the captain's open-door policy and concern for his deputies. The captain admired the young deputy's work ethic and genuine attempts to make his co-workers' environment safer.

After the election, the captain did some investigating on his own in regard to Falcon Sane. The more he heard the more he liked. Every corporal and sergeant wanted him on their shifts because he worked hard. Scuttlebutt had it that he didn't take any crap either. This led some of the lazier deputies to resent him, but gave him an excellent behavioral advantage working with criminals; as the captain knew all too well, a weak link could get you killed. The captain smiled to himself as he remembered a story he'd heard. An inmate had called Sane a bitch and threatened him through his locked cell door. Feeling secure he was warning further that once out of jail, he was planning to kick the deputy's ass. Apparently Deputy Sane didn't care for the conversation.

"Why wait?" he said, and ordered the control tower to open the inmate's door. He walked into the cell. "If you're man enough, give it a shot."

The prisoner said, "I would, if you wasn't wearing that badge."

The captain chuckled to himself, as the next part was what he enjoyed the most.

The young deputy, right handed, placed that hand over his badge.

"Go for it, tough guy," said Falcon. "I won't even move my hand."

The inmate stared dumbfounded.

Sane lost his patience and verbally opened up at him.

"I'm right here you fucking coward. You wanted to flap your gums and show everyone in the pod how tough you are. Let's go! You want to kick my ass, here's your chance. Badge doesn't matter."

The inmate gulped and sat down on his bunk.

Deputy Sane stepped forward and smiled. "Good choice, asshole. You'd have found out the hard way who the bitch was."

Captain Writer laughed. He'd checked the kid out and found him legit, which was why this notification to investigate Sane made no sense. He searched out the Lieutenant in charge of investigating Falcon. "Dave, what's going on with Deputy Sane?"

Lieutenant David Tanker was a dry, quiet, fit man with the classic-cop moustache trimmed neatly at the sides that gave a perpetual stern countenance. Employed by Messmate for 10 years he was considered a company man. "There's a complaint that Sane choked out one of the inmates."

Captain Writer rolled his eyes. "Give me a break."

The Lieutenant shrugged, "The sheriff brought it to me himself."

"When?"

"Yesterday, said get on it."

"Meaning what?"

The lieutenant didn't answer. They both knew what it meant.

"When are you interviewing him?" asked the captain.

"Twenty minutes."

"I want to be there."

"You can't. Just me, Sane, and his lawyer."

"I'll watch and listen through the two-way," said Captain Writer.

"Fine with me."

The captain's stomach tightened. "Dave, what's this all about?"

The Lieutenant scanned the room ensuring no other ears. "I heard he had a little sit-down with Georgia Blanco."

Captain Writer's eyes widened. The election was in full swing and got nastier by the day. "Who'd you hear that from?"

The lieutenant paused. "Rumor mill."

In the parking lot surrounding the jail where recording a conversation would be impossible, Falcon's DSA attorney William Norris ESQ prepped him on what to expect. "First off, they're going to read you your rights."

Falcon's head snapped as if he'd been punched. Fury didn't even touch the emotion he felt. "My rights, like a freaking criminal? A lying felon and his pal make up a story, and I'm being read my rights?"

"Yes. Something's not right, Falcon, I know. The County Sheriff's election is close and I'm aware of the political undertow. Let's focus on the present situation. When asked a question, pause before answering in case I want to stop you. Do not go on and on. Answer only the question asked, in brief, short sentences. Don't speculate or try to remember. If you don't know or don't remember say so. Also, the law dictates you don't have to speak. Once he reads you your rights you'll exercise your right to remain silent.

Bile burned Falcon's throat, "Seriously?"

"Yes. Then he will order you to speak. At that time you'll have to speak but nothing you say can be used against you in a court of law."

"That doesn't make sense."

"It's set up so law enforcement can get answers without violating your constitutional rights."

"What if I don't want to answer his questions?"

"Then they can fire you for insubordination."

"Are you freaking kidding me?"

"No, I'm not. I did some research. I'm not sure why, but some friends of mine in the department think you're being used as an example and a scapegoat, so you need to be careful."

"This is total bullshit!"

"Yes, it is. Welcome to politics Mr. Vice President."

Falcon and his attorney entered the Sheriff's Department and a room normally used to question suspects.

The lieutenant was waiting.

"Lieutenant," Falcon nodded.

"Deputy, Counselor," he said.

The attorney said, "Hello Lieutenant."

Captain Writer, who viewed them through the two-way window, reached over and turned up the volume knob. "You have the right to remain silent. You have the right to an attorney. If you cannot afford this right one will be appointed to you. Do you understand these rights as I have given them to you?"

Do I understand my rights ... you fucking asshole! I'm the only one in the room who even cares about my rights! Falcon took a long look at the Lieutenant and then turned to his attorney.

He nodded.

Falcon struggled to control his voice. "Yes," he said, louder than he'd meant to.

"Very well, I want to ask you about a situation that happened a month ago."

"My client will be exercising his right to remain silent."

"For the record, you have exercised your right to remain silent.

Now I'm ordering you to answer my questions."

Falcon again checked his attorney.

He nodded again.

This is freaking surreal.

The lieutenant started again. "I want to talk to you about a situation in V-tank a month ago. We received a complaint, with witness accounts that you assaulted an inmate."

Falcon, as calm as he could, responded. "That's not true. While passing out laundry in V-tank, one inmate refused to leave his bed and receive the clean laundry. I completed the task, and as I began to leave he jumped from his bed screaming at me, calling me a punk motherfucker. He then threw his dirty underwear and socks at the cell door and continued to scream how he was going to fuck me up. I went back and opened the cell. Because he was in an un-secured pod with five other bunk mates, I told him to come out with his hands behind his back. He told me to fuck off. I called for backup, stepped inside the pod, and escorted him out of the cell, up to booking, where I locked him in a cell by himself."

"He said you choked him out, and he almost pissed on himself," said the lieutenant.

"He's wrong."

"That's not what one of his cellmates said."

"How would his cellmate know if he almost pissed on himself?" said Falcon.

Still viewing through the two-way, Captain Writer nodded. *Good question.*

The lieutenant paused and stared at his notes. *Good question.*

"He said he was lying on his bunk when you walked up to him and ripped him out of his bed."

"He's wrong."

"They're both wrong, and you're telling me the truth?"

Falcon's anger started to rise in his chest. He faced his attorney.

"Are you accusing my client of something?"

"No," said the lieutenant. "But the witness to this event, Wayne Kenneth, is a pretty hardcore guy who I've known for a while."

Falcon said, "Kenneth?"

"Yes Kenneth, he's pretty hardcore."

"He's a convicted lying piece of crap who abuses women. I wouldn't call that hardcore. Obviously, your definition of hardcore is different than mine."

"Okay. So you're denying this happened?"

"I told you what happened," Falcon said. "I'm not denying anything."

"Fine. Anything else you want to add?"

"Yes sir," said Falcon. "I want to make sure I understand this correctly. You hire me and provide zero training, then question the way I deal with an inmate who is combative toward me. An inmate who I guarantee doesn't have a mark on him, at least not from me. He waits weeks to make this complaint, and the only other witness is a convicted felon."

"Okay," said the lieutenant, "we're finished here."

"Is my client under any type of constraint from this moment further?"

"Not at this time. He will continue on with his regular schedule."

"So, to be clear," said the attorney. "You just accused him of a crime, yet he's clear to resume his duties?"

"I did not technically accuse him of a crime. He is clear to resume his duties until further notice."

Captain Writer turned the volume knob back down and slipped around the corner as Deputy Sane and his attorney left the interview room and exited the building.

Lieutenant Tanker walked into the hall and bumped into the captain. "Well what do you think?"

"You tell me."

Lieutenant Tanker said, "If that kid's lying he's the best I've ever seen."

"What are you going to tell the sheriff?"

"I don't think it matters what I say, Sane's in trouble."

Captain Writer shook his head. "This can't be happening."

"I think it is."

Falcon and his attorney remained silent until they reached the parking lot.

"Well?" Falcon asked.

"Who knows? Your question about the peeing remark threw him off though."

"This is all happening because of an election?"

"Look Falcon. You're intelligent, young and confident, but you need to wake up. Your elders don't want you rocking the boat."

"I don't care. They're wrong and certainly not following the law."

"I'm not disagreeing, but they have the power. Americans are getting exactly what they vote for, shit heads, while guys like you will always be slaughtered for trying to stand up."

"I'd rather be slaughtered standing up than lay down and take it."

"I get it. I really do, but you better get used to it because the system will eat you alive."

"You're a freaking attorney. How can you say that?"

"There's no justice in the world anymore. I see it every day. Criminals have all the rights, politicians have all the power, and people like you are pawns. Come on Falcon, do you think the sheriff or Georgia Blanco could do your job?"

"No."

"Yet they're in charge of you. We give them power, which they abuse and use for their own benefit. They know you're smarter and quite possibly will challenge their domain. They'll use you until you become a liability or a danger and then throw you away like the nightly trash. Wake up pal and smell the garbage."

Falcon fell into deep thought on his drive home. *Throw me away like trash. Was it really that easy for people to dispose of others?* The inmates he oversaw every day were more than capable, but he wanted to believe authorities would draw the line. *Maybe not.* His memory brought back the many worthless adults who had surrounded him as he'd grown up. *What the hell is wrong with the previous generation? What happened to honor, humility, and integrity? They seem to be just words now; where is the meaning? I need to talk to Dad.*

5

*T*he reporters were scribbling notes and undoubtedly tipping their caps to Jeff Laffer for doing his homework.

Next up was Sophie Gonzalez from GNN, a young, solid reporter who hated Bush, had loved Obama until the AP reporter scandal, and now believed America was too far gone to fix. The banks, economy and the dollar were all being manipulated by the government regardless of party. Falcon Sane seemed to understand the enormity of the situation yet was still willing to try and outrun the avalanche. She doubted his sanity, applauded his courage, and said a small prayer. *Please let this guy be real.* "Thank you for sharing your last story without making us browbeat you."

Low laughter rumbled throughout the room.

"I doubt anyone present would disagree that our collective systems in America are broken or badly damaged," she said. "What makes you think you can repair the damage?"

"First off I won't do it alone," said Falcon. "A good leader recognizes superb talent and surrounds him or herself with those people. The American people possess amazing abilities, energy and patriotism. Many are waiting for the call to defend freedom and reestablish the Constitution. I believe it will be harder to get elected than to fix our problems. The American people will respond to hard-working, intelligent, ethical leadership. I live by those standards, and I plan to demonstrate them consistently at these press conferences and during this race. If the people are ready to make a difference and fix our problems, I'm offering them a way. If elected, I will bring excitement to work seven days a week for the next four years with a staff that will do the same. Our problems are not a crisis of lacking talent, but rather a crisis of lacking ethics."

The next question was easy.

"So you won't be taking vacations?"

Falcon almost snorted, "Why would I want a vacation? I love my life and will love it from Washington D.C. Who needs a vacation from helping restore freedom?"

The next reporter honed in on Falcon's term statement, "Why only four years? What about eight?"

"If elected I will not run for a consecutive second term. Presidential consecutive elections are about ego, money and power. Ethical leaders realize the positive potential of others and guide that potential to bear and benefit the country and society. No one person should ever want to be in power for eight consecutive years. That is not about service; it's about power."

The reporters sat up with that statement; they'd never heard that before.

Henry Gator from ABS jumped in, "I appreciate everything you just said, but admittedly you left us hanging with the Messmate County story. Would you mind continuing?"

Falcon nodded and resumed.

"Prior to my meeting Ms. Blanco, I applied to the Messmate County Dive and Rescue team also known as D.A.R.T. Multiple members of the DART team, including my shift sergeant, gave their written recommendations for me to join the team. During the physical test, I swam faster and more laps than any other applicant. One guy stopped during the swim and quit, which was supposed to disqualify him. During the running portion I lapped two of the other four candidates and beat the other two by a full minute in the timed mile. At the end of the tryouts, the sergeant in charge of the team unofficially welcomed me to the team. Five days after meeting with Georgia, I received a letter informing me I was not selected. Two other candidates were invited to join, one of which was the individual who gave up during the swim, and, I had lapped during the mile run."

Falcon's brain kicked back to the conversation he'd had with the sergeant in charge of the dive team. *Seems like yesterday.*

Falcon didn't know the man, but he seemed to run a tight program. He approached the D.A.R.T. leader. "What happened, Sarge?"

The sergeant understood exactly what he was being asked.

"I turned your name in as my first choice. It was kicked back down and I was told to pick someone else."

"Why?"

"Politics young man."

"Politics?" repeated Falcon.

"Yep. It's election season, and rumor is you met with Georgia Blanco. The sheriff didn't like that."

Falcon was stunned and stared. He hadn't even met with his fellow deputies yet about the meeting with her. Besides, it was his duty to talk with both candidates as a representative of the DSA and report back to his constituents. "Why would he keep the most qualified candidate off a team meant to protect the community? That's ridiculous."

"I agree, and furthermore I like that you talked to her. She used to work here in the investigator's office."

"I didn't know that."

"Yeah, she'd been around quite a while until the sheriff fired her."

"Fired her?" Falcon's head began to ache.

"Fired her. Some crap about insubordination, and now

apparently, it's your turn. You got screwed on the DART team. Everybody knows it, so be careful. And be careful with Georgia too."

"I barely know the woman. We met once, and I listened to her views of how the department should be run."

"Like I said, be careful. Both of them are politicians who only look out for themselves. They're like ticks waiting to drop out of a tree in search of new blood, parasites. Besides, you should know by now the rumor mill is wicked, doesn't have to be true. Someone in the wrong position just has to believe it."

Falcon didn't know what to say.

"Gotta go," said the Sergeant. "Keep your eyes open kid."

Three days later, Captain Writer sat at his desk going over the morning reports listening to the Undersheriff give him an earful. "You need to let Deputy Falcon Sane go today."

"Why would we let him go? He's one of our best deputies."

"It isn't working out with him," said the Undersheriff.

"What are you talking about? I just signed off on his last evaluation; everything was fine. He's the best applicant for the Dive and Rescue Team, not to mention he's the DSA Vice President."

"You need to wake up. Someone else has already been picked for the DART team. It ain't gonna be him."

"This is crazy. I'll talk to the sheriff."

The undersheriff leaned in, as a nicotine stench assaulted Captain Writer. "Who do you think sent me down here, dipshit? I don't know this Sane guy, just get rid of him today. And don't make any noise about it, or you could be a lieutenant by dinner tonight."

Falcon and Patrick stood in Control Room Bravo as they oversaw the maximum-security inmates. Falcon's regular eight-hour shift had ended four hours before at 7:00 a.m., but due to a staffing shortage, an issue Falcon brought up with his supervisors almost daily, he'd been ordered to stay over. Now at 11:00 a.m., his body clock was calling for sleep. The Control Room phone rang, "CRB" he answered.

"Deputy Sane?"

"Yes."

"Captain Writer needs to see you in his office after you're relieved."

"Ten four." *Probably wants to discuss the new jail protocol.*

Patrick and Falcon continued to scan the area.

"You know," said Patrick. "We've worked together some time now. I've told you about my wonderful wife, but you've never mentioned anyone."

Falcon grinned, "I never kiss and tell."

Patrick chuckled, "Wasn't asking for details, just wondered if you were married or had a girlfriend?"

"Neither. Been searching for the right one my entire life."

"Really?" said Patrick.

"Yep. Appears I've been looking for love in all the wrong places."

"Johnny Cash?"

"Johnny Lee."

Patrick said, "I was close."

"Hardly."

"What do you mean all the wrong places?"

Falcon described crossing America and parts of Europe.

"Let me get this straight. You've been all over the world, London, Paris, Dublin, Madrid and in nearly every state in America looking for one woman?"

Falcon turned his head as his eye swept across the other pods and smiled. "Not one woman, my friend. The woman."

Patrick scrutinized his buddy. "You hitchhiked, drove, walked, and slept on planes and trains …"

Falcon nodded as he still eyed the inmates.

"… Over the Rocky Mountains, up through the Midwest into

Minneapolis and into Maine during the winter?"

Falcon laughed, "Did I mention the blizzard in Kentucky?"

"You did all that and more, for a woman?"

"Not a woman. *The woman*."

"Wow," said Patrick, "I thought I was a romantic."

One of the inmates started to dig in the trash.

"Get out of the trash, Lickes," Falcon said over the intercom.

"What were you thinking when you started this, this, search?" Patrick asked.

How do I explain it? This calling — since I was little I knew my life would be about finding her and helping others. What words would describe a desire so strong I found myself constantly searching every situation for clues as to where she is? "It wasn't so much thinking as a feeling. Feeling her out there and knowing it was my calling to find her. My guess is when I do, I'm going to find out she is quite a traveler. That's got to be the reason I've been to all these places. I didn't go to Europe to sightsee. I kept moving, talking to new faces looking for her. I might still be there if I hadn't run out of cash."

"Why Europe? Do you think she's English or French?"

"That's a good question. I've wondered about that too. No, she's definitely American. I feel it in my bones. I don't know why I went over there. I just had to."

"Have you ever heard of Match.com?"

Falcon laughed, "The Internet dating thing?"

"Yeah."

"Isn't that for people who can't find dates? I don't have that problem."

Patrick laughed, "No, I have some friends who were very successful. They swear by it."

Falcon studied his friend. "Really?"

"You should try it. Can't say why I've suddenly become a

matchmaker, but I think you should check it out."

"Match.com?"

"Match.com," said Patrick.

Match.com? An Internet website? Could it be that easy? Is she there, right now waiting for me? The telephone rang.

Falcon answered, "CRB."

"Deputy Sane?"

"Speaking."

"Captain Writer needs to see you in his office after you're relieved."

"Ten four. Heard you the first time."

"What's up?" Patrick asked.

Falcon hung up the phone. "Writer wants to see me in his office after shift."

"Is this normal?"

Falcon shrugged, "We sit down once a week since the DSA election. But it's usually before shift not after."

The phone rang again.

"CRB."

"Is Deputy Traveller in there?"

"Yes," said Falcon.

"Good. Tell him he's been assigned to CRB. You are clear to go home."

"Ten four," Falcon stood and stretched. "It's all yours big man. Looks like coming up to see me before your shift started earned you CRB duty for today. I'm off to see the wizard."

"Remember that Internet thing I told you about."

"What's it called again?"

"Match.com."

"Got it Suzy matchmaker." He patted his friend's back. "I'll try and check it out today when I get home."

Captain Writer waited solemnly at his desk for Deputy Sane.

He heard his secretary greet him in the outer office when he arrived.

"Go on in Falcon," she said. "He's ready for you."

"Thanks, Betty," Falcon smiled bright. "How's your day going?"

Betty had been with Captain Writer five years and the department 15. A sweet, competent woman, she appreciated the difficulty of the job these young people attempted to accomplish. She liked Falcon very much, who was always polite and friendly, unlike some of his fellow deputies. She knew what was about to happen and struggled to hide her feelings.

"I've had better. Just go on in, honey."

"Sorry to hear that. Is there anything I can do?"

"Unfortunately no."

Betty's heart ached knowing what awaited Falcon.

"Okay," he said, not wanting to pry. "Please let me know if I can help."

She nodded and tried not to cry.

Falcon entered Writer's office. "Hey Captain, what's the good word?"

The captain motioned toward a chair and in a very professional manner said, "Take a seat."

Falcon sensed something wasn't right.

"There's no easy way to say this so I'm just going to say it, Falcon. The department is releasing you on probation. I need your badge and your weapon."

Falcon leaned forward as he considered what the captain just said. "Are you serious? I just finished working a 12-hour shift."

Captain Writer stewed over that fact, and that the order came in an hour ago. *They worked the kid overtime and then made me fire him! Unbelievable assholes!*

"I was not aware of that Falcon. I am sorry. I'm simply following orders."

Falcon felt stifled, his natural inclination to talk through difficult situations to find a solution wanted to engage, although he sensed it was useless. However he pressed his search for a crack in the door. His recent application to the FBI appeared hopeful after scoring high on their first written test. How would he explain to the Bureau or any future employer being fired? "Why am I being let go, captain?"

"I don't have a reason for you, Falcon. I don't know."

"Don't you have to have a reason to fire someone?"

Writer's sighed heavily, "Technically no; you're still on probation so we don't need a reason."

"Have you ever fired a person without having a reason?"

Good question, kid. "Not that I'm aware of."

"So there is no reason why I'm being fired?"

"I'm not aware of one. This was not my call Falcon."

It finally sunk in what was happening. Just like Falcon, Captain Writer was the sheriff's pawn. Falcon liked Captain Writer, so there wasn't any point in yelling at him, which the sheriff probably wanted anyway. A few months ago, per Falcon's request, Captain Writer had written him a letter of recommendation to use and apply to graduate school. "Is it okay if I use the letter of recommendation still?"

"Absolutely, son, absolutely. It's the least I can do."

"Okay. Thank you," Falcon said. He sat for a brief second and gathered his thoughts. "Be back in a minute."

He returned from his locker with his badge, ID card, weapon and magazines, extra clothes and the rest of his lunch. Placing the items and unloaded Beretta on the captain's desk, he extended his hand. "I guess this is it, captain."

"I am sorry about this," said the captain as he shook Falcon's hand.

"Me too," he said then exited out the door. "Goodbye, Betty. I hope you feel better soon."

Betty forced a smile as she thought it wise not to speak or she might start to cry again.

Falcon closed the door behind him and hurried through the corridor he'd entered 15 months ago for the first time. Popping out the back security entrance, he hustled down the stairs and walked quickly toward his truck. After five steps he broke into a run and then a sprint. He had to get out of there before anyone saw him. He didn't have time for tears – theirs or his. Although the job had its challenges it met his need to belong. Once again Falcon felt ostracized from society.

Captain Writer watched the young man stride away then stepped into his secretary's office.

"This is so wrong Betty," he said.

"Yes, it is," she murmured.

A few hours later the rumor mill caught fire. *Was it true? Did they fire Sane? Why?* Gossip has a wicked way of moving at the speed of light. Some said he quit because he was tired of the political crap. No one believed it; he would never quit. The second story was he'd roughed up an inmate. Everyone knew that was impossible. After enough chatter, the truth had burrowed through. The sheriff was scared of losing the DSA endorsement, which could possibly cost him the election, and the message to everyone in the department was: If he'd fire Sane, no one was safe.

Falcon drove home and spat expletives. *Freaking unbelievable! Bust my hump for what, thrown out like trash!* That last thought reminded him of the conversation with the D.A.R.T. sergeant. The words, "be careful," kept running through his head. *Be careful. Be careful. It's too fucking late to be careful now! Now what?*

The Undersheriff informed his boss the dirty work was complete. Sane was technically released on probation and had left the premises. Free from confrontation, the rotund sheriff waddled toward Captain Writer's office. *That's what democracy is all about, power in the hands of the few, elected by the ever-decreasing intelligence of the many.* He'd realized long ago most citizens didn't bother to vote. With that little nugget of information he targeted only the people who voted consistently. *Who cares what the others think? If you can't get off your lazy asses and vote then you get what the elected fed you.* He knew Deputy Falcon Sane was different.

"That motherfucker was dangerous," he muttered to himself ignoring Betty and wobbled into Writer's office. "I hear it's done."

Captain Writer hated this man. The sheriff was a conglomeration of everything wrong with politics and leadership.

He said flatly, "What's that sir?"

"Don't fuck around. You know what I'm talking about."

The captain's eyes narrowed in anger for a brief second before self-preservation kicked in. He succumbed to the same belief system perpetuated through most of his generation. *Live for the moment. Don't worry about the future or anyone else.*

"I apologize sir," he capitulated. "Yes, it is done."

The obese man eyed the captain. "You know Writer, there are three lieutenants begging to be a captain right now."

"I am aware sir."

"I'm not sure you are."

"Sir?"

The sheriff glared at him. "The undersheriff told me what you said."

Writer felt sweat drip from under his armpits as the sheriff bore down on him. "My apologies sir. Won't happen again, I appreciate all you've given me."

The sheriff kept glaring then sneered, "That's a good boy. I'm glad we had this little chat."

"Me too sir." Writer clenched his jaw as another layer was shaved off his soul.

Falcon hadn't slept in 24 hours but adrenaline was speeding

through his veins. He changed clothes and put on his running shoes, slapped on an old Walkman he'd hung onto, and sprinted down the stairs to ACDC's "Back in Black". Stride after stride he ran through his neighborhood and worked out his frustration. He stopped to pop out 50 pushups and jumped back up and took off again. *What do I do now? Obviously I need a new job. That shouldn't be too hard. I'll make a couple of calls and should be set.* Two group homes he had worked for previously always needed staff. That short-term problem solved he focused on Messmate County. Legally there wasn't much he could do. Although they'd never sent him to any training this would be a difficult thing to argue in a court of law. *I was never trained so I should get my job back ... probably not a winner. Maybe challenge the firing or being released on probation, but lawsuits cost money*. He was a saver, but didn't have the funds to throw into a lawsuit that may or may not work. After dropping down for another 50 pushups, Falcon bounced back up. Stable financially, he'd been trained as a child to put money away in case of an emergency. Besides, he knew he'd have a new job shortly. One last set of 50 pushups and he'd finally locked onto the injustice of it all. This entire situation was entirely wrong, and there appeared to be nothing he could do about it. He was a cog, a piece of trash to be thrown away whenever his skills weren't useful or became dangerous to the ones in power. So much rage stirred in him that his hands shook. He banged out shadow punches one after the other as he ran down the street. Left right, left right, his arms pumped like pistons as his lungs screamed for oxygen and his heart worked overtime trying to provide it. Left right, left right, he kept punching with only one thought in mind: *I'm coming for you, you piece of shit sheriff*!

"Revenge!" he screamed into the sky. "I want revenge!"

Falcon's heart and legs required him to come to a stop. He gasped for air and walked in a circle with his hands above his head and a strange quiet filled his body. *Is that what I really want? Revenge?*

His breathing began to return to normal as he continued circling and contemplating the question. *Revenge ... revenge ... revenge*? His mind worked through a conversation he'd had years ago while traveling, and on a whim gone with a friend to a palm reader. *What had she said?* The sound of her voice floated through his mind.

"No, you don't believe in revenge. You believe in retribution."

He hadn't thought of that in years. She was right. *Not revenge. Revenge was filled with hate. Not justice. Justice was blind, and apparently deaf and dumb. Not justice. Retribution.* Falcon glanced toward the sky. *I hear ya Big Fella. I understand. What do we do now?*

That night and a few Cokes later, Falcon and Charlie sat on their couch as Falcon finished his story.

"What an asshole." Charlie fumed.

Falcon nodded calmly, his anger now channeled into moving forward.

"What are you going to do? I know you'll never do it but there's always unemployment. You did pay for it." Charlie asked.

"Not in a million years. I'll dig ditches the rest of my life before I sign up for that."

"I get it, just thought I'd mention it. Don't worry about the rent or anything else. I've got you covered."

"I appreciate it, really, but please don't ever say that to me again. I have plenty of money saved and nothing around here will change."

"You'd do the same for me."

"And you'd say the same thing I just did."

Charlie smiled, "So true."

"Nothing changes brother. Not interested in pity. I've already got a new job lined up beginning this weekend. It's a Friday through Sunday gig. Think of all the couch time you and Lara will get," he winked.

"Good point. Always a silver lining with you."

"Nope, make mine gold," Falcon laughed.

"What's the job? Back with the abused kids?"

"Yep. That's a job I fear will always be available."

"Not when you become President."

Falcon smiled wryly, "Yeah we see how well I'm doing in government work."

"I'm not sure why but I have a feeling one day we will be talking about that again, and when we do I want it on the record, that I will be your Chief of Staff," said Charlie.

Falcon laughed, "Sure why not. And when I'm Santa Claus you can be Head Elf."

"No, if you're Santa Claus I want to be Rudolph."

"Rudolph? Why Rudolph?"

"Because when Santa needed help Rudolph led the way."

Falcon looked at his best friend and extended his hand. "Deal."

"Deal Mr. President."

The new job consumed Falcon's weekend. The kids were like a tornado, and their house was a mess. By Sunday night the residents were exhausted from 10-mile hikes through the mountains and secure in the fact an adult was finally in charge. None bothered to ask for dessert, as they knew the new counselor would say to eat fruit. They brushed their teeth for the third night in a row and collapsed into bed. Falcon arrived home later that night, worn out but at peace. Working with kids always filled his heart. He found Charlie and Lara lying on the couch watching a movie. "Hey buddy. How was the new job?"

"Good. Really good. Hi Lara."

"Hi."

"There's a message on the machine for you from Georgia Blanco."

Falcon's entire body turned to stone. He'd forgotten about the Messmate County drama over the past few days.

"What'd she say?"

"I didn't listen to the whole thing, but she was apologizing for getting you fired and wanted to help."

Falcon contemplated the machine and pushed the button.

"Hello Falcon. This is Georgia Blanco. I just heard about you being fired, and I'm so sorry. I feel responsible and want to help. Please give me a call."

Maybe I'll call, or she can cool her jets for a while. He went back to the front room in time for a commercial for Match.com. He remembered Patrick's comments. *That's two. Things usually come in threes.* The commercial finished.

Charlie muted the TV. "You know I've heard people have pretty good success with that Internet dating thing."

And that was three. Charlie had Falcon's full attention. "Really?"

Lara looked at Charlie and raised her eyebrows.

He nodded, "We didn't say anything because some people think it's weird, but that's how we met."

Falcon was surprised by his best friend. "I'm pretty sure my Chief of Staff can't be keeping secrets from me."

"Not secrets. Just things you don't need to know Mr. President."

"We've had too many presidents who've worked the 'I-don't-need-to- know' policy. My need to know is very clear. I need to know everything."

"It wasn't a secret. It was a superstition."

"Wow, we're splitting hairs already. I can't wait to hear your version of welfare and immigration."

"Oh no, I'll leave that stuff up to you. I'm the guy that keeps the car filled with oil and gas. You're the one driving it." He joked with all sincerity.

"You're quick with the answers, I'll give you that. Match.com?"

"Yeah check it out. It's really easy to sign up."

"I will. See you tomorrow Lara, Chief."

Charlie said, "Do you want me to save the message on the machine?"

"Nah I have her number. I'll call her in the morning."

"All right. Goodnight Falcon."

"Goodnight."

Calling Georgia Blanco kept Falcon ruminating for a week. His radar up, he understood some people had a voracious appetite for power. A desire to control others was a foreign concept to him. Financial freedom, yearning for space, yes, but he didn't want authority over people. Ingrained in him was to lead by example, coach others to success that they might enjoy the fruits of their labors, not someone else's. *The woman seemed pleasant enough. What else could possibly go wrong? I can't lose my job again. My reputation is already part of the gossip tree. What more could they do me?* He didn't want to think about that, he knew the answer. They could charge him with a crime. Didn't matter he had done nothing and no proof. *Yep, politics could get pretty rough.* Still, it wasn't in his nature to stand down and allow someone to abuse him. He made the call.

"Hi, Falcon!" said Georgia. "Thank you for calling back. I'm so sorry about your being fired. Actually shocked. I feel responsible."

"Thanks. Yeah, I'm not quite sure what happened. Meeting with you wasn't a secret. I was performing my duty as DSA Vice President. I'm glad he didn't find out about Patrick."

Georgia made a mental note to his comment. The fact that Patrick Traveller still had his job meant only part of the meeting was reported to the sheriff. This didn't surprise her since the mention of Patrick's presence was insignificant to her. It was Falcon who worried the sheriff. She just didn't think he would stupidly fire a sitting DSA board member, especially one with the reputation Deputy Sane had built in a short time. She knew she was responsible for Falcon's predicament, but her call wasn't about helping him, it was about him helping her.

"Falcon, I promise this will be corrected. I have an attorney friend and a contact with the local newspaper, *The Republic Reveal*. I'll have them contact you. With your permission of course. The attorney is in a trial right now and very busy, so he'll call you next month." *Which is better since it'll be closer to the election.*

Falcon listened and weighed this information.

"He's an expert in employment law," Georgia continued, "and can file a legal action against the department requesting you be reinstated with back pay and possible punitive damages."

"I can't afford an attorney, Georgia."

"He's agreed to work pro bono. It won't cost you a thing. He's a friend of mine and hates the sheriff. Honestly, he can't wait to help us."

Falcon did not miss the usage of the word *us*.

"Furthermore, Falcon, I'll personally guarantee if I win this election to reinstate you, with back pay. I need good people like you, leaders who aren't afraid to do the right thing. We can fix this mess together."

Falcon twisted the phone cord around his finger. *How much worse could it really get? Besides, friends told me about the lies being spread regarding my being fired and it pisses me off.* "Other deputies are being warned to watch what they say or they could be next."

"Yes, I've heard."

"There's also garbage floating around that I abused an inmate."

"I know. Nobody believes it, most deputies are pissed, but some are real scared. If someone like you could be discharged, anyone could be let go or demoted."

Falcon's mind waded through his options. He remembered the D.A.R.T. sergeant's description of the sheriff and Georgia being parasites. *Still, what else is left? Fight with the tools available or surrender.* "Okay, Georgia, I'll do it."

"Perfect, I guarantee if I win this election you'll have your job back the day I'm sworn in."

"I like the sound of that."

"Me too." She imagined the sign on her office door: Sheriff Georgia Blanco. "I'll set up a meeting with my newspaper contact. The three of us can get your story on record, and then I'll comment about the legality and corrupt punishment pressed upon on you."

"Thanks," said Falcon.

"No need to thank me. I know I got you fired. Time to clean up my mess, and I'll see about a settlement too."

"I don't need a settlement. All I want is my job."

"Trust me Falcon," Georgia purred. "I'll take care of everything."

After hanging up, Falcon mulled over his next move. Working with kids would keep him going for now, but no longer was it the career path he wanted to follow. As he perused the classifieds once more, a position with the Watch County Probation Department looked promising, a mere 30 miles from his apartment. He hoped to get his job at Messmate County back, however he was now experienced enough to know, hope had nothing to do with success. Hope was something children believed in at Christmas time or the sensation lottery ticket buyers embraced – that is, before somebody else's numbers were called. *Success is about perseverance.*

Falcon paused when the next reporter in line raised his hand. "I hate to stop you, but did you ever go to Match.com?"

Falcon grinned, "I did."

He pointed to a stunning blonde who stood quietly off to the side.

Every person in the room followed Falcon's gaze and a chorus of voices exhaled a collective sigh as all eyes focused on Avery.

"Ladies and gentlemen," said Falcon, "my beautiful wife, Avery."

The magnificent, svelte woman glided across the stage and joined her husband.

"And yes," added Falcon, "we met on Match.com. Gotta love the Internet." Falcon kissed Avery gently on the mouth, and she slipped an arm around his waist.

A voice from the back of the room said, "Might we have permission to ask Mrs. Sane a few questions?"

Falcon cocked his head toward Avery as a cue to see if she was interested. Words were unnecessary; she smiled at him and their communication was complete. Falcon adjusted the microphone and stepped aside for his leading lady.

"Good evening ladies and gentlemen," she said. "So, who is next?"

"James Bunky, NBS. Who contacted who on Match.Com?"

Avery laughed, "Enquiring minds want to know, hmmm?"

The reporter completed the line from the old commercial, "I want to know."

She stole a quick look at Falcon and grinned. "He contacted me of course."

The crowd laughed as Avery continued.

"My wonderful husband sent me an email filled with hilarious jokes."

"Tim Angelo, MSNBS News. Do you still have the email?"

Avery shook her head, "No, unfortunately it was deleted. Kind of like the emails from Lois Lerner."

The reporters took note of the comment about the former head of the IRS. Avery Sane was not just another pretty face.

Avery flipped her long hair over one shoulder.

"Paul Roark, Wolf News. Did you answer him?"

"No Paul I waited. My female intuition told me he would try again." She smiled sweetly. "Obviously he did, and since I have the mike right now I'll give you my version of the story. My

'Baby-Cakes' might have a little different slant."

Avery regaled the reporters with their first short encounter. She'd had a BBQ to attend, and didn't have time to meet him. Falcon, as Falcon does, talked her into a quick 20-minute rendezvous, in the parking lot of a local restaurant. Lilli, Avery's puppy, had bolted from the car and scampered to Falcon as though she'd known him forever. She'd jumped into his arms, and had given him kisses as Falcon and Avery stood by their cars and chatted.

Falcon edged up behind Avery at the podium and leaned into the mike. "This gorgeous woman, with the sweetest little dog, gave me a few brief minutes, shook my hand, and then drove away!"

The reporters appeared enchanted by the winsome, engaging couple, except for the crotchety old goat next in line. He could appreciate the woman's beauty, and the story of how their relationship had begun, but the romance between the candidate and his wife didn't interest him beyond an eye-blink. He pressed forward and did not even formulate an appropriate question. "So, you were talking about Watch County."

Falcon shot the man a stern look. "Yes, I was." He turned to Avery. "Did you have anything more to add sweetheart?"

She flashed a genuine smile, kissed Falcon's cheek and sashayed away from the podium.

Still captured under Avery's spell, most occupants in the room watched her as she headed toward her spot off stage.

Falcon beamed. "By the way folks my wife is an Air Force Veteran."

A syncopated cadence of applause broke out.

"Thank you darling," said Falcon, "and thank you for your service to our country." He winked at her.

Avery's cheeks flushed crimson. *It was the best part of my life until I met you baby!*

Falcon smiled at her. *That's my girl.*

The crabby reporter cleared his throat, "Ahem!" He raised a disapproving eyebrow at Falcon.

Falcon's face tightened as he acknowledged him with a stare. *Freaking boomers never learn do they?*

"Okay we were talking about Watch County. The Watch County job with the Probation Department was an entry-level position, but through hard work and persistence I believed opportunities to move ahead would present themselves. The hiring process was quite an eye-opener on many levels. After receiving written documentation that my application was being considered for candidate selection, I procured a high score on a written exam, stayed focused during an incredibly uncomfortable psych evaluation, and finally met with the hiring coordinator who requested clarification regarding my resume."

Bert Holt, Chief Employment Officer at WCP, scanned the papers on his desk. "I'm reading here that you were released on probation by Messmate County. Tell me about that."

Falcon summarized the information Bert Holt had before him.

"I worked at Messmate approximately 15 months, copies of my reviews indicate my behavior was acceptable or above. I was voted VP of our association and attached is a letter of recommendation from my acting captain who thought highly of me. Officially I was given no reason whatsoever for my release. The rumor being spread is I assaulted an inmate, which is completely false. As part of my responsibilities as Association VP, I met with the current sheriff and the woman running against him. Following the meeting with Ms. Blanco I was released, I believe due to a political agenda."

Bert observed Falcon while he spoke. Plenty of people on both sides of law enforcement had lied directly to his face. *If this kid is lying he is a master.* The sit-down was a mere formality, as Bert had already personally completed a background check, which was rare. Anyone with Falcon's resume and incredible test scores was the kind of talent he made it a point to employ. They just didn't fit his applying for such a low position. However after being fired from a law enforcement job, getting a new one was difficult. Being young Falcon was going about it the right way, starting over at the bottom, and counting on his skills to succeed. The Messmate County Sheriff's management was very tightlipped about Falcon and stated nothing good or bad. On the other hand the deputies told a different story regarding Sane; the alleged assault on an inmate was complete garbage.

"I watched him on camera the entire time," said the deputy on duty during the incident in question. "Nothing like that happened. Falcon was fired because the sheriff was sending a message that all deputies better support him for re-election or else."

Others spoke highly of Falcon too, although doing so put their jobs on the line. Bert admired Falcon for standing against corruption still he needed to know if the kid had anger issues. He telephoned the psychiatrist used for evaluations and placed an order to "push the kid's buttons." He received the results over the phone, and days later the outcome still made him smile.

Dr. Rob Embree called Bert on the phone. "Hi Bert, just finished with your new protégé."

"How did it go?"

"Quite well, but I have to admit it was painful to watch."

"Why?"

"I asked him how he would respond to someone screaming in his face. He answered perfectly. I repeated the question. He paused for a second and answered as before, perfectly. He demonstrated no signs of aggression or temper, just puzzled, which is normal when you're asked the same question twice. I put my pen and notepad down, stared at him, and said, 'I'm going to ask the same question one more time. Really think about your answer; the first two were completely wrong and if you don't answer correctly this time I'll fail you on the spot.'"

Bert said, "Geez … I told you to push his buttons Rob, not kill the kid."

"You asked me to make sure."

"Then what happened?"

"I said to prepare for his last chance. If he screwed up he was done, then asked if he had anything to say. He responded clear and calm. He was happy to answer my question again, but his answer wouldn't change. He didn't want to fail, but wouldn't change his mind based on the outcome of my decision. He nodded and said he was ready to answer again if I wanted him to. I glared at him and told him he'd just failed the test. He definitely appeared frustrated, but in full control of his emotions. He stated he thought he answered the question quite well and told me he disagreed with my assessment. I switched to a few garbage questions, giving him time to explode. He didn't. I told him to wait in his chair, that I would be back in a minute. I returned 10 minutes later. Still calm, he asked if I had any more questions. I said no. He asked if we were finished, I said we were. He shook my hand and thanked me for my time. I watched him walk back to his truck. He wasn't happy, but he certainly wasn't out of control."

"Anything else?"

"Yes. Obviously I can't read his mind, but it appeared once I told him he had failed he seemed to process the information quickly, weighing the ramifications, then zipped through the stages of grief in seconds, except a moment of frustration and moved to resolution. Threatening to fail him would have set off anyone with anger issues. They always see themselves as the victim. That young man is no victim and doesn't have anger issues. If anything he's a protector, not an aggressor."

Bert was impressed with Falcon. The kid was collateral damage of a corrupt department. It was unfortunate good guys like him were sacrificed due to an irresponsible culture perpetuated by lying power-hungry people.

"Okay, Falcon. I did your background check myself and confirmed your story, and you passed your psych eval with flying colors."

The sheer relief on Falcon's face was apparent. He thought Bert had called him in as a courtesy to say he'd been turned down.

Bert smiled at his relief. "The doc said you did very well."

"That's not what he told me!" Falcon laughed.

"I had to check you out. Your story is rare. Actually, I've never heard one quite like it."

Falcon shrugged; he'd received the short end of the stick more times than he could count, but the reassurance and knowledge of passing the psych evaluation was comforting. Although he never doubted himself, he was beginning to doubt his opportunities in law enforcement.

Bert offered his hand. "The job at Watch County Probation Department is yours son, welcome aboard."

Days turned into weeks. Falcon worked at Watch County and filled in with on-call shifts at the group home managing to save 50 percent of his paychecks by living well below his means. A month passed since he'd last spoken to Georgia and finally an appointment had been arranged for Falcon with her attorney friend.

Richard Lemontree, a practicing defense attorney in Messmate County, had known Georgia Blanco for 25 years. His prime motivation this year was getting her elected sheriff. He would rid himself of a nemesis in the current sheriff, and his access to power would improve with her in office. Despite the 12-pack of Mountain Dew and two packages of Marlboro cigarettes Lemontree consumed in any 24-hour period, obesity, kidney stones and emphysema had not stopped him yet from making a decent living. It was, after all, Mess-mate County with plenty of criminals to defend.

Falcon refrained from normal breathing as he sat downstairs in the waiting room. The wretched odor of stale cigarette smoke and a smell he could not quite discern assaulted his senses. *Let's get this over with and get out of here!* The dimly-lit room created an ominous feeling of impending doom. Heavy energy hung in the air probably due to the revolving door of criminals passing through each day. Falcon recognized the feeling from having worked at the county jail.

"You must be Mr. Sane!" A voice boomed from nowhere, and a man as tall as he was wide hobbled down the staircase.

Falcon stood and stared at the massive wreckage who barely made it down the stairs. He cringed. *This is my attorney? I guess you do get what you pay for.*

Lemontree extended his arm.

Being well-mannered Falcon didn't refuse the man's hand.

"Yes, I am," Falcon answered.

The pear-shaped man wobbled around and headed back toward the stairs. "Come on up, and we'll talk in my office. Anything to drink?"

"No, thank you."

"Suit yourself."

Falcon kept a distance between them as he followed Lemontree to his office.

"Have a seat." The attorney motioned to a chair across from the messiest desk Falcon had ever seen. Staggered files piled a foot high, crumpled fast-food wrappers, molded paper plates, and empty Mountain Dew cans littered the entire room.

Falcon reluctantly sat.

As the attorney wheezed, he steadied himself against his desk. He rifled through a drawer and procured a bottle of whiskey. Not bothering to offer again, he filled a large water tumbler to the top with Jim Beam then collapsed into his huge, sagging creaking chair.

"So I hear the three of us have a problem with the sheriff."

Falcon noticed his usage of the word *us*. The same pronoun used by Georgia Blanco. "I know I have a problem, and understood you could help me out."

Lemontree gulped half the glass of JB. "I don't see why not. I've heard the story. You're meeting with Georgia and a local reporter later today to give your version of events. I'll file a claim for you against the county requesting your immediate reinstatement, which will probably be refused. Then we move to a hearing where I'll present our case. With any luck, Georgia will win this election next month and per my conversation with her, you'll be rehired and rewarded back pay. Once that happens I'll close your case, as that's the outcome we're all hoping for."

Falcon wasn't big on the word hope. People who hoped for things to occur rarely endeavored to work toward making things happen. "Okay, but what if she wins and doesn't reinstate me? Will you still be my attorney pro bono?"

"Of course …" Lemontree dug a thick finger into a crumpled cellophane package and fished out the last cigarette. "I'm here for you Mr. Sane, but I don't see that as the outcome. I personally guarantee once she's elected you'll have your job back. She's going to need people like you."

That's exactly what Georgia said. "You personally guarantee this?"

"Yes, she told me she planned to make this right."

The attorney patted himself down in search of a light and came up empty-handed. He paused to study Falcon, who was fit, well-spoken, and cut right to the chase when he asked questions. He exuded a certain dangerous energy. The kind fools met with when they searched for trouble. It didn't usually go well for his kind, people who lived by morals and ethics, something those playing the power game in the gutters of government rarely possessed.

"As I said, I've heard most of your story. Anything to add?" asked Lemontree.

"No sir."

The attorney emptied his glass, sat forward, and refilled it again.

In 34 years he couldn't remember ever having had a case like this one. He'd gotten guilty sentences reduced with plea bargains, and even freed a murderer through a technicality. He rocked in his chair, thinking, *If only I'd taken care of myself this case could have put me on top.* He still dreamed of one day being the District Attorney. But his poor diet, alcoholism and usage of prescription pills made for a sorry sight and even worse demeanor. His view of life, like millions of his generation, was to live for today. When he was completely honest with himself he knew that was a big lie. His once-sharp mind now a sad mixture of Valium, whiskey or gin, he simply couldn't keep up with the hard work required to be successful anymore. Fortunately for him, he'd been a good enough attorney and made enough connections to not have to pay alimony to any of his wives. He made an agreement with each one of them on a certain amount of child support and only occasionally missed payments. He helped two of his three wives work the system and got them both on SSI or long-term disability. Neither of them had real issues other than laziness, but he figured his taxes were paying for them, or "my paycheck," as wife number three called it. Besides, then it didn't come directly out of his pocket. He'd given up on guilt and shame decades ago and couldn't remember the last time he even thought about the morality of his decisions. That he was thinking about it now was due to the young man in front of him. Strangely, he didn't hold it against him as most of the people he knew would. There was a sense of peace about the young man that he seemed to exude, and it covered the entire office.

"Okay. Any other questions?" asked Lemontree.

"I don't think so," said Falcon.

They wrapped it up.

"You have my number. I'll be in touch in a couple of days with an update."

Falcon said, "Thank you for your time."

"Sure … sure. On your way out if you see a woman downstairs tell her to come up. I have a proposition on how to keep her out of jail, *again*."

"I will."

Falcon moved swiftly and quietly down the staircase; he couldn't wait to leave this place behind.

In the lobby stood a pale woman maybe 50, who wore a skirt too short and heels too high. Her hair was bleached and frayed, and multiple tattoos covered her bony shoulders. Thick clown-like makeup hid her natural features, and the heaviness of her perfume mixed with the cigarette smoke was nauseating.

"Mr. Lemontree said you could go up," said Falcon.

She focused on the voice, and flashed a smile, devoid of top teeth. Taking a drag off her cigarette she exhaled and checked Falcon over. *Yum! Who's this hot, tall drink of water? I'd do him for free.*

"Mister Lemontree!" she cackled and hacked out a smoker's cough.

Falcon didn't know the woman, but he'd seen plenty of her type come through the jail on a variety of charges, usually prostitution, shoplifting, and sometimes possession of meth. He rarely dealt with the female inmates. He felt sad for most of them, but any compassion demonstrated in that setting was a recipe for disaster. He treated them like men, for the most part, and only verbally cracked down when they tried to flirt with him. He had zero tolerance for that, and the women learned quickly to save that technique for other officers. The inmates knew who the good and bad deputies were. If you were doing something you shouldn't, you didn't want Deputy Sane around. If you were being threatened or getting the crap beaten out of you by other inmates, you wanted Deputy Sane to be the first one there.

"I call him Dick," she snorted, "and he likes it!"

Falcon didn't bother to answer. He held his breath and headed straight for the door and fresh air.

"That ain't all he likes neither baby! Dick likes it when I suck his dick!" The diseased-ridden woman coughed through another spell.

One more step to freedom, and Falcon heard her for the last time.

"I'll suck you all's dick for free!"

Falcon hit the sidewalk and almost ran. Shaking his head, he tried to rid the scene behind him from his mind. He whispered a silent prayer for the two wretched souls and a prayer of gratitude that the good Lord had him on a dramatically different path. *But for the Grace of God go I.*

The prostitute watched the young man disappear. She had a few more puffs on her cigarette. Dick wouldn't let her smoke while she "paid her bill". The last time she did, busy on her knees with her head in his lap, they both forgot the cigarette was lit. Neither one noticed his pants catch on fire until he started to scream and jumped out of his chair, threw his back out for a week, and slammed her head against the desk. She took one last drag, flicked the butt onto the floor, and swallowed a couple of Darvocet procured from a trick last night. Dick was a fat prick who made her work off her bill in 15-minute increments. She owed him 20 hours for keeping her ass out of jail a month ago. *It would've been cheaper to just plead guilty* was her last coherent thought as the Darvocet numbed her body and mind. It was a lot easier to sell your soul while high on drugs.

Falcon met with Georgia and the reporter from the Republic Reveal. Georgia Blanco sat next to the reporter and listened intently while Falcon answered easily. *Of course it's easy.* He thought to himself. *The truth is never difficult to remember.*

The reporter scrutinized this man, Falcon Sane. He'd heard quite a bit about this situation and relished writing the story. He considered Georgia Blanco a friend and abhorred the current sheriff. *This piece will be a dream.* Yet, now as he met the guy this political drama engulfed, he felt bad for him. *Politicians will sacrifice anyone to win. He won't be the first casualty or the last.* "So obviously you are unhappy with the decision to fire you."

Falcon remained silent and shot the reporter a disgusted sarcastic facial expression. "Obviously."

When Falcon answered with the reporter's own word, "obviously," his hair prickled beneath his shirt collar as he realized the degree of the deputy's irritation. Pity for the man turned to respect, and perhaps a little fear. *Let's see if I can backtrack.*

"No disrespect intended," the reporter said.

"None taken," Falcon smiled, although his eyes did not soften.

"Living well is the best revenge."

Falcon laughed at the implication. "Revenge is for the weak and shortsighted. If you plan to travel any road, grab retribution in both hands and clear a path for others."

"Isn't that what justice is for?" asked the reporter.

Falcon's face tightened slightly. "A philosopher trapped in a reporter's body, huh?"

"A philosopher perhaps," the reporter laughed. "But one with money in the bank. What about criminal justice?"

"Criminal justice is an oxymoron," replied Falcon. "There is no justice for abuse of a child. No punishment or time spent makes someone's abuse of others justifiable. Anyone who thinks so is perpetuating a fraud onto the people and themselves."

"It's the best system in the world."

"No, freedom is the best system in the world." Falcon leaned his elbows on the table and laced his fingers together. "The consistent falsehood that we are fine, because the rest of the world is worse than we are, is exactly the small-minded thinking of revenge types. With this premise, the trash in your yard doesn't smell so bad because you live next to a dump. It's called a race to the bottom."

Georgia felt a need to redirect the conversation. "Okay, okay. I think we're getting a little off track here," she said nervously.

Falcon and the reporter glared at her with disdain.

The reporter wished to continue the conversation.

Falcon simply didn't trust her. "Actually, I have to go."

"Okay," said the reporter. "I'll finish up with Georgia. May I call you if I have other questions?"

"Certainly, Ms. Blanco has my number."

"Great. Nice to meet you Falcon."

"You too."

Falcon shook their hands, strode quickly to his vehicle, buckled up, and drove the speed limit as he left the town behind him. He exhaled deeply as he passed the county marker. Free of the cesspool known as Messmate County he smiled in anticipation of the weekend.

Early Saturday morning Falcon and Charlie laced up their shoes and jogged to the neighborhood park to seek a basketball court. These days most kids stayed indoors due to crumbling neighborhoods, video games or childhood obesity. Thus the half-mile run rewarded them with not one, but five empty courts that begged for attention. Scrutinizing each one closely for cracks, weeds and graffiti, the two friends surmised which court was the best.

Charlie stood on court three. "This one's pretty good buddy."

Falcon hustled over.

As they briefly stretched they took a few practice shots.

Falcon bounced on his toes. "I'm ready; let's go."

"Sounds good, shoot for outs?"

"Fire away superstar," Falcon beamed.

Charlie took a fade away 20 footer that just rimmed out.

Falcon grinned and gathered the rebound. "So close. I was really feeling it for you."

"You're gonna feel it in a minute," said Charlie.

"Bring it on Superman."

Falcon flipped the ball behind his back and started up court. As he glided past the half-court line, he head-faked to his right, crossed Charlie over, and blew by him.

Charlie realized his mistake, reverse-pivoted, gave chase, and took a swipe with his hand as Falcon drove for a layup. His elbow smacked the back of Falcon's head and knocked his sunglasses sideways as the ball rolled out of bounds.

Falcon stopped, and turned toward Charlie. His sunglasses covered one eye like a patch and the frame barely clung to his head. "One of these days little man, one of these days."

"I'm sorry but hey, I gotta do something otherwise these games aren't even fair."

"Hammering me in the head isn't an option lover boy."

"I'm just saying."

Falcon warned, "You know I have an elbow too."

Charlie laughed as he chased down the ball. He knew Falcon could throw haymakers, but their friendship was so strong Charlie never doubted he could get away with almost anything.

Falcon took the ball out at the top of the key.

The two men played full court hoops whenever they could, best of five games, usually to 21, each bucket counting for one, winning by two. When finished they were typically exhausted.

Falcon gave a drop step, faked right then went straight up and drained a 14-foot jumper. "That's right! Karma little man!" He back-pedaled down court.

Charlie jogged up and used a left-handed dribble, pulled up

from 22 feet, and let it fly. Swish.

"That what I'm talking about," he grinned. "Karma from the corner."

Falcon retrieved the ball and barreled up the right side as he looked for an opening and chirped at Charlie. "You're just too afraid to bring it inside. You know it's coming back in your face."

"Keep talking big man. I'll climb on your back if I have to."

Falcon laughed, drove to the middle, went behind his back, and used the backboard to flip the ball under the rim. Charlie leaped in the air and clobbered Falcon's wrist.

The ball hung in the air for a second and then fell through the basket.

"And one little man!"

Charlie shook his head. *Unbelievable.* He grabbed the ball and sprinted down the left side of the court. A quick head-fake got Falcon in the air, and Charlie headed for daylight and a layup. All of a sudden it got dark. Charlie felt Falcon right on his back. He contorted his body, switched hands, and flipped the ball behind his head as he never even looked at the basket. He felt the wind of a long arm whoosh over him, but the ball was away as he danced out from under the rim and turned around just in time to see his shot fall through the hoop.

"Give me a break! You didn't even see the rim!" said Falcon. "What a joke!"

Charlie jogged back down the court as he laughed and got back on defense. "The joke's on you superstar. Have a 'Coke and a Smile'."

Saturday games with Charlie were Falcon's only break in an incredibly busy life. Working long hours and saving his money, his life was on fast forward. Before he knew it the Messmate County voters exercised one of their rights.

The election results were in.

There was a new sheriff in town, and her name was Georgia Blanco.

Georgia, still high from her victory, headed to the law office of her old friend Richard Lemontree. He had issues, but he'd been loyal to her, and she would return the favor. It had taken her five years to get revenge, but get it she did. With her victory in hand the power she dreamed of awaited her. She was top cop, and it was time to wield authority. *Reward my benefactors and punish my detractors. It's going to be so much fun!* She floated up the stairs to celebrate with Lemontree. She rounded the corner, and pranced into his office.

He motioned for her to sit as he finished talking on the phone. "Thanks for calling me back, Mr. Sane. Good news, Georgia is the new sheriff. No doubt you'll be back to work once she's sworn in."

Georgia listened as Richard lied to Falcon. She wasn't bringing him back. The election was neck-and-neck before the deputy's story broke, but after the huge coverage Falcon received, the race was hers. She didn't like owing anyone, and not the type to experience guilt she figured the kid served his purpose. *Better to cut him loose now.*

Richard hung up. "I did my part. I rescinded the lawsuit against the Sheriff's Department today and will be sending a termination letter to Falcon tomorrow. You just heard me tell him you were going to hire him back, so what's the plan?"

"We'll see. Maybe he'll fade away. I don't get sworn in for another month."

Richard frowned. *This guy wasn't fading away.* He'd argued with her to reinstate him and got nowhere. Her rationale didn't make sense. She was making an enemy she didn't need just to prove she was in charge. Lemontree held no loyalty to Falcon; it just seemed like a dumb move.

"Why don't you reinstate him, give him his back pay, and let him resign on his own?"

"What if he won't?"

"What's your problem with this kid? He went out on a limb for you. He's one of the good guys, I know, because I'm not one of the good guys."

Georgia admired her manicure. "Bringing him back will make me look weak."

"How do you figure?"

"It just will," she snapped. "I don't want to discuss it further."

Richard lit a cigarette. "Whatever. I still think it's a dumb move."

She leveled him with her eyes and growled, "So you've said."

"When are you going to tell him?"

"When I get around to it; I'm busy, you know." She sat high in her chair. "I'm the sheriff."

"If you think you can ignore him you're sadly mistaken. He's one of those people you want on your side, not the other way around."

"Yeah, yeah, yeah, so you keep telling me."

"Okay. Don't say I didn't warn you."

Crossing her legs at the knee, she bounced her foot. "What's he gonna do? I'm the sheriff and a woman."

"You're not thinking rationally. It won't be a physical thing. This kid is bright. It may even take some time, but eventually he'll come for his pound of flesh, metaphorically speaking."

"Like what?"

"I don't know, maybe run for office himself. Maybe he's kept a journal of this entire fiasco and will find someone to do an exposé on you, or maybe write the exposé himself. Don't mistake kindness for weakness. If you do, the mistake will be all yours."

"You're his attorney."

"Not anymore. I told him because you were going to reinstate him our agreement was complete."

Georgia didn't want to think about Falcon Sane anymore. *I'll just ignore his calls. What's the worst thing that could happen?*

After Falcon concluded his business with Lemontree with the promise of Georgia reinstating him, he left messages for Georgia over the next few days. Falcon tried to think positively, but his experience with politicians hadn't been good. He continued with his current working situation. Unsure of wanting to return to Messmate County, he definitely wished to be reinstated to leave on his own terms and clear his name. Explaining on every job application the rest of his life regarding the termination from Messmate County did not sit well. While he contemplated his next step the phone rang.

"Hello?"

"Hi Falcon, it's Georgia."

Falcon's heart rate picked up. "Hello Georgia. I was wondering when I would hear from you."

"I've been busy with all the hoopla."

"Yes. It appears congratulations are in order."

"Ah, yes. Thank you."

"You're welcome. So when do I start, or should say, return?"

There was silence on the line.

Falcon doubted the woman planned to keep her word.

"Ah … we have … a little problem."

"What's that?" said Falcon.

"I'm not going to be able to bring you back."

Falcon counted slowly to ten. *Politicians.*

"Why not?"

"I just can't."

"Of course you can. As soon as you're sworn in you can reinstate me immediately, just like you promised."

"Uh … I can't … it would be showing favoritism …"

"How is that?"

"Uh … it just would."

"No, it wouldn't." Falcon's voice lowered, "It would show a

wrong being righted. It would show integrity if nothing else," Falcon pressed her. "It would show you're able to keep your word!"

"Look Falcon, I just can't."

"Can't or won't?"

"What's the difference?"

"Can't means you don't have the capacity. Won't means you do, but are unwilling!"

Georgia became snippy, "Sorry Falcon. Politics are rough."

"At least reinstate me and let me resign so I can clear my record."

"No, can't do that either. It's too bad this happened to you but you're incredibly smart, you'll land on your feet. I have to go now."

Click.

Falcon replaced the phone in the receiver. His mind sped through the stages of grief; denial, anger, bargaining, depression and acceptance. Trying to find a resolution, he sifted through and landed on his only real option. *Call the local reporter Georgia set me up with and tell my side.* Might work for revenge, but wouldn't get his job back. Lemontree had dropped Falcon through a letter as soon as the election was over and wasn't returning his calls. He didn't have money to retain an attorney, to fight for a job, and both sheriffs stood against him. It wasn't in him to relinquish, but he was out of options. Falcon headed to the bathroom where he splashed cool water on his face. He stared into the mirror as his mind worked to accept being used, abused and screwed. His eyes screamed for justice. His face contorted as the anger tried to escape his body. Both hands were unconsciously clenched so hard pain finally allowed his fury to ebb. He slowly settled into a resolute state. Justice was indeed a myth. *It's simple ... retribution.*

"I know God. One day she'll pay her pound of flesh."

6

*H*ours had evaporated as the press conference began to wrap up the Messmate County saga. The reporters would have a week to research the facts and delve deeper into Falcon's past. One reporter seemed to be a little ahead of the others.

"One last question for the night?" asked Angela Hector from NBS.

Falcon nodded.

"Were you aware Georgia Blanco had a stroke and was removed from office only six months into her role as sheriff?"

The surprise on Falcon's face said it all. "No I was not."

"Any comment?"

The reporters looked curiously at the candidate. Most politicians were seasoned liars, and when hit with new information they talked up and down about nothing, eventually losing the question in the answer. This candidate remained quiet and looked thoughtful before he answered.

Falcon stared straight into a camera. "That was a long time ago. I do not hold any ill will toward Georgia. Wherever she is." Falcon said goodnight and exited the stage.

Tommy, on security once again, thanked the press and locked up. "The Boss Lady slipped out an hour ago with the mini Boss Lady," he told Falcon as he entered the candidate's office. "She said Lilli was going crazy in the office with all the people around."

Falcon sat at his desk as he jotted down a few notes.

"Great job boss, see you tomorrow?"

"Thanks brother. Enjoy your evening and take the weekend off. We'll fire back up on Monday.

"Thanks!" Tommy grinned.

"Hey buddy is Maya still here?"

"Yes sir, she never leaves before you."

They spoke their goodnights.

Tommy left the office with the evening events playing reruns in his mind. Deep down he sensed his boss could handle himself, and while his stories were exciting, Tommy felt concerned too. His ranger days taught him to battle an enemy he could see. How would they battle the invisible duplicitous world of politics? Falcon had said once, "When things seem out of control keep things simple." Stripping away all the spin and garbage Tommy cut to the chase. *We keep electing people who are lying to us.* That truth had never occurred to him before, and for the first time in his life he was embarrassed to be a part of such an ignorant generation. Yet old habits die hard, and Tommy's sexual appetite still dictated his private life. He hadn't seen her in months. One phone call later the deal clinched he headed over to her place for a late night rendezvous. Turning the dial around on his Sirius Satellite Radio he flipped back and forth between FOX, CNN, CNBC, MSNBC and FOX Business. Nightly topics covered quite a spectrum and as long as the love-fest for Obama didn't get too bad, he could stomach most of the liberal shows. He enjoyed FOX as well, but tired of the ranting coming from people like Sean Hannity.

Hannity for the most part was correct, but day after day he pissed and moaned about the things Obama was doing and still gave George W. Bush a pass. He also had a nationwide audience but didn't seem willing to put his name on a ballot and put himself on the line.

"If it's so important," Tommy yelled at the radio. "Run for

something. Stand up! Stop whining! Step into the arena!" He recalled Falcon once reciting Teddy Roosevelt verbatim from a favorite quote that hung in his office.

It is not the critic who counts; not the man who points out how the strong man stumbles, or where the doer of deeds could have done them better. The credit belongs to the man who is actually in the arena.

Tommy agreed. *Step into the arena otherwise have a "Coke and a Smile".* Spinning the knob he landed on CNN.

"Why do we need AR-15's?" Piers Morgan's replacement didn't have his haughty English accent but nevertheless picked up where the retired British talk show host left off.

Tommy shook his head. *Still banging on the guns, huh, never going to happen. You would never get Americas' guns without a war.* This was something liberal America didn't understand. Most of the citizens voting for Obama were one-issue voters and that issue wasn't guns. It was skin color, amnesty, a women's right to choose, homosexuality, or guilt. *It's almost impossible to hang on to a voting majority when those issues are so different.* Still the Republican politicians were doing a great job of giving the Democrats fodder by constantly talking about abortion. "What a bunch of morons." He turned off the satellite, punched in good old-fashioned A.M. talk radio, and struck gold on the seek button.

"This Falcon Sane guy might be someone to give serious thought to," a male caller said.

Tommy removed his finger from the button and waited.

The caller continued, "I'm a registered Democrat, but not one of these liberal jackasses who think welfare and unemployment checks stimulate the economy."

The host interrupted, "Sir this isn't satellite radio, you'll have to clean up the language or those liberals you referred to will send the FCC thought police down here and yank us off the air."

"Oh yeah, sorry, anyway I read this guy's book, and he's exactly what we need. Did you listen to his press conference earlier?"

"I did."

"He tossed a lot of good ideas out like a consumption tax, and border security, which I agree with, but the most impressive thing he said was he would not run for the job two terms in a row. Have you ever heard a politician say that?"

"No, but I didn't think much of it," said the host. "What did I miss?"

The caller's voice rose in pitch. "First off that's true leadership, someone who is willing to step down before they have to."

"Good point, good point."

"But that's not the best part; he's showing a new strategy for America. He didn't say it out loud, but underneath he said he would do everything he could in four years, and then hand it off to someone else."

"So, why is that important?"

The caller laughed, "Are you joking, the man's playing chess while everyone else is playing checkers. He knows he can only serve two terms, but if things get screwed up again he can come back. It's brilliant!"

The DJ sat on the talk button for a second, dead air rolled out. "I didn't think of that."

"Well think on this — politicians, men or women, do not say things like that. They're not willing to give up that power. This guy actually loves America!"

The caller enlightened Tommy too. *I never thought of it quite that way, but I'm sure the boss has, and that guy sounded excited about America! No more wet-blanket Obama or flip-flopping Republicans, because the American voter has a choice this time. Life is about to get more exciting. It always is around Falcon.*

The A.M. channel went to commercial.

Tommy clicked off the radio and his mind fast-forwarded to what awaited him this evening. He hummed a song by Chris Isaak he couldn't remember the words to. As he parked in front of her condo, he grabbed the flowers he'd picked up on his way. His breath quickened with each step toward her front door, and a smile parted his lips, as he knew she'd be ready. Two knocks and turn the handle. He practically danced down the long hallway and into her bedroom.

As expected, she was already in bed with candles placed strategically around the room.

He set the flowers on the dresser and stared.

The only thing she wore was a yellow bow.

Wow ... she definitely knows how to embellish her glorious physical attributes.

Pushing her lush auburn hair off one shoulder she purred, "Don't you want to unwrap your present?"

His knees buckled and he placed a hand on his chest. *God Bless America.*

The evening had not ended for Maya. She diligently held down the office, crunched numbers, and strategized on how to win the election. Her mind worked like a Rubik's Cube; and though she hated to admit it, she loved politics. Falcon was lukewarm at best on political discussion, didn't care about politics, and hated politicians. His only concern was making America better. That mattered to Maya too; but the energy that surrounded government fascinated her, and the increased pressure of their burgeoning campaign seduced her like ice cream did a child.

Falcon leaned into her office doorway. "You should get some sleep. Remember it's a marathon not a sprint."

Maya glanced up. "The same to you Mr. President."

"Thanks for the promotion. But let's stick with Falcon."

"Yes sir." In all her life Maya had never met anyone with such genuine humility. However Falcon's modesty was a stunning contradiction to his hyper-competitive spirit, which his stories today proved.

Falcon said, "I'm done for the day; see you Monday. And no working this weekend. We have plenty of long days and nights ahead. Let's be consistent with our—"

"Sleep patterns." Maya finished his sentence, and then added, "Water, food and shelter are important, but sleep is the only thing our body forces us to do."

They both laughed.

Falcon said, "I guess I won't be repeating that speech again, at least not to you."

"No sir. I'll get some rest, I promise, but it's hard to stop. This is incredibly exciting," Maya shined.

"Wait until the mudslinging starts."

Her dark eyes widened. "How bad do you think it will be?"

"Easy on us, because we won't do it. Either America is ready for ethical leadership or not. We won't change who we are."

"Yes sir!"

Falcon piled into his 10-year-old Hummer H3. It still looked new, ran even better, and best yet, was paid for. Switching on his Siri satellite radio he stopped on FOX business for a final wrap-up of the markets. Gold was in the toilet along with everything else. The federal government had given up on manipulating the dollar and interest rates. Instead they threw everything left in the piggy bank at the housing market in an attempt to pump up home prices by offering loans that would never be repaid. Falcon was disgusted and flipped to Eighties on Eight, the music from his teenage years. Falcon sang along with Paul Young's "Every Time You Go Away". The lyrics reminded him of Avery and the words tugged at his heart. *This political crap is already stealing precious time away from her, and I hate it*! He cranked up the volume and followed along until it ended, and then clicked the radio off. *The pressure cooker is just beginning to build steam, I'm ready for whatever comes, but how can I shield Avery from the stress?* He sighed deeply. *How can I when stress is everywhere in America today? Serious conversation regarding foreclosures, unemployment and bankruptcies happens every day over water coolers, and those are the topics for the fortunate still employed. Anxiety is a side dish at the dinner table. America is getting the stuffing kicked out of her. Even my relationship with Charlie is almost nonexistent.* Falcon felt a twinge in his heart he couldn't quite describe. *I never thought our friendship would be lost, particularly over political views. It hurts like losing my brother.* His eyes began to sting. *Stay positive.* He blinked rapidly and allowed his thoughts to amble toward Avery. Avery – his gorgeous wife. *She's everything, my favorite everything ... nothing can change that.* Falcon made a quick stop to pick up a surprise for his girl. Now pulling into their driveway, Falcon's heartbeat quickened. Thinking about Avery made Falcon's blood pressure rise, knowing she was so close. He maneuvered into the garage, grabbed her presents, and ran up the stairs to the rear slider.

Their tiny dog Lilli welcomed Falcon home with her original barking that sounded like a baby chick peeping.

"Where's Mommy, Lillers?" Falcon scooped the bouncing fluff up with his free hand.

Lilli wiggled and peeped as she tried to lick his face.

The twosome headed toward the bedroom.

When Falcon heard the shower running, he set Lilli down and hid Avery's presents behind him. After entering the bathroom, Falcon's pulse banged through him. He stared at the vision behind the slightly steamy glass, her eyes closed, water tracing the curve of her back as she rinsed her silky blonde hair. A broad grin spread across his face. *Thank you Big Fella!* His voice sounded husky when he said, "Hey beautiful, need me to come in there and wash your back?"

Avery turned, opened her deep green eyes, and smiled. "Hi

Baby-Cakes!" Shutting the faucets off, she slid open the shower door. "What are you hiding behind you?" She tried to peek around him.

"Why don't you come and see, little girl." Avery's beauty was undeniable, surpassed only by her heart. But what really moved Falcon was her delight in small things. He held out a tight bouquet of pale peach roses and a bag of Peanut M&M's, the economy size.

"Oooh," she squealed, "you brought me treats!"

Joy encompassed them like two enchanted children.

Avery wrapped a towel around her damp body, and then wrapped herself around Falcon. "I love you," she whispered in-between tender kisses.

"I love you too, sweetness."

Not to be left out, Lilli seemed content as she licked drops of water off Avery's toes.

Falcon bowed, "My Lady." He handed her the flowers and candy.

Avery giggled, accepted them with a curtsy then headed toward the kitchen in search of a vase.

Falcon followed Avery, and Lilli followed Falcon, which made a small private parade.

"Are you ready for our daily election chat?" Falcon pulled out a stool in the kitchen.

Twenty minutes each day they discussed the election, and if need be, cleared the air about feelings or concerns. While this appeared to be a necessity for both of them, it was really for Avery. If something bothered Falcon, he lacked patience or willingness to hold in pain and would blurt it out almost immediately. Avery would put on a brave face and stockpile. Falcon knew for both of their sakes it was better to vent than to allow her to let it marinate.

"Don't I look dressed for an election chat?" She twirled and showcased her after-shower attire, then focused on arranging the roses.

"Works for me … no …" Falcon acted as though deep in thought. "Maybe lose the towel."

She smiled, "You are such a bad boy Falcon Sane."

Falcon sat scrutinizing Avery; although she was smiling, he knew his wife well. "So what's up?"

"Nothing sweetie, everything is fine."

Her "fine" did not convince him. "Really?"

"I'm just tired."

Prior to the presidential run their lives had been busy, and now time evaporated into thin air. Avery still flew regularly around the country for work, and Falcon left before the sun rose and rarely made it home until it set.

Avery placed the vase on the bar in front of Falcon, gently gathered the rose heads in her hands, leaned forward, and inhaled their fragrance. "Thank you Baby," she said. Her eyes remained lowered and thick lashes brushed the tops of her cheeks.

Falcon studied the love of his life. He knew what was bothering her. He sighed. *I feel the same way. She'll never say it. She doesn't want to make me feel guilty.* Falcon pushed away from his stool, stood behind Avery, and enfolded her into his body. He whispered in her ear, "I miss you too."

Avery closed her eyes and melted into his embrace. She loved when he held her; feeling him near made the rest of the world disappear. Her voice cracked. "How did you know?"

Falcon turned her to face him, lifted her chin, and kissed away a single tear. "Don't cry baby, everything will be all right."

She wrapped her arms around his waist. "I know. I'm just tired."

Falcon scooped his beauty into his arms and carried her to bed.

"I feel better now," said Avery, as Falcon laid her down. Keeping her fingers laced around his neck, she pulled him to her, and kissed him deeply.

Falcon brushed his lips over her eyes, her cheeks, and once

again enjoyed her mouth.

Their lovemaking was slow and tender, mending all the bruised places in their hearts.

Avery lay on Falcon's chest and fell asleep.

Falcon stroked her back, and intertwined his fingers through her damp hair. Sleep would not come as his mind worked overtime for a solution. There was no way he would let their relationship fall apart. *Nothing is more important than her. I spent 30 years searching for her. Before her, my life was incomplete. Now each day is pure heaven, I can't lose any part of her.* He smoothed her hair and held her close. Falcon closed his eyes and hoped his brain would land on an answer. Instead, a crushing doubt crept into his soul. *Is it possible to serve the country and not lose his wife? Can I keep her safe?* His eyes sprung open. Only once in his life had he experienced such powerful uncertainty. He was not foolish enough to challenge it again. This time the Late Bird begged for support. Staring at the ceiling, he pleaded, *Please help me Father... you know my life is nothing without her.*

The weeks piled up and pushed through Thanksgiving. Falcon had a press conference the following day. Christmas would fall on a Friday, and a reporter asked if Falcon planned to give his normal press conference on Christmas Day.

"Of course I will," he said. "Freedom never takes a day off."

A voice from the back said, "Even God rested on Sunday."

Falcon's eyes narrowed. "I'm not building an entire universe from scratch." He paused to gain their attention. "Besides, I'm not God. Didn't we get enough of the Messiah complex with the last president?" Actively engaging the reporters he said, "This is part of free will. I choose to be here. It's up to you whether you will join me." Then he added, "Bring your families if you like. We're all in this together."

Christmas evening they did just that. Spouses, babies, teenagers and a grandparent or two crowded into the warehouse along with the reporters.

Horton Hooray received a belated holiday gift with first ups. Hooray, a television personality on a very liberal network, possessed a too-sharp wit and equally annoying French accent. The star of MSNBS loved to grandstand and zing his guests. He slyly waited until time became short, attacked with a one-liner, and cut immediately to a commercial to leave the interviewee, who would then appear insignificant and enraged. "The stories you have shared over the last few weeks have been of a personal nature. Having the impression that you didn't trust or even like the press, I must admit surprise."

Falcon leaned on the podium. "First of all, Merry Christmas to everyone. We still say that kind of thing around here."

A chorus of voices filled the room with holiday wishes.

Falcon said, "What gave you that impression, Mr. Hooray?"

"Your unwillingness to grant interviews following the popularity of your book, and I'm equally surprised that you know who I am."

"I do watch television once in a while."

"Yes sir, apparently so. My question then is which network do you watch the most?"

"Which do I watch or enjoy the most?"

Hooray wanted an answer to both, but if he played this right perhaps Falcon Sane would agree to come on his show. "Let us go with watch."

Falcon forced a straight face. "FOX News."

Everyone in the room roared with laughter, even Hooray as he scribbled in his notepad: sense of humor, check.

Falcon wasn't kidding about FOX News or watching television. He enjoyed it most of the time despite their attempt at "fair and balanced" reporting, or the bitterness of MSNBC on the left that screamed racism or homophobia and pointed fingers on every issue.

The questions continued with only gentle probing; after all, it was Christmas. Ten minutes left on the clock, and the last reporter posed an unusual scenario. "I brought footage my producer discovered of what appears to be you handing out money at a fast-food restaurant called Chick-Fil-A. I'd like to show it prior to asking my question if we might use your PowerPoint."

"You sure did your homework." Falcon regarded the reporter with respect. "Sure. Email the file to Tommy, and he'll put it on the PowerPoint."

Tommy went to work on the file. With a few clicks of his mouse the footage appeared on the screen attached to the wall behind the podium, which Falcon had pulled down.

Maya clicked off the lights from the back and everyone settled in.

Falcon watched too as he came to life on the screen.

A gentle male voice began to narrate the footage. "It is a blistering summer evening in Roseville, CA. Today is Chick-Fil-A Appreciation Day. At this local Chick-Fil-A, nearly 1,000 people wait in line in support of comments made by the Chief Operating Officer: 'I pray God's mercy on our generation that has such a prideful, arrogant attitude to think that we have the audacity to define what marriage is about.'

"Due to that comment," continued the narrator, "The mayors from Boston to Chicago to San Francisco attacked and threatened Chick-Fil-A with the Mayor of San Francisco stating: 'Closest Chick-Fil-A to San Francisco is 40-miles away, and I strongly recommend that they not try to come any closer.'

"The peaceful protest has packed the small drive through and parking lot. The line extends around the corner and out of sight. I'm about to approach a fit young man, perhaps 30, who is speaking to folks in the line while handing out $20 bills."

The camera zoomed in on Falcon's face.

Falcon smiled at the guess of his age. They were only off by a decade. *Mom was right. Keep eating those fruits and veggies young man.* He watched curiously as he'd forgotten all about that day and had been unaware of the taping until the crew approached him. His words seemed to jump off the screen.

Falcon approached a family. "Why are you here today?" he asked a pregnant mother.

The woman with three young children answered, "We're here to protect our freedom of speech."

That was the answer Falcon hoped for. "I'm glad to hear that ma'am. Please allow me to pay for your dinner." He held out two $20s.

The woman stared at him in disbelief.

Her seven-year-old son extracted the money from Falcon's hand. The camera came in for a close-up of the giddy child who waved $40 like a flag.

Sweat beads rolled off Falcon's forehead and disappeared under his sunglasses as he moved to the next person in line. He repeated his question.

"Freedom of speech young man," said an elderly gentleman who sported a WWII Veteran's cap. "Right honey?" he addressed his wife.

She nodded.

Falcon pulled out a $20 and offered it to them. "God bless you sir and thank you for your service. Dinner is on me tonight. It's the least I can do."

The old man tipped his hat.

His wife said, "I'm very proud of you young man. God bless you."

The picture became blurry as the camera person jiggled it trying to get a better shot of Falcon.

He stopped in front of a teenager and his girlfriend. Before he could even ask his question the couple blurted, "Freedom of speech!"

Falcon laughed, "Really?"

"You know it man." The skater grinned.

Falcon handed them a $20. "If you don't use it all please pass it back to the next person in line or tip the staff, but keep the money moving."

"You got it bro."

The camera crew followed close to Falcon. His shirt was glued to his back from perspiration, but he continued to work the line and hand out cash as he discussed freedom of speech. The video froze on a frame where Falcon broke into a genuine smile, and then continued rolling.

The voice of the narrator broke in. "Excuse me sir, could we ask you a few questions?"

Surprised by the crew, Falcon turned and tilted his sunglasses above his eyes. "What can I do for you?"

"We are a Christian organization doing a documentary. Are you a Christian?"

"No sir I am not. I'm an American."

"From what I can tell, you seem to be passing out money. Why?"

Falcon faced the camera. "I'm here today because of freedom of speech. When elected officials attack any business because of something someone said, it is our *duty* to stand and make our voices heard. I'm not affiliated with Chick-Fil-A in any way. I've never even eaten at a Chick-Fil-A. I'm merely doing my small part to maintain freedom."

"It appears you've been passing out $20 bills. I wouldn't call that small. Do you mind if I ask how much you passed out?"

"I don't mind. $500, and I wish it could've been $5,000. Actually, I wish the elected officials would remember what their jobs are."

"And what is that?"

"To serve the people."

"What do you think of homosexuality?" the interviewer asked.

Falcon stared directly into the camera. "I don't. What people do in their own bedrooms is their business, so long as they aren't hurting anyone else. This show of support today isn't for or against homosexuality. It's about the elected officials who threatened Chick-Fil-A. Last time I checked," Falcon paused, "this was a free country; people are free to decide upon one's own sexual preference. We cannot allow government to crush any business because of a personal statement made."

The footage stopped there.

Tommy clicked off the screen; Maya hit the lights.

Falcon acknowledged the reporter who'd brought the footage.

The reporter said, "So to verify, that was you?"

Falcon could not hide his disdain. "You tracked down four-year-old footage, taped by an amateur who showed my face at least five times. That's amazing investigative journalism and now your one question, the last of this evening, is 'Was that you?' Come on! You're better than that!"

The reporter's face flushed. Without thinking his mouth opened and the truth came out. "Mr. Sane, for two months you've told stories about bullies, rapists and thugs, governmental abuse, and how bad the freaking boomers are! You tell me then — what the hell are we supposed to be asking?"

Falcon grasped the podium, considering the frustrated man. His demeanor mirrored the mood in America. Americans had endured enough, but had no idea where to turn, or what to do. Falcon stepped away from the podium and strode over to the reporter. Extending his right hand he said, "I'm sorry brother. I was wrong."

The journalists and their families sat hushed, awaiting the shocked reporter's response. He gazed at Falcon's hand, looked him straight in the eyes, and said, "Thank you, I appreciate your apology."

The people in the room exhaled in sync when the two men shook.

Falcon returned to the podium. "One of your brethren just posed a thought-provoking dilemma. What do we ask and of whom? What do we do with the corruption and moral decay in our society? What are we supposed to do?" Falcon paused for effect. He glanced across the room to a mother who cradled her sleeping baby. "Today is Christmas, a time when we honor the birth of a child. Jesus' life demonstrated what we are supposed to do … love, and forgive. On this holy day, we follow His example." His eyes tightened. "But tomorrow. Tomorrow is a new day when we follow Washington, Abraham and Ike, Patton, Teddy and Truman. Tomorrow is about another special child." Falcon pointed toward the baby and other little ones as he spoke. "Tomorrow is for every single child in this room. Tomorrow, my friends, we fight for America."

The crowd responded for the first time with applause.

Falcon stopped talking. *Less is more.* Besides, it was Christmas and he had a surprise in store. "I thank you all for coming tonight and look forward to next week. Again, Merry Christmas." Falcon left the platform and headed for Avery. "How did I do, beautiful?"

Avery sparkled brightly. "You were great!" She slipped her hand inside his, and they locked fingers.

"Maya?"

"Perfect boss. I think they'll be squeezing you harder next time though."

"Me too. They're still trying to figure me out."

"Once they do they'll love you as much as I do," beamed Avery.

He gave her hand a squeeze. "I hope so Boss Lady." Falcon winked at Tommy. "Are we all set hero?"

"Yes sir. Santa is outside waiting for the kids."

Avery studied Falcon. "Santa?"

Falcon's eyes shined. He loved the glow of joy on little faces when children saw Santa, and a Saint Nick lived inside Falcon too. Borrowing a rendition of a time-honored tradition from Falcon's favorite teacher, Mr. Albert Jacobsen, Falcon and Tommy had spent hours filling stockings with candy; an American flag, a pocket copy of the United States Constitution, a CPR face shield, and a small box wrapped with gold foil paper tied with a ribbon of red white and blue. Every stocking also included a tiny typed note.

The note said: "Merry Christmas to you. Each gift bears a special meaning. The candy is for you to enjoy. The United States Constitution is the reason you can. The American flag stands for your freedom. Wave it proudly and ensure it never stops. The CPR face shield is used to protect you while giving mouth-to-mouth resuscitation and is a reminder about life. Always be prepared. In the toe of your stocking you will find a tiny wrapped present, which comes with a choice. If you open it, enjoy; it pleases our hearts to give to you. However, because America is the most generous country in the history of man, we offer you the opportunity to join the practice of giving and sharing. If you decide to pass your gift to someone else, please let us know. We would love to hear the story behind your giving, and how it changed your heart. God Bless America young ones; freedom knows no bounds.

Liberty's humble servant,

Falcon Sane"

With his arms around Avery, Falcon enjoyed the holiday scene from the open warehouse door. He'd done his part and contentedly watched from the shadows.

The hired Santa was topnotch. He even sported a real fluffy snow-white beard. Tommy and Maya donned fir-green elves' caps, and the bells on the tips jingled while they jubilantly assisted the stocking distribution.

Santa roared in rare form, "Ho, ho, ho!"

Children squealed with delight and anxiously waited a turn to sit on Saint Nicholas' lap. The entire procession lasted almost an hour, and then the last car pulled out of the parking lot.

Tommy disappeared too and headed for a hot date.

Maya's family already met for Christmas brunch, so she joined a group of reporters for a late-night dinner. *She did love politics.*

Hand-in-hand, Falcon and Avery gathered Lilli from his office. She'd been kenneled for her own good, and the good of the carpet. Now freed from jail, she bounced up and down as excitedly as one of the children waiting for Santa. Falcon opened the car door for Avery, and she leaned across and opened his. That one small gesture Avery had performed on their first date went straight to Falcon's heart.

In staying with their tradition Falcon and Avery headed toward Granite Bay, California. Lilli bounced around the backseat like a jumping bean and left puppy kisses smeared on the windows. Every year the Christmas luminaries put out by the Granite Bay community bore a magnificent sight. Miles upon miles of candles spaced a few feet apart beckoned viewers to come, in celebration of the birth of a child. With his running lights on, Falcon drove slowly through the welcoming "All-American" neighborhood.

Avery's eyes glistened as she commented on the different decorations adorning each house. "Ooh, that's my favorite!" she cooed and pointed to a nativity scene aglow in twinkling white lights.

Falcon smiled in the darkness of the Hummer, enchanted by her excitement. "You are my favorite," he said.

Avery reached for his hand. "Tell me what I'm thinking right now?"

"I love you."

"I know you do, but what am I thinking?" She giggled at the little game they often played. "Yes, that was it, my beautiful husband. I adore you."

Falcon's heart was full as they glided along. *Thank you Big Fella.*

7

arch marched in, as the crowd of reporters grew every Friday night.

Maya scrutinized the group as she waited for her boss this evening. She'd established plenty of contacts over the last five months and recently heard the same thing from each of them. Story time was over. It was time to talk policy. "I see too much fidgeting," she told Tommy as they waited for Falcon to emerge from his office.

Tommy shrugged, "They look the same as always."

Maya could not put her intuition to rest. The reporters planned to pull out the big guns tonight. "What should we do if they go after him?"

Tommy laughed, "What do you mean what should we do? The Boss Man will light them up."

"I'm being serious." She fretted, "We should have a code word or something in case he needs help."

Tommy patted her shoulder. Maya was wickedly intelligent, definitely smarter than him on policy, statistics, and all that crap, but she'd never been in a real fight. He couldn't explain that Falcon didn't need help. In fact, they might even get in his way. The boss needed to be out front during battle, unencumbered by the responsibility of others. Falcon led by example. Rather than the Obama way, from behind, or if stated truthfully, following. "Trust me, he'll be fine." Tommy smiled at her.

The reporters seemed wired, and they filled the room with a high-pitched buzz.

Maya said a prayer as Falcon took the stage.

Whether members of the press had previously discussed hitting Falcon hard that evening or if, belonging to the same breed, they instinctively sensed it, clearly they were gearing up for a battle. Skip story time and head into the land of real political issues, top on the list – immigration.

"Ben Johnson, MSMBS. About immigration, in your first press conference you stated you would secure the border. The terrain alone makes this a difficult task. How would you physically accomplish it?"

"Good evening, Ben. We've been led to believe the border is impossible to close. This is ridiculous and insulting to the American spirit and creative ingenuity. People daily are walking through these supposed impossible areas to secure. Walking indicates there is soil under their feet. Where there is soil, construction can take place. Ben, I must admit, I'm tired of hearing how difficult securing our border would be. That is the Boomer culture. I belong to the American culture, the same one that built the Golden Gate Bridge, the Erie Canal, and, need I remind you, that put man on the moon. Seriously, a space shuttle averages a wingspan of 78 feet and a lift-off weight of four-and-a-half-million pounds. The machinery must endure a temperature of 1,650 degrees C upon re-entry, be maneuvered outside of Earth's gravitational pull, complete the job it was created for, and safely return the astronauts inside, to our planet. How long will we continue to buy into the lie that we can launch a rocket to the moon, but cannot secure miles of dirt along our border?"

Falcon recognized the next in line. "All good points, Mr. Sane, but you didn't answer his question. How would you physically secure the border?"

"By providing leadership."

"You still are not answering the question."

"Okay," Falcon said, "in 2013 the federal government thought they could set the bar low and the people would go for it. Does anyone in here remember that?"

"Jill Jennings from Wolf News, are you referring to the 90-percent plan?"

"Yes, politicians floated an idea about sealing the border so only 10 percent of illegals would get through. Once the 90 percent could be verified everyone here illegally would get amnesty."

Several people nodded.

"Let's ignore the fact that this is pure stupidity. To ascertain a percentage of anything requires real numbers. It would be impossible to count who made it and who did not. If we didn't catch them how would we know they exist? Putting that aside, here in America we give 100 percent. Actually we give 100 and 10 percent! We use this verbiage because it is ingrained in us. When any leader begins a program with an expectation of 90 percent, it has already failed the American people. Leaders do not set the bar low. Leaders establish a goal that the masses believe to be unobtainable, and then lead us there! Nothing is impossible in America unless you think it is." Falcon refocused on the reporter who originally asked the question. "I don't need to know how the border will be physically secured. I need to know where to find engineers and construction companies who can fulfill the vision in my head – that is leadership. Leaders don't know everything, and anyone who thinks they do isn't a leader. Come on people, does anyone in this room think securing the border would be harder than walking on the moon?"

Silence filled the room, which left Falcon optimistic that his explanation might make all the irrational arguments slip away. "My guess is 24 hours after my request to the American public hundreds of responsible, cogent specs would land on my desk for approval.

I'll also speculate quite comfortably that private American construction could seal the border in three months, if not sooner. The problem isn't the private American workforce. The problem is our corrupt, lazy, unethical government."

"Michelle Roberts, MBS News. Then are you saying all the Latinos should go home?"

"What's a Latino?" asked Falcon.

The reporter scrutinized the candidate. "My error, are you saying all the Hispanics should go home?"

"What's a Hispanic?"

Excitement bounced around the room as the reporters sensed the upcoming conflict.

Falcon studied the reporter who mulled over Falcon's responses.

With great deliberation, the reporter chose her words. "Are you saying you want to send all the Mexicans home?"

Maya sucked air. *Uh-oh.*

Tommy set his jaw and stared straight ahead.

They both knew Falcon didn't care about skin color. He cared about behavior. They also knew their boss hated racism – all racism.

Falcon's eyes closed. *People, people ... use the brains God gave you.* He shook his head slowly, opened his eyes, and fired away. "The term Latino or Hispanic is racist. There is no home for Latinos or Hispanics to go to. This is a white guilt creation trying to pigeonhole humans with brown skin. It's disgusting and one of the worst things fabricated by the 'Me Generation'. I was born to American parents, which makes me an American. Not a Cracker, White Trash or a Haole. Individuals born to Mexican parents are Mexican. Not Wetbacks, Latinos or Hispanic. I consider those terms profane, and I abhor the usage of profanity!"

A voice from the back shouted. "Those terms are used every day--"

"And it needs to stop!" Falcon said. He momentarily scanned

the occupants in the room. He'd heard the third rail of politics was social security and that no politician should ever touch the third rail. If that was true the fourth rail in America was skin color, and he was going to grab it with both hands. "I don't care what you look like, believe in, or sleep with. As long as you are kind to others, obey our laws, are willing to work hard, and believe in freedom ... America will always have a place for you. Our prisons are overflowing with Americans who don't do those things. If you're here illegally and not part of the American dream you're going back to whatever country you came from, whether that's Mexico, Vietnam or Russia." He paused. "If I am elected, our laws will be enforced. All of them."

There were plenty of other hot button subjects the reporters could've run with, but they weren't letting this one go.

"Ken Dewsh, MSNBS. What about all the anchor babies? What will you do with them?" he asked dramatically.

Falcon said, "Are you talking about children? Are you calling children, anchor babies?"

Dewsh backed up. "I didn't mean it like that. So what will you do with all these children?" The drama in his voice faded away.

"Excellent question; it's nice to know someone cares about the next generation."

Maya bit the sides of her mouth as she tried not to show she appreciated Falcon's sarcasm.

Tommy didn't bother. His smile was wide.

Growing weary of spinning his wheels, Falcon replied, "The children will remain with their parents. Next question."

"Ann Rogers, Wolf News, what is your official position on abortion?"

"Abortion is something I pray will end soon. When will America wake up and practice safe sex? We have condoms, oral medication, and the day-after pill available at Wal-Mart! Come on people, we have to be better than this! We have to stop creating unwanted life. With that said, I will always be on the side of freedom. A woman must always be the ultimate authority on what she does with her body. Case closed." The candidate appeared to be tiring.

Ann Rogers took a chance and followed up. "What about," she winced, "late-term abortions?"

"All of this is so reactive. We have to be proactive. We need to educate children about abstinence and the importance of waiting. We must raise them to have sex responsibly." Falcon plugged away.

The reporter stared him down. "That wasn't an answer."

"Late-term abortions are disgraceful! Do you recall the doctor who made a practice of snipping spinal cords of babies who survived late-term abortions? Thank God he's in prison now!" Falcon's face contorted into such a painful clench, the reporters gasped at the rage on the man's face. He slowly refocused as he tried to remove the image of a little baby who tried to live while being murdered. He stared into the crowd. "Such things are abominations. That's what happens when people are irresponsible. If you're looking for me to fix this I can't. I don't control or want to control others' decisions. Once again, a woman must always be the ultimate authority on what she does with her body. I simply pray women do everything in their power to make sure this option never be used again."

Maya exhaled slowly and glanced toward Tommy who gave her a confident nod.

Falcon took a sip of water, and the next reporter stood.

"Hello, Mr. Sane, Nicole Harness with the *Wall Street Gazette*."

"Hello, Nicole."

"Sir, could you respond to comments others have made about your book?"

"Asking me about other people's comments is a form of gossip and harmful. Ask me anything you like, just make the question yours. Don't ask a question you aren't comfortable with by using someone else as the scapegoat."

The reporter flushed and set her jaw.

Falcon noticed. *I didn't mean to embarrass or anger her.* "Let's try again, Nicole."

"Absolutely," she snipped. "To make sure I understand you correctly, you're willing to answer any question as long as we ask it the way you want. Sounds like you have a control issue Mr. Sane."

Falcon exhaled. He knew this subject would arise. Americans stuck in the current culture loved to use the word control. There was nothing wrong with America. *But there was definitely something wrong with some Americans.* "I believe in freedom not control, not only am I not trying to control you, I'm not willing to control you. Government controls us through Social Security, Medicare, Medicaid, and now Obamacare. We are forced into paying for these things. Our children are controlled by the Department of Education, Common Core and public teachers unions. And what do we get with all this control? A bankrupt retirement system, crashing health-care programs, children who can't read. The list is endless." Falcon inhaled. "When I address the way I'll answer a question, I'm not attempting to control you. I'm establishing boundaries so you can't control me. I believe in freedom, but if you think freedom allows you to behave any way you like without consequences, let me be the first to tell you, Ms. Harness, you are very wrong. As my father says, 'Your rights stop at my nose.'"

The reporters responded in a plethora of ways. Some shifted uncomfortably, others talked in low murmurs, a few sat straight up and simply gaped, and others scribbled furiously. Politicians didn't talk this way, at least not to them. They'd been taken to task, and it was anyone's guess how they felt about it.

Falcon regained their attention. "This passive-aggressive usage of language is an example of the corruption of our culture and country. A term you're all familiar with is Political Correctness. Politicians love that phrase. It gives people cart-blanche to misbehave and everyone else is supposed to keep quiet about the outcome. Multi-cultural is another favorite." He paused to make certain everyone was still listening.

Every head in the place popped up.

"There is no such thing as multicultural. There is a superior culture and inferior cultures. The culture of America is very easy to understand, but since we seemed to have lost our way let me say it again. Our original culture is freedom. Why do you think people continue to come here? To be free."

Nicole Harness waited as Falcon took a drink of water and the rest of the room watched. Most doubted he could win but many were starting to hope so. His passion combined with the truth was something America sorely needed.

Falcon knew he was getting angry. He paused because his next thoughts weren't pretty. He thought about what he really wanted to say. What he really wanted to talk about was a quote where Warren Buffet said he felt he should pay more in taxes. *Then do so, Oracle of Omaha!* He also heard Bill Gates say he felt guilty about the lifestyle he was leading. *Then stop leading that lifestyle, richest man on the planet!* Classic Me Generation culture: *"I'm too successful." "Woe is me." "My life is too good." "I shouldn't be allowed to live like this." "Oh, well, I guess I'll continue." "I'm such a bad person." Pathetic.*

Falcon nodded to Nicole.

She decided to change gears. "What about your foreign policy?" she asked

"Can you be more specific?" Falcon replied

"Would you follow the Bush Doctrine?"

The expression on Falcon's face said everything you needed to know. "If you're asking if the United States will defend itself from terrorism, then yes."

The reporters seemed to be willing to allow multiple questions to occur from one individual so Falcon continued. His point about working together seemed to be taking shape. As any good leader he stepped aside when growth occurred.

Nicole posed another follow-up. "Do you have an opinion on Mr. Bush?"

"I do."

"Will you give it to us?"

Falcon had mulled this question over long before it was asked. Discussing Bush, Obama and even Bill Clinton was something he struggled with. He truly believed in "If you have nothing nice to say, say nothing at all." He had nothing nice to say. However remaining silent would be detrimental to America. "I remember Kanye West declaring George W. Bush didn't care about black people during Hurricane Katrina. His statement was right and wrong. George Bush and the politicians don't care about black people, but not because they're black. They don't care about people period, black, white, brown or yellow with pink polka dots. They only care about *votes*. Mr. Bush also cost us thousands of lives from our best and bravest. Politicians like to use words like 'blood' and 'treasure' when refer-ring to our military or the American dollar. I hate those inferences. Someone please tell John McCain our money isn't treasure. It's the sweat of American labor. Maybe it feels like treasure to him because he keeps digging our hole deeper, searching for more! But the worst part is the usage of the word blood by Barack Obama. American men and women in our military aren't blood. They aren't blood to their children who will grow up not knowing the hugs and kisses from a mommy or daddy. They aren't blood to their wives or hus-bands who will never hold or be held by their best friend again. They aren't blood to their mothers who silently cry and die a little more every time they enter their child's room which waits in a permanent state of limbo, screaming out an empty promise for those sent to fight Bush's or Obama's war. They aren't blood to their fathers who choke back tears while rising every morning, realizing it wasn't just a horrendous nightmare.

"Barack Obama is George Bush on steroids. Starting with the Clintons through Bush and into Obama, they've left America broke and dysfunctional. We have to stop digging the hole."

The next reporter burrowed in on the current President. "Kimberly Hansen, MPR News. Any more thoughts on Obama?"

The night was wearing Falcon down. His childlike spirit felt buried under the depression of America's former presidents. He knew he'd had enough tonight. The fatigue from the pressure, the frustration of having to explain things over and over and the distance between he and Avery was stirring his temper up. "Thoughts on Obama? Here's my first thought. Hurricane Katrina. Many parts of New Orleans still look like a war zone. It's been years. Where are you 'Chosen One'? To use Obama's own words there are lots of Americans struggling in Louisiana because of Katrina *who look just like him*. He could care less. Let's talk Obamacare. The Affordable Care Act is a joke without a punch line. The fattest generation in American history now wants their grandchildren to pay for their healthcare."

Tommy nodded along in agreement while Maya prayed her boss wouldn't blow a gasket.

Falcon's face began to flush. "The joke is on them. Their grandkids are too busy smoking all that pot their grandparents thought was so cool. They might smoke a joint with their grand-pappy but they aren't paying for his rectal exam!"

Tommy burst out laughing along with a good portion of the reporters. *Tear 'em up boss*!

Maya frowned at Tommy but had to admit Falcon was right.

Falcon stopped, lowered his voice, and finished. "For Barack Obama to carpetbag himself to Chicago professing concern for the plight of the poor children *who only look like him*, is despicable. His power reaches the corners of the Earth, and yet what has he done? Seven-plus years later murders continue. Google the name Hadiya Pendleton. Welcome to leading from behind."

Although Falcon had enough, the reporters weren't letting him go. Sensing he was on the ropes, they continued pounding away, some hoping for a Howard Dean moment.

"Charles Davis, *The Economizer*. Would you comment on the shots you're taking from the Democratic and Republican parties? I'll not offer quotes, but surely you are aware both sides are giving it to you."

"Hello, Charles. Yes, I have caught a glimpse, and I'm very excited I was able to bring these two parties together." Falcon's slight levity lessened the tension briefly toward a serious issue. The vitriol thrown by the two political parties was beyond lunacy. That they spent time and money attacking him only proved he was having an effect. "I'm not surprised. After the last election I thought I'd seen it all. Calling Mitt Romney a killer? Unbelievable." He shook his head. "I thought that stuff only happened in *The Enquirer* but, lo and behold, every news show, newspaper and radio program ran it. I don't watch the 24-hour news cycle of drama. It is amazing though what happens when you flash some sunshine on those people. They scurry like cockroaches!"

The reporters laughed and penned the comment about both political parties resembling cockroaches.

"I shouldn't say cockroaches. Cockroaches have a purpose," he smiled.

The press howled as Falcon winked from the podium and appeared to have gained a second wind.

Stretching his back he straightened up. "So Charles, to answer your question there are some quality people in both parties, just not enough to make a difference. What we need are responsible Americans to step forward, small business owners, school teachers, law enforcement and fire personnel. Rid ourselves of the attorney and lobbyist and get back to American ideals. Serve as an elected official for one term, not a lifetime. Mr. Davis, did you say you represented *The Economizer*? I used to read your magazine."

"Used to?"

"Yes. After the Romney-Obama election I felt the coverage in your magazine was factually incorrect. I can email a copy of my cancellation letter to you if you like."

"I would appreciate that."

Falcon glanced at Tommy, who went to work forwarding the letter to the reporter, then gave Falcon a quick signal the task was complete. "Mr. Davis the cancellation has been sent, but I'd like to display it on PowerPoint for everyone to see."

Tommy didn't need a cue. He was already on the same page as Falcon. The letter came up on the screen.

The reporters shifted and began reading as fast as they could. Some clicked pictures with their phones; photographers busily snapped away.

Falcon and the entire podium lit up like the Fourth of July. His fingertips suddenly numbed, then his lips, and within seconds his vision had blurred in one eye. It was only a matter of minutes before he was completely blind. If he didn't catch it quick then nausea and crushing pain would ensue, encapsulating his entire head and neck. The following 12 hours would be complete agony that only sleep would mitigate. Even after sleeping for at least several more days his neck would ache as though he had been in a car accident. His extreme sensitivity to flashing lights slammed him into a sledge-hammer migraine headache. Two packets of an over-the-counter medication called Exaprin and a large Coke was a miracle he'd accidentally stumbled across, which usually stopped the oncoming train of pain from worsening. Immediately wasn't a fast enough word.

Falcon shielded his eyes and held a hand up toward the

photographers. "Please! Please stop with the pictures. We will post the letter on our website for anyone wanting a copy."

The flurry of wanna-be paparazzi ceased.

Falcon lowered his hands and a lone wolf snapped one more photo. The flash that banked off Falcon's eyes seemingly lit up the room. The candidate was not smiling as he trained his eyes on the photographer. *There's always one who thinks they're above the rules.* He bored visual holes into the photographer.

"Sorry," muttered the man, and he focused on the ground away from Falcon's piercing stare.

Falcon hadn't experienced a migraine in two years, but the potential was always there. Too much salt or too many nuts could set it off. Stress alone could be the culprit, but he made a point to exercise, stretch, and eat well to minimize how stress affected him. Flashing lights were the only things he didn't have a correction for other than abstinence. "Tommy, would you do me a favor and bring me a Coke, please?"

"Yes boss." As he hustled off, Tommy questioned the strange request. He'd never seen his boss drink soda of any kind. Falcon believed aside from cigarettes, narcotics, and laziness, there may not be a more dangerous substance for people than high fructose corn syrup. Tommy was unaware of Falcon's migraines.

Falcon addressed the last person to snap a photo. "Mr. Photographer."

"My name is Joe."

"I'm sure it is," Falcon said curtly. "This ..." he pointed at Joe, "is a perfect example of today's culture. Even when a directive was given and an alternative provided, this selfish culture continues to do whatever they want regardless of outcome."

Tommy handed Falcon a Coke.

"Thank you my friend." Falcon took several swallows and waited for the Coke to interact as he prayed the tingling in his fingers would subside. *This better work or I won't be able to see in a second.* Falcon paused for another long drink of the Coke. Squiggly lines aggressively took over his right eye; in a moment his sight would be gone. "This reminds me of one definition of insanity: Doing the same thing over and over and expecting a different result. I do not practice insanity. Joe and his belief that he's more important than the rest of us are wrong. The consequence for his behavior is an abrupt end to our night together. It's time everyone realized ignorant behavior from others has consequences for us all. Tonight because of Joe's behavior your questions will have to wait another week. God Bless the United States," he said, and strode from the room.

The confused reporters continued to stare as Falcon walked out. They had no idea what had just happened, or what specifically had set the presidential candidate off. Time, pressure, and the race might present an answer somewhere down the line, but there was one point everyone in the room could probably agree on, *they were glad they weren't Joe.*

Tommy looked at Maya and grinned. "Told you he didn't need any help."

"What was the Coke about, and why did he cut the night short?"

Tommy's smile faded, and he followed after Falcon.

Falcon shut the door to his office, felt his way around the room, and retrieved the packets of Exaprin. Downing four tablets with the remaining Coke he lowered himself gingerly into his chair.

Maya tapped on Falcon's door. "Are you in there, Chief?"

"Yes, come in."

Maya and Tommy entered the darkened office.

Tommy reached for the light switch, and then thought better of it. "Is everything okay boss?"

"Fine. Tommy, would you mind getting me another Coke, please?"

"You got it." Tommy bolted out.

Maya asked, "What's going on Falcon?"

He smiled at her perceptiveness and genuine concern. "I get migraines sometimes."

"And you have one now?"

"Yeah the flashing lights set it off."

"Is it bad?"

"Nothing I can't handle."

Tommy returned with the soda.

Falcon didn't like mothering so Maya let the subject go. Relieved he was okay, she quietly started rehashing the press conference.

Falcon listened as he swallowed half of the second can.

"You really let the Boomers have it tonight," Maya said.

Falcon took another long drink. "I call it my Shakespearean approach."

"What's that?" asked Tommy.

"Either one of you ever been to a Shakespearean play?"

They both shook their heads.

Falcon couldn't see them. "I'll assume from your silence the answer is no. Years ago I went to one in Ashland, Oregon. Beautiful setting, wine and beer garden, and ice cream while watching the actors perform."

Tommy laughed, "Let me guess, you went with the ice cream."

"You know it brother. After the first 20 minutes it seemed the actors kept repeating the same lines over and over, with just enough subtly to keep you interested. This went on for hours, and is the prime reason why most Americans have no interest in Shakespeare. Browbeating eventually turns off your crowd."

Tommy asked, "Did you ever go to another play?"

"Shakespeare. Heck no. The guy was brilliant, but I don't need to hear anything a hundred times. I thought I would lose my mind. No wonder they serve alcohol at those things."

Tommy and Maya laughed.

"It's getting late. You two should head home. I think this circus is about to begin. And Maya, I appreciate your concern, but don't worry about me. I'm at my best out front alone because I trust you both to watch my flanks and keep orchestrating our plan."

"Yes sir." Tommy snapped a crisp salute.

"Absolutely Chief."

Maya and Tommy locked up and headed home.

Falcon drained his Coke and tried to fight off the inevitable. It was too late. The numbness dissipated and his vision improved some, but the searing pain pounding in the back of his head was only beginning. He grabbed his cell.

Avery answered, "Hey Baby-Cakes."

"Hey beautiful."

"How did the press conference go?"

"Good until a cameraman flashed one too many."

"Are you okay? Do you have one of your headaches?"

"Unfortunately yes sweet girl."

"I'm on my way."

"Okay baby, thanks." He massaged his closed his eyes and leaned back in his chair. "Hey sweetie?"

"Yes?"

"I love you."

Avery smiled. Even in excruciating pain her husband amazed her. "I love you more. Close your eyes; I'll be there in 20 minutes."

"Okay baby." Falcon hit the button that ended the call and put his feet on the desk. As he tried to relax and will the pain away, he disappeared into the darkness. *Freaking Boomers, they just never stop.*

8

*T*he first Friday in July delivered a scorcher with a presidential campaign to match. Escorting in the blazing Sacramento summer was the red-hot attention of the Republicans and Democrats trembling over the real prospect of a third-party candidate. Not since Ross Perot had there been this much interest regarding a candidate who did not parade a D or an R behind their names. In secret, Republican and Democratic strategists shared information and misinformation about the Independent candidate. Both sides pounded away with negative ROBO calls, radio and television ads. This strengthened voter determination as the American people were outraged by the two parties colluding to push them into wars, massive debt spending, and corrupt bank bailouts. Many in their 60's felt desperate as they hadn't saved any money for their golden years, and the struggles of their grandchildren to make any caused problems. Because of this the Republicans and Democrats were panicking and pulling out all the stops while Millenials screamed with rage at their student loans, Obamacare premiums or fines while crushing unemployment offered them no hope. They needed change fast as their grandparents took their jobs in the fast food and grocery markets as they tried to survive.

Tommy waded through the hate propaganda and searched for something positive to share with Falcon before the press conference that night. Not that Falcon needed a pick-me-up; it was really more for Tommy. "Hey boss?"

Falcon glanced up from his computer. "Yes sir."

"There's a message on my voicemail I thought you might enjoy."

"Oh yeah?"

"Yep. Remember the little wrapped boxes we tucked inside the Christmas stockings for the press conference? Here's another call." Tommy pressed the button on his iPhone.

"Hello Mr. Sane, my name is Abby Adams. I am nine and a half. I wanted to wait until I decided what to do with my gift to thank you. Anyway I know it is July now, but it took me that long to figure it out. First I stared at the pretty box wondering what was inside. I asked my parents what they thought. They smiled and said it was up to me, which was no help at all. I read your letter over and over. I wanted to open the box, but I also wanted to be that part of the America that gives and shares. I took it to school and showed my teacher. She did a whole hour on the gift of giving the next day, which was pretty cool except we had homework after class. She said she is voting for you. I would too if I wasn't a kid."

Falcon and Tommy chuckled.

Abby said, "I took it with me almost everywhere, and the wrapping paper tore on a corner. To be honest I peeled back a little trying to see what was in there. Didn't work, you wrap presents pretty good Mr. Sane."

Falcon's face radiated listening to the entertaining-and-honest Abby.

"One of my mom's friends is a producer cuz, you know, my mom's a reporter. Sorry if she said anything you didn't like. She does it to me all the time, eat your vegetables, clean your room, brush your teeth … Anyway the producer had a great idea. A Marine lives in our neighborhood who was hurt really bad in Afghanistan. His name is John. The producer thought we should do like an auction for the box and then give the money to him, but I thought it would be better to just give him the present. So I did. The producer filmed me doing it and put it on YouTube. I guess it was pretty cool cuz it had so many hits it raised almost $50,000. So I gave him that too. Since then everyone's been calling me Abby Adams, lil Marine. I like it. I guess that's it. I wanted to let you know cuz you said you would like to know. Have a great day and God Bless America."

Falcon sat motionless, immersed in her story, and then swallowed the knot in his throat.

Tommy powered off and smiled at his boss. "Just like you told the reporters about that kid Flint, the gift that keeps on giving is the gift of you."

Falcon remained silent. His expression said it all.

"Should I call Abby Adams back or invite her to visit, maybe a little photo shoot?"

Falcon shook his head. "Give her a call and tell her thank you for her story, but no need to bring her in. She's not a prop. That little present will unfold on its own. We put the ball in play now let's see how many lives it will touch."

"Okay, switching gears back to work stuff. My voicemail filled up again overnight just like normal. I've got quite a list. Are we still on the no-interview policy?"

"Who's calling again?" Falcon asked.

Tommy pulled out his list. "That guy from MSNBS."

"No"

"Just no?"

"Anyone foolish enough to say only white people can be racists is simply too irresponsible to sit down with. Besides, I don't think I could sit across from a man who admits to getting a tingle running down his leg at the sight or sound of Obama."

"Okay. Bob Bailey from Wolf News," Tommy said.

"I like Bailey. He's on point with protecting the kids, as well as supporting the troops, but his interview style is abrasive. And what's with the thought for the day always in the negative? How about the glass is half full, rather than half empty?

"Peaches Carlyle is next."

"That'll be the day." Falcon huffed, "She can't even moderate a debate factually. Next."

"Dave Broker?"

"If I wanted to talk to a George W. Bush apologist maybe but seeing as I don't, no."

"Crystal Mello?"

"No she did some quality reporting on the condition of our brave soldiers in Afghanistan. Aside from that, she's a Bush hater and Obama apologist. That makes her a hypocrite or wildly uninformed. You remember that commercial, this is your brain on drugs? Well that's Obama. He's Bush on drugs. They should go find Clinton. At least he didn't inhale. If their decisions weren't so dangerous these guys would be laughable. How many more do you have left?"

Tommy looked at his list. Common sense took over. He knew the entire list would be a no. Falcon was very consistent. Besides, 'if it ain't broke, don't fix it' and not meeting one-on-one was working. "That should do it boss. It looks like we'll have a full house tonight. I need to go set the microphone up. Can we catch up on this later?"

"Yes, we can."

"Hey, that sounded like the Obama chant," Tommy teased.

Falcon shot Tommy the steely expression he'd inherited from his mother when she was cross.

"Just kidding boss, just kidding."

In a low growl Falcon said, "I'll see you in five."

"Yes, you will." Tommy ducked out of the room while he still could.

Falcon thought about the chants the American people bestowed on Barack Obama. *Yes we can! Yes we can!* Although Falcon had doubted Obama's competency when first elected he had definitely hoped he was wrong. He sadly wasn't. Obama had been a tsunami of lies, distortions and incompetence, and with the help of Chief Justice John Roberts, had stripped medical privacy away from Americans. It was just the latest abuse allowed by the people. Benjamin Franklin had said it best, "People willing to trade their freedom for temporary security deserve neither and will lose both." Bush and Obama had taken advantage of the fear Americans felt on 9/11 and crushed the country with the Patriot Act, Homeland Security, secret courts, and warrantless searches. Americans' personal medical information was just the next thing to go.

Falcon recalled the chanting some of the American people did during Obama's first election. It was eerie to hear 100,000 people chanting one man's name. *O-Bam-A! O-Bam-A!* It reminded Falcon of the bizarre chanting done in Iran or North Korea. *The only time I enjoy that kind of chanting is done using three letters in places like Lake Placid, New York in 1980 at the Winter Olympics. USA! USA! Do you believe in miracles? Yes!*

As the campaign thrust forward the reporters gained momentum and pushed hard for the answers they sought; this night no doubt would prove more of the same.

Falcon had given leeway on the one-question-only scenario as long as everyone worked together. Some people preferred listening more than speaking, and the questions normally followed behind one another smoothly. He stood at the podium and observed the reporters settle in as he'd done for months. They'd spent hours together in this room questioning, sometimes interrogating each other – and Falcon gave as good as he received. He'd begun to feel a certain amount of affection for most of the journalists; after all, they belonged to the American people he desperately wanted to help. Although he was not convinced they understood how important their roles were to freedom, he did appreciate a healthy work ethic, and most of them were consistent and respectful.

"Good evening, sir," said Cynthia Chelsea of the *New York Patriot*.

Falcon said, "Good evening to you."

"If it's okay with everyone, I would like to recap your positions to make sure we've covered all the bases for the American people."

"Sounds good to me," Falcon replied

"Okay. We know you believe in securing the border using troops if necessary, are against abortion as a practice, but believe free will and freedom requires women have the right to choose."

"Yes."

"You also believe politicians taking campaign contributions should be illegal, all income tax should be erased and replaced by a consumption tax and global warming or climate change is not something man can control."

"That is correct. We need to be better with pollution, but we don't control the weather or the climate."

Cynthia continued, "You believe in God or a higher power, but don't practice any particular religion; quantitative easing is a crime; public unions are strangling our states; with a few exceptions Republican and Democratic politicians are essentially the same; and the federal government needs less money, not more."

"With a few exceptions, yes."

"You believe in living presently, abhor the abuse humans are piling on each other, love dogs, practice personal responsibility, and are not an attorney."

Everyone laughed, as Falcon had made clear his disdain for elected officials who were either attorneys or bankers.

"No, I am not."

"You believe the Affordable Health Care Act or Obamacare is horrible for our country and society because there is nothing 'affordable' about it; it restricts free will and confiscates patient medical information."

"Not to mention it does nothing to benefit health," said Falcon.

"What do you mean?"

"Our hospitals are filled with obesity-related problems. Without them we'd have plenty of space for accidents, surgery or the elderly. The Affordable Health Care Act or Obamacare will never survive in today's America; like Medicare and Medicaid it will eventually fall apart. Our society is breaking down. Fifty years of *living for the moment* — or, as the kids these days call it, YOLO, 'You Only Live Once'— has left us not with a mess ... but an emergency. A time will come when the money runs out. What will become of those truly in need? There will be a day when police or fire personnel will not answer your 911 call. What then? In many parts of our country that moment has already arrived. If we do not resume responsibility for our country now, this generation will be denounced as the worst in American history and judged rightfully so."

"How would you change things?" asked the reporter.

"I'll do what I have always done, live responsibly and require responsible behavior of others. These aren't policy issues to be legislated by lawmakers. We're talking about moral issues that must be dealt with in the home and our neighborhoods. We cannot turn a blind eye to irresponsible behavior anymore. It is killing the American dream, people. The dream of freedom."

"That's it. You'll live responsibly?"

"I will lead by example. Responsible Americans don't want someone telling them what to do. They want someone enforcing the laws on the books and locking up the problems in their neighborhoods. Responsible Americans want to breathe free, not eat a free lunch. Once the shackles of complacency, corruption and cronyism are removed, America will flourish again. Until then there will be pockets of America that are free and increasingly larger pockets of America that are not. It's our choice. It's your choice as individual citizens. Earn a living or expect a handout. Which America do you want to live in?"

"Maggie May, MSMBS. What about gay rights?"

"First of all there is no such thing as gay rights. All American citizens are afforded the same rights under the Constitution. You don't have more or less rights depending upon your sexual preference."

"What about gay marriage?"

"Marriage isn't a right. Marriage is a choice. There are plenty of people willing to marry gay couples."

"But what about their rights as a married couple?"

"There is no such thing. Your rights don't change whether you're married or not." Falcon paused. "Some of these things are frankly a waste of time. If I'm elected I'll implement a consumption tax and completely remove the inheritance or death tax, taking all the drama and perceived unfairness away from many issues, including this one. I find it easier to explain situations using my own life. I'm the owner of a small business who for many years paid for my own medical insurance. I had a PPO and paid a fairly large medical premium every month. In 2011, after the passage of Obamacare, my premium skyrocketed. I, like many others in the private sector of America, knew this was only going to get worse. My wife worked for and still works for a large well-run company. She's had her medical insurance through them for many years. Although her premiums were going up as well, they weren't as bad as the premium increase for the little guy at the time. I switched to her company and saved quite a bit of money in the beginning. My first point is this: Obamacare is killing the small business owner. The larger corporations will survive by passing the cost to their employees as well as the consumer. If this doesn't work they will lay people off. Small companies keep the big companies honest and the marketplace competitive. Without them we have monopolies. This one law by itself is crushing competition which makes all of us less free."

"Okay. But do you think it's fair that you could switch to your wife's program but a gay couple couldn't do the same?" pressed the reporter as the July heat matched her intensity.

"First off your inference is incorrect. I call Avery my wife and she calls me her husband. Actually, I call her sweetheart and she calls me Baby-Cakes, but that isn't the point."

The reporters laughed at the joke.

"We aren't *government* married. We didn't see the need to get someone else's approval to us being together. As she likes to say, we're married in our hearts."

"Then how can you say you're married?"

"It's called the First Amendment, you know, freedom of speech?"

"But that's not legal."

"Of course it is. Tell me what law is being broken by saying we're married?"

The reporter remained silent. "Well, it's not accurate, so it's not right."

Falcon studied the reporter closely. *This is why America is on the decline. Reporters like this one too busy giving their myopic prejudiced opinions on social issues rather than reporting on the collapse of our monetary and educational systems, not to mention the war profiteering happening.* Falcon leaned into the microphone. "Not that you're entitled to an explanation, but I'll give you one anyway. The First Amendment grants me the right to call her my wife. It also gives me the right to call you a few things right now. However I'll refrain and provide an example of responsible usage of the First Amendment by not practicing the biased and hypocritical speech we all just witnessed."

Everyone in the first two rows turned around to face the reporter. She flushed and wilted slightly.

Maya inwardly smiled. It appeared things were about to get good!

The MSMBS reporter carried a boulder on her shoulder as a self-proclaimed lesbian who lived every issue through the lens of homosexuality. What she failed to comprehend was Falcon didn't have issues with homosexuals. He believed homosexuality or heterosexuality weren't things anyone had a choice in. You were born one way or the other, no better or worse. He felt compassion for people who were homosexual. With the hypersexual environment America had succumbed to, it had to be rough on a teenager to be unable to discuss the confusion surrounding his or her bodily functions and feelings due to a legitimate fear for one's own safety. Still, Falcon's compassion and the compassion of others was now being used by many in the gay and lesbian world to attack and label people as intolerant, particularly religious groups. In the end most Americans didn't care about a person's personal lifestyle or what happened in their bedrooms, but being called a bigot or a homophobe definitely enflamed many parts of the population.

"In response to your statement, it's not only right but very accurate. My wife and I practice the same rights, as you call them, of any couple, gay or otherwise. Unlike many government-married couples, straight or gay, we love and care for each other. We share a home, finances and chores. We have medical coverage through her company. Something afforded to all couples through her company. We also have life insurance policies in case something tragic occurs so the other isn't left in debt. It's called loving, responsible behavior. This is something all couples have the option to do, although many do not. I thoroughly enjoy her company, and she is my best friend. So back to your statement, everything I just said is accurate, and I believe most Americans would agree with me. However, whether America or you agree doesn't matter one bit. My wife and I demonstrate responsible behavior, which is the right thing to do, and I'll call it anything I like … including married!"

The reporter remained tenacious. "What about the death tax?"

"What about it?"

"If a heterosexual member of a marriage dies the surviving member doesn't have to pay any death tax."

"That's not accurate but, okay, I'll accept your inaccurate premise, and?"

"Gay couples don't have that right because they aren't legally married," she proclaimed triumphantly.

"That isn't factually accurate. Wills or living trusts are available to all citizens regardless of their sexual preference. Current tax policy allows couples who aren't legally married to enjoy less taxation. It's wrong and morally bankrupt to tax government-married couples more than other couples, but it's the latest punishment the federal government has come up with in order to squeeze us for more money. I agree with you on the Death Tax. But rather than punishing the heterosexuals, I'll remove all of these taxes and replace them with a consumption tax. Then it will be left to the individual to disperse their money how they see fit. You shouldn't have to pay any more taxes once you've left the planet. Or as a friend of mine once said, 'I cannot believe I have to pay a fee in order to die.'"

The parry was entertaining but the subject played out. There were too many issues the press wanted to tackle.

"Danniel Dustin, *Joshua News*. I know you've said and described securing the border as a top priority for you. Then what? What will you do with the millions of illegals here now? Do you have some type of plan?"

Falcon smiled. He'd been waiting for this question. The reporters had spent most of their time picking through his life and vetting him. As the polls climbed and his election became a possibility they were now playing catch-up. "Do I have a plan? As a matter of fact Mr. Dustin, I have that plan here with me now. It's called the United States Personal Responsibility Act. Tommy?"

Tommy excitedly distributed copies down the rows and flashed it on the overhead. He'd waited months for this question and wondered if it would ever surface. Falcon had told him it would eventually, but the dispassionately-lax decorum of the press was startling. Sex, drugs or scandal and they were all over the place – serious policy and moral propriety, *boring*.

"Okay," said Falcon, "everyone has a copy, and it's on the screen. Let's call it for tonight." Some of the prior sessions had gone on for hours, but Falcon knew he needed to start weaning the time down. Two hours had already passed. "This will give you a chance to really dig into the U.S. Personal Responsibility Act during the week. I'm sure you'll have questions, and I look forward to answering them next Friday. Have a good weekend."

As Falcon exited the stage one reporter sat quietly looking at his copy. The entire document was less than three pages, which was two pages more than the Declaration of Independence and thousands less than the Affordable Care Act.

The United State Personal Responsibility Act of 2017

(1) All federal income tax will be abolished. No tax shall be levied on anyone or anything, including or pertaining to income, capital gains, death, payroll, alternative minimum, corporate, etc.

(2) A federal consumption tax will be instituted in the place of federal income tax. All products sold or services rendered will be subject to the federal consumption tax unless exempt. A list of exemptions will follow.

(3) Federal Consumption tax rates are as follows:

All products/services purchased at or under $500.00 will be taxed at eight percent.

All products/services purchased at $501.00 to $5,000.00 will be taxed at 10 percent.

All products/services purchased at $5,001.00 to $20,000.00 will be taxed at 12 percent.

All products/services purchased at $20,001.00 and over will be taxed at 15 percent.

These rates cannot be increased or decreased without an enactment of a new law voted on and passed by the Congress and signed into law by the President of these United States.

(4) Exemptions are as listed.

(a) All fresh fruits and vegetables (nothing canned), nuts (unsalted), refrigerated meat and dairy (excluding anything with added sugar or sugar substitutes) will be tax free.

(b) The purchase and ownership of one (1) residential house (home) will be tax free. The tax-free allocation does carry to the next home as long as previous home is sold within a 90-day window. All other purchases of homes will be taxed at allocated rate.

(c) All stocks, mutual funds, exchange traded funds, bonds, etc., will only be taxed at time of purchase and not at time of selling.

(5) A yearly United States Military and Protection Tax will be implemented on all United States citizens and legal residents at or above the age of 18. These monies can only be used for the domestic protection of the United States. The yearly U.S. Military and Protection Tax will be $250 per citizen or legal resident due each year by July 4th. Any citizen or legal resident abrogating their responsibility will be subject to fines and/or imprisonment. These monies will be allocated by Congress and used only by United States entities listed: Army, Navy, Air Force, Marines, Coast Guard, CIA (Central Intelligence), FBI (Federal Bureau of Investigation), Dept. of Defense., U.S. Marshals, and U.S. Border Patrol. Exemptions to this tax are as follows: All currently serving military members will be exempt. Any military personnel injured while engaging the enemy will be exempt for their lifetime. All military spouses or children having a parent killed in action, will be exempt for their lifetimes.

(6) All healthcare coverage and retirement package(s) given to current and all former members of Congress will be repealed. Only the sitting President, Vice-President, Speaker of the House,

and Senate Majority Leader will have healthcare coverage provided by the American people and only while in office.

(7) A United States of America Federal Voter Picture Identification card will be required by all United States citizens in order to vote in all federal elections. This identification card will be given free of charge.

(8) All banks and brokerage houses, investment firms, private equity firms, etc. will be separated. No bank will be owned, leased, rented, shared, or have current ownership in any of the listed entities above. No company shall be created to circumvent this separation.

(9) The United States Federal Government will have no financial role in housing. All federal government housing programs will be discontinued.

(10) The United States Federal Government will structurally and electronically secure and physically man the United States Southern Border. After, and only after, the border is secured will immigration reform begin. Immigration reform is stated as such:

(a) All persons living in these United States without legal documentation (U. S. birth certificate, Passport, Work Visa, etc.,) will be given six (6) months to register with U.S. immigration.

(b) All persons registering with factual information will be processed and checked for any committed crimes (misdemeanor or felony).

(c) All persons registering with factual information and no criminal history will be given a three-month temporary status visa and temporary status card that must be available to present to law enforcement at any time.

(d) Temporary status will be removed upon completion of items listed below:

(1) Proof in writing and verification of current employment.

(2) Administrative check verifying individual is not receiving any federal government assistance, financial or otherwise.

(3) Proof of residential address.

(e) A 24-month Permanent work status visa will be awarded after all above items have been completed.

(f) Any arrest of a Temporary work status individual will be subject to deportation and immediate forfeiture of their Temporary status visa card.

(g) Any criminal conviction of a Permanent work status individual will be subject to deportation and immediate forfeiture of their Permanent work status visa card.

(h) All Permanent work status individuals must re-register before 24-month expiration date.

(I) All Permanent work status individuals must apply to become United States citizens immediately after receiving Permanent work status.

(j) All Permanent work status citizen applications, to become United States citizens, will be addressed after 10 years of appropriate behavior, and after every person applying for citizenship legally before them, has been addressed.

(k) United States citizenship may be earned with eight years spent in any of our Armed Forces with good conduct.

(l) Any person living in the United States of America after the allotted six-month period of time without proof of citizenship or work visa will be immediately deported.

9

*T*he summer heat seethed and punished the earth as it cracked her dried soil. Fear and frustration gripped America as her citizens screamed for relief from government intrusion and choking unemployment. The six-year drought in California, America's largest individual economy, bled the United States as decades of over-population, high-density housing and political refusal to build more dams and reservoirs crippled California farmers. Skyrocketing water and sewer charges crushed the little guy. Drab, spiritless lawns became the norm and mirrored the suffering of America. The massive public pension system in the Golden State known as CalPERS wreaked havoc, took cities, districts and other municipalities to court, and demanded money that no longer existed.

In the midst of this Falcon's life had been filleted for all to see yet not one private interview had been granted. The latest topic was whether he would travel and meet America face-to-face. There was also the debate issue. In recent times presidential candidates had debated three times head-to-head in a type of verbal judo. Currently things harkened back to the John Anderson days with three candidates in the running; but unlike Anderson, Falcon actually had a chance to be elected. Falcon's entire platform had come from his book, which millions across the world read and reread. The Friday night press conferences became legendary as he sparred with the cream of the reporting trade, giving him no quarter since he wasn't a Democrat or a Republican. The Independent Party fretted over his unwillingness to tour the country kissing babies and pressing the flesh, but the party was so thrilled at a chance to change America that they waited like wallflowers at a dance as the one-man campaign continued to wake up the United States. With the election 13 weeks away, Falcon met with three representatives from the Independent Party. Numerous questions about scheduling, interviews and fundraising ensued.

Tommy filled out the five-man meeting. He knew Falcon, and this cacophony of noise was about to come to an end.

At the five-minute mark Falcon raised his hand. "Please stop. I need only one thing from you gentlemen — get me on every ballot in every state. Fifty should be fine, but the 57 Obama thinks actually exist may increase our chances. It certainly didn't hurt his."

A twitter of nervous laughter escaped the three representatives. They wanted to win. America had already slipped into a third-world nation in some locations; a generation or more of this and Americans would not recognize their own country. The wealth gap had exploded. *If something wasn't done soon the forces of human behavior and the economic invisible hand would crush America.*

"We were thinking," one of the reps waded in slowly. "We could do a few commercials." He paused and smiled, "That is, if you're available?"

Falcon cringed. "I'm not doing commercials. Things have changed. There's no going back to, 'My name is Earl and I approved this message.' Now that racial politics have come to the forefront, it's only a matter of time before entire counties transform into Detroit, San Bernardino or Oakland. This election is our last chance to turn America around."

Tommy nodded in agreement.

Police across America chose to contain mobs rather than arrest and prosecute. Hordes of law enforcement retired early, moved to safer, smaller communities, or just plain quit. Protestors screamed their rage in front of capitol buildings and large banks. It took almost eight years, but the Obama Administration had successfully accomplished something the Bush administration could not – it united America.

One of the reps panned an Obama slogan, "Looks like half a loaf. Hope is gone, but we definitely got change."

Tommy saw no reason to respond. *If I never hear Obama's name again it will be too soon.*

The third rep said wistfully, "Romney declaring we don't have to live like this does seem a long time ago."

Falcon envisioned debilitating headaches in his future. *They're not even talking about Russia, China or terrorism. Do I really want this job? Do I want the responsibility of deciding when bombs drop and lives end?* Falcon continued giving eye contact to the three men in front of him.

Tommy knew, although Falcon continued to acknowledge the reps, he was in deep thought. He shot his boss a quick glance.

Falcon felt Tommy's eyes on him and nodded, then flipped a switch reclaiming the meeting. "Gentlemen, I appreciate your nomination. I'm modeling to the American people a different type of leadership. Commercials, fundraising and interviews are antiquated and will only get in the way. I plan to travel the U.S. for 30 days, stopping at 15 locations. Use your assets to secure venues for potentially thousands of excited, perhaps frightened, and even angry Americans. Not productions with music or guest speakers. I'll stand alone, present a 10-minute speech, and take questions."

The three men sat taller and nodded their approval, as they were unable to hide their pleasure. *This was an unexpected turn.* Only a few months ago the party had run some commercials to show support for Falcon. He ripped them at his weekly news conference, angry that they had wasted American dollars on garbage television. On the record he warned he would switch to the Freedom Party if they did it again. The ads were pulled immediately. His approval rating gained 10 points overnight as America's voice roared throughout the nation for a real leader.

One rep took the lead. "May we send you a tentative list of 15 cities, for your approval naturally?"

"Absolutely gentlemen, and we'll return it in 48 hours," said Falcon.

"Sounds wonderful," one of the reps gushed.

"One last quick question guys," said Falcon. "I have a dinner date with my lady."

Two men blurted at once, "Debates?"

Falcon had known this was coming. The press had tried to wring it out of him for months. So far he'd done nothing normal during his campaign. Some said he hadn't campaigned at all. Frustration was mounting from every side for a debate. Some wanted to see him trade blows under pressure. Most just wanted to watch a heavyweight fight and see a knockout. *Either way they knew it would be must-see TV.*

"I'll get back to you on the debate idea. He stood and extended his arm. "Thanks for coming out. Let's meet again at the end of the week after the press conference."

Falcon drove home and into his garage, not bothering to close the door since he and Avery would be headed out for dinner soon. He bounced up the exterior steps anxious to tell Avery about the decision to go on the road. When he reached for the door handle he heard.

"Hey Baby-Cakes!"

He turned and saw Avery who waved from the upper deck.

"Wow!" Falcon's heart flip-flopped as he hurried toward her. "You look hot."

A shimmering cerulean dress caressed her voluptuous curves and grazed the tops of her knees. Her golden hair danced around her shoulders as she walked across the deck.

"Look," Avery gestured toward her three-inch strappy heels. "I'm as tall as you are now." She beamed and threw her arms around his neck.

"Shoes like that were made for a woman like you," he growled.

She giggled, stepped away, and spun around as she modeled every angle.

Falcon pulled her close again. "Maybe we should skip dinner and start with dessert."

Resting her hands on his chest, she pushed off. "Oh no you don't," she grinned. "We are having dinner first. Then maybe if you're a good boy, dessert later."

Falcon scooped her up and headed for the house. "And what if I'm a bad boy?"

Avery laughed and borrowed a line from Seinfeld. "Then no soup for you!"

He laughed, settled for a kiss, and put his prize down. "I'm going to jump in the shower. Where are we eating?"

"Cascada. I made a reservation."

Falcon stopped. "Did you give them our name?"

"No, I learned my lesson last time, Mr. Rock Star."

He groaned. "Baby, don't say that. That's what they called Clinton and Obama."

"Oh yeah, sorry. How about my star?"

"I like that. I can work with that."

Apparently bored with scouring their yard for adventure, Lilli suddenly joined the couple as she peeped away.

Avery translated, "She said you're her star too."

Falcon smiled at the two females in his life. "I don't know about being a star but I sure am blessed."

Avery ran her finger coyly over her husband's chest. "Another blessing might be coming your way tonight too."

"Do we really have to go out for dinner?"

"Yes! Now off to the shower for you."

The following morning Tommy and Maya entered Falcon's office. One rule on the short list, never arrive late. If the boss called a 6:30 a.m. meeting, it was wise to punch in by 6:15 a.m. The closer it got to the scheduled time the less patient he became. Maya was early everywhere. She enjoyed life and passed on the stress of rushing. Falcon's motto fit her to a tee. *Be quick but don't hurry.* Punctuality didn't come natural to Tommy, but over the years he'd learned life was easier being on time. Maya and Tommy nestled into the supple black leather couch across from Falcon's desk.

Falcon's office conveyed his belief in a minimalist lifestyle. One wall held framed copies of the United States Constitution and the Gettysburg Address, gifts from Charlie from a trip to Washington D.C. a long time ago. Framed Asian symbols meaning peace, strength and sensitivity, and a ceramic copy of the poem "Footprints" rested nearby. A stone water fountain from Avery gurgled below a stunning wooden sunburst mirror made by his father, while a photograph of Falcon and his brother Deeter as toddlers splashing in a wading pool with the caption: "The greatest gift to a mother is the love between brothers" finished decorating the walls. Pictures of Avery and Lilli, and a plaque inscribed with "Living the Dream" adorned his desk. It wasn't a collection of wealth. It was a collection of love.

Falcon walked in sipping a venti, decaf, nonfat latte. Avery had introduced him to this decadent beverage, and he had become addicted to it. Before meeting her he had never drunk coffee. Now his Starbucks Gold card got a workout almost seven days a week, and their product, and customer service reminded him how much richer life was with Avery. He even used Starbucks to measure the financial heartbeat of America. He called it the "Starbucks Economy". Government stats and reports could not be trusted, and economist's opinions paled in comparison to the consistent profits that embraced the coffeehouse chain. He ascertained if Americans could afford to shell out for a $5 coffee, and Starbucks could grow through the "Great Recession", the real underlying economy was hanging tough. One more drink of the steamy delight and Falcon was revved and ready to reclaim freedom for his country. He carried a cardboard box that held coffee and tea for Tommy and Maya. "Okay," he handed Maya her drink, "where are we?"

"I've been talking to reps for the other candidates regarding the debates," she said. "That political science degree is finally coming in handy. The Dems are pushing for three, hoping to stockpile enough time for damage control if need be. The RINOS believe 10 couldn't vanquish their man of words."

"Vanquish?" Falcon smiled.

"What can I say? Words are to be used." Maya replied with a nod.

Falcon smiled again and turned his attention to Maya's usage of RINO or Republican In Name Only. *What had happened to the Republican Party? Did they think because Obama was so bad America had forgotten about George Bush? And the Democrats? Wow. It's like witnessing the last dying gasp of a huge predator mowing down everything in sight as it crashes to earth. The cleanup will take generations.* "I am not doing three debates," Falcon replied sternly.

Maya said, "I think you should do at least one. We'll request a Friday the same as the press conferences – millions have been watching those. It's a perfect segue to the next level of communication. I know you'd prefer one-on-one, but with three of you it provides for a unique situation."

"And that is?" asked Falcon.

"To let you shine Chief." Maya smiled. "The Democrat has a

temper and frequently loses it at inopportune times, *for her*, that is. Remember when she freaked out in front of Congress when they questioned her about Fast and Furious? The press tried to spin it as passionate, but trust me, the country felt disgusted with her. The RINO is smart, but he talks too fast and comes across as constantly needing a drink of water. They'll try to dominate the platform, but fat chance standing beside you. Because there are three of you, they'll both push for the middle of the stage. We'll announce at Friday's press conference where you stand on the stage is not an issue; it's about where you stand in life, and that's what counts."

"I like that," said Tommy.

"Thanks. Once position is decided it will tell us more about their game plan. If you're in the middle they plan to tag team you. If not, one of them sold their soul for the power position. We can strategize off this decision alone."

Falcon smiled, "You're getting excited about this."

"I enjoy tactics. Remember Chief, we'll be playing chess while they're only playing checkers. Besides," she shrugged, "we have a huge advantage. We have you! So, the question is how many debates?"

"Let me think about this for a second," said Falcon. "Tommy what about the tour list from the Independent Party?"

"They sent 30 cities and want to start ASAP."

"How did they choose the cities?"

"It's insane. They have us crisscrossing all over the nation like a spider web."

"Thoughts?"

Tommy said, "If we start on the West Coast, arranging them in order of proximity and work toward the East Coast, we'll finish in New York City."

Falcon grinned, "Originally I told the party 15 stops, but let's make 64 in 30 days. Two stops on each week day, and six over the weekend."

"Whoa!" Tommy raised his hand for a high five. "They'll love that."

Falcon slapped his palm. "I'm sure they will. Organize their list, and then you and I will add to it. So far our costs have been minimal, but this will take some cash. We'll accept the offer of the party's private jet. Tell them they can select a few people to come on the trip. Otherwise it's the three of us, Avery, and as many press corps as we can pack in."

Tommy jumped out of his seat. "I'm on it boss."

Maya waited expectantly for her marching orders.

Falcon said, "One debate — any more will be a waste of time. As far as subject matter goes, everything is open. I'll announce it Friday so don't say anything during the negotiating."

"How long?"

Falcon smiled, "It doesn't matter."

"Okay. How about 90 minutes?" asked Maya.

"More than I'll need." His eyes sparkled.

"I'm sensing you're five moves ahead of me."

"The rest is up to you, time, place and moderator. I trust your judgment."

"That's my cue." She picked up her coffee and headed for her office. *One debate is perfect. The others could do two more on their own.* Mentally listing the particulars needing to be addressed, she focused on one issue. *If I can get them to agree to only one debate and convince them it was their idea it might keep them from doing the other two.*

An hour later Falcon sat reading Porter Stansberry about the relationship between China and Japan while Stuart Varney's English patter ran down stocks in the background.

Tommy popped into the office. "Okay, boss. I've got it mapped out, but one thing puzzles me. The weekly press conferences seem to be working. Why change now?"

"Great question." It appeared Tommy had finally broken the

pattern of out-of-control playboy to a critically thinking adult. "It's the right thing to do. We aren't campaigning. The American people need to talk face-to-face to their chosen leaders."

"Still no interviews though, right?"

"Right."

"Okay, but I received a request for an interview with me. What-taya think?"

"Do you want to give an interview?"

Tommy smiled, "It might be fun."

"Who's it with?"

"A new magazine called *Peace*."

"*Peace*?"

"Yep *Peace*."

Falcon paused, "What's her name?"

The boss doesn't miss much. "Hilary," he answered lamely.

Falcon shot Tommy an amused glance. "I believe in free speech, so have at it. Remember though, freedom comes with responsibility."

"Don't worry boss, I'd never do anything to hurt you, I swear."

"I know. At least not on purpose."

"Not even accidentally. It'll never happen. Our campaign is too important to you, for us, and to the country."

"Okay. Be smart. Let's see the list."

"I have a pretty good idea where to kick this off. If the polls are correct—"

"The polls." Falcon stared at Tommy with disdain.

"Sorry, but I've been studying this stuff like you suggested. If we begin on the West Coast we can build momentum toward NYC. In fact, I think we should visit every capital starting with Juneau and Honolulu."

"I like it. Why the capitals?" asked Falcon.

"So we can capture the energy from each state. It'll demonstrate the passion Americans have for our country and send the message to all sitting politicians."

"What message?"

"We're coming for you."

Falcon mulled over this information. "We're coming for you. I like that. I'll work it into one of the speeches if you don't mind."

Tommy beamed, "What's mine is yours boss."

"If we cover each capital we're left with 14 more cities to visit. Coordinate that schedule with the Chairman so we aren't flying back and forth. Stay on the same time zones moving across America, and please reiterate, I will be the only speaker, will talk no longer than 10 minutes, and then take questions from the crowd. This is interactive. I don't want hero worship."

"I'm fairly certain you made that clear last time," said Tommy.

"Make sure. Now I plan to write for about an hour — when the list is complete, buzz me. And Tommy, I'm very pleased with your job performance. Your efforts allow me to be more productive. Thank you."

Tommy straightened and his ego swelled. Maya's voice immediately filled his thoughts, something she'd said years ago. *Pride goeth before the fall.* He centered himself and answered, "Thank you, Falcon. Your words mean a lot to me."

Falcon smiled at his friend. Moments like this make life worth the ride. "You've earned them, brother. See you later."

Tommy left, quietly closing the door behind him. He'd almost reached his office when he remembered the interview with Hilary. *Oh yeah ... this day keeps getting better and better.*

The blazing mornings and nights of August pardoned California with something folks hadn't seen in almost a year – rain. Falcon enjoyed the solitude in his office on the first flush of an early Thursday as he watched the stock futures expand on his computer screen. The TV in the background squawked that the markets appeared hopeful with the upcoming election.

"If this Sane guy gets elected, no pun intended," remarked a reporter. "We might actually have an adult in the White House."

Edward Snowden's blowing the whistle on the U.S. government reading and listening to Americans' emails, texts and phone calls was on Falcon's mind as he perused articles on Yahoo and Google. Troubled regarding the probability of the NSA super computers located in Utah were monitoring him, he clicked on koala bears, rose bushes and the Pizza Guys just to throw them off. He laughed at the thought of some "genius" at the NSA trying to tie food, flowers and bears together, only to sober quickly at the idea of being spied on. *The days of privacy are over. Technology and the Me Generation have changed our lives forever.*

An article about Steve Jobs caught his eye. Falcon paused. He'd read a biography on Jobs once. The guy's life was filled with aggression toward others yet he was hailed as a great communicator and inventor of the iPhone. *Now we pay for the right to broadcast our thoughts, dreams, and nightmares into the universe where Big Brother is listening.* Thanks to Steve, Orwell was right. Jobs created a wormhole into every American who carried a cell phone and a built-in tracking device that allowed anyone with a smart phone to be tailed or located at any time.

Falcon closed the Jobs article and tapped Thomas Jefferson into the Yahoo search engine as he sought a specific quote. *The tree of liberty must be refreshed from time to time with the blood of patriots and tyrants.* He clicked on the quote and could almost hear the humming of the supercomputer trying to decipher any hidden messages. He thought about the mixture of beauty and horror in the quote. Jefferson's hypocrisy wasn't lost on him. Jefferson loved to pontificate about liberty and justice, but had personally owned slaves. *Justice. Justice isn't just blind ... she's also deaf and dumb. Justice is so reactionary. No wonder the Me Generation loves talking about social justice. The only thing social justice is bringing to the country is social injustice and unrest to every hardworking, ethical, responsible American.* In some cases the Internet was beautiful. Information moved quickly and easily, almost like a godsend. Of course, propaganda moved just as fast. The information age had given way to the incessant need and desire to gossip and perform voyeuristic acts via the net. Falcon skipped through multiple polls on the upcoming election when a caption caught his eye.

"UNNAMED SOURCE IN THE PRESIDENTIAL INDEPENDENT PARTY CAMPAIGN CALLS FALCON SANE A TYRANT." Falcon cared little about what others thought of him or the ridiculous stories that were just that – ridiculous. A supposed love child tucked safely away, a direct blood link to Abraham Lincoln, and Falcon's ability to verify that UFOs did in fact exist were the craziest of all. The fact these stories held zero truth did not stop the papers from printing, or the current culture from frothing at the counters hoping to invade another person's life. *Misery does love company.* The "Tyrant" story was published in *PEACE* magazine and written by Hilary Temple. *Of course it is.* Falcon shook his head. *What did Tommy say? Hilary was straight out of an Eagles' song. Raven hair, ruby lips, and he didn't mention sparks flying from her fingertips, but Don Henley was probably being creative. Tommy was mooning, and she'd spun him like a top.*

Her exposé quoted an unnamed source that bemoaned the fact that "the hours were long" and "sometimes there wasn't enough time to even do his laundry." The story continued without further quotes but painted quite a picture of a tough taskmaster who ran his business more like Patton than Gandhi.

Falcon considered the comparison of Patton and Gandhi, who had held completely different views about life and their struggles with human oppression, while his temper gave birth to a slow burn. *Freaking Tommy*!

As he streaked toward work, Tommy turned on the car radio

to a call-in talk show. "I thought that Sane campaign was a buttoned-down program. Now someone's leaking like a sieve. Getting elected as an Independent is hard enough, can't have drama, no sir, can't have it!"

What are they talking about?

A second voice added, "And who's talking to *PEACE* magazine? I've never even heard of this rag!"

The speaker's statement made Tommy gasp, and his knuckles whitened from gripping the steering wheel.

"Hilary Temple?" continued the radio voice. "Who the bleep is Hilary Temple?"

Tommy switched to another station.

"So Falcon Sane is Patton or Gandhi. Which is it? I wonder what was in that reporter's Shirley Temple," said the morning drive DJ to her co-host.

"Who knows? The real question is who gave her the information? I guess this Falcon Sane guy puts his Underoos on one leg at a time like the rest of us. Shoot, his book about growing up in America is probably a fairy tale, just like Obama's. All character composites and fantasy."

"We do not need another Blobama," blurted the female announcer.

"We couldn't afford the first one, missy; he maxed out our credit cards."

Tommy loosened his tie and cranked up the AC. *What the hell happened? I gave an awesome interview. I thought this chick liked me!* The DJs interrupted his thoughts.

"Do you think we'll ever get a real person for President?"

He replied, "Unless science discovers how to freeze-dry me for later, not in my lifetime."

"I'm serious Bob. Don't we have anybody out there who isn't a complete tool?"

"Maybe a couple of screwdrivers if you know what I mean ...

bada-bump! I'll be here all week folks whether you like it or not, and please tip your waitress."

"Okay Howdy Doody let's reel it in. Don't we have anyone out there?"

Tommy screamed at the radio, "Yes we do! His name is Falcon Sane!"

Falcon finished the "Tyrant" article as he scrolled down to read the comments written by other readers. Although aware of his throbbing temples, he believed he had his temper under control, until he read the first comment.

"What did you expect? He's just another fucking politician."

Adrenaline raged through his body. He took a deep breath, but deep breathing wasn't going to do it this time.

A thumbs-up or down was placed next to each comment. Readers could click if they agreed or not. The first comment had two thumbs down. Falcon felt mild relief and continued reading.

"I don't know about this story but if the worst part is Sane runs his company like Patton with the peacefulness of Gandhi, my question is, what's the problem? Falcon Sane for President 2016." Thumbs-up: 6028. Thumbs down: 123.

Falcon's temper resumed a level of normalcy.

"If his campaign is already leaking what will happen when he's president? A person is measured by the company they keep. What kind of people does he have surrounding him?" Thumbs up: 3243. Thumbs down: 2987.

Falcon agreed with the measurement statement, and he also believed even the best of people sometimes make mistakes. *But I cannot afford mistakes.* He massaged his temples, closed the screen on his computer, and stared at the wall. What to do? *I love him to death, but Tommy has always been a wildcard. Can the country afford to have him in the White House? Will he do something that puts someone in danger or worse?* Falcon looked toward the ceiling for guidance. *Well Big Fella? Here we are again. I need a hand Father. Are you sure I'm up for this? Things are coming a bit undone. I hardly see the best part of my life anymore. My company is financially taking a hit because we're spending so much time dealing with this crap. Maya's hanging in there but she's only human. I'm tired Father. I'm tired of people hurting each other. I'm tired of reading about children being murdered. I'm tired of being called a racist cracker who hates women and wants to kill babies. Please Father I'm begging you for direction.*

A knock came at the door.

Not waiting for Falcon's approval, Tommy burst into the man's office and words raced out of his mouth. "Boss I'm so sorry! I didn't say any of those things. I talked about love for the country, how it's our duty to stand up and be counted. I told her you kind of saved my life and got me back on track—"

"Stop!" Falcon raised his hand, stood and glared at Tommy. Pointing to the couch he said, "Take a seat."

"Yes sir." Tommy sat straight as a board as he waited for the firing squad.

Falcon crossed the room several times as he tried to calm down. In all the years they'd known each other he'd never yelled at Tommy. *We've done everything right! We're so close!*

Tommy prepared for the worst. *Let me have it, Boss! Please let me have it! Fire me if you have to.*

Falcon ceased pacing, closed his eyes momentarily, and spoke almost in a whisper. "Do you realize how close we are to helping children who've had no chance? Do you have any idea how close we are to changing America for the better? Can you comprehend how close we are … to obtaining the most influential position on the planet?"

Tommy's head dropped into his chest. He would have preferred being yelled at.

Falcon's voice grew dangerously low as the storm of outraged passion gained momentum in his soul. "Do you know how long it took me to write this book? Two years. Two years of writing, rewriting, editing and enduring criticism and opinions about my life. Two years of painstaking work to put us in a position to help others. And for one night you were willing to jeopardize everything! Are you ever going to grow up, Tom? Are you ever going to get it?"

Tommy peered at the man he admired and loved, while guilt and shame wrenched his very core. His eyes began to blur. "I'm sorry." He stopped to clear his throat. "I never meant to hurt you."

The anguish on Tommy's face softened Falcon's heart. He let out a heavy sigh. "It's not about me, brother, it's about our country."

"I know, I know. I really am so sorry." Tommy didn't want to say the last thing on his mind, but he saw no recourse. "Please accept my notice; maybe that will—"

"You think you're going to quit on me? On America? Oh no! You're one Baby Boomer who is going to stay put and help clean this mess up!"

Tommy jumped to his feet. "Anything you want boss. Just tell me what to do. I can do a press conference this morning and fix this."

Falcon glared, "Are you kidding me? We see how well that worked the first time."

"I'm so sorry, boss."

"Just stop talking!" Falcon stared at his friend. In a low voice he said, "We're going to let this go on one condition."

Tommy gulped. *Here it comes*. He stood tall and took the request like a good foot soldier. "Anything sir."

"No more comments about this incident. It's only a story if you or I become further involved. There are plenty of good reasons why I don't give interviews. This is one of them."

"Don't worry. It's over, boss."

Falcon briefly shut his eyes. "Not exactly, but we will not belabor the point. And Tommy please tell me you did not fall in love last night?"

His face flushed. "Not even close. She shut me down at the door."

"Good, she did you a favor. Now start thinking north of your equator and go get the list. You did finish the list of cities, right?"

"Yes. It's in my office."

"Well, let's get moving, looks like it's going to be one of those 'long work days' I just read about. Hopefully, you washed and changed your shorts," Falcon smirked.

"I'm so sorry, Falcon."

"I know you are, George. Get the list."

"I am. I really am."

"Yes, I know, Mahatma. Go get the list!"

Grateful the Earth was spinning again Tommy left Falcon's office with his job and integrity intact, and an unforgettable lesson under his belt ... literally.

Maya poked her head inside Falcon's office door.

"Good morning, superstar!" Falcon waved Maya in.

"Good morning, Tommy's at it again, huh?"

"You see the story online?" Falcon asked.

"Yes, same silliness we've dealt with before. Remember the article wanting me to proclaim whether I was a Hispanic, Latina or a White Latina?"

"I do, and I remember your articulate letter setting them straight. The depth of America transcends skin color, race, gender or religion. We are from a fruitful land, measured individually by our pursuit of happiness and thankfully born free." Falcon looked at his second-in-command as he dropped his voice to underscore the seriousness of his next words. "It was awe-inspiring."

"Thank you. I did cherry-pick the 'born free' from you," Maya said as she tried to deflect the compliment.

"Imitation is the ultimate form of flattery."

Maya smiled, grateful, but embarrassed at her boss' words. "Okay, switching gears, the latest on the debate."

"Hit me."

"The other parties want at least two. We're still standing at one, right?"

Falcon nodded, "I know it would make your job easier if we agreed to two, but the way I plan to debate will only be powerful the first time around. Debates lose their steam quickly, and frankly most Americans lose interest. We don't play the Super Bowl three times a year."

Maya laughed, "True. My concern is they will have one or two more on their own."

"Let 'em. The weekly press conference is keeping America excited about the book and more importantly, informed and educated. It won't matter what happens in those other debates – their only audience will be people planning on voting for one of them. What names have come up for the moderator?"

"Same as always, one from NPS and another from ABS. A panel was suggested too, I think because they're hoping to fill it with their people."

"I like panel moderating. Keeps the room equal," said Falcon. "A trio … I like that idea."

"Any preference?"

"No, not really; moderators all do the same job, ask open-ended questions. It would be nice to balance the room though. With two men and one woman debating perhaps we could request two women and one man to moderate."

"That's a good idea," said Maya. "I'm sure everyone will be agreeable to that. The RNC will be sorry they didn't think of that first. They could spin it to show the War on Women is over."

"They'll probably spin it anyway. The Democrats will take

credit as well as the only party who cares about women's rights anyway. Let them. One last detail I want assurance on though."

Maya's interest piqued. Falcon showed little concern regarding the specifics and left all the debate prep to her. He said if speaking from the heart and mind wasn't enough then it wasn't enough.

"I want the audience able to participate with applause," Falcon added. "I do not want a dull, quiet arena. Let's allow the anger, fear, frustration, excitement, and the adrenaline coursing through the crowded space to run free. I also want the podium microphones to be cordless."

Maya's imagination turned somersaults. *These requests would be easy to get. One of the Republican negotiators already posed the idea of allowing applause.* She'd watched Falcon work a room of people multiple times, but never with combatants on both sides and moderators. Studying Falcon she felt his charge of excitement. His demeanor was calm but his eyes shined. *The boss is going to light a fire under America on that stage and burn the Boomer Culture to the ground.* Maya left his office and closed Falcon's door.

Falcon lifted his eyes toward the ceiling. *Thank you Father, I'm back on track.*

10

September slipped in without notice, and just as all the attention had piled on Falcon, it now fell to the leak in his camp.
Americans bought in just enough to the Independent candidate to now care about his leadership capabilities. The country liked
what they were hearing but needed assurance this man could handle
having the nuclear codes and his proverbial finger on the button.
As voters screamed about the corruption coming out of Washington
D.C., they fiercely readied to tune into the popular Friday evening
press conference, only eight weeks away from the election.

Hilary Temple of *Peace Magazine* sat outside Falcon's building
in her rental car and chirped on her cell. "Thank you, easier than
taking candy from a baby. What's that? No problem, I own the guy.
What do you need?" She listened. "That'll cost more than last time,
a lot more. Un-uh. If you want that kind of dirt, I want my own
television show. Not cable either, I want network." Hilary ended the
call and smirked at her reflection in the rearview mirror. *One more
garbage story and I'll be an anchor!*

The political operative hung up his phone and smiled. *One more
garbage story and Falcon Sane is finished.* Karl Berkel was a well-
paid hatchet man. Unlike Falcon, the operative tracked every poll.
He held no loyalty to any party let alone America. He pulled a pack
of Camels from his pocket and shook one out. Using the last match
from Garth's Diner from somewhere in Oklahoma, he struck, lit,

and inhaled deeply. *What a ditsy broad. She'll never be an anchor.* He inhaled twice more and then flicked the still-lit cigarette into the dried brush. *And fuck you Falcon Sane, you and your righteous bullshit you Generation X, Latch Key fucking prima donna!* He mentally grabbed his crotch. *I got your Boomer right here!*

As Tommy prepped for the Friday night press conference the acid in his stomach could've burned a hole through lead. *The Tyrant issue is settled between me and Falcon, but who knows what the reporters will do.* He adjusted the projector, the computer, and positioned his chair where he could see Falcon, and more importantly Falcon could see him. Nearly every seat was filled when Hilary Temple of *Peace Magazine* strut into the room. Prior to today, a woman like Hilary could have burned him repeatedly. *No woman is worth the humiliation and disloyalty I put the boss and myself through.*

Hilary smiled sweetly at Tommy.

He nodded in return, like two boxers acknowledging one another before a fight. *Keep your friends close and your enemies closer.* Tommy wasn't so much angry with her as he was with himself. He'd been with Falcon over a decade and once called Falcon the Godfather. Falcon laughed asking if Tommy was his Luca Brasi. Tommy replied absolutely. Falcon reminded him, these were fictional characters engaged in immoral, unethical and criminal behavior.

"If anything we're exactly opposite of this," stated Falcon.

"I know," Tommy replied. "I just meant the loyalty factor."

Tonight Tommy felt disloyal and guilty. Not only had he left his boss unprotected, he'd created a new issue for Falcon to deal with. This was one evening Tommy wished he did not have a ring-side seat. As Tommy's stomach seethed, Falcon entered the room and advanced to the podium.

The reporters settled in, ready for a good verbal tussle. They had come to really enjoy the banter with the candidate. Accessible and willing to deal with them respectfully, his words didn't need to be deciphered for hidden meanings. Plus, his approach to this campaign forced the Republicans and Democrats to think outside the box and find new ways of communication, which is always beneficial to a free society.

"Good evening my friends and a few others."

Earnest chuckles rumbled around the room. It was an inside joke gone mainstream. He'd addressed the press many months ago by saying good evening friends. Although most of the reporters weren't friends with him they were at least friendly. His comment played on every channel across America as Republican and Democratic pundits tried to turn it into an issue.

"Now the reporters are his friends," opined a Democratic wonk.

"Sure getting cozy around the Independent candidate," whined a Republican strategist.

When asked about the complaining from the other parties Falcon's answer was simple and to the point. "Had they done their jobs, serving the people by enforcing rather than interpreting our laws for their own personal benefit, the country wouldn't be ready to be rid of them. Besides, have they grown so bitter and controlling they cannot allow people to be friends? Why are they so afraid? There's a humorous yet profane statement made by Richard Pryor years ago that fits here. 'Have a Coke and a Smile'. Can anyone finish the sentence?"

A voice from the back of the room answered, "And shut the fuck up!"

Falcon grinned. "Now let's be accurate and not quote me as the one who finished that line."

The reporters belly-laughed. This candidate held nothing back. He was a regular guy who believed in freedom. His message was simple, and the American people were beginning to pick up what this man was putting down: freedom, truth and personal responsibility.

The reporters continued to work together, which made the press conferences zoom by and still yield plenty of information.

Falcon assumed the hot items for that night would be the debates, campaigning, and the *Peace Magazine* article. The order in which they were addressed said a great deal about the press and what they thought the people most wanted to hear.

"Phillip Garrett, NBS News. We all want to know about the debates and campaign trip across America, but my first question is about the article in *Peace*."

And people wonder why our country is in such bad shape. Falcon said, "And your question is?"

"Do you know who the anonymous source is?"

Falcon considered the reporter and then shifted his gaze to Tommy.

The entire press corps followed his gaze.

Tommy wanted to melt into the chair. *Sit tall and face the music.*

Falcon sized up the reporter. "Is this really something you want to discuss? You consider it news?"

The reporter grinned. "I don't know if it's news but we definitely want to talk about it."

"Yes," said Falcon.

"Yes?" repeated the reporter.

"Yes," Falcon said again.

"Yes what?"

"Yes, I know who the anonymous source is, next question please."

"Jennifer Day, CBC News. Can you tell us the name of the anonymous source?"

"Yes, I can. Next question please."

The reporters stirred. It appeared the candidate was giving another lesson on the usage of language. Although the information held no real value, it was slightly juicy. The reporters weren't letting it go.

"Vince Gamboa, ABS News. Will you tell us the name of the source?"

"Yes, I will. Next question please." Falcon laughed to himself.

"David Flynn, WOLF News. What is the name of the anonymous source?"

"Finally, people. I thought we might be talking about Tommy all night rather than issues important to America."

The press paused for a long second and then collectively stared at Tommy.

Tommy did not squirm or blink. He stared directly at his boss and ignored the jumbled thoughts that tried fiercely to permeate his attention.

"Patricia Tornada, MSMBS. Can … may we ask Tommy some questions?"

"Sure. As I told my friend when he asked permission to give an interview, we live in America where you can say anything you like without fear of government persecution or prosecution although these days … well," Falcon tailed off. "As did most of us in this room, Tommy had the privilege of being born free in the United States of America, and even served our great country in the military." Turning toward Tommy he smiled. "In what branch did you serve my friend?"

"United States Army, Staff Sergeant, Rangers."

"If anyone has the right to free speech it is our veterans, so let's move this along. Tommy would you care to take questions from these nice freedom-loving people whom you helped defend?"

Tommy paled and appeared as if he might vomit.

Maya stood in the wings and tried not to laugh.

Falcon held an amused expression. *Every action has a reaction Buddy. Be humble and smile. The country will love you for your sincerity.*

"No sir. I think I've said enough."

"Are you sure? Everyone's curious about the *Tyrant* story. I mean, seriously George, are the hours too long?"

Maya choked down her laughter. She knew Falcon loved Tommy and was having some fun with him and the press. This was a lesson Tommy needed to learn, *right now*.

The press began picking up on the tone the Presidential candidate was emitting. He was teasing and teaching at the same time. After all, loose lips sink ships. The holes needed filling to keep the boat afloat – Falcon's boat.

Tommy grinned. "No sir. The work hours are amazing. I cannot think of a better way to spend my time than protecting freedom." *Provide answers, a bit of humor, and then send a message.*

Falcon approved of his answer. *Good one, buddy.* "That's good to know because, according to the story, you didn't have time for some chores. Did you get your clothes washed, Mahatma?"

Everyone in the room roared with laughter, everyone except Hilary Temple.

Tommy nodded and continued smiling, hopeful his part in this play completed.

Falcon glanced across the room at the reporter who'd meant to embarrass his friend and create conflict. He remained silent as he continued to focus on the woman until the laughter subsided. "I'm always appreciative of a good laugh Ms. Temple. Thank you for providing the material this evening for our comedy routine. Now let us move on to important things. As my friend mentioned a few moments ago," Falcon gestured toward Tommy, "let us focus on freedom."

The presser barely finished and Hilary Temple checked her iPhone. It held one text message from Karl Berkel. *So much for the anchor job.*

After watching the press conference on his laptop, Berkel

grudgingly shook his head. *This Sane guy's pretty smooth.* His phone started ringing. He recognized Hilary's number, declined it, and deleted her from his contact list. He let out a sigh. He'd taken money from the Democrats and the Republicans, and both expected results. Although the two parties pilloried each other in the press both knew they couldn't allow an outsider to win. Decades of illegal agreements based on coercion, lies and blackmail would come crashing down. Berkel stared at his phone and beads of sweat formed on his forehead. *Who do I call first?*

With the press conference finished, Falcon and Tommy took a red-eye flight from Sacramento to Phoenix to make a Saturday morning meeting with the Independent Party campaign coordinators. It was time to plan the campaign trip across America or, as it was named, "The Freedom Train".

Avery flew in as well from the East Coast.

Maya finished negotiating the final details for the debate. Surprisingly all parties agreed on one debate. The Republicans believed their only chance would be to blow their competition out of the water and leave no time for damage control. This was a gamble. Although their guy was a sitting senator, strong debater, and quick-witted, he needed a huge wave to propel him into the lead. According to the polls he'd never recovered from an ill-advised attempt early in his senate career to coerce the American public into Reagan Amnesty number two.

The Democratic candidate, who was the only woman in the race, banked on that fact being a major ace in the hole. Her background read like a four-star menu: decades of government experience, a sitting senator from the nation's largest state, and a family relation to a former president. Name recognition worked against and for her, as some dyed-in-the-wool Democrats thought she could do no wrong. Oddly enough, other Democrats hated her almost as much as the Republicans. She had a taxing case of entitlement and believed she deserved to be president. Rumor was the senator made statements like, "It's my turn," and "It's rightfully mine."

The only reason Maya could think of the DNC agreeing to one debate was that they doubted their candidate could pull off three positive showings. She was indeed a polarizing figure with an invigorated case of "It's all about me". With her kind of attitude, the door opened for Falcon's label of her generation, blazing a trail across the nation with the power of typhoid. "Boomeritis," it screamed from front yards, windows and bumper stickers. No surface was exempt from the generational disease.

Three hours later at the airport in Phoenix, Tommy stood with Falcon in the desert night as he drank a bottle of water. The September sun had been down for hours, but the heat still reminded them why they lived in Northern California.

Tommy looked down as his phone buzzed. "It's Maya, Chief," Tommy said and handed his phone to Falcon.

Falcon had stopped carrying his cell a while ago. It never stopped ringing.

"Good evening," Falcon's voice came through her earpiece.

"Back at you Chief. I have good news and a little bad news. Which do you prefer first?

"Let's have dessert first."

Maya laughed, "When's the last time you ate dessert?"

"Hey I need to stay in tip-top shape. Being President seems to age people pretty quickly. At least I won't have to worry about my hair turning grey." He ran his hand over his smoothly shaved head.

Maya said, "Everyone agreed to one debate. It will last 90 minutes and cover five topics.

Ninety minutes. Falcon smiled to himself. "That's fine."

"Do you want to know what the topics are?"

"Sure, go ahead," Falcon said mildly interested.

"The topics are the economy or lack thereof, the Patriot Act,

Abortion, the IRS, and of course Obamacare."

"Nothing about immigration?"

"No sir," said Maya. "They don't want to talk about it. From what I gather, they both feel it's too hot to touch. We've heard nothing about it the last couple months. I think a backroom deal was made agreeing to shelve it."

"Your opinion or you talked to someone?"

"On the record, no. But several groups are trying to stir the immigration topic up again and are getting nil from both parties. It appears the D and R's plan to ignore it continuing with the status quo, no enforcement, no fence, less and less border security. Big business wants the cheap labor, the unions want a guarantee the new 'legals' as they call them, will sign up and get on board. Nobody in organized labor is screaming to start picking fruit and vegetables in the fields every day. As always, the real problems of border security are ignored, and our cities continue to be inundated with more mouths to feed, bodies to cloth, and children to educate. The RNC knows their guy almost lost any chance at being the nominee with his shot at pseudo amnesty and the DNC knows no one in the pro-immigration camp believes anything they say after they were promised by Obama last time for their votes."

"Okay," said Falcon. "They really want to talk about abortion?"

"Yes sir. The DNC thinks they can continue with the War on Women program. I don't think they really want to talk about abortion, but because the RNC continues to deal with abortion as something that should be illegal rather than a freedom issue, they give the Democrats one strong pillar able to balance a bunch of shaky smaller constituents. I know we haven't sat down and talked about the debate, but I think once you're done explaining the right to choose as a freedom issue the DNC will be in free fall. They won't have anything left."

"I agree. Good job, anything else?"

"With your approval I can get the contracts signed tonight. The moderator panel consists of two women and one man. I'll receive their info soon. You'll be unencumbered on stage, independently miked in addition to a cordless microphone."

"Did you tell them I would be moving around?"

"No, I couldn't tell them anything. I don't know what your plan is. Not knowing made negotiating easier. Had I known, I would've nitpicked each thing, which could've made them less compliant. Being we're new to the game, I'm sure they think they laid down all the ground rules."

Falcon smiled – that's exactly what he wanted. He knew both political machines would start spinning as soon as the deal was struck. He wanted them twirling while he was thinking. And he wanted them at their best so there would be no excuses. *Ninety minutes ... I'll only need two. For society to improve and break free from its current state of affairs a new idea has to be presented. Einstein said it perfectly. "No problem can be solved from the same level of consciousness that created it. It's time for a new level of consciousness.* Falcon finished with Maya, "Okay, catch up to us when you can. We'll be holding the Friday press conference down here, and then begin the Freedom Train."

"See you in a couple of days, Chief."

Karl Berkel began his calls. First, the Democratic candidate. Normally someone in Berkel's line of work never spoke directly to any candidate, but he'd known Sheila Reid Arnold nearly three decades. He was still amazed by the level of energy the 70-year-old woman could muster. Maybe 'muster' was the wrong word. Consumed was a better description.

The Democratic candidate's long-deceased, communist-leaning parents had instilled in her a hatred of guns, grace and God. By age 22, she blamed those three G's for the state of America. Swearing to eradicate them and make the world equal, her battle cry was,

"America isn't special, and Americans aren't any different than anyone else."

She had married a charming man who loved two things: sex and the sound of his own voice. While she ignored his dalliances, they used her inherited fortune and began politicking after law school. Manipulating every situation to their benefit and willing to cross ethical and legal lines at will, the power couple had appeared unbeatable. A bout with cancer for her husband, and a long line of unexplainable deaths surrounding former co-workers or lovers removed any chance he had of pursuing higher office. Sheila Reid Arnold, on the other hand, would not be denied. She continued up the ladder, carpetbagging herself to California where, after Reagan's Amnesty, only Democrats were elected. After her fourth term in the United States Senate she knew the 2016 Presidential Election was her last chance, to change the world, to be the first woman President in American History, and to be the most powerful person on Earth.

Karl Berkel knew she would pick up after two rings.

"Karl."

He could hear the desperation in her voice. "Hello Sheila."

"Just finished watching 'Friday Night Live'." Sheila's name for the Sane press conferences.

"Yes, it didn't go as expected."

"Obviously not."

Karl sat quiet. Four calls in three weeks, and nothing had worked as they'd planned. "Karl, we've decided on one debate."

"Not sure that's a good idea, Sheila."

"I disagree. I'm going into debate prep in two weeks while 'Boy with Many Stories' is on his Freedom Train," she said with disgust. "You know I have high cheekbones too!"

Karl grimaced slightly at her Boy with Many Stories name and high cheekbone comment. After an exhaustive background check, Karl had discovered Falcon had a grandfather who was one-quarter

Kickapoo American Indian, a nomadic tribe who were treasured for their phenomenal storytelling abilities. "You know it's not smart to call him that even in private. Someone might hear you."

Sheila snorted her derision. "What difference does it make? Do you have anything for me or not?"

Karl shook his head. *She's too angry to be the finger on the red button. Boy with Many Stories is sounding better every day.* "Sheila, I've done all I can. Good luck in the debate. If anything comes up you know my number. I look forward to your inaugural address in January."

"I do too Karl."

Karl disconnected and quickly called the campaign manager for the Republican candidate.

"Hello Karl."

"Hi Raul."

"Looks like Friday Night Lights had a trick play up his sleeve," said Raul.

Karl almost laughed at him. *These guys are in way over their heads.* After checking with Sheila first, he'd taken the Republican money. Her only comment was that she wanted a discount since both sides ordered the same meal: the destruction of Falcon Sane. He knew what to expect with Sheila, an obnoxious, two-faced liar, who only cared about herself. She was all carnivore.

The Republican candidate was anything but a carnivore. He did however fit exactly the new Republican mantra: *If you can't beat them join them.* Senator David DeJesus was the perfect size: smart, flashy smile, quick-witted and Latino or Hispanic depending upon which state he was in. His résumé was a trifle weak, and he used campaign contributions for his personal use without a second thought; but he'd made his way through the Republican Primary gauntlet, despite an attempt at Amnesty number two nearly derailing his campaign. He never thought being compared to Ronald Reagan would be a bad thing. DeJesus quietly listened to his campaign manager, Raul, speak to Karl on the phone.

Karl cracked back, "Friday Night Lights. Didn't know you played football, Raul. Thought you were more of a soccer fan."

"No Karl, you stole our name. Real football isn't played with pads like a bunch of pussies." Raul looked at DeJesus who smiled.

"Anyway," said Karl, "I've done everything you paid me to do."

"Yes, it looks that way. Doesn't really matter anymore. We've settled on one debate," Raul bragged.

"That's probably not a good idea, Raul."

"Yeah I thought you'd say that. Now I really like it!" he laughed.

Karl shook his head. "Vaya con dios Raul."

"Do you know what that means Karl?"

"Yeah it means go with God."

"We don't need God Karl ... we have De-JESUS!"

"So you do." Karl disconnected the line. *What a dumb fucking wetback.*

Raul extended his hand toward the senator for a fist bump.

The senator fist-bumped his campaign manager.

"These stupid gringos have no idea," said Raul. "When we win and make our people legal, we'll own this country in 20 years. Then we'll start making up names for the color of their skin. Forget about taking back California. We're taking it all. This is for La Raza!"

DeJesus nodded, "This is for our race."

11

*T*he last week in September The Freedom Train kicked off to a roaring crowd in Juneau, Alaska. Six weeks away from the election, Alaskans disgusted with Washington D.C. came from every town and borough and packed their capital. The massive turnout convinced Falcon to reconsider the protection offered from the Secret Service months ago. In July when the independent polling put him ahead of the Republican candidate, he was appreciative of the offer, but graciously refused and left the SS in a quandary. Now the crowds were too big. They had no choice. They had to protect him. Fortunately Falcon agreed.

With the current mood in America hundreds of thousands of trained militia members watched and waited. Backing Sane 100 percent, they weren't shy about what actions they were willing to take if something happened to him.

One militia member went on the record and paraphrased the *Godfather*. "If Falcon Sane has a heart attack we're holding the government responsible. If Falcon Sane drowns drinking a glass of water we're holding the government responsible. If Falcon Sane is struck by lightning we're holding the government responsible." When a reporter asked, "What do you mean by holding the government responsible?" Armed with an AR-15 rifle, the member had stared steely-eyed at the reporter and said, "Don't ask stupid questions."

After Falcon's refusal in July, the Secret Service placed 24-hour surveillance on him and Avery by staking out his office and home. They weren't alone. The diligent, well-trained militia outnumbered the Secret Service 10 to one and silently provided a peripheral presence. After the huge crowds in Alaska, with pressure building and death threats piling up, Falcon acquiesced to the Secret Service's request to adequately protect him and Avery.

He also met with the leaders of the militias. "I appreciate what you men are doing. I really do. Please give the Secret Service a little room. I've accepted their offer to protect me, my wife and my staff while we're on the road. I believe them to be good people and better equipped than I am at this juncture."

One man stepped forward and extended his hand to Falcon. "Robert Collado, sir. I served in the Marine Corp, three tours in Vietnam." He looked around at the other militia leaders. "We'll follow your orders and give them room. Just know if you need us we'll come running."

Falcon shook the hardened Marine's hand. "I appreciate that more than you know." He acknowledged the other men. "I sincerely thank you all. We have to trust there are some good people left in our government."

The men nodded in respect, although most doubted he was right.

Falcon continued, "We also have to trust that God will see us through on our journey."

Every man snapped to attention, shoulders squared.

"But so help me God, should something happen to me, swear that you will protect my family." Falcon looked each man in the eye.

All 12 militia leaders, former U.S. decorated military, fired off a simultaneous salute.

Falcon's voice became grave. "And once my family is safe ... I want your word that you will take back our country. So that my death and all the deaths of others who have fought for freedom will not be in vain!"

"Yes sir!" exclaimed the 12.

Not another word was spoken as Falcon shook each of their hands. None was needed.

Sheila Reid Arnold stared into the mirror as she fretted over the ill-fitted pants suit women of her generation loved so much. The waddle of skin under her neck went well with the dark circles under her eyes. Never a picture of health, the dozen or so medications she needed daily to stay alive or comfortable ate away at her body. They would have consumed her soul – if she'd had one.

One of her many staff rushed into the room. "You should check this out. He's at it again." The young woman turned on the television.

Sheila groaned.

The Freedom Train had been chugging along for the last two weeks. The crowds grew at every stop as thousands of Americans drove from state to state to follow the message of love of country, personal responsibility and freedom.

"This guy thinks he's Truman. Where is he now?" asked Sheila.

"He's at the Alamo. There are at least 200,000 people according to the press."

Sheila frowned and swallowed hard. *What a bunch of losers! The only thing I ever followed around the country was the Grateful Dead.* She glared at the television.

Homemade signs decorated the massive Texas crowd. The camera closed in on a few: *"Don't Mess with America," "Texas Bleeds Red, White, and Blue," "Falcon Sane is a Texas Son".*

The television blared Falcon in full throat. "Remember the bravery of Americans facing a tremendous army, knowing full well they would die if they did not surrender. Surrender is not an American attribute. We're not being asked to die for America at this time. No one is asking us to storm Normandy Beach or death march to Bataan. But let's remember the legacy of the brave Americans who stood on this hallowed ground and gave their lives to take back our country. Let's embrace their courage and make a stand for freedom!"

"Remember the Alamo?" Sheila blurted. "What an asshole." She muttered as she watched Texans of all colors cheering. *What the hell are all the blacks doing there? How many times does the press have to call this guy a racist before it sticks? He's got a shaved head and lived in Idaho for Christ's sake! Dumb jungle bunnies. If they vote for this guy their welfare is gone.* She peered closer to the screen. *What the ... what are all those Mexicans doing there? He wants to close the border!* "Turn it off!" Sheila snapped. "And get me Karl Berkel!"

Senator DeJesus and Raul sat glued to the TV in a hotel suite in Washington D.C. while Falcon Sane continued his speech in San Antonio.

"Thank you for your time, energy and presence. You humble me." Falcon placed his hand across his heart.

The crowd quieted enthralled with the passion coming from the man on the stage.

Falcon searched the sky for the right words to close with. "Without a doubt, God blessed Texas."

Raul clicked the remote off and scrutinized his boss. "Lots of brown faces in that crowd."

DeJesus scratched his head. *Raul's right. What are they doing there? This guy wants to make them all sign up for citizenship and work? Any illegal here that's committed a crime or on the government dole will be deported. He stated it and wrote it down in his book. What the hell are those Mexicans thinking?*

Raul watched the senator with concern. He'd never admit it, but they were out of their element. Even if Sane hadn't appeared from nowhere, he doubted they could beat Sheila Reid Arnold. Raul's bluster and bravado were just that. *Frankly I'm still in shock we got the Republican nomination. White Guilt is a powerful thing.* He waited for his boss to respond. Hopefully the senator would know what to do.

The senator could feel his chance slipping away. Turning to Raul he said, "Call Karl Berkel."

Avery and Maya, escorted by a dozen Secret Service, and the invisible presence of militia, entered the Winnebago that they, Falcon and Tommy would ride in to Oklahoma City. Falcon's 10-minute speeches were having a tremendous effect on America. Short and concise, the networks easily fit them into their time slots. Each speech shared his passion for freedom, and for the first time in modern politics, a candidate spoke the language of the people. No speech writers or Hollywood hires moved pen to paper. It was all Falcon, and the people loved him for it. Headlines across American newspapers shared the sentiment. *There is no stopping the Freedom Train. Soar Falcon soar! America has found a leader worthy of the word.*

Falcon, his constant shadow Tommy, and the Secret Service made their way toward the Winnebago.

Falcon couldn't see the militia, but they were present. *Not sure if I'm the safest I've ever been or in the most danger.*

Tommy watched his boss with concern. Falcon was tired, but in front of the crowd, the fatigue seemed to melt away. America was pumping her energy into him.

"Stop staring at me Luca. I need food," Falcon growled.

"I'm hungry too."

"You're always hungry."

"I find food calms me," said Tommy.

Falcon eyeballed Tommy briefly, then they both burst out laughing. Falcon tapered off and quietly said, "Anything I need to know?"

Tommy hesitated before answering. At Falcon's request he checked in frequently with the militia leaders. As a former ranger, he fit comfortably in with the collection of operators. Death threats continued to increase; even Tommy received a few. With four weeks until the election he never left Falcon's side until Falcon clocked out for the night. Today word from the militia was someone with serious money was making threats – big threats. The Secret Service added an extra team. The militia called for reinforcements and doubled their coverage on Falcon, Avery, Tommy and Maya. Tommy learned all this information during Falcon's speech. *I don't want to tell him but I have to.* Tommy chose his words carefully. "Apparently a pretty big player is out there."

Falcon stopped to listen.

"The militia doubled the guard on everyone and will double it again if needed. I reiterated your top concern – to keep Avery safe."

"Did you mention Maya too?"

"I did. Maya seems to be off the radar fortunately. I'm getting pretty popular though," Tommy said.

"That's to be expected since you're like a Rottweiler at my heels."

"Just doing my job boss, covering your back."

Falcon smiled at his friend. "I know brother. I appreciate it."

They approached the Winnebago and climbed inside.

The call sign went over the Secret Service radio. "Late Bird is in the nest."

The Winnebago was loaned to the Independent Party from a private citizen. It slept 10 comfortably and could be easily secured.

The owner, Malcolm Morgan, was a good man. A former Army Paratrooper, retired deputy sheriff, and current militia member he felt honored to drive the carriage. His motor home lumbered down the highway toward Oklahoma City with thousands of other vehicles ahead and behind. The Freedom Train was hot to crash the party in Washington. American flags, which waved from every car and truck, put a smile on his face. *This is exciting! America's on her way back!* Malcolm knew what he volunteered for could be dangerous, but danger was nothing new to him – he'd protected his country every day of his adult life. *I'll serve my country until the day I die.*

When some distant relatives heard he joined the Freedom Train the jokes ensued. He'd laughed at the one about *Driving Miss Daisy*, but when a snide comment made at a party inferred he was an Uncle Tom, Malcolm squared off with his low-life ex-con cousin and knocked him clean out with one punch. Then he turned on the group, rolled up his sleeve, and flashed the American flag tattooed on his right shoulder. "I've defended America my entire life, and she has defended me. If I hear another word about any uncles, it better be Uncle Sam."

The sky blushed a soft crimson framed in indigo, while the sun closed her eyes for the day. As he drove, Malcolm hummed along with the tunes of classic country radio. He didn't care much for "new country". *Everything's about pickup trucks, beer and more beer.* He chuckled. *I'm just fine with losing my woman, my house, and my dog. Well maybe not my dog.* He heard movement behind him.

Falcon stepped forward and eased into the passenger seat. "I needed a clear view of the road." He smiled at the man driving. "Sometimes I get a little car sick."

Malcolm nodded. After two weeks with the Freedom Train, this was the first time the Presidential candidate had ridden in his vehicle. For safety purposes, the SS agents moved the candidate, his wife, and team each night. Although vetted weeks in advance, Malcolm was informed only one hour ago of his honor for that evening, and then ordered to stay with his vehicle and immediately surrounded by the protection detail. Attempting to send a text message to one of the militia leaders, he discovered his phone stopped receiving service. He didn't worry. The Secret Service undoubtedly jammed all communications. Malcolm knew his guys were nearby, tracking the candidate every second of the day. Now he was hopefully sitting next to the next President of the United States.

Falcon stared at the road and hoped his stomach would calm.

Avery arrived and handed him a Coke.

"Thanks baby."

"Are you sure you are okay?" she asked.

"Yeah I'm fine. Try and get some sleep," Falcon said. Her love and genuine concern kept her tossing all night.

She scowled at him, and her lips pressed into a tight smile.

Falcon knew that look. She would not leave his side unless her concerns were calmed.

Falcon changed tactics and flashed his brightest smile. "I'm great baby, just enjoying some road time." He winked at her. "And you'll feel better if you get some sleep."

Sleep sounded so appealing to Avery. *But who'll watch out for my man?*

As if reading her mind, Falcon turned toward the driver. "Hi, my name's Falcon, what's yours my friend?"

"Malcolm Morgan sir."

"Malcolm will keep an eye on me sweetie, won't you Malcolm?"

"Yes sir I will. My job is to keep you safe," he said with such strength and assurance both Falcon and Avery took a second look at him.

"See sweetie, I'm in good hands. Malcolm's in charge. Go get some rest."

Avery wrapped her arms around her husband and kissed him. "I love you."

Falcon played along. "I love you more."

"I love you the most." She kissed him again and headed to their room for the evening. *Time to get some sleep.*

The Coke settled Falcon's stomach, and he watched the road, which helped too. *Buckhorn Summit all over again.* Falcon took another swig and couldn't stop himself from asking, "So my friend, do you think someone's going to shoot me before November fourth?"

Malcolm regarded Falcon and quickly returned his eyes to the road. "Not if I can help it sir."

"Military?"

"Yes sir."

"Thank you for your service."

"Thank you sir."

Mesmerized by the drone of the road, Falcon stared into the darkness.

Malcolm said, "Sir?"

"Please call me Falcon my friend."

"Yes sir. Falcon, are you okay?"

Falcon thought about the question before he answered. "You ever had somebody threaten the one person you love most in the world and are helpless to do anything about it? Not knowing who they are, you wait and pray it never happens."

"No, Falcon I haven't."

Falcon stared out the window in silent contemplation.

Malcolm wasn't much of a talker but for some reason he spoke up. "Falcon?"

"Yes?"

"If you don't mind my saying sir, we have your back. We've been waiting a long time for a leader like you. We won't let you down."

Falcon continued staring. The pressure of the death threats on Avery was taking its toll. *None of this is worth it if I lose her.*

As though Malcolm could feel his pain he stated, "Falcon my friend, God is my witness, we have your back sir."

Falcon's head snapped, and he took a long look at Malcolm. *God is my witness? Is that you Big Fella?*

"Yes sir," Malcom repeated, "we have your back."

Falcon stared in amazement and then settled back into his chair. The Big Fella did have his back. *That's all I need.*

The roaring crowds grew at every stop, as Falcon spoke with

passion at each capital. Twenty-five miles outside of Rapid City, South Dakota, Falcon stared in awe at the greatness of Mount Rushmore.

The beauty however was lost on one, most assuredly lost. Karl Berkel leaned against his rental car in the Rushmore parking lot. He needed a vacation and probably a psychiatrist. Due to threatening messages on his voicemail from Raul and a scream-fest with Sheila, his Camel habit had climbed to four packs a day. He replayed his conversation with Sheila three days ago.

"What do you want me to do, Sheila?"

"Whatever it takes Karl! Get him out of the race! Perot him!"

"What the hell does that mean?" Karl asked exasperated.

"Do whatever they did to Perot to make him drop out. I'm serious Karl! Handle it! I will not be screwed again," she screamed into the phone and hung up.

Karl opened his third pack of cigarettes for the day. Central Park in NYC was booked for Sane's last speech. That gave him two weeks from Thursday. The only debate fell on the next night. *Sheila and DeJesus made a huge mistake scheduling only one,* but the die was cast. Somebody had choreographed the Sane campaign well. *The election is a week after the debate. Perot him? How I am supposed to get this guy to drop out of the race with just three weeks to go?*

Sheila's reference to Ross Perot was clear but virtually impossible, besides Karl had spent the last six months trailing, bribing, and trying to crush Falcon Sane at every turn. It didn't surprise him to learn Sane was emotionally solid and couldn't be bought or threatened. What surprised him was that no one close to him could be either. Karl had shelled out nearly a million dollars to PIs to comb through Falcon's past. He'd read his book at least a dozen times and burrowed into the subtext. Nothing. He'd honestly never done any drugs, and while the guy wasn't perfect, when he made mistakes he owned up and learned.

Karl found a few things on Tommy, but everyone knew he was a player. His military jacket provided some interesting background. Tommy's smile and demeanor hid one scary dude. *I wouldn't want to piss him off or threaten anything he cared about.* Maya seemed to walk on water. A half-dozen PIs couldn't find one person to say anything bad other than she worked too much. No alcohol or drugs, and she had a long-term boyfriend who almost caught one of his detectives in her trash can. Then came Avery. Karl squirmed a little when checking her out. He felt certain Falcon would destroy anything in his path to protect her. Karl had actually sighed in relief when the worst they came up with was a dopey boyfriend she'd dated in high school. America loved her. One magazine referred to her as "America's Diana" with serious chops, due to her military service. Karl burned his cigarette to the nub and rubbed it out on his shoe. *Fuck this. He's right. My generation sucks.* Pulling out his phone he made a call he never thought possible.

"Go for Eichelberger," came the voice on the end of the line.

"Still using that name, huh?" asked Karl.

"Yep. I'll remember that prick the rest of my life."

"He's a charmer," Karl said.

"He was a fat fucking prick who had his clock punched much too late."

"He's dead?"

"Yep," answered the voice. "Fucking Boomer finally bought it. Three wives, a beer belly and Viagra. Heard he lost his fortune to his 30-year-old wife just seconds before the tax man planned to beat down his door. Couldn't have happened to a nicer guy."

"Boomer huh?" Karl laughed at the voice's usage of Falcon Sane's word.

"Oh yeah. I'll tell you what, Sane's right. Your generation killed our country—"

Karl cut him off, "I think it's finally time."

The voice was quiet. "Time? You mean retirement?"

"Yep. Time to hang it up. Getting too old for the stress. Got some Viagra I want to use myself before my ticket gets punched." Karl paused, "I'm giving you the okay to take over my clients. I've done well. First up, Sheila Reid Arnold. Be careful. She's a hateful woman. Next..."

Karl smiled sardonically after hanging up and piled into his rental car. *Old Boomers can learn new tricks.* Karl howled as he drove away with dueling thoughts that raced through his mind. *Fuck you Sheila you rotten bitch.* He laughed uncontrollably at the insanity he left behind as his mind cleared and he wiped his eyes. *Why not Falcon Sane? Go get 'em Boy with Many Stories!*

Eichelberger watched his two young sons play catch in his backyard. Karl's retirement would open many doors for a political operative like himself but would also come with strings. Strings that felt more like a noose as he thought about what people like Sheila Reid Arnold and David DeJesus would require of him. He watched his eight-year-old fire a fastball to his older brother. *What kind of world am I leaving for my kids?* He'd read Falcon Sane's book and loved how loyal Falcon and Deeter were to each other. He'd never had that as a child. Now watching his sons, he knew if he truly loved and cared for them a choice had to be made. Karl's entire client list had just arrived via email. Eichelberger stared at the unopened file for a brief second then hit delete. *I'm sure they'll find somebody else to do their dirty work but not me. Sane is right. It's time to make a difference one American at a time.*

Falcon felt like a newborn child bathed in sunlight as he beheld the beauty of Mount Rushmore.

Avery kissed him tenderly and straightened his tie.

From habit Falcon smoothed it with his right hand and sat

momentarily in the memory of Matthew.

Avery said, "Matthew?"

Falcon nodded. *She knows me so well.*

"He'd be proud of you today, baby. We all are."

Tommy lingered in the background as Maya approached the couple. "We're ready to go Chief," she said. "Reportedly a half-million people are out there."

"Choo-choo!" Tommy called. "Bring on the Freedom Train!"

Falcon kissed his wife and still held her hand as he stepped onto the stage. "Walk with me beautiful. I want you to feel how much America loves you."

The roar was deafening as Avery smiled and waved to the crowd, "This is amazing" she said to her husband.

"Yes it is sweetheart." *Nothing like American freedom.* Falcon removed the microphone from the podium. Normally chilly in October, an Indian Summer blanketed everyone in warmth. With Mount Rushmore framing him, Falcon waited peacefully for the cheering to stop. It waned and he dove in forcefully in full stride. "For a moment disregard the faces on this prestigious monument and let us focus on the American spirit, the drive and determination it took to blast an entire mountain into a national treasure. The love of America drove this individual to leave behind a reminder of American greatness, strength and might. No one is asking us to move mountains. We're being asked to stand for freedom! Who will stand for Freedom? Who will stand up for America?"

Five-hundred-thousand Americans jumped to their feet chanting, "USA! USA! USA!" Raw emotion suppressed for far too long exploded into the atmosphere.

Avery stood beside Falcon on the stage, and was nearly thrown off balance from the sheer force of America's voice. *Amazing isn't a strong enough word* as she watched Falcon pound away at the corruption that brought America's passion to a boil.

Falcon continued, "I recall a quotation from my youth that captured my attention. 'If Mohammed won't come to the mountain then bring the mountain to Mohammed.' Our federal government believes it is Mohammed ... and has forgotten about the mountain."

An avalanche of boos cascaded off the granite walls.

Falcon raised his hand and a hush fell over the crowd.

"It's time our federal government understands ...WE are that mountain. And this Freedom Train is coming for you!"

The booing paled in comparison to the roar that ensued. Clanging off the mountain like a bell, freedom rang ... in the Dakotas.

Pleased, Tommy smiled. *The boss used my line.*

12

*S*heila Reid Arnold stared at the television as her staff worked the phones. The newest poll was out, and she couldn't believe it.

A cowering temp quietly informed her, "If the election was today Ms. Arnold, Falcon Sane would carry enough states to not need California."

"You're fired," shrieked Sheila. "Get out of my sight!"

Fired from what? The 20-old girl took off like a shot. *I'm a volunteer you cranky witch.*

Sheila listened as the commentators confirmed what she'd just heard.

One host on Wolf News laughed, "If she wants to be President she better have a whale of a debate that's all I'm saying."

"As a fact of the matter," said the female democratic strategist paid to say positive things, "she's been prepping for the last two weeks and is more than ready for Train Man."

"She might be *as a fact of the matter* but *as a matter of fact* I believe the Freedom Train will roll right by or over her if she gets in the way."

"Don't discount her because she's a woman," said the Democrat.

The host scoffed, "There you guys go again with your girl that cried wolf. No one is listening anymore."

"There you go again calling us girls!" pounced the Democrat.

"Oh please! You really think that's still going to work? America needs a leader, not another equal-rights, equal-suffering-for-all, Me-Generation facelift. Americans want a cheerleader and they've found one, and his name is Falcon Sane."

Sheila glowered at the screen. "Turn the channel!" she screamed. Another volunteer raced to the television and turned to the next channel where a reporter stood and asked a man his opinion on the presidential candidates.

"So far I like what I'm hearing from the new guy," the man answered.

"You mean Falcon Sane?"

The man looked at the reporter in derision. "Is there somebody else we don't know about? The other two are rejected retreads."

The reporter honed in. "So as an African-American you support Falcon Sane?"

The rage in the man's face boiled to the top. "My father is a proud black American! My mother is a wonderful woman from Puerto Rico! Where do you hear Africa anywhere in there?"

The reporter's shocked face displayed his mistake. "I didn't mean any disrespect. Should I have said Latino?"

"Latino!" the man almost screamed.

His wife patted his shoulder. Her husband was a good man, but she worried about his blood pressure. "Remember what the doctor said, honey."

The man regained composure. *The doctor also said it was more dangerous keeping things bottled up ... especially the truth.* The man gently took the position of the reporter. The reporter handed him the mike. Staring into the camera American anger went off. "All the politicians and you guys in the media have been pushing us too far. Everybody's a racist, we all hate gays ... enough! You're telling our children it's okay to smoke dope, borrow money, and get fat. You've been slinging the bull but now the bull has turned." The angry American glared into the camera. "And now you're gonna get the horns!"

Sheila yelled, "Turn it off and let's go! The debate is tomorrow. I need more prep people!" She stormed down the hall with her staff as they trembled behind her.

David DeJesus, already in debate prep, felt good. Unlike his democratic counterpart he had style, good looks, and an excellent grasp of the issues. Raul and his team had been hitting him with every possible question or counter Falcon Sane might have. "I don't care about Sheila." He shut down one of his assistants when asked about the war on women. "The country is looking for a reason to not vote for her. They found one in Falcon Sane. It's our job to take him down tomorrow night."

Raul stepped into the debate room to listen.

David saw him and raised his eyebrows.

Raul shook his head. They were still in third, *or if he wanted to spin it, tied for second.*

David questioned. How would Falcon Sane play this? Surely he was aware he was in the lead. Would he be cautious and try to hang on like Romney did after his first debate? "How do we think like him?" The senator posed the question to his staff.

Silence covered the room.

"No one has any idea how to get inside his head? Come on people, he's just a man."

One brave hand rose in the back.

"Yes?" David said.

"It's not me," stammered a young female intern. "It's just, well, I don't think this but …"

"Go ahead." David flashed his perfect teeth as he tried to charm the young girl. "Speak your mind."

She relaxed for a second and blurted out, "He's easy to figure out. You just have to love America."

David DeJesus eyes darkened although the smile never left his face. "Thank you for your input." Nodding at Raul, he motioned with his hand. "Let's get back to work."

Raul asked the young girl to step outside with him while the staff continued to pepper the senator with questions.

"Yes?" asked the intern.

"We won't be needing your services anymore. Goodbye." Raul left the stunned girl in the hall and returned to the staff room. He gave a quick nod to David to indicate that the deed was done. Raul was a bit saddened by the small turn of events. *Too bad. She was cute, just not my flavor.*

The Freedom Train caravan had rolled into New York City the night before. The tour had been a whirlwind but the best part was yet to come. That night, Falcon was excited about Central Park.

Avery worked the phones in their hotel room. With Maya, Tommy and Falcon on the road, Avery had taken over the day-to-day operations of Responsible Recycling. Falcon employed only quality people, thus the small company continued to perform. Besides, Falcon wasn't willing to take a salary as President, so R&R was still a primary source of their income. Avery asked someone to hold while she took the other line. It was one of her general managers with a question. She was still the vice-president in her travel agency, but if they were elected, her leave of absence was already green-lighted.

As the morning passed Falcon's fervor began to escalate. It was the night of his last speech and, if reports were correct, the largest crowd to ever gather in the Park would join him. "I'm too revved up to stay in the hotel," Falcon told Avery. "I'm going to check out the setup for tonight. Be back in a bit."

"Okay baby." She returned his kiss and went back to the phones.

Falcon, Tommy and dozens of Secret Service exited the hotel and loaded into the waiting vehicles.

Words spilled out of Tommy, who shared his excitement about

the approaching evening.

Falcon let him go; his juices were flowing too. *Tonight is going to be fun!* Arriving at their destination, Falcon sprang out of the car as though he was heading onto the baseball diamond at Trinity High.

Tommy sprinted to catch up, still lost in his zealous monologue.

The speech was scheduled for 8:00 P.M. Eastern time. Ten hours away, and already enthusiasm crackled like a power line.

Not wanting to interrupt the preparations with his arrival, Falcon wore a baseball cap and sweatshirt. The Secret Service did not blend in, but with so many floating about all morning long, the setup crew seemed unaware of the candidate's presence.

The outer half of Central Park was surrounded with dutiful Freedom Train followers who awaited the inner gate to open, swapped stories, and shared food. As Falcon watched from his position he felt inspired by their vivacity as they anticipated the big night.

Tommy grew silent and stared into the ocean of people. "This is going to be awesome tonight, boss."

Falcon said, "It certainly is my friend. We're making a difference …" His voice tapered off when he spotted a little girl who jumped and waved seemingly at him. *With my hat on and hood up it isn't likely she recognizes me.* Falcon returned a small wave.

Her bouncing became more emphatic, and she waved faster.

Falcon nudged Tommy. "See that bouncy little girl?" He pointed in her direction from the wings of the stage.

Tommy glanced over the crowd until his eyes landed on the human pogo stick. "Yes boss, I see her."

"She sure is energetic," he chuckled. "Do me a favor. Without attracting attention go see what she wants."

"Yes sir." Tommy and his Secret Service entourage headed toward the child. He assumed the man and woman who stood beside the hopping sprite were her parents and casually asked, "Are you folks ready for tonight?"

Before they could answer the child said, "I need to talk to Falcon Sane."

Tommy glanced down at the tiny girl and guessed her to be about six. "What makes you think he's here little lady?"

"Cause I see him over there in that hoodie and baseball hat." She pointed toward Falcon.

"What do you 'need' to talk to him about?"

"I can't tell you. It's a kind of a secret."

Tommy laughed at her spunk. "Well unless you tell me." He froze when the girl pulled out a crumpled red, white and blue bow. Tommy recognized it immediately.

Her mother said, "She's been saving that a long time."

Tommy smiled, "Okay folks, let's go."

A SS man whispered in Tommy's ear, "They need to be checked out."

Tommy turned to the parents and said, "Would you mind if they screened you first? Security has been tight since we've been on the road."

"Not at all. We've been with you since Wisconsin and read the papers. We know about the ..." the father paused, aware his little girl was hanging on every word. "... issues of safety. What do you need?"

Tommy waited as the Secret Service did their job. As he recognized a face in the crowd he smiled.

Robert Collado sidled over decked out in jeans and an Old Navy sweatshirt. The two men shook hands.

"Big night tonight," the former Marine and leader of the militia protection said. "Tell Falcon we're damn proud of him, of you, of our country."

Tommy's subtle head nod said thanks, "Wait until tonight."

"Looking forward to it."

When The SS waved they were ready, Tommy shook his friend's

hand again. "See you brother."

"That you will brother," Robert replied.

Tommy escorted his train of three VIPs back to Falcon. The child struggled to keep up with the adults so her father reached down in an attempt to pick her up.

She shook him off. "No Daddy. I'll walk. Uncle Jonny said Americans carry their own water. I'm walking for Uncle Jonny."

Pride filled the man, and he acquiesced to her request with a caveat. "All right, but hold tight of my hand."

"Okay Daddy."

Her mother smiled, "Uncle Jonny is very proud of you sweetie."

"I know Mommy, I'm proud of him too."

Tommy silently led his troop toward Falcon. *The boss is going to love this.*

Falcon descended from the stage and removed his hood as the small group approached. The SS fanned out, and the little girl marched bravely right up to him. Falcon admired her spirit.

Her face was painted with horizontal stripes of red and white, and a square patch of midnight blue adorned with three tiny white stars that covered the area around her right eye. As she extended a hand to Falcon she said, "Hi, I'm Ava." She examined him closely as a young one does a department store Santa. "Are you the real Falcon Sane?"

Falcon smiled, "The only one I know of. I like your face paint, Ava."

"Thank you, I'm Old Glory." The R in Glory sounded like a W. "That's what my teacher calls our American flag."

A wide grin covered Falcon's face. "Well Old Glory, what can I do for you?"

"My uncle Jonny is a Marine." Her cherub face darkened. "Uncle Jonny's legs are gone now. He can't walk anymore cause he got hurt in the war."

Falcon crouched down to eye level with the tender-hearted child. "I'm so sorry Ava. So truly sorry."

"It's all right Ava." Her mother gently hugged her.

Ava blinked back tears. "Uncle Jonny told me not to cry. He said Marines don't cry."

Falcon waited silently.

Ava let out a deep sigh. "Why are there so many bad people out there, Falcon?"

Tommy stared in awe. *From the mouths of babes.*

Falcon ached for the pint-sized American angel. "I don't know Ava. I really don't. But there are more people like your Uncle Jonny than the bad ones. Good people who protect us. And just like your Uncle Jonny, we must all do our part to protect our nation's freedom."

Ava's solemn face returned to life. "Freedom. I love freedom. My uncle says nothing is more important than freedom."

Falcon smiled with genuine appreciation for her parents. *Here stands the greatness of America, a generation being prepared to appreciate the gift of freedom, unlike the next generation of little girls in the Middle East.*

"Falcon?" asked Ava.

"Yes?"

"How much does freedom cost?"

Fascinating. It was a topic he planned to address tonight and was still searching for the exact words. He closed his eyes briefly. *I'm listening Big Fella.* "What do you think, Ava?"

"I don't think you can buy freedom with money." She paused, "It's more like the first time I wanted to ride my bike to the corner by myself. Daddy said I'd have to stay on the sidewalk, and Mommy said only when she was watching from our house. Mommy gave me a hug and said it was my choice. Freedom is like that, doing the right things and hugs from Mommy."

"Yes it is." Falcon was transfixed by the wisdom of this little female Yoda.

"Falcon?" Ava cupped her hands around her mouth and whispered, "I have something for you." Reaching into her pocket she pulled out a small box. It was dented and the gold wrapping paper had seen better days, but Falcon recognized the red, white and blue bow on top, he'd put it there himself. She handed him *the gift that keeps on giving.* "This is from my uncle." She gave him a folded paper.

Falcon unfolded the hand written note and read:

Dear Mr. Sane,

Although not in person, it is my honor to stand with you today. My love of country and respect for you sir knows no bounds. This gift, that originated with you and came to me from a little girl, touched me in ways I will never be able to repay. The outpouring of love I have received from my fellow Americans has been a Godsend. Because of this love I have recaptured my freedom through the use of a TRACK CHAIR. American ingenuity knows no bounds. Through learning how to use the chair I met the love of my life, Samantha.

I cannot declare my entire journey has been fun, but I believe God works in mysterious ways. Through your generosity and one special child, my prayers have been answered. I am now returning this gift to you through another special American child.

Semper Fi

Respectfully,

Corporal Johnathon Craig Zetterberg,

United States Marine Corps.

A single tear traveled slowly down Falcon's face. He made no attempt to stop or conceal it.

Ava's mother gasped.

Her father stoically blinked back his own unfettered emotions. Johnathon Craig Zetterberg was his oldest brother.

Falcon composed himself and said, "Thank you sweet child."

Ava nodded, but her mission was not complete.

Falcon waited. It appeared she had more to say.

She motioned Falcon closer.

Falcon took a knee and leaned in.

"I said my prayers last night like always, for my family, and especially for Uncle Jonny. I prayed for you too Falcon and for freedom." With the sincere face of an angel and twinkling eyes Ava whispered to Falcon, "God said I should tell you not to worry, Big Fella's got your back."

13

*T*he setting sun in New York City brought Central Park alive. The sheer beauty of the impressive trees and vegetation was awe-inspiring for those who noticed such things. From the New York Philharmonic to the Supremes, Elton John to Bon Jovi, Central Park had been host to countless concerts over the years. According to the FDNY a Garth Brooks Park performance pulled in almost one million. Like the country Falcon believed in, the Garth Brooks concert was free. According to reports that record would be dwarfed tonight.

The Freedom Train had arrived. Nearly three million Americans, a sea of humanity, waited to hear the candidate's final speech. The Presidential Debate was tomorrow night in Washington D.C. and then the election only a week away.

What a ride. Falcon smoothed his tie, strode out onto the stage, and approached the podium.

The crowd jumped to their feet and cheered for the man whose book brought to life this peaceful revolution. The voices grew louder, and Falcon smiled as he accepted the wave of love from the American people.

He leaned into the microphone. "I wish each of you could stand in my place and feel the energy up here tonight. Before we begin please clasp hands and join me in the three word celebration of freedom!"

Millions created a physical chain and chanted, "USA! USA! USA!"

The stage trembled from the vibration. Falcon let the joy bathe him in the beautiful song of freedom, secure in personal responsibility, and protected "upstairs". Falcon was steady, his head clear, but the raw emotion emitted from the masses overwhelmed his sensitive heart. The man with a lifelong desire to help others could not hide a boy's wonder and humility. His eyes welled up with tears.

"USA! USA! USA!"

Television crews waited for his first word. Cameras ricocheted the historic moment all over the world, and it was anyone's guess how many millions sat glued to their TV sets. Ten seconds turned to 30 as the crowd awaited the American believer of freedom to speak.

"USA! USA! USA!"

Falcon took in the awe-inspiring moment and as he stood there he knew *the* moment had arrived. Embracing the microphone he began, "We the people of the United States of America ..."

His historical beginning detonated another clap of thunder.

"We hold these truths to be self-evident that all men and women are created equal. That they are endowed by their Creator with certain inalienable rights and that among these rights are life, liberty and ..." Falcon lifted his hands to the crowd to join him.

"... the Pursuit of Happiness! USA! USA! USA!" broke out again and reverberated through the trees.

"As we stand together on this historic day, let the word go on, that this day was the day, Americans joined hand in hand, to assertively thrust freedom forward. Let it be written that the United States, in all her glory shall never bow from forces abroad or tyranny within. That this nation, conceived in liberty and dedicated to the proposition ... that all people are created equal shall not perish from the Earth!"

Falcon raised his hand to quell the deafening clamor. America was ready, ready to give. They hushed.

"We have a dream. A dream of love, peace, and freedom. Knowing full well love must come with discipline, peace through strength, and freedom for all. As we gather today, cast off erroneous premises. Reject the supposed heroes and embrace heroics! Throw off false prophets as we need more godliness and less gods and open your hearts to freedom. Destiny is not a matter of chance. It is a matter of choice!"

"USA! USA! USA!" the crowd continued.

Enamored with his brothers and sisters, who bonded as one beside a leader they'd all yearned for, the massive crowd blurred, and their thundering voices faded in Falcon's mind. He laughed, the laugh of freedom, and thanked God for this opportunity.

"It is our time and that time is now!"

14

*F*alcon lay in bed with Avery the next morning. The passion and excitement from last night's speech mixed with exhaustion from the entire process had found both of them staring at each other hungrily late that night in their hotel room. Sitting in a chair across from her, Falcon had watched her move as she uncorked a bottle of wine. Pouring a glass for herself she motioned to him. He shook his head as the shape of her body mesmerized him. She took a drink, slowly put down her glass, and looked over her shoulder coyly. *I know what you want. I want it too*. Deliberately teasing him, she removed her clothing, one piece at a time.

Falcon could feel his heart starting to race. He wanted her now as much as the first day he laid eyes on her.

Completely nude, Avery said, "Come and get me Mr. President."

Soon they were asleep in each other's arms the world of elections seemed far away.

Sitting at a Starbucks nearby the Waldorf Astoria Hotel in Washington D.C., Maya still felt chills from the previous night. The morning papers spread out on her table, she scanned every one. Although her boss's speech was well under 10 minutes, he was being hailed throughout the media as the "next great American communicator." One paper called him "a combination of Lincoln strength, Reagan idealism, and William Jennings Bryan fire and brimstone."

A British editorial consumed by the raw electricity stated,

"Were it possible to insert a plug somewhere into the crowd I dare say the entire Eastern Seaboard may have been powered by the ever-famous American love of country. The beautification of freedom and the presence of an old soul burning brightly into the night encapsulated us all with the nectar of passion flowing from a free man born in a free country."

Falcon had his detractors. One editorial, whose writer already endorsed the Republican candidate, referred to his speech as "elegant plagiarism of past poets only surpassed by his 'Hollywoodesque' timing for drama." A liberal newspaper, soon to be bankrupt, referred to the speech as, "a moving message worthy of PT Barnum." Yet the same writer referred to Mr. Sane as "a worthy adversary in the destruction of big government and even bigger corruption." For every negative comment, hundreds lauded and applauded Falcon's words, timing and structural usage of time. Americans were tired of long-winded speeches that promised everything and delivered nothing. The country was fed up with bickering "Washingtonites" misbehaving like undisciplined children. The masses demonstrated their opinions through their support as they longed for the voice of freedom they'd heard the previous night.

Maya's favorite article depicted the scene perfectly.

"The candidate, who abhors the word politician, seemingly floated onto the stage. The depth of love for this man, this American, was surpassed only by the perpetual voice roaring through the most Central of Parks. USA! USA! USA! Reverberating through this valley of freedom, never lingering, never wavering as if led by the freest of conductors, unleashing volley after volley of the noblest song ever played. The song known as the United States of America."

Maya relaxed in her chair, sipped her latte, and was filled with equal portions of peace, elation and exhaustion. *It's almost beyond belief that this all happened so fast.* She and Falcon had already started discussing her next steps with the increasing possibility the

American people might elect the first Independent Party candidate ever. Falcon's goals and leadership skills never waned, and he pressed Maya to decide where she would be the most beneficial to the country.

"Quite a speech last night," Tommy's voice yanked her back into the present.

She smiled at her friend.

Wearing a new suit and a big smile, Maya couldn't help but reflect on how much Tommy had grown in the last year. Rather than a lovable goofball who made her cringe every time he opened his mouth, he'd become a trusted confidant and loyal friend. Just as Falcon had seen the potential in her, he'd also seen it in Tommy whose charm and je ne sais quoi had become quite valuable in the last six months. With his self-esteem rising and his testosterone in check, he'd become a trusted friend and sounding board. He seemed to have turned everyone, regardless of party, into an ally, and at the same time kept an eye on Falcon's back.

"The speech, yes the world loved it and him," Maya answered.

"He was on fire, never seen him quite like that."

"Wait until tonight. I think this debate is going to seal the deal."

"I think the deal is already sealed," said Tommy.

"I agree, but we live in a weird and dangerous time. Anything is possible."

"The only way he doesn't get elected on November fourth is voter fraud. No other way around it."

"Let's head toward the center," said Maya. "I want to double-check everything."

"Sounds good, let me grab a veggie breakfast sandwich real quick."

"Vegetarian?" Maya tried not to smile.

"Yeah, one of the reporters asked the boss last night why he never seemed to eat any meat. I'd never heard the story about the commercial with the cow lying on its side while a man had his foot on its head holding it down before slaughter. The way he explained the look in the cow's eyes waiting to die. It was horrible."

Maya had heard Falcon tell that story twice, and it made her cry both times. She wasn't a big meat-eater before, but she'd stopped eating "anything with a face" after that.

"That bacon sure does smell good though," Tommy said wistfully.

Maya laughed and headed for the door while Tommy chomped down.

Sheila Reid Arnold was wreaking havoc on her staff. A bear to work for, this election alone she'd run through three campaign managers. Considering her state of mind, a fourth might be produced before the evening was over. "The debate is tonight, and you're telling me we still do not have a strong answer for the economy! What the hell am I paying you guys for?" she screeched. "Write me something! Eight years ago one of you gave Obama, 'We aren't red states or blue states, we are the United States!' That line was genius! I need a rerun of that!"

"We're working on it, Sheila; these things take time," said the new campaign manager.

Sheila shrieked, "Time! We don't have time! Get one of those snooty high-priced Hollywood writers on staff to give me some lines. This stuff I have right now is garbage. 'For the betterment of the people.' Who the hell talks like that?"

The campaign manager stood quietly. *People who actually care about the country you miserable wench! Maybe you should get laid sometime.* "You're right. I'll have something for you soon."

"You better and where is Karl Berkel?"

David DeJesus reclined in his hotel room as he attempted to quiet his mind. His freshly starched shirt hung in the corner. Clothed in a luxurious hotel robe, he tried to visualize a debate victory. He answered the three knocks on the door. "Come in Raul."

Raul entered with faux enthusiasm only to quickly drop the facade. He was tired. He knew the senator was tired and they both knew the chance of winning this election was minimal. Between the energy from the Sane Freedom Train and the unstoppable force known as Sheila Reid Arnold, who was willing to do anything to win, the senator had been relegated to the sidelines.

"After this is over we need a vacation," David said to Raul.

Raul didn't even bother to argue. "Someplace warm with lots of beautiful women?"

David raised his eyebrow, and they both laughed.

The senator stood and dropped his robe.

Karl Berkel shielded his eyes as he glanced up from his pool lounge in Maui. "Yes my dear, I would love another beer," he leered at the scantily clad server. It'd only been 10 days but he'd never felt better. *Massages every day, hours by the pool, and lots of poi.* For some reason he'd fallen in love with the stuff. He'd even figured out the E-cigarette and was off the Camels completely. He closed his eyes. *Why didn't I do this before?* Berkel had done some questionable things in his life, but he wasn't stupid. With a new exterior and ID that would impress the witness-protection people and a fat nest egg, he was set. *I'm done with politics and the games. This is the life.* He grabbed his new burner cell phone to make a call then laughed at himself for having the throwaway. *Who's listening to me now? Force of habit I guess.* He dialed the local number he'd used every day since his arrival last week. "Hi, yes room 346. No, tonight I want a blonde. Eight o'clock is fine." Ending the call, he gulped down a swig of ice cold beer. *God Bless America.* The debate was the last thing on his mind.

15

*T*he traffic was stifling, as the regular DC commuters were engulfed by the caravan that traveled overnight from Central Park. The Freedom Train, now consisting of over two million Americans, had come to DC to watch the debate and make their presence felt. The location was the Eisenhower Theatre in the Kennedy Center. The Eisenhower Theatre, named after President, General and Supreme Commander of the Allied Forces in World War Two, Dwight D. Eisenhower, seated 1,200 patrons. The room was elegantly decorated and perfect for the type of debate Falcon envisioned. The acoustics were incredible, and the orchestra pit converted into a stage, which had been done.

Entry tickets had been split between the parties, and outside of the center a ticket war was being waged for the coveted seats. The Republican and Democratic bigwigs distributed theirs to VIPs or in, layman's terms, anyone who donated over a million bucks to their campaigns. The Independent Party wanted to reward their donors as well, but had learned the hard way it was better to leave such decisions to their candidate.

Falcon and Avery arrived. Both appeared refreshed and focused.

Tommy grinned. He recognized that look and hoped he'd be wearing it the next day. The lady he'd been dating back home on the QT was flying in that nigh*t. As long as the debate goes well*. His mind took an R-rated mini vacation.

Maya's steady beau was in town too, but Maya was all business. *The Freedom Train's a success. The debate is almost here and Tommy's under control.* She beamed at Falcon as she brought him the box of theater tickets. "You're out in front tonight all on your own Chief. Just the way you like it."

Falcon smiled, took the box, and immediately headed outside into the tremendous crowd gathered around the Kennedy Center. The uproar was deafening. The Secret Service went crazy trying to keep him surrounded. Falcon smiled as he waded through his brothers and sisters. He felt safe in his crowd. The chanting from the previous night continued, "USA, USA, USA!" It was an exhilarating party of freedom no one wanted to end. Falcon continued to wade through his brethren and paused often to ask, "Are you ready?" The crowd's passion ensued, and he gleefully handed out tickets like candy on Halloween. After 20 minutes the box was empty. Falcon saluted the crowd and started to walk back inside. He paused at the door to the theater and looked out over the crowd once more. Walt Whitman had once talked about this. *That you are here, that life exists, and that you may contribute a verse.* Falcon exhaled deeply at the poet's words. *It's time to contribute my verse.*

The packed theater buzzed with anticipation. Every news organization had cameras trained on the stage. Rumors spread that tickets were scalped for thousands of dollars. Some Americans were seen pooling their resources to pack the house. Others hovered around cell phones, laptops and portable televisions; the people weren't going anywhere. Falcon trusted the tickets he'd given away would not be sold.

Dressed in a navy-blue suit and crisp white shirt, Falcon stood with Avery, Maya and Tommy in the wings of the stage. He smiled. The fatigue was long gone, the fire inside him readied to roar. His eyes gleamed. "It's game time baby," he said softly to himself. He gave his wife's hand a gentle squeeze, winked at Tommy, and nodded his appreciation to Maya.

Maya put her hands together and bowed slightly. "It's your time Chief."

Tommy saluted sharply. "Go get 'em boss."

Falcon glanced over the theater and his past flooded in. *How did a little boy from California make it here?* He pictured Del Loma: Deeter the Spider Monkey made him chuckle, his loyal dog Amber, and his work in the family business. With a quick look up he thought of Mike. *Thanks for watching over me brother.* Mr. Jacobsen, Ricky and Lloyd followed as he recalled Trinity, his first baseball field and Pluto's last words. A camera on him caught a faint smile as his memory brought his Uncle Chip to mind. *Look at me now Chip, long way from Weaverville.* And Flint ... he'd never forget the greatness of Flint. He paused to thank God for two loving parents, without whose nurturing, guidance and protection none of this was possible. Avery squeezed his hand and brought him back to the moment. He grinned at her. *What a woman. I am the luckiest man on the planet.*

One of the producers flashed one finger at him. "One minute."

Falcon surveyed the perimeter.

Sheila Reid Arnold and David DeJesus stood silently beside each other on the opposite side of the stage.

Falcon reflexively ran his hand down his tie. His pulse quickened and his body tightened as the adrenaline spiked.

The producer yelled, "Ten seconds!"

Falcon turned to Avery, smiled, and laid one on her. "I love you my favorite everything."

Momentarily speechless, Avery kissed him passionately in return. Regaining her decorum she whispered, "My man is a marvel."

The countdown occurred and the three candidates for President of the United States walked onto the stage. Flash bulbs fired from the crowd as the adversaries headed toward each other.

Avery had mentioned the flash probability to Falcon the night before in regards to his migraines. He'd smiled wanly, "Won't be up there that long." When she pressed him, his lips formed a secret smile. "I want it to be a surprise," he said.

As insurance though, Falcon kept his eyes focused straight ahead, away from the impromptu firework display.

The Republican and Democrat both approached from the left, opposite of Falcon. While his opponents moved casually, smiled and waved to the audience, an advantage, not lost on Falcon, presented itself.

Larger than both, and in much better shape, he closed the distance quickly and walked with a purpose.

As the gap narrowed the other candidates paused and then stopped.

Falcon chuckled to himself at their mistake and settled behind the center podium.

Sheila Reid Arnold, although a weathered combatant of political battles, was no match for the raw physical energy of the Independent candidate. She quickly peeled off and found refuge behind the nearest podium on Falcon's left.

David DeJesus realized his error and headed directly for the middle podium with a big smile and hand extended. "Big night tonight!" said the Republican candidate as he approached Falcon.

Falcon advanced to meet him.

With two steps left between them DeJesus paused again.

Falcon took immediate advantage, slipped his arm around the shoulders of the Republican and whispered in his ear. "Leadership isn't about popularity; it's about being honest with the people … and yourself." Falcon turned and good-naturedly waved to the crowd.

For months DeJesus was asked by reporters what Falcon Sane had said to him that made his face contort and freeze into a mask of confusion. His answer was always the same. "It was a private word among friends."

Falcon continued to wave then guided DeJesus toward his podium with a playful athletic push.

DeJesus advanced to his spot, grabbed the bottle of water placed next to his podium, and downed a big slug.

Falcon watched and smiled as the Republican put his bearings together on Falcon's right.

The three moderators stared at the interesting situation unfolding, not sure what had happened, and then trained their attention on Falcon.

He noticed, and winked at them. His illuminating smile appeared to appease their concerns but to those who knew Falcon well, that smile meant one thing: A reckoning.

The crowd responded to the candidates' presence then sat quietly watching the drama unfold. Of the 1,200 seats available over a thousand of them were filled with Falcon supporters. They realized the Central Park speech was huge, but this was political combat. Hard-earned American dollars packed the house.

The television producer counted down from five and pointed his finger at the female moderator in the middle.

"Good evening. We welcome the audience and our candidates. Tonight will be the one and only Presidential Debate of the year. Due to time constraints, each candidate has two minutes to introduce themselves, and then we will move on to our first item. According to my notes, we are to begin with the Senator from California, Sheila Reid Arnold."

Falcon suppressed a laugh when the moderator smiled sweetly at Sheila. He hadn't bothered to press Maya to negotiate the moderators. They were known friends or close acquaintances with the Democratic Party. *They could have whomever they wanted.* As long as the microphone could be removed from the podium, it wouldn't matter. While Sheila gave her introduction, Falcon slightly tested the mike to make sure it would exit the holder. He and Maya had tested it earlier, but he wanted to make sure nothing had changed. It hadn't. He focused on Sheila. *This politician is going to use every second of her two minutes to ramble.*

"And let me end by thanking the Kennedy Center for the usage of this beautiful theater. I've enjoyed many showings and plays here over the years," the Democrat concluded.

A tiny smattering of applause came from different sections as the moderator thanked the Democrat profusely and turned to the Republican candidate.

David DeJesus started in on his two minutes.

Falcon touched his tie and his thoughts drifted to his last conversation with Matthew so many years ago.

As Falcon stood beside his dear friend's bed, Matthew had pulled him close. "You're meant for special things Falcon. When you're finished I'll see you on the other side. Now it's time to go to work." Matthew closed his eyes and an ethereal light encompassed his entire body. One final breath, and a peaceful presence took the good man home. Falcon's attention returned to the Republican as he finished his intro.

"And, finally," said DeJesus, "I echo the gratitude of the former speaker and give my thanks to the wondrous Kennedy Center. I, too, have enjoyed a few presentations here while in Washington D.C."

Again a tiny smattering of applause trickled in the auditorium.

The moderator thanked the Republican mildly and curtly nodded toward the Independent candidate.

Falcon faced the moderator and sent her an icy stare.

As if cued to do so, the audience leaned forward in their seats.

Falcon held her gaze. Every television camera stayed on him and recorded his hand as he smoothed his tie. *Thank you for the platform Big Fella. Time to go to work Matthew.* "Let me first thank the generations of brave Americans who have joined and defended freedom at home as well as abroad so these politicians on my right and left could attend their presentations and plays in safety."

Genuine laughter pealed in the room.

"Our first thank you must always go to the American Patriot, Militia, Minuteman, Army, Navy, Air Force, and Marines!"

The audience came alive and leaped to their feet as the Freedom movement cried: "USA! USA! USA!"

Falcon leaned forward and raised his voice so he could be heard. "Our next piece of gratitude goes to our fellow taxpayers who have been carrying the burden of this diseased culture known as Boomeritis far too long!"

"USA! USA! USA!"

One moderator checked the clock. *He still has 90 seconds to go!*

Waving toward DeJesus and Arnold, Falcon fired away. "These politicians are well-named. 'Poli' means the people and 'tician' means to be lied to. There is no doubt we need *more* of our people and *less* of their lies!"

The roar coming from the crowd outside could be heard. "USA! USA! USA!"

The clock seemed to be moving in slow motion. *Forty-five seconds left.*

"I'm a big believer in less being more." Falcon motioned toward his adversaries again. "Undoubtedly the less these politicians speak the better."

The audience energy cascaded over the stage in waves. Falcon removed the mike from its holder, advancing forward. His internal clock kept perfect time ... *thirty seconds.* Reaching the middle of the stage he raised his hands for calm.

Immediately the crowd quieted, eager for whatever was to come.

The countdown was in Falcon's head. *Twenty five, twenty four, twenty three, twenty two* ... He scanned the crowd. "Friends, allies, Americans, lend me your voices." *Twenty-one, twenty, nineteen, eighteen, seventeen, sixteen* … As he placed his right hand over his heart, he faced the stars and stripes displayed proudly on the stage. He addressed the crowd, "Please stand with me!" Then he began reciting the pledge of allegiance. *Allegiance to America.*

The strong voice of America rippled inside and out of the theater, across the nation, in homes, and in front of TVs, a prideful voice alive and hungry for the meaning behind the words. Hats removed, backs straightened, Americans spectacularly pledged to the country they loved with full hearts.

"I pledge allegiance to the flag of the United States of America," led Falcon. The clock kept ticking *fifteen, fourteen, thirteen, twelve, eleven*... "and to the Republic for which it stands,"

The Democrat and Republican candidates both jumped in and started pledging their allegiance as the camera crews tripped all over themselves trying to discern where to point their equipment.

Ten, nine, eight, seven… "one nation under GOD,"

All three moderators finally leapt to their feet and put their right hands over their chests.

Six, five, four…"indivisible, with liberty," *three, two, one* … "and justice for all!"

Falcon stood at the top of the stage and ran his hand down his tie one last time.

"That was for you, Matthew; that was for you, my friend," he murmured.

Falcon Sane smiled as wave after wave of the sweetest song ever sung rained down on him.

"USA! USA! USA!"

As he enjoyed each moment, he began to walk down the stairs. Over the singing he heard the moderator screaming for him to return to his spot. He turned toward the screaming voice of the moderator, completely forgetting he still had the microphone.

The moderator continued, "Mr. Sane! Mr. Sane! You still have a job to do here!" she ranted.

Falcon smiled and trained his eyes on the screaming woman. Raising the mike to his lips he said loud and clear, "I don't work for you." Pointing to his brothers and sisters, his fellow Americans, he finished his sentence. "If they'll have me, I'll work for them!"

The crowd inside and out along with the millions who watched TV roared at his leadership.

"This is not a civilized way of conducting business!" shrieked the moderator.

Falcon's entire body seemed to clench; the muscles in his face and neck appeared granite-like. He clenched his fists twice as his body filled with rage. The room hushed at the transformation that happened to the man in front of them. Camera crews zeroed in on his face as millions of Americans across the country nodded in agreement as they recognized their own pain. Deliberately he glared at the audacity of the Boomer culture before he answered. "It's a lot more civilized than devaluing our money. More civilized than pitting one American against another because of the color of our skin. It's certainly more civilized than lying and sending our children, mothers and fathers off to war. But I'll tell you what, we have a saying where I come from." Motioning to the crowd and cameras trained on him he asked, "Are you ready?"

The crowd along with every freedom-loving American across the nation roared, "YES!"

Falcon faced the moderators, the Democrat and Republican still on stage, then stared straight into the camera, he grinned and said, "Have a Coke and a Smile." Laughing like a child. An American child. Born free.

A Late Bird had arrived.

16

November 4, 2016. The Democratic presidential candidate paced in her rented hotel suite above the fray. Downstairs, multiple TVs blared in unison with the musical loop of Springsteen and Jay Z, reverberated through the rented ballroom at the Democratic headquarters in Chicago, Illinois. Balloons and streamers frozen in place appeared to defy gravity. Cristal, Heineken, and a rowdy crowd waited for the signal to cut loose. Hushed groups of exhausted year-long campaign volunteers huddled to watch a collection of news networks break down every possible voter scenario. A drunken sex-fest was going to happen, one way or the other.

In Tallahassee, Florida, the Republican presidential candidate stared out the window from the sixth floor in his rented hotel suite above the fray. The Republican headquarters' multiple TVs blared in competition with a mariachi band. Based on amnesty, the party had stretched their plan to court new voters as far as they could. Balloons and streamers suspended in place appeared to defy gravity. Margaritas, Coronas and a riotous crowd waited for the signal to cut loose. Hushed groups of exhausted yearlong campaign volunteers gathered and watched a collection of news networks break down every possible voter scenario. A drunken sex-fest was going to happen, one way or the other.

The Independent candidate Falcon Sane stood on his deck in

Liberty, California and admired the mountains that surrounded his home. He squeezed the hand of the woman beside him. After 15 years together he still thought of her as his beautiful bride.

A sprinkling of close friends and family gathered with anticipation in the couple's understated 1,800-square-foot house nestled at the top of the valley. Over the years as Falcon's disillusionment with manipulative politicians grew, he hoped a real leader would emerge. None did. Trusted colleagues and family suggested Falcon toss his hat into the literary ring, and a new voice was born. A positive message chronicled through his life's challenges, triumphs and loves. A song of freedom, with devotion to country Americans could relate to. It became his platform and the very spark America desperately needed. The outcome of this election would determine if his message had reached their hearts.

America needed a leader, not another president.

The people had not elected one in decades … would they do so tonight?

*J*ason Kraus is an author and entrepreneur. His background includes a BA in psychology, counseling of troubled youths, and law enforcement. He writes a regular column for the purpose of breathing appreciation, freedom, and responsibility back into America. He lives in California with his wife.

Facebook: Jason Kraus
Facebook page: Jason Kraus
Email: Falconsane@yahoo.com
Twitter: @falconsane